ANCIENT APPETITES

ANCIENT APPETITES

The Wildenstern Saga, Book One

Oisín McGann

OPEN ROAD

INTEGRATED MEDIA

NEW YORK

Cover design by Jason Gabbert

978-1-4976-6570-5

Published in 2015 by Open Road Integrated Media, Inc.
345 Hudson Street
New York, NY 10014
www.openroadmedia.com

FOR MY SISTER, ERIKA,
WHO LOVES LIFE . . .
IN ALL ITS FORMS

ANCIENT APPETITES

PROLOGUE

THE BEAST OF GLENMALURE

IT WAS GERALD WHO SAID that the Beast of Glenmalure could be tamed, but it was Nathaniel who said that it would be. Gerald had plenty of time to regret his confident claim as he trudged up the hill after his cousin, constantly glancing around at every suspicious sound that pulled at his ears as they ascended through the trees. And to Gerald, every sound the forest made was suspicious. It took great self-control not to raise his double-barreled shotgun at each crack or rustle. Nate glanced back to check on him every once in a while, noting with some small satisfaction that his cousin was struggling to keep up.

It was the last hour of dusk and it promised to be a bright night, but that would not help them. Mist hung in strands in the beech trees, and the higher up they went, the thicker it got. The woods around them were already a mottled mass of grey shadow. Nate had made it clear that they were not to use the lamps, and that they must wear earth colors to blend into the landscape. Their tweed suits and flat caps were of the latest cut—the finest money could buy; but Nate wore his with the carelessness that came from being born obscenely rich.

His well-worn boots sank into the soft turf. The soil was a thin skin over the mountain's rock skeleton, and there were grains of silvery-white granite in the mud, catching the last of the evening light.

"We'll follow the waterfall up when we meet the stream," Nate said softly, pulling up his collar against the damp evening air; the moisture was already dripping from his blond hair and down his neck. "It'll mask the sound of our approach."

"And the sound of anything sneaking up on us too," Gerald muttered.

"You insisted on coming." Nate stopped and turned to him. "I could have brought someone else."

"I thought there'd be more of us," Gerald replied with a scowl as he hefted the gun cradled in the crook of his elbow. "There's safety in numbers. This thing maimed two men last week and sent another one home gibbering. It doesn't make sense to take it on alone. We need some more bodies—I mean, someone to carry the *equipment,* at least."

They had driven a gig to the end of the road in the valley below, before tying up the horse and continuing the rest of the way on foot. Gerald was not accustomed to carrying heavy loads, and the straps of the bag on his back were biting into his shoulders. He resented being used as a pack animal; that was the whole point of having servants, after all. The gun was getting heavy too, but he had ignored Nate's demand that he leave it behind, so he wasn't going to mention it now.

"Are you going to moan the whole way up?" Nate asked.

"You could have brought Clancy."

Nate looked back up the hill.

"This has nothing to do with him."

Gerald rolled his eyes, finding it hard to believe that Nate still had issues with his manservant. Nate set off again, even faster than before, his hands gripping the straps of his backpack, and Gerald urged his tired legs after him. Nate was eighteen, his cousin a year and a half older, but they still shared a schoolboy competitiveness.

They had to cross an open area, the ground beneath the yellow grass damp and boggy after the recent rains. It was difficult to keep their feet from making squelching noises, and both of them kept their eyes anxiously on the tree line ahead, eager to get back under cover. At the edge of the trees they came upon a track, and followed it to where it met the stream that flowed down Fraughan Rock Glen, a steeply sloping valley pinched between two grassy cliffs.

Upstream there was a waterfall, with a rough, rocky, path rising alongside it. The fog was getting heavier now; they could no longer see the tops of the hills against the sky. The creature could be anywhere out there. It could be a few yards away and they might not spot it until it was too late.

"This is where it was last seen," Gerald panted, wiping his

forehead with his handkerchief. "The men in the pub said there'd still be tracks."

They both surveyed the surrounding land, looking for any movement, any lights or telltale sounds.

"I'm still not sure that three men in a pub is the best source of information on which to base a hunt," Nathaniel grunted.

"You said you wanted local knowledge."

"I was thinking more along the lines of someone who could *lead* us to the bloody thing."

"Well, the last man who managed to find it had his leg broken in three places for his effort, so he won't be leading anyone anywhere for quite a while. Three men in a pub was the best I could do—What is it?"

Nate had stopped suddenly. Gerald looked round his shoulder at the spot on the ground that had seized his cousin's attention. There, in the soft ground near the base of the waterfall, was a single linear track, winding like a rigid snake into the heather that covered part of the hillside.

"It looks like the drinks are on me," Nate breathed shakily. "See the size of that? It's a foot wide if it's an inch."

"I told you it was big," Gerald said, nodding. "I've wanted to catch sight of this creature ever since Clancy used to scare us to bed with those stories of his. All these years, and nobody's managed to trap it."

He gazed expectantly at Nathaniel, his blue eyes, flushed cheeks and damp black hair making his unhealthily pale face seem as if it were glowing.

"But you handled bigger things than this in Africa, right? You haven't steered me wrong, have you? We can still go home and get more men."

"And have a bunch of bog-trotters traipsing around, making enough noise to wake the dead?" Nate snorted. "That's exactly why nobody's caught the thing. No, we can handle it."

But looking at that track, he was beginning to have second thoughts. After finishing school he had decided to defer his place at university in favor of traveling. While some of his friends had gone off on jaunts to London, Paris or even New York, Nate had wandered further afield. His family had made part of its vast fortune capturing and selling engimals, and he wanted to see how it was done. And the biggest, most dangerous engimals were to be found in Africa.

The family employed the services of the famous American hunter and trapper, Peregrine Herne, and Nate had defied his father, using the family's connections to get a place on an expedition to the Congo. He had spent over a year traveling with Herne across the Dark Continent, studying the various species through books and observation in the wild and, of course, joining in the hunts.

He had thought that after helping trap berserkers and behemoths, he would be well able to handle whatever minor predator Glenmalure had to offer. Now, without Herne's practical wisdom and the teams of wily black guides, Nathaniel was beginning to feel out of his depth.

"They say there's not a horse in Ireland that can outpace it," Gerald said over his shoulder. "And it's particularly partial to crushing people against tree trunks. So, are we going, or what?"

"We're going," Nate retorted. "I'm going to need a lamp to follow this. The heather's thick."

He had a small oil lamp in his bag, with a red lens and a metal hood over the glass to allow only a sliver of light to show. Lighting it, he followed the track carefully through the bent heather. The hill grew steep, and he could feel the burn in the muscles above his knees and in the backs of his calves as he climbed. Behind him, Gerald's breathing became shorter and more strained.

"You sound a bit pursy," he hissed to his friend. "You should walk more. This is an easy trek. You wouldn't last a day on the trail in Africa. You're breathing like a steam engine."

"Funny then that you're the one blowing all the hot air," came the caustic reply.

The trail wound through some thigh-high growth, and crested a ridge. There were some sparse, stunted trees dotting the hillside, sucking a living out of the marshy soil. Nate and Gerald were peering into the fog, trying to make any kind of sense out of the blurred grey, when they heard the low rumble of a growl far off to their right.

"Did you hear that?" Gerald gasped.

Nate held up his hand for him to be quiet. There came another growl. The fog made it impossible to gauge the direction properly, but it was close enough to set their hair on end.

"This will do, right here," Nate whispered, beckoning his cousin into a stand of heather at the base of a fir tree. They crouched down in the soft, rough foliage, and Gerald gratefully propped the shotgun up against the tree trunk.

"If we can hear it, it can hear us," Nate added. "That's all I need. Hand me your bag."

Gerald shrugged off the backpack and handed it over. Nate pulled out a wooden cube no larger than a shoebox, and then another object, covered in cloth. Unwrapping it, he revealed a funnel-shaped piece of metal, much like the end of a trumpet, with a bend at the narrow end.

"A music box? What, you're going to play it a tune?" Gerald smirked. "I think you spent too much time with those bloody snake-charmers."

"Watch and learn," Nathaniel replied as he fit the narrow end of the horn into the top of the sandalwood box. He inserted a small handle into the side of the music box and started to crank it around. Gerald looked on in fascination, his curiosity winning over his sarcasm.

"Most of the larger, lone enginals are territorial," Nate explained quietly as he finished winding up the box. "They don't take kindly to challengers. The Boers use these things as decoys."

There was another mumbling growl, low and menacing. In the grey, cloudy air it was hard to tell how close it was, or in what direction. Gerald took his small hip flask from his jacket pocket and took a swig of brandy. His fingers were shaking as he tried to screw the top back on.

Nathaniel took off the gold rings he wore on each of his middle fingers.

"I would have thought you'd need those," Gerald muttered. "You're going to need all the health you can get."

"I saw a man tackle a berserker on the Cape," Nate replied. "His ring caught on its carapace; it pulled his finger off."

"Ah, right. Well, give them here, so."

Nate handed over his rings and dragged a large coil of rope from Gerald's bag, pulling one end free. It had a loop tied into it, not unlike a hangman's noose.

"You're going to hang it now?" Gerald shook his head in puzzlement. "Or is that for you, in case you should fail? You can take this whole "honor" thing a bit far, you know—"

"It's a lasso," Nate told him. "The ranchers use it to catch cattle and horses in America. Herne taught me how to use it."

"Nate"—Gerald frowned, looking serious now—"you can't catch this thing with a bloody *rope.* I don't know what you thought you'd—"

"Quiet!" Nate was peering into the fog. There was the sound of movement nearby. "It's closer than I thought. Stay put. Don't make a sound . . . And don't bloody shoot anything."

Gerald swore under his breath, fervently wishing he'd never proposed this stupid idea. Shifting the coiled rope onto his shoulder, Nate picked up the box and crept out into the open. He carefully placed the box down in the damp grass and then pulled out the handle. Instead of music, a metallic chugging sound erupted from the horn, the sudden noise harsh in the muffled silence of the fog. Nate sprinted to a nearby Scots pine, dropping the rope onto the ground, making sure that the looped end was free. Wrapping the other end several times around the stout trunk of the tree, he tied it off and sank down into the heather to wait.

He had hoped for more time to prepare, but the beast had obviously heard them. Damn Gerald and his prattle. The box's noise made it hard to hear the sounds of the creature's approach, but Nate knew it was coming. It would not come stealthily, not with such a blatant challenge to its territory.

And then he heard it: a deep throbbing, rising to a rasping roar. Two pinpricks of light appeared through the fog, growing steadily as they rushed towards him. The creature roared again, and its eyes blazed, the mist igniting with a white glow around it. He could hear the sound of its passage through the undergrowth now, as it crushed the heather beneath its wheels. And then it charged out of the fog towards him, its engine bellowing.

It was the biggest, most savage velocycle Nate had ever seen.

He lay frozen for a second, terrified. For that instant his nerve failed him, and all he could do was look. Its wheels must have been more than two feet in diameter, its body nearly half that again in width at the cowl. The silvery metal and black ceramic of its torso bulged with power, veined with jagged, angry markings of gold and red. It stood four feet tall at the shoulder, and must have been nearly eight feet long from nose to rump. Its cowl and horns were painted with the dried, rusty-brown blood of its most recent victims. It had raced across the clearing and screamed past him before he had time to flinch. A magnificent beast. Nate closed his eyes and let out a shuddering breath. He was a fool. He should have brought more men.

But the wet tearing of soil as the velocycle skidded into a turn told him he had seconds before it came back. There was still a chance that he could defeat it. It would be confused. The decoy gave the impression of a large, aggressive engimal, and the velo-cycle would have been expecting to be met by a rival. It probably hadn't even seen the box. The next charge would be slower, less confident.

It didn't roar this time, rushing through the grass as if hunting for prey. Its lights were hooded as it came into sight through the mist, and then Nate was up, swinging the lasso over his head. The beast swerved past him, unprepared for a charge, and Nate pivoted and, with a deft flick of his wrist, looped the lasso over the creature's horns.

He stepped clear of the rope just before the coils started to whip away. The engimal was accelerating into the mist, trying to shed the snare. And that was its mistake.

When the velocycle was forty feet away, the rope snapped taut like a fishing line, anchored by the stout Scots pine. The engimal's head and shoulders were wrenched to a complete stop, and its legs and hips swung around it, throwing it onto its side. The creature lay there, stunned. Nate crossed the distance to it at a full sprint, seizing it by the horns and leaping onto its back. Then he loosened the lasso and cast it off. It would just be a dan-ger to him now.

"Right, let's see what you've got, you beauty!"

The thing didn't need any goading. It thrashed around on the marshy ground, trying to get back onto its wheels. The hind legs holding its rear wheel bent at the knees, pushing its rump up, and its front wheel twisted under it. Leaning on one knee, it flicked itself upright, lifting Nate with it. Its engine roared with outrage, and he held on for grim death as it bucked and pivoted, its spinning back wheel sending up a fountain of mud. The beast reared and then took off across the mountainside.

Nate's pulse was pounding as the wind blew his hat off and rushed past his ears. The ride was rough; the engimal swerved and bounced and tried to make sudden stops, but the swampy ground hampered its efforts. Too much turn and it would slip onto its side, and any attempt to skid to an abrupt halt ended in a long slide. Keeping his arms taut and his body supple, Nate foiled one move after another. But it would take a long time to tire, and he wouldn't. The constant shaking was jarring his senses, and he was in danger of having the teeth jolted out of his head. And all the time, Gerald's words echoed in his mind: *You only have to hang on long enough. Long enough to make it remember.*

He hoped it would remember soon. The creature raced back and forth across the ridge, twisting and bucking and tossing him like a rag doll, but he clung on. It jumped off humps and hags, trying to lose him in mid-air, but anything that came close to throwing him also risked turning it on its side again. It would not have that.

The enraged engimal leaped off a low embankment and Nate found himself lifted off its back as it soared, the momentum carrying him into the air. He went with it, following its movement, and as it hit the ground again, he landed back on it . . . his full weight crushing his groin against its metal frame. Pain drove like spears up from between his legs and he let out an embarrassing, high-pitched squeal. But he kept his grip.

The thing picked up speed, and he forced himself to ignore the excruciating pain. Tears were swept from his cheeks by the wind, chilling his face; grass and heather lashed past his legs. Every bounce over the rough ground threatened to reduce him to a blubbering baby, but he held on. The beast slowed, turning in tight jerks, smacking one horn and then another against his thighs, but he refused to let go. It bucked again, twisting and thrashing and throwing its wheels up, but he screamed in defiance at it.

"You won't beat me, you cur! You're mine! You're mine! *You're mine,* y'hear me, you goddamned machine?"

His head was spinning, and he tasted blood in his mouth. His body ached and with every move he felt weaker. His hands and arms gripped the beast's horns with a will all their own. The engimal's thrashing seemed to be growing weaker. Nate's head lolled back and he saw stars above him. Stars in the fog. He slumped forward over the creature's back. It was some time before he realized he was no longer moving.

The engine was throbbing quietly beneath him. Nate raised his head and stared. The velocycle was standing still, heat radiating off it, steam hissing wearily from its nostrils.

"Bloody marvelous," Gerald laughed.

He was leaning against a tree a few yards away, holding a cigarette in one hand.

"Best show I have ever seen, bar none," he declared, tapping some ash off the gasper. "My God, we could take it on tour. I haven't had this much excitement since that young Lady Haddington flashed her calves at the spring ball. You're a bloody star."

"Ah thunk ah bit muh tongue."

Nate pushed himself upright and worked his jaw around. He still had all his teeth, at least.

His hands were clamped around the creature's horns. Stalks unfolded from the metal bars and locked into place within reach of his fingers. Brake levers. It was giving him its brakes. He had tamed the Beast of Glenmalure.

He squeezed the front brake once, to acknowledge the gesture, and then peeled his hands off the horns and uncurled his stiff fingers.

"Are you going to ride it home?" Gerald asked him, stubbing his cigarette out on the tree trunk and picking up his shotgun.

"I'll have to." Nate leaned back to ease the pain in his groin. "Or at least as far as the gig anyway. I don't think I can walk."

Gerald chuckled, but then his smile faded, and he gazed at the engimal for some time. "I was right, wasn't I?"

Nathaniel nodded. "Yes," he said. "It remembered."

I

A DEATH IN THE FAMILY

THEY MADE THEIR WAY DOWN the hillside together, Gerald striding and stumbling, Nate riding the cowed velocycle. As he rode, his hips rocked in reflex. Gerald noticed this and laughed.

"It's not a horse, y'fool! Stop your bouncing. You look like you're trying to rattle the thing! Haven't you bruised your tackle enough for one night?"

Nate chuckled ruefully and settled himself more comfortably on the engimal's back. He had put his rings back on, but he knew he'd need to apply more gold to his skin to speed up his healing processes. And it wasn't on his fingers that he needed it.

"The sooner I get a proper saddle on this thing the better," he commented, rolling his sore tongue around his mouth.

"You going to make it a mare or a stallion?" Gerald asked.

Engimals were asexual. Their owners referred to them as "he," "she" or "it" depending entirely on their taste.

"Oh, I think I'll leave it as the mysterious cur that it is. And it goes like a flash, so that's what I'll call it."

"'Flash,'" Gerald mumbled, lighting another, cigarette. "I like it. And the girls will go potty over it. They'll be like flies to honey."

Nate gave a satisfied nod. He eagerly anticipated riding into town on his monstrous new mount. He would be the envy of every man, and an object of wonder for every young filly who saw him. For once he and not his eldest brother, Marcus, would be the talk of the town.

The mist was thinning out as they descended, and through it they saw a figure climbing through the heather towards them. Nate and Gerald exchanged puzzled looks. The man was quite short, with square shoulders and a ramrod-straight back. He wore a long tail-coat and buckled shoes. He made no attempt to greet them until they had stopped before each other.

"Master Nathaniel, welcome home, sir. Master Gerald." He bowed stiffly, doffing his cap to them.

"Clancy." Nate frowned. "How did you find us?"

"You make your presence felt wherever you go, sir," came the reply.

"I didn't think we'd made *that* much noise."

"Perish the thought, Master Nathaniel." A pause. "That's a fine beast, sir."

His manservant had an ugly face. Bushy, greying eyebrows hung over lined eyes; his wide, prominent cheekbones combined with a nose that had been squashed flat in his youth to give him features like broken stone. He looked weary now, and not from his climb up the mountain. If he felt any surprise that Nathaniel was riding a wild engimal, he didn't show it. Staring at the ground at their feet for a moment, he took a breath and continued.

"Sir, I'm afraid I bring terrible news. Master Marcus is dead. A climbing accident in the Mournes, I'm told. I'm very sorry."

Nate felt as if the air had been drained from his lungs. "Are you sure?" he gasped in disbelief. It was immediately replaced by suspicion. "Who declared him dead? Has Doctor Warburton examined him?"

"Yes, sir. I'm afraid there can be no doubt. There . . . there was extensive damage to the body. There was no chance of recovery. The family are being gathered. Master Roberto will be confirmed as the new Heir after the funeral."

No member of the Wildenstern family could be confirmed dead until one of the family doctors had examined the corpse. With the Wildensterns' special physiology, the opinions of ordinary doctors could not be trusted. Nate twisted the rings on his fingers. Gerald's hand squeezed his shoulder. He barely felt it.

"I'm sorry, Nate." He heard his cousins voice as if from a distance. "It's the damnedest luck."

"Are they sure it was an accident?" he demanded.

"Yes, sir. He was with two friends, and was being watched by more people from below. Master Marcus was climbing ahead of the other two when he fell."

Because of the peculiar traditions of the Wildenstern family, every accident was treated with suspicion. One could never be absolutely sure.

Nate stood there, saying nothing for some time.

"I want to be on my own," he announced at last, handing his backpack to his manservant. "Clancy, you go back with Gerald. Tell them I'll be along later."

And with that, he kicked his heel against the velocycle's side. Snarling eagerly, Flash's wheels gouged holes in the turf and they set off down the hillside. It took only minutes to descend to the bottom and cross a rough stretch of ground, plunging through a stream and scrambling up onto the forest track, spitting mud and pebbles in their wake. Instead of heading down to the road at the bottom of the valley, Nate turned left and raced deeper into the forest.

Marcus was dead. It made no sense. A man like Marcus did not die in some freak accident. His elder brother was the kind of figure that people told stories about, the type of man everyone wanted to have as a friend. He was everything Nate wished he could be. Uncommonly clever, witty, generous and good-natured. Blessed with a natural sense of style, he cut a dashing figure at parties, but was equally at ease in the wild country; when it came to seeking adventure, he had the heart of a lion.

And he was dead.

Marcus was . . . had been the Heir, groomed from birth to be the future head of the family. He shouldn't even have been in the country. His place was in America now, where the family carried out most of its business. He had come back for a holiday, and to see his kin.

And now Roberto would be Heir to the massive fortune. Poor Berto; he wouldn't take the news well. Like Nate, he had no interest in the family business. A warm-hearted, social animal, he was happiest amongst his friends, or immersing himself in poetry and music.

Nate rode the forest roads for nearly an hour, and then slowed the engimal as the track in front of him withered to a narrow trail in the glow of Flash's eyes. He had no idea where he was going. Bringing the velocycle to a halt, he climbed off, confident now that the creature would not wander. Gazing down at it, he ran his hands over its back, remembering the letter he had received from Gerald; the one where his cousin had explained why he thought this beast *wanted* to be tamed.

Gerald had been studying a new work by a man named Charles Darwin, called *The Origin of Species.* This man, Darwin, claimed that animals were not created in six days along with the Earth as described in the Bible, but had in fact evolved over time, through a process he called "natural selection." Gerald said this was not the first time somebody had proposed the idea, but Darwin had put forward such a thorough and convincing case, he had thrown the world of science into turmoil. And Gerald believed that it could mean the end of religion as they knew it by the beginning of the twentieth century.

Darwin's supporters went on to say what he had not dared— that mankind too had evolved and was in fact descended from apes. This didn't go down too well either, and caused much consternation in polite society across the civilized world.

The church had, of course, denounced him as a heretic, despite the fact that he was a devout Christian. They also pointed to engimals as a failing in his logic. These creatures—named for their engine-like internal organs—had long been held as arbitrary, divine creations, because they were clearly machines, and yet were for all intents and purposes alive. Their flesh could heal to some degree, but they could not reproduce like animals, so they had to have been created somehow, and yet their physiology—their *mechanics*—were beyond human understanding. These creatures had not evolved; something or someone had made them, and this offered the most obvious challenge to Darwin's reasoning.

Yes, Darwin conceded in his book, engimals seemed not to have been shaped by their environment, and since any given species of engimal did not seem confined to one geographical area, like marsupials in Australia, or the giant tortoises in the Galapagos Islands, it supported a further theory of his. That they were made by a civilization before that of Man; one which had disappeared before the beginning of recorded history.

This was truly the *de rigueur* topic of conversation at parties, and the cause of much frothing at the pulpit. And Gerald was hooked. He knew that while engimals had been tamed throughout history, the breaking of these animals had been carried out as if they were actually *born* wild. The more he studied their shapes, forms and behaviors, the more he became convinced that they were merely *feral*—that they had been built to perform some function for a master, and had happened to escape captivity, living out the rest of their lives in the wilderness.

Like a farrier judging a horse, Nathaniel ran his fingertips over the creature's curves, feeling the weathered metal, the myriad scrapes in the ceramic, the joints and hinges, the muscular shock absorbers. Its sides were hot from the exercise, and its breath plumed in pale vapor against the dark air. It bulged with power.

Gerald theorized that serving a function for a master should be a natural state for these machines. It only remained to find out what each engimal's function was, and place it in a situation where it would be compelled to carry it out. From drawings of the Beast of Glenmalure, it was clear to him that, like other velo-cycles, this creature was made to be ridden. Its back was slightly bowed as if to fit a saddle, much like a horse's, and its horns were the perfect shape for handlebars, almost like a bicycle. If it had brake levers, like others of its species, that would be the final proof. All Gerald needed was someone who would be brave, reckless and foolish enough to try and get on this thing's back and stay there long enough for it to remember its true purpose in life.

So he had put pen to paper and presented his thoughts to his cousin, who was away chasing wild engimals around the Dark Continent.

Nathaniel stroked the beast's back and its engine purred. There had been times on the long voyage home when he had doubted himself. With few distractions aboard for a virile young man, he had been troubled by nightmares of injury and failure. There had been every chance that he would ridicule himself, and be maimed or killed in the process. Not wanting to present himself at the house until after the hunt, he had Gerald meet him at the docks and he had booked into a hotel. Two days later, they had the information they needed, and they had set off into the hills.

But now the Beast of Glenmalure was his. And he had been denied his triumphant arrival home atop his prize by the ill-timed demise of his big brother. Even in death, Marcus had stolen his glory.

Despite what Clancy had said, Nate knew that the family would look on this death with great suspicion. They would not believe that this was an accident, any more than he believed it himself. And since everybody knew that he had the most to gain, most of their suspicion would be directed at him.

"Damn you, Marcus," he breathed through tense jaws. "Look where you've left me now."

It was getting late, and now that they knew he was back, the family would be expecting him. It was time to go home. He swung his leg over Flash's back and groaned slightly as he made his tender groin comfortable. A long soak in a hot bath was in order, perhaps with some of those Eastern bath salts he'd picked up on the Cape to sooth his frayed nerves . . . and his other bits.

"Right, let's go home, old boy," he said, feeling suddenly exhausted again. "And mind the potholes, if you please; I won't be walking right for a week as it is."

II

THE TREASURE MAP

FRANCIS NOONAN WALKED on tired legs along Sackville Street, making his way home. Most of the lights had gone out now, and the street had lost its glamour to the night. Even the pubs were quiet at this hour. Nelson's Column towered into the night sky, and he looked across at the Imperial Hotel, the most brightly lit building on the street. It reminded him of the times he and the lads would hang around on the corner, watching the "lords and ladies" strut like peacocks; laughing when the toffs had to cross the mucky side streets—acting like they were fording a river, trying to avoid getting mud on their fancy duds.

He didn't laugh at them now. Not now he worked at the Wildenstern stables, earning a good wage. Nowadays it was all "yes, sir," or "no, ma'am" or "thank you kindly, sir" whenever they saw fit to talk to him directly, which wasn't often. Mostly they just spoke to Old Hennessy as if the others weren't there, and the old timer passed on the instructions to the rest of them.

There was a man out in front of the hotel, leading an engimal back and forth over the flagstones of the path. Francie stopped to watch for a while. He had seen this one before, many times. The hotel had been using it for years. The thing was roughly the size and shape of a large chest of drawers, and was rolling along with its downward pointing mouth, licking the muddy footprints off the stone and buffing the surface with its soft, rough tongue. It seemed happy enough, being led on a rope as placidly as a cow, and getting an occasional friendly pat from its keeper. Francie watched until he got bored and then carried on walking.

He shouldn't have been out. He'd hitched a ride into town with the coalman, but he wasn't sure how he was going to get back to his bed in the loft above the stables by morning. He could lose his job if Hennessy discovered he was missing. But they might put him in jail for the piece of paper he had tucked into his shirt. Francie's father had said to let him know if anything big happened in the Wildenstern house; any inside information he could pass on for a price. Francie's da had friends who could use that kind of information. Francie would do anything for his da, and he had a right juicy bit of gossip for him this time.

He crossed Great Britain Street and made his way round Rutland Square. Further up he could see the silhouetted shape of the Black Church. Legend had it that if you walked three times counter-clockwise around that church, reciting the Hail

Mary backwards, the devil would appear to you. Francie had once managed two and a half circuits before his nerve had failed.

A metallic noise near his feet made him start, and his heart leaped into his throat as something brushed against his arm. For a silly moment he thought that the Wildensterns were on to him, that they had sent the peelers . . . He blinked, squinting into the gloom. Instead of a hulking policeman, he saw it was a small engimal, with rotating blades around its mouth, a wheeled base and a long arching tail. The kind of creature that could be used to mow rich people's lawns. Francie had nearly stepped on it. The thing had probably just escaped from its owners. It stared at him with its tubular eyes and then scurried away down the street. Francie gawked at it for a second, and then sprinted after it. He didn't have time to be chasing around after a lawncutter in the dark, but it was too great a temptation to resist. A good healthy engimal was worth a lot of money.

It was dark, and the streets off the main thoroughfares were badly lit, if at all, but Francie knew these streets blindfolded. The lawncutter led him a merry chase, zigzagging away from him, bouncing up onto the curb, its motor making a shrill whirring sound. He hoped nobody else would hear it. Francie wanted this prize for himself. He was breathing hard and his trousers were spattered with mud by the time he cornered the machine in a dead-end alley. It had turned round to look at him, humming warily. He advanced slowly, making comforting sounds, but it backed away from him into the shadows until its tail touched the wall that blocked off the end of the alley.

"Here . . . thingy, thingy, thing," he called softly. "I'm not goin' ta hurt yeh. Come 'ere to me now. Come to Francie. That's a good girl."

He didn't know if it was a boy or a girl, but it probably didn't matter anyway. He wondered where it was from. Not from around here, that was for sure. Nobody in this neighborhood had a lawn, let alone an engimal to mow it. He edged closer, admiring the sweeping patterns on its humped carapace.

"Shhh. That's it. That's a good girl. Easy now."

Francie was good with animals. He got on well with the horses and dogs that were kept at Wildenstern Hall. The stable boys weren't let anywhere near the engimals, but he was sure he could win the lawncutter's trust. Having seen machines like this used on the estate, he knew he had to grab its tail. It should be tame enough once he got hold of it. Its little engine gave a nervous growl. It shifted from side to side, but Francie had his arms out ready to grab it if it tried to get around him.

"Shhh. Come here to me now. That's it. I'm not goin' to hurt yeh—"

It swiveled and he lunged for its tail. The lawncutter turned and went for his feet, and he barely got out of the way of its spinning blades in time. The machine let out a screech and came at him again, its rotating jaws snatching at his ankles.

"Aaah!" he yelped. "Holy Mary—!"

Francie jumped clear of the gnashing blades and turned to run. It clipped his heel as he took off, and he thanked the good Lord that he was wearing shoes. He could hear it behind him as he ran, its blades whining with speed. Clattering round a corner, he slipped in the mud and fell hard on his side, jarring his senses and badly scraping his elbow. The lawncutter was only a few yards behind him and, with an agility born of fear, he leaped to his feet and hurled himself at the top of the high wall beside him. His fingertips caught hold and he scrambled up and onto it, flopping down to try and catch his breath. The engimal looked up at him, giving off a petty little growl and spinning its jaws in triumph.

"Get lost!" he yelled down at it. "Get away from me, yeh maggot! Go on!"

It snarled back at him.

"Go *away,* I'm tellin' yeh! If I have to come down there, I'll hit yeh so hard I'll make yeh cough up three-penny bits. Away with yeh now!"

The lawncutter was unimpressed. It crouched there, waiting for him.

"What's all that noise there?" a voice called down from a window above them. "There's people tryin' to sleep here. Have yiz no homes to go to?"

The engimal flinched from the voice, its newfound savagery disappearing at the sound of another adversary. It flashed its blades once more at Francie and then scurried off down the dark street. Francie waited for a couple of minutes to be sure that it was gone. Then he climbed down and brushed down his clothes as best he could. He was plastered with mud all down his left side, and the left elbow of his shirt was torn. His elbow was bleeding and it was starting to hurt. There was no way he'd be able to get his clothes clean by the morning. He was going to be in for a right hiding from Hennessy when he got back to the stables.

He found that the tails of his shirt had come out of his trousers and gave a start. Checking around his sides and back to be sure, he uttered an earthy curse. It was gone.

Desperately casting his eyes around, he searched the ground where he had fallen. It wasn't there. His heart thumping, he worked his way back along the road where the lawncutter had chased him until he saw a pale square in the mud a few yards away. He could easily have missed it in the darkness. Francie picked up the folded piece of paper, wiping it down. Checking that it wasn't damaged, he tucked his shirt into his trousers, tightened his braces and slipped the large folded piece of paper back inside. He breathed a sigh of relief. It had fallen less than a foot from a stream of raw sewage that was oozing down the gutter. And he was lucky the lawncutter hadn't shredded it.

Francie's family lived in the tenements not ten minutes from the bright lights of Sackville Street, in a Georgian house that had once been a fine building, according to his father. Fit for a lord, he said, before the Famine emptied the country, and thousands had moved to the city. Now there were eight families living in that house. Eight *large* families.

Francie found his way down the gloomy lane, past the one outside toilet that served four houses, with its rusting tap where they took their water and rinsed out their privy pails. He clambered over the wall into the yard that led to the back door of his house. Somewhere a cat yowled like a hurt child. Another one answered it. Patting his shirt to make sure the folded piece of paper was still tucked into it, he lifted the latch.

His family lived on the third floor, and he climbed the bare wooden steps, wincing at the familiar squeaks. He had never been embarrassed by his family's poverty before. But after nearly a year of working for the Wildensterns, he had become painfully aware of the sordid life he had grown up with. From behind the door of one of their neighbors he could hear arguing and crying. From another, the sound of a tin whistle being played with vigor. The third door he passed was hanging off its hinges, the frame splintered. There was no warmth or sound from the darkness within. The O'Malleys must have been evicted. That room would be filled soon enough by some other desperate bunch. Some of these rooms housed as many as twenty people.

He reached his family's door, and knocked before opening it. There was only one candle lit, and his mother sat by the light, darning a hole in the elbow of a jumper. The rickety wooden chair scraped on the floor as she stood up.

"Francis, pet! You're home! Oh, praise be to God, you're home!"

She was always like that. Stating the obvious—and then thanking God for it.

"Shay! Francie's home!" she cried as she rushed over to give her youngest child a smothering hug.

"Can't I see that with my own eyes, Cathy?" came the answer from across the room.

His father stood up from his place by the small cast-iron stove and came over, giving Francie an excuse to extricate himself from his mother's embrace. Shay looked his son in the eye and held out his hand. It still made Francie proud, to have his da shake his hand like he was a grown man. Francie was almost as tall as him now, tall enough up to see his da's bald spot under the thinning brown hair.

But he could see the curiosity in his father's gaze too. Shay knew his son had broken rules to be here.

"Have a seat, son," he said. "Sit down there and have some tea. The kettle's just boiled."

"Look at the state of you!" Cathy scolded her son. "Is it swimmin' in the mud you were?"

Taking a damp cloth, she cleaned up his bloody elbow and then wiped as much of the mud from his shirt and trousers as she could until he squirmed. Then she got on with making the tea.

"Aren't they missin' yeh at the stables?" his father asked, giving him the shrewd eye.

Francie shrugged.

His mother fussed about, putting tea leaves in the teapot and pouring in the water. She made a good cup of tea, did Ma. Francie sat down at the table with his parents, sipping the hot, milky tea and taking a look around to see what had changed. Nothing much. They had neighbors who lived in worse conditions. But the room was still sparse: a threadbare rug on the bare floorboards, the stove in one corner, the table in another. There were no curtains on the window, but it was so dirty on the outside that it didn't matter. And there was the trunk that held most of the rest of their possessions, which also doubled as a bench when some of the neighbors came round for a session. The folded blankets in another corner would make the beds that his folks and older sisters slept in.

"Where are the girls?" he asked.

"Away working," his da replied.

"They both got placed in houses," his ma added. "Chamber-maids. We don't see so much of them any more. Peggy's all the way out in Dundrum."

Francie was disappointed that nobody had seen fit to let him know.

"What brings you out, son?" his father asked.

He was a lean man with a worn, ruddy face and had little patience for prattle when something had taken his interest. Francie took a breath. He'd been dying to tell them the news, but it was nice to just sit there and talk about the little stuff.

"You said to tell you if anything important happened up at the house," he began. "Anything like . . . y'know. Interestin'."

"Yeah, so?" his father nodded insistently.

"Well, it's the first son. Master Marcus. He's dead. Was out mountain climbing and fell off, they sez. There's goin' to be a huge funeral; deffiney some time next week—it looks like Saturday, but they're not sure yet. They won't announce it for a couple of days."

"That's terrible," his ma gasped, her hand to her mouth. "God help his poor mother."

"His poor mother's in her grave these past eight years, woman," Shay snapped. "No doubt she'll be glad of his company. What else, son? There's more, isn't there?"

Francie bit his lip and reached into his pocket. Taking the folded paper from inside his shirt, he laid it on the table. The expression on his face was a mixture of excitement and fear. He was even trembling a little.

"What is it?" Cathy asked.

Shay unfolded the sheet of paper and flattened it out. It took up the entire top of the table. Father and son shared a look. Francie's mother could not read.

"It's a map," Shay said, studying it. "A plan of the house . . . Wildenstern Hall."

"One of the lads working on the new railway gave it to me," Francie lied. "I just wanted to show you what it was going to be like. The railway, I mean. And what some of the house looked like. This is only one floor—not even a floor; this is just the cellar."

The architectural plan showed where the basement level of the house connected to the underground station; where the Wildensterns would be able to board their private train. It also showed every other room on that level, and every room was labeled.

"This is marvelous, Francie," Shay praised him cautiously. "What a place this must be. Have you ever seen the like, Cathy? Look," he said, pointing at one of the rooms. "An armory! What kind of family has an armory in their home? Those Wildensterns are a breed unto themselves and no mistake. Bloody rich people!"

"Shay!" Cathy exclaimed. "Language!"

"Sorry, love."

Francie stared into his father's eyes and discreetly tapped his finger on another room marked on the paper. Shay gazed down at the plan and exhaled quietly.

The label for that room read "TREASURY."

III

A TAINTED HOMECOMING

NATE AND FLASH COULD SEE the silhouette of Wildenstern Hall against the night sky long before they reached it. Set on a hill at the fringe of the mountains that bordered the south of the city, its jutting rooftop was the highest point on this side of the country. As Nate and his mount approached at an easy pace, he gazed up at the house and felt a welling up of homesickness. It was good to be back.

There was no question of riding up the main road to the front gates. He could not arrive home on his new steed like a conquering hero; nothing would be said, of course, but it would be considered bad form. Instead, he took the back roads, entering the grounds through the rear gate and rolling past the cabins where the railroad crews would be sleeping, or drinking and carousing the night away. There were nearly two hundred of these laborers living here, out of sight of the main house; they were working on the private railway line that would eventually stretch from the underground station beneath the house, to Kingsbridge Station in the city. Another branch would eventually lead east to the docks of Kingstown on the coast.

The gravel road led past the hamlet of rough buildings through the woods to the manicured lawns that skirted the lavish, exotic gardens. Gas lampposts illuminated the grounds near the house, the gravel road joining a wider, cobbled thoroughfare lined with cast bronze sculptures holding flaming torches in glass shades. To the west Nate could just hear the mewling from the zoo; the cages and pits where the family had its menagerie of untamable engimals. Too savage to be useful, but kept out of curiosity and a hunger for unorthodox entertainment. Nate wondered how much of that would change once Gerald's theories could be tested.

The cobbled drive took Nathaniel and his mount up to the yard past the stables, then further round to where deliveries were made. A wide, ornate marble staircase led up to the rear entrance. Below it, and to one side, a more utilitarian brace of double doors marked the tradesmen's entrance, and the doors to the kitchens, the storerooms, the servants' quarters and the service elevators. Further round to the right again, below a wing of the house with no windows, was another door, which led down to the dungeons, deep in the foundations. They were disused now, a relic of Norman times, when the house had started life as a keep.

Nate gave a start, turning in the saddle, sure that he had just seen a small shadow darting across the grass and in behind the stables. He was tempted to take Flash after the figure to investigate, but he was too tired to be concerned. It was probably no threat at all; most likely just some groom returning after a frolicking with one of the housemaids.

To refer to Wildenstern Hall as a house was a pitiful understatement, but there were few words that could do it justice. It was far too tall to be just another manor house, but too grand to be a tower. At its highest point it was thirty stories of gothic magnificence; a monolith, a cathedral of commerce. The smaller wings around the main structure were older, but just as grand in their own way. Wildenstern Hall had grown over the generations, and now, in the mid-nineteenth century, its new size reflected the unprecedented wealth the family enjoyed.

The lights from the courtyard only illuminated the bottom two floors; above, there was just a shape, dotted with the occasional lit window. Near the top it was difficult to distinguish them from the stars.

"Welcome 'ome, sor," a voice greeted him in a thick Donegal accent. "I 'eard yeh come en. I see yev find yerself a new wee animal there, sor."

"Hennessy." Nate smiled wearily at the lithe middle-aged man with the enormous white sideburns who stood before him. "Yes, it's a fine brute, isn't it? Its name is 'Flash.' Would you find it a stall, and water it for me? And I'll need a saddle. Whatever fits for now, but have one ordered to measure as soon as possible please."

He climbed off the velocycle, and Hennessy went to take one of its horns. It snarled its engine at him, making him jump.

"Ah." Nate raised his hand. "Perhaps I should put it to bed myself. You lead, and I'll follow."

With the velocycle ensconced in a comfortable, straw-strewn stall, complete with water trough, Nate bade the head groom goodnight and trudged across the yard to the house. He took his mucky boots off by the door and walked in through the servants' entrance, causing alarm among some unfortunate members of staff who had been relaxing, thinking themselves safe from the eyes of their masters. He handed the boots to one of the young kitchen boys playing marbles in the corner, confident that his footwear would be spotless within the hour, and waved to the cook, who was tucking into the leftovers of an expensive dessert normally reserved for them upstairs. He ignored the flustered parlor maid who was warming her bare feet on the lap of a helpful pageboy.

Nathaniel did not feel ready to greet his whole family—and particularly not his father. Nobody would voice their suspicions, but they would all be thinking the same thing. It was an incredible coincidence that he had arrived home on the same day that Marcus had died. Too much of a coincidence.

The men would be in the smoking room now that dinner was over, and the women would have retired to their own recreations. His arrival would be greeted with more fuss and bother than he could bear. He took the servants' mechanical lift up to the residential floors, and watched the brass needle turn as the lift rose. The elevator car stopped with a barely perceptible settling, built to limit any noise that might disturb the family. The doors opened with a quiet slide, and he stole down the rich pile carpet of the sumptuous, gas-lit hallway to his sister's room.

Tatiana's maid was fast asleep in an armchair outside the door. She shouldn't have been napping—there was no way that Tatiana would be asleep yet. He tapped gently on the door. The maid woke with a shudder, but Nate put a finger to his lips and waved at her not to get up.

"Who is it?" a voice chirped from inside.

He opened the door and poked his head in.

"A great big pirate, come to steal you off to Africa!"

His fourteen-year-old sister, Tatiana, threw her book down, jumped off her bed and rushed over to the door.

"Oh, Nate!" she exclaimed, pulling him into the room. "You're back! Oh, it's so—" She stopped in mid-sentence. "You do know about . . . about Marcus?"

He nodded. She buried her face in his chest, wrapping her arms around him. Despite her ongoing attempts to act more like a lady, she could never contain her wild emotions. He found it as endearing as ever. Nate knew that Tatiana would never believe him capable of killing their brother and he drew great comfort from that. Tears were welling in her eyes when she pulled her face out to gaze up at him.

"I still can't believe it," she said in a small voice. "It's so terrible."

Her forehead thumped back against his chest, mussing her wavy blonde hair.

"I know I should be grief-stricken. I've read all about how it should feel, and yet . . . I don't . . ." She sniffed. "I should be so poorly that I must take to my bed. I'm supposed to be overcome with heartache. But I hardly feel *anything*, really. I mean, I feel sad that I don't feel sad, if you know what I mean . . . but . . . Oh, Nate." She lifted her face to meet his eyes again, and whispered in a frightened voice, "Do you think I'm evil?"

He smiled and took a handkerchief from his pocket to wipe her eyes, brushing her blonde locks off her face.

"Of course you're not evil, Tatty. Don't be so melodramatic. You don't have a wicked bone in your body. You're just overwhelmed, that's all."

"Thank God," she breathed. "I was so worried." She wiped her eyes with the back of her hand. "Let's sit down. There's so much you have to tell me."

They sat down together on the edge of her bed as they had done since they were children. Nate cast his eyes around the room, which was lit on either side by two small lamps with stained glass shades. Little had changed. There was the pink and gold floral wallpaper, the matching curtains and the ornately dressed fourposter bed that must be getting a bit small for Tatiana now. One corner was completely given over to her collection of porcelain dolls, with their fashionable dresses, and her favorite stuffed bears.

The roll-top desk where she spent so much of her time was littered with notepaper, pens and different-colored bottles of ink. He knew all the letters he had written her would be tucked away safely in one of its drawers. The gifts he had sent from Africa— the wooden mask, the metal tusk of a berserker, and the short Zulu sword in its leather scabbard—had all been given pride of place on top of the desk.

"So, did you bring me back anything?" she asked, her attention having returned to less spiritual matters.

"Yes, of course," Nate replied. "But it's down with my luggage on the boat. I wanted to surprise everyone . . ." He paused. "Clancy will be having my things brought up, but it's late. I'll have your present for you in the morning. You'll just have to wait until then."

Tatiana gave an exaggerated moan and flopped back on the bed.

"Tell me what I've missed while I've been away," he prompted her. "How is your new governess?"

"She's a cow."

"She can't be any worse than Mrs. McKeever. You said *she* was a kraken sent from the depths of the sea to torment you."

"This new one's *much* worse."

"How can that be? Worse than the kraken? I don't believe it," Nate scoffed theatrically.

"Mrs. McKeever was *ancient*. She was bound to kick the bucket eventually. This new one can't be more than thirty years old. She won't die for *years.*"

"You must never give up hope, Tatty."

"Can't I have my present tonight?" she whined.

"No. Don't be such a spoiled brat. Tomorrow morning."

Tatty gave another frustrated moan and thumped the bed.

"Very ladylike," Nate told her. "If you keep that up, I won't show you the monster either."

"What?" Tatiana sat bolt upright.

"Didn't I mention that? Big brother caught a monster tonight." Nate pretended to study his nails.

"Really? Like the ones in the zoo?" She clutched his sleeve.

"Better than those old things. I can ride this one. I've tamed it."

She gaped.

"But you can't see that until the morning either," he said, getting to his feet. "Now you go to bed, and I'll see you before breakfast. And don't sit up late, reading—you'll strain your eyes. Go straight to sleep."

"Oh please. I'll never sleep *now!* You're so mean!"

"It's for your own good," he retorted as he opened the door, imitating their old nurse in one of her favorite phrases. "You'll thank me in years to come."

A pillow hit the door as he closed it behind him.

His room was on the next floor; he took the stairs up. His door was open, and Clancy was inside with Nate's trunks and cases from the ship. The manservant already had most of the clothes put away. There was a nightshirt laid out on the bed, which had been freshly made.

Apart from the new clutter, Nate's room was exactly as he had left it. It was still a boy's room, really; full of sporting trophies, framed daguerreotypes and lithographs of wild engimals; shelves of adventure books and penny dreadfuls. That would all have to change.

Clancy was looking over some of the shoes Nate had bought in Capetown, obviously unimpressed with the stitching. As he noticed his master, he stood up straight and gave a stiff bow of the head.

"Welcome home, Master Nathaniel. You're looking well. Africa seems to have suited you."

There was pride in the older man's eyes. Nate was different now, a grown man, mature for his eighteen years. His shoulders filled his jacket and his body was strong and agile; his hands had been roughened by work that did not befit a gentleman, his skin darkened by long days in the sun.

Nate had known Clancy all his life; this short, ugly man had served as his manservant and bodyguard for several years, and had been Marcus's before that. Nate had done most of his martial training with him, including boxing and wrestling, fencing and shooting, as well as many of the other skills a young man needed in an increasingly complicated world. Clancy had been his mentor, his guide and his shadow as he grew into manhood, but Nate had left him behind when he had escaped his family to travel the world.

"Thank you, Clancy. It's good to be back."

He sat heavily in one of the armchairs, feeling all the aches and bruises of his night's adventure. His tongue was slightly swollen, and the dull pain in his groin was still there.

"What would you like done with these, sir?" Clancy asked, pointing to a number of packages laid out on the floor.

"Just leave them." Nate waved his hand dismissively. "Just leave everything. It'll all wait till the morning."

"Yes, sir."

The man sensed that his master was not finished with him and so he hovered for a minute by the door.

"Clancy," Nate said at last, "if there is any word among the staff about . . . about my brother's death, you'll let me know, won't you? If you hear anything at all."

"Of course, sir," Clancy replied. "Am I to take that to mean that you don't believe Master Marcus's death was an accident?"

With some of the predators in this family, Nate thought, you can't take any chances.

"It's just a feeling," he said out loud. "There's still too much I don't know. And now there's going to be the funeral too—it's going to bring all the dregs out of the woodwork. This house is full of people who'd do anything to—" Nate stopped himself. Sometimes he forgot that Clancy was only a servant. This was no business of his. Another thought occurred to him. "What's the word on the rebels?"

"The family is facing a great deal of unrest in the country-side," Clancy began, the faint Limerick accent just detectable beneath his cultured tones. "After the Famine, and the failure of the last rebellion, people have grown ever more discontented with their lot. They are giving more sympathy to violent men. There is a new breed of rebel appearing, better organized this time, and there are rumors of funds and arms from America. But I've never believed that one should allow fear to dictate one's actions, sir. I think most people would rather talk out their differences than resort to violence."

"Not in this family," Nate snorted. "And Marcus's funeral is going to have everyone gathered together in one place—along with every important figure this side of the country. You're telling me the rebels wouldn't be tempted by that kind of target?"

"With the number of guns being carried at this funeral, sir," Clancy replied, "I think the rebels will be the least of your problems. Would you like me to arm the booby traps on the way out, sir?"

"Yes, please." Nate nodded.

All the key members of the family had their bedroom doors and windows booby-trapped. It didn't pay to take chances. As he flopped back on the bed, Nate reflected on the fact that he had felt no need to take such precautions when he was away from home. After all, none of his relatives were in Africa at the time. He turned onto his side, intending to relax for a few minutes before undressing. But his exhaustion finally conquered him, and moments later he was drawn down into a deep but disturbed sleep.

IV

TEA AND TOAST

FRANCIE DID NOT GO STRAIGHT TO BED when he reached the Wildenstern estate. One of his father's friends had taken him on his drayhorse, riding at a canter to get him back before he was missed. He was running across the grass towards the stables when he saw the mysterious gentleman ride in on a monstrous velocycle. Francie ducked in under the stairs that led up to the grooms' quarters and peered out at the courtyard. Old Hennessy had come out to greet the stranger and inspect the magnificent engimal.

He heard Hennessy call the man "Master Nathaniel" and he knew immediately who it was. The third son, the one who had disappeared off to Africa before Francie had started work at the stables. Nathaniel must have heard of his brother's death and hurried home. Could he really have come back so quickly?

Maybe on a beast such as this one. A mighty African berserker that could eat up distance.

Francie watched as they led the velocycle into the stables, and waited until Hennessy had filled the engimal's water trough and gone back to where he lived in the cottage at the bottom of the gardens. With his heart pounding in his chest, Francie crept up to the door of the huge stables, lifted the latch and slipped inside. A single lantern burned near the door—Hennessy must not be finished here. He'd have to be quick.

There were a couple of other engimals in the stalls of this wing, along with most of the coach-horses, but he ignored them all. The deep rumble of the new machine's engine could be heard throbbing at the far end. He tiptoed to the door of the stall and looked over. The thing was guzzling water, sucking it up through its vented nostrils.

"Lookit you, yeh beauty," he whispered. "I've never seen nothin' like yeh!"

Its flank was just within reach, and he reached out tentatively, stroking his fingertips along the smooth metal. The engimal flinched and twisted round to look at him, and Francie whipped back his hand for fear of losing it.

A sharp smack to the back of his head knocked all thoughts of the creature from his brain, and he turned round in time to catch another blow on the ear.

"Ow! Jaysus!" he cried.

"Jesus wuz born en a stable, son," Hennessy growled at him. "So ah'll have no blasphemin' on sacred grind!"

"I was just lookin'!" Francie protested.

"You look wuth your eyes and not wuth your hands, yeh wee gastral," Hennessy lambasted him, smacking him around the ear once more. "That's the master's beast and don't you go touchin' it again! An' whut have yeh done to yer clothes? Git up thar nye and clean yerself up 'fore I take a crop to yer arse!"

The old man aimed one more blow for good measure, but Francie ducked and darted to the back door, flipping up the latch. He stole a last glance at the velocycle. The creature regarded him for a moment, and then turned its attention back to the water. Francie let himself out through the door and closed it behind him. Hurrying round the building, he climbed the stairs that led up to the loft. The stable boys slept at one end of the space, in narrow beds with lumpy straw-filled mattresses. This end was always damp, which was why the other, dry end was used for storing the straw and feed. The stables had been built for the benefit of the family's horses; the boys who tended them had to fit in wherever they could.

Working his way across the creaking floorboards in the musty gloom, he kept one hand up ahead of him at head height. That way he would feel out the low roof beams before he hit his head off them. This was not the first time he'd had to make his way to his rickety-framed bed in complete darkness, so finding it was easy. The boys had to sleep two to a bed and his usual bed-mate, Patrick, was fast asleep, dreamily mumbling to himself and licking his lips.

Wrinkling his nose at the rank smell of moldy feet, Francie shucked off his muddy clothes and climbed into bed, pulling some of the thin woolen blanket over himself. Patrick snorted and rolled after it, but didn't wake up. Francie sighed as he tugged to get more of the blanket, but was glad of Patrick's warmth. They were getting too big to be sharing a bed, and he could feel the wooden frame digging into his side. He lay awake, waiting for sleep to take him away. Below the floorboards, the bass engine sounds of the velocycle soothed his nerves.

He dreamed of owning his own engimal. Not even in his wildest imaginings would he have believed that he would ever have something like the creature downstairs; but maybe something small, like the lawncutter he had tried to catch, or one of the other machines he saw around the grounds of the estate.

Maybe when he was rich. His father was always telling him he could be rich if he tried hard enough. It didn't seem to be working for his da, though, and he was *always* trying stuff. But then, they'd never had a really big plan before. And now they did.

Francie was proud of himself. He couldn't make up plans; he didn't know how to do things like his da. But he'd come up with the idea, and that was what they really needed. Da would look after all the planning. He'd already said they'd need Francie's help. And he said that if they pulled this job off, Francie would be able to buy a whole stable-full of engimals all for himself. That's how rich they were going to be.

He lay there, picturing all the creatures he'd collect, and tried not to listen to the scratching of the rats in the roof. Some day, he thought. Some day soon.

Nathaniel woke late and lay huddled in the warm blankets for some time, savoring the comfort of a real mattress after more than a year of ship bunks and camp-beds. He had woken during the night, undressed, and crawled under the covers. His whole body ached from the struggle with the velocycle. His tongue was painfully swollen.

In the drawer by his bed was a small purse of gold sovereigns. Lying back in the bed, he laid three of the coins under his nightshirt, down along the bare flesh of each leg, and three more on either side of his ribcage. His arms would be all right after some stretching. He slipped another of the gold coins under the hem of his underpants, gasping as the cold metal touched his skin. He took one more sovereign from the purse and put it in his mouth, sucking on it to ease the pain in his tongue.

Before long the pain was forgotten, replaced by the excitement of what he'd achieved. He had tamed a wild engimal. Not some would-be tool or piece of furniture, but a true beast. He couldn't wait to go and see it in the daylight, but first he would have to traipse downstairs and greet the family. And the sooner he got that over and done with, the better.

When he was satisfied that the gold had suppressed the worst of the aching, he gathered the coins up and put them back in their purse. Reaching out for the cord that hung by the side of the bed, he rang the bell, and a minute later Clancy knocked and came in.

"Good morning, sir."

"Morning. I suppose they're all downstairs?" Nate asked.

"Actually, most of the family are out by the stables, sir," the manservant replied as he took a shirt and trousers from one of the wardrobes. "Word has got round about your velocycle; it's been up half the night, scaring the wits out of the horses."

Nate grinned and threw the covers off, sitting up on the side of the bed.

"If you think they're prattling now, Clancy, wait till they see it run!"

"I have no doubt its running will be the subject of prattle for days to come, sir. But I'd suggest some breakfast first. Your father is in his study with Master Roberto; he has asked to see you when they are done."

Nathaniel's face dropped. So it had already started. His life as he knew it was over.

"Would you like me to run a bath for you, sir?"

Nathaniel had already taken off his nightshirt and was standing, waiting for his trousers. He frowned.

"Is that a hint?"

"I'd venture to say, sir, that the velocycle wasn't the only thing you brought down from the mountains."

Nate smelled his armpits. "Yes, of course." He grimaced. "Of course. What was I thinking . . .?"

"Are you all right, sir?"

"I'm fine!" he snapped, scowling.

Clancy had become far too comfortable in his position, but Nate never had the stomach to pull him up for it. Servants were not even supposed to speak in their master's presence unless they were asked a question or were delivering a message. They were supposed to be invisible. But Clancy's extra duties as tutor

and bodyguard had made him more familiar than a typical footman. It was particularly irritating when the servant pointed out
his master's mistakes.

It was strange how quickly Nate found himself returning
to his old habits now that he was home. He had done his own
shaving while he was away, but after his bath he let his manservant
scrape the stubble from his cheeks. And then he was assisted in
dressing. As Clancy helped him into his shirt and started to do up
the studs, Nate's mind came back to his impending meeting with
his father. He swallowed a lump in his throat and found that his
palms were sweaty.

"Clancy . . ."

"I shall make sure that the toast is freshly made, sir."

"Thank you."

Nate swallowed nervously as he regarded his reflection in the
full-length mirror. The freshly starched collar felt like a blade
against his neck.

The dining room where the Wildensterns took breakfast faced
east, its French windows looking out over the misted blue and
purple hills to the cool grey of the sea beyond. The breakfast room
was big and airy, warmed by a hearty coal fire in the huge marble
fireplace. The five tables, with their crisp, white linen tablecloths,
could comfortably seat six people each, but it was rare for the
entire family who lived in the house—more than thirty in all—to
eat breakfast together. There were only two other people there
when Nate came down: Tatiana and their sister-in-law—Roberto's
wife, Melancholy. Or "Daisy," as she preferred to be known.

Nathaniel would never have suspected Roberto of harming Marcus. But he wasn't so sure about Melancholy. He didn't trust her at all.

Breakfast was over, and she and Tatiana were sitting together, discussing something over tea.

"Good morning, Tatiana," he greeted his sister, and in a frostier tone he added, "And to you, Melancholy."

Tatiana rolled her eyes and sighed. Nate insisted on calling Daisy by her formal name whenever he could get away with it, because he knew she hated it. He was not taken in by her innocent doe eyes or charmed by her delicate, dark-haired beauty. Nate knew a gold-digger when he saw one. And she didn't like him any more than he liked her.

"Welcome home, Nathaniel," Daisy said politely, her voice tinged with ice. "It's good to have you back."

I'm sure, Nate thought to himself.

"Is Berto down yet?" he inquired.

"He's still with Father," Tatiana told him. "When can I see the monster, Nate? Nobody will let me near it. I'm fourteen now, you know. I'm not a little girl any more."

"After Father has finished with me," Nate told her as he made for the sideboard. "Not until then. We need time to introduce you properly!"

Surveying the empty dishes on the sideboard, he was about to mutter a string of curses when a parlor maid came in with covered platters of eggs, bacon, crumpets and kippers. But it was the thick slabs of fresh toast that he'd really been waiting for. In a manor house, everybody served themselves at breakfast, and he took ample portions of the bacon and eggs from the heated silver serving dishes, as well as plenty of toast—done on one side only, as all civilized toast should be. Nate could face any morning as long as he could have his hot buttered toast.

Sitting down opposite Tatiana, he poured himself some tea from the pot and reached for the sugar.

"Is Gerald up yet?"

"You must joking." Tatiana smirked. "He was first down. Apparently he's made a discovery that could change the course of science. He's been rabbiting on about your adventures last night to anybody who'll listen."

"Has he really?"

"Oh, yes," Daisy spoke up. "You were quite the hero, he says. Right up until that part where you . . . injured yourself. The hazards of riding bareback, I suppose."

Nate coughed into his tea, and Tatiana giggled.

"Are you sure you're comfortable?" Daisy added. "Should we get you a softer chair?"

Tatiana was noisily blowing her nose in her handkerchief, her cheeks blushing violently.

"Gerald has a habit of stretching the truth with his story-telling," Nate grunted.

"I hope so"—Daisy sipped her tea—"for the sake of the family line."

Nate threw her a savage stare, and she put her hand to her mouth, turning crimson. It was not the thing to say to a man who had just lost his brother.

"I'm sorry," she stammered quietly. "I . . . I wasn't thinking—"

Nathaniel continued to glare at her.

"Gerald's giving everyone else the tour down at the stables," Tatty whined, her mind still on the monster. "They wouldn't let me go. Said it wouldn't be decent for me to see the thing. It's so unfair."

"Well, don't you mind them." Nate winked at her. "None of *them* will get to *ride* it."

"Oh, yes *please!*" she exclaimed. "Do you think I could—?"

She was interrupted by the appearance of Roberto at the door. Nate stood and hurried over. Berto gave him a grim smile.

"Nate! God, it's good to see you! Welcome home!"

"How the hell are you, you old rogue?" Nate grasped his hand. "You haven't changed a bit!"

It wasn't true. Berto looked pale and shaken, and Nate couldn't tell if it was the shock of Marcus's death or the realization that he was now the Wildenstern Heir. Or it might just have been the result of a morning spent in the company of their father.

"How is he?" Nate asked.

"Like a bear with a headache," Roberto replied wryly. "I feel as if I've been put through the meat-grinder. Even the dogs are scared of him today—God, I hate those dogs. I haven't seen him in such a foul temper for a long time. He . . . eh, he wants to see you immediately."

Nate looked over at his breakfast.

"I wouldn't keep him waiting," Roberto urged him.

"Right, then." Nate glanced uneasily towards the open doors of the elevator at the end of the corridor.

He wondered if all sons were as terrified of their fathers.

"It'll be fine," Berto said in an effort to reassure him. "I've . . . I've softened him up for you."

Nate gave his older brother a sour look and strode out the door and down towards the elevator.

"We'll all be thinking of you!" Roberto called from behind him.

V

THE PATRIARCH

NATE STOOD MOTIONLESS in the mechanical lift. A teenage boy in a braided uniform hovered in the corner by the door, with his hand on the brass control lever. It was pushed all the way forward. The elevator climbed steadily through the floors. Nate ran his sweating hands down his jacket and tried to loosen his stiff collar. He had told himself many times that there was no real reason to be intimidated by his father. The old man had never hurt him, had never laid a hand on him or brutalized him in the way that some of his classmates had been by their fathers. In fact, his father had paid little attention of any kind to his children. Except for Marcus, of course. But there were no other patriarchs like Edgar Wildenstern. And few other families shared the ruthless Wildenstern traditions.

Few other families tolerated assassination as a means of achieving one's ambitions.

The Wildenstern family valued ambition above all other qualities. It was how they had achieved their success, and how they had accrued one of the largest fortunes in the world. The family possessed more wealth than many a sovereign nation. They were a breed apart, not only in terms of their wealth, but also in the physiology that had helped them attain it.

Wildensterns lived longer, were fitter, stronger and recovered from injury and disease far quicker than the average human being. They were blessed with what was known as *"aurea sanitas;"* what their doctors (all drawn from the family itself) sometimes referred to as "a hereditary resistance to death." This was bolstered by the effects of gold on their powers of healing. For reasons that were still not fully understood, placing pure gold in contact with their skin increased their healing abilities many times over.

These characteristics were shared by a few of the most powerful families in the world, but were rarely spoken of outside this select company. The families were also careful to marry into one another, to keep these powers amongst themselves. When one was so blessed by God, one had to be careful not to waste His gift on the undeserving.

But with so many of them living so long and producing proportionately large broods of children, there was fierce competition for the control of the resources of these families. And over the generations, a system of traditions had been put in place to hone these conflicts for the good of the families.

The Wildensterns were a perfect example. The eldest son of the family was the Heir, and took over as Patriarch when his father died. If there were no sons, one of the Patriarch's brothers could take his place, but sons always took precedence. The Patriarch controlled the family's resources and distributed the wealth and responsibilities as he saw fit. If the next son in line thought he could do a better job or, more to the point, was greedy enough to try it, he had the right to kill his brother and ascend to the position of Patriarch. The family would see to it that the death was ruled an accident, and no outside authorities would be permitted to involve themselves.

The same went for any male member of the family. If he wanted to improve his position, he could kill his way closer to the top. It was a tradition that had endured for centuries, and was seen as an essential way of honing ambition and ability, and rooting out any of the few weak individuals that arose in each generation.

It was not as straightforward as plain murder; there were some strict rules laid down—the Rules of Ascension—and anybody who failed to follow them would be ostracized—barred from any further contact with the family. Also, every male member of the Wildenstern clan within conceivable reach of the title was trained from birth in the techniques they would need to defend themselves, so it was not as if they would be easy targets. These skills included, but were not limited to, mastering unarmed combat, fighting with a range of edged weapons and firearms, the mechanics of trap-setting and the chemistry of poisons. These were taught with the emphasis on protecting oneself, but

Nathaniel had gradually come to understand that if he should feel the need to use his skills to advance his position, the family would understand.

Female members of the family could not hold any positions of importance apart from those of wife and mother, but they were welcome to assist their male relatives as they saw fit. Some also chose to take advantage of the training where they could.

Edgar Wildenstern, Duke of Leinster, was the current Patriarch—and it was expected that he would hold the position for some time to come. At 123 years old, Nathaniel's father had survived countless duels, several assassination attempts—including stabbings, shootings, a house fire, a crossbow bolt, a poisoning and a mathaumaturgical curse—and had outlived three wives (at least one of whom was thought to be every bit as fierce as he was). Apart from his advanced years and growing obesity, he suffered from gout and syphilis, was deaf in one ear, blind in one eye, was missing his right hand, and limped on a twisted left leg. And still he was considered indestructible.

It had been decades since anybody had made any attempt on his life, or on the lives of his remaining children, as Edgar had imposed order on his house with a will of iron. His fifty-year climb to the top had been marked by one of the most bloodthirsty periods in the family's history, during which he had killed two of his brothers, and had been forced to do away with three of his own sons and one of his daughters in self-defense. The remaining two sons from his first marriage had been exiled for breaching the Rules of Ascension and had not been heard of since. He had decided that enough was enough, and had made it clear to the family that there would be harsh punishment for any further transgressions. They would all just have to wait for him to die of old age.

It seemed to Nate that the old man had been in a bad mood ever since. And the recent death of his favorite son would have done little to improve his temper.

"Shall I wait, sir?" the lad asked.

"What?" Nathaniel replied absent-mindedly.

They had reached his father's floor. The lift doors were standing open.

"Shall I wait here for you, sir?"

"No, thank you. I may be gone for some time."

He stepped forward, turned, and made his way slowly down the gloomy corridor towards the door to his father's study, which faced him at the far end. He rarely came up to this floor. Much of it was off limits to everyone but Edgar and his small cadre of slaves. It was always dimly lit, and the décor was . . . unsettling. The walls were lined with dark oil paintings of ominous biblical scenes, particularly those of the Old Testament. The design of the carpets and the wallpaper suggested sharp edges and raw flesh. Wildenstern Hall was riddled with hidden rooms and secret passageways, and Nate suspected that this floor had more than most. When they were younger, Nate and Roberto would talk in hushed tones about how they sometimes thought they heard a ghostly wailing from the vast attic above their father's quarters. Nate shuddered at the memory of those sounds.

The door opened as he drew near to it, and a large man in an expensive but tasteless suit, carrying a bowler hat, emerged from the room. His chest and shoulders bulged under the well-cut jacket. His dark, oiled hair was slicked back from his broad face and a neatly trimmed moustache perched on his top lip. The expression in his eyes was more akin to that of a reptile than a human.

"Master Nathaniel," he smiled, showing a mouth interspersed with gold teeth. "A pleasure, as always!"

"Mr. Slattery." Nate nodded to the man and went to walk past. The man didn't move out of his way.

"Looks like you've moved up a rung, Master Nate. You'll do well out of this, I expect, eh?"

Nate glared at him. Slattery worked for his father. He was a bailiff, but Nate knew there were other kinds of work he carried out—more secretive work. There was a hardness and a cruelty to the man that unnerved him.

"You're in my way," he muttered through gritted teeth.

"So I am, so I am. Sorry about that." Slattery stepped to one side. "Just wanted to pay my respects to your father. He was as sound as a bell, your brother was. A fine fella, and no mistake. He'll be sorely missed."

Slattery was a Dubliner who'd spent time in Liverpool, and it had given him a strange mix of accents.

Nate nodded again and brushed past him. The bailiff was making his way down the corridor when he stopped and looked back.

"So I reckon you'll be off in his place, eh, Master Nathaniel? You'll remember old Slattery when it's you that's makin' the decisions, eh?"

The nerve of him, the conniving crawler. Nate ground his teeth. Marcus wasn't even in his grave, and the man was already trying to curry favor with the new bosses. Slattery stood at the door to the elevator, looking expectantly at him.

"I doubt I'll be making any decisions that concern you," Nate snapped at him. "And I think you'll find the *servants'* elevator is at the end of the corridor. Good morning to you."

Slattery's expression froze, and Nate was struck with the certainty that he would be regretting that remark before too long. He put it to the back of his mind. There was enough to be worrying about. Knocking on his father's door, he steeled himself for what was to come.

"Enter!" a voice barked.

And he did.

There was a giant, dark-brown bull mastiff lying just inside the door, and Nate stepped over it gingerly. Two more of the dogs, one tan-colored, the other black, lay before his father's desk. The room was huge, with a vaulted ceiling supported by carved oak beams. The walls were lined with bookshelves, hunting trophies and paintings, and above the fireplace, a display of arcane weapons from all over the world.

In the corners of the room behind the Patriarch stood two elegant black men—taken as young children from a Maasai tribe in Kenya—each nearly seven feet tall and dressed in the uniform of a footman. Trained from childhood to serve and protect their master, they would wait silent and unnoticed until he beckoned them.

His father's desk was nearly ten feet wide, and made of solid teak. Behind it, dressed in a burgundy waistcoat over a white shirt, a cigar clamped between his teeth, sat the Patriarch. Ensconced in a tall teak and leather chair, his large head hunched over an obese body, Edgar Wildenstern resembled some kind of albino razorback boar, but for the eyes—one startlingly blue, one milky white—that fixed Nathaniel in their gaze. All he was missing, Nate thought, was the tusks. Whiskers swept down his cheeks and joined his sideburns to frame his pale, scarred, wrinkled face in thick grey bristles.

"Father." He bowed his head.

"Hello, boy," Edgar uttered in a bass rumble. "Did you enjoy your time in Africa with Mr. Herne?"

"Yes, thank you, sir," Nate replied after a moment's hesitation. "Mr. Herne sends his compliments."

"Of course he does," Edgar grunted. "I pay for his gallivanting, after all."

Nate was going to reply that Herne had made the family a great deal of money with his "gallivanting," but he stayed silent.

"You disrespected the family by running off after you finished your schooling, to satisfy your ill-conceived notions of adventure," his father continued. "But I suppose a certain amount of disrespect must be expected and tolerated in one's youth. You, my boy, have well and truly used up your quota."

Nate's eyes fell on the crab-like claw that took the place of Edgar's right hand. It had been torn from some engimal, and he could open and close it at will, through small movements of his wrist and elbow. Its tips clicked together when he was agitated. Nate had just heard the first click.

"You will take Marcus's place at the head of the company. There is much you have to learn about international commerce and the sooner you start the better. Once you have acquainted yourself with the fundamentals of our business, you will go to America, and when you are deemed to be ready, you will take control of our interests there. You leave in two months."

Nate's heart sank. He had known this was coming.

"But Roberto is the Heir now—"

"Roberto is a buffoon!" Edgar snapped.

Nate ground his teeth at hearing his brother insulted in this way, but he knew better than to argue with his father. Berto had fallen out of favor long ago; with his kind-hearted, affable nature, he lacked the ruthless qualities valued in a male of the Wildenstern line. Berto hated Edgar, and while Nate had finally rebelled by fleeing the family home, Berto had always sought out more subtle ways of defying their father's will.

But now he was the Heir, and Nate had no wish to usurp his position. Particularly as it was a position he didn't want.

"Roberto will run the estates here," Edgar told him. "And I fear even that will stretch his abilities."

"I have taken a place at Trinity College, sir," Nathaniel began. "Engimal Studies, under Professor—"

"There will be no more talk of engimals, safaris, zoology or any of that confounded nonsense in this house," his father cut in with a growl. "You will study commerce, economics, law—an education that will prepare you for your future: overseeing the business of this family in the United States."

"I don't—"

"You will go to America—to Washington and New York—and you will assume your brother's responsibilities. This family's fortune is dependent on the firm control of our dealings with those Yankee dolts, and that is now *your* duty, God help us."

"I'm not—" Nate tried again.

"This couldn't have happened at a worse time, what with talk over there of a civil war and a slave revolt—as if the black wretches had the wherewithal to organize a bloody tea party, let alone a revolution—"

"I'm not going!" Nate exclaimed.

He lifted his eyes for a moment, amazed at his own courage. He would never have dared to raise his voice to the old man before. But he couldn't hold his father's fierce glare, and he dropped his gaze to the floor once more. The claw's tips clicked together like a telegraph. He could feel Edgar's eyes bore into his skull. There was menacing silence.

"A bit of time with the savages has given you some nerve," Edgar growled finally. "I'm glad; it was sorely needed. You're still not half the man your brother was. I suppose there's nothing that can be done about it; I put it down to your mother's weak blood."

Nate flinched, but said nothing. Edgar rarely mentioned his dead wife and he had never insulted her before.

"But you are a man now, whatever kind of man that might be. The time for frivolity is over."

Given that most of his childhood had been divided between his formal education and the family's inevitable self-defense training, Nate felt that he was due a few more years of frivolity yet. But to make such a remark to the old man now would be a step too far.

"You will listen now, boy. Because I will not repeat myself again." Edgar pushed his chair back and stood up. Even slightly hunched as he was, he stood over six feet tall, and his bulk was still almost as much muscle as fat. "The funeral is on Saturday. The archbishop will perform the ceremony. Once it is over, Silas will begin teaching you the fundamentals of our business.

"You will learn as much as you can from him. Then you will go to America and take up the reins there. And by the time I shuffle off this mortal coil—and we can only hope that is after you have aged enough to have developed some sense of propriety—you will take over the company that has made this family what it is today.

"Roberto is the Heir, through this capricious act of fate. But given that he is a feckless dandy wastrel with less sense than God gave a giggling dolly-mop, it falls to you to shoulder Marcus's responsibilities. And you will. You *will* do your duty. Do I make myself clear?"

Nathaniel was trembling with suppressed rage and frustration. It wasn't right. The old man had all but ignored him for most of his life. Everything had always been about Marcus. Edgar had never given a damn about the rest of his children—Nate had never understood why. And now he was expected to step into this role that had been shaped for his favored brother, and give up all his own hopes and ambitions. It wasn't right.

"*Do I make myself clear?!*" Edgar bellowed.

The brooding dogs in front of his desk flinched. The two Maasai servants did not.

"*Yes!*" Nathaniel shouted back, with tears in his eyes. Then, more quietly, he added: "Yes. Yes, I understand."

"That will be all," his father said.

He eased his bulk down into his seat and opened a thick leather-bound accounts ledger.

Dismissed as if he were a lowly servant, Nate stood listlessly for a moment, staring into space. Then he turned and walked unsteadily to the door, stepping over the reclining hound that blocked his path. He glanced back once at his father, but Edgar paid him no more attention, the tip of his crab claw tracing columns of figures in the book.

Nathaniel closed the door behind him. At the far end of the corridor was a window, and he made his way slowly towards it. It faced south, and looking out and down, he saw the grounds: the beautiful gardens, the woods beyond, and the hills that stretched away to the horizon. And far below, the roofs of the surrounding buildings. His eyes fell on the grey slate tiles of the stables, and he suddenly knew what he had to do.

VI

A DISCUSSION ABOUT FAMILY TRADITIONS

MELANCHOLY WILDENSTERN, or Daisy, as she was better known, sat with her husband in the breakfast room. She was drawing him as he sat there, staring into the fire and fretting away to himself. The sliding, squeaking of the charcoal was the only sound that could be heard, apart from the crackling blaze in the fireplace.

"Do you have to do that now?" Roberto asked, playing with the watch chain that dangled from his waistcoat pocket.

"Would you rather I just sat here and brooded with you?"

"Well, yes I would, frankly." He frowned at her for a moment. "You're not even getting my best side."

"Then move, darling."

Silence again, while the charcoal traced Berto's contours.

"The old cove just doesn't listen," he said at last when he

realized she was not going to offer any comfort. "I don't *want* to be the Heir! I don't even want to manage the estates. It's a soul-destroying job and I have no interest in it—it'll bore me sense-less. And we do such horrible things to the peasants sometimes. Debt collecting! Evictions! I haven't the heart for it, Daisy."

Daisy knew it. That was one of qualities she loved in him. He was the gentlest man she'd ever known. An extraordinary thing, when one considered his upbringing. She wondered if this was the right time to bring up her suspicions about Nathaniel. Rober-to's younger brother was not so gentle. And everybody knew who would wield the real power in the family now that Marcus was dead. Berto had always claimed that he and Nate were eager for Marcus to marry, so that their big brother would have a son and take them out of the running for Patriarch if anything happened to him. But Daisy suspected Nate had more ambition than that.

"I've no head for numbers either," Berto grumbled. "I'll never keep track of everything. Do you think Father would notice if I just sold all the land and bought myself a little island in the Indian Ocean? I quite fancy Madagascar."

"I've said I'd help you with managing the books," she told him as she shaded the creases on the arm of his jacket. "And you'll have accountants to deal with all the little details. It won't be all that hard, you know."

Daisy had mastered all the skills required to become a good wife. Drawing, painting, poetry, music, croquet, crochet, embroi-dery, interior decoration and domestic management; there was little that she couldn't do if she put her mind to it. She had a keen eye for fashion and could maintain a polite conversation with tedious house guests for hours, before forcefully ejecting them from her home in such a way that they would sing praises about her hospitality. And she was so incredibly bored by it all.

Before her marriage she had been one of the first women and possibly the youngest ever to attend London University and had graduated with honors. For nearly a year she had helped to run the accounts office for her father's cotton mills, and saw for herself how his gambling debts were costing him dear. He had come close to losing everything. Roberto Wildenstern had been courting her by this time and, with her father facing ruin, Daisy did some simple arithmetic and then did what any good daughter should. She married into money.

It wasn't that Daisy didn't love her husband. She could have done a lot worse. Berto was kind, considerate and sensitive; an amusing and entertaining companion. He would read her poetry and sing to her. He took her rowing on lakes on long summer afternoons.

But he lacked ambition. He had a wonderful way with people—he was warm and witty and had scores of friends—and that seemed to be all that mattered to him. He paid no attention to all the plotting and backstabbing that went on in the Wildenstern family, preferring instead to laugh at their vanities and taking a perverse delight in infuriating his father at every opportunity. There were times when she suspected he had only courted her because the family considered her to be *nouveau riche* and therefore unsuitable for him.

She would never forget the month of torture when he decided to teach himself the trumpet deliberately choosing a small room directly below his father's study to practice. Thankfully he stopped when the Patriarch finally responded by having the room's doorway bricked up . . . with Berto's trumpet still inside.

There was a less frivolous side to Berto too. She knew he had secrets; there were times when she detected shame in his voice when she innocently inquired where he'd been. She wondered if there were things about this unusual family that he still had not told her.

"Where's Tatty?" Berto asked abruptly, hoping for some more sympathetic company.

"She's out playing with the spaniels," Daisy replied. "I think she's looking for a way to sneak in and see the beast."

"I think I'll go and join her."

"Just let me finish your shoes first."

He was a devil to draw. He fidgeted constantly and kept heaving great sighs. Looking over at her, he tilted his head to one side. She glanced up at him and then back at the paper. The drawing was almost finished. It wasn't one of her best.

"I know what you're thinking," he said.

"I have no doubt."

"You're thinking that Nate had something to do with Marcus's death," Berto told her solemnly. "He hadn't."

Daisy laid the board on her lap and met her husband's gaze.

"I wasn't thinking that," she said. "But now that you've brought it up, perhaps we should talk about it. You have a rather . . . *special* family, Berto."

"I like to think so."

"You know what I mean," she retorted impatiently. "There aren't many families that encourage murder. They say Marcus's death was an accident, but who really knows? Isn't that what you do here? Somebody does away with somebody else and it's all covered up? Your so-called 'Rules of Ascension?'"

"That's old hat." Berto waved his hand dismissively. "It hasn't happened in years . . . decades."

"How do you know?" she persisted. "How many of your relatives have kicked the bucket under mysterious circumstances? But that's not the point, Berto. The point is that this is Marcus we're talking about. He was the Heir. He dies, and the whole family changes. And who benefits most? Nathaniel, that's who. Everybody knew he'd be put in charge of things if anything happened to Marcus. How can you not be suspicious?"

"But I'm the Heir now!" Berto protested. "And Nate just wouldn't . . . he just wouldn't do that, Daisy. I was next in line, so I had most to gain. You might as well be suspicious of me!"

"Oh, Berto, who's going to suspect you of murder?" She put the drawing board down, gathered the bulky folds of her tiered skirt and moved over to the chair next to him, taking his hand. "You wouldn't hurt a fly . . ."

"I might," he sniffed.

Daisy smiled despite herself, but she worried that Berto's loyalty to his brother might be blinding him. He always took Nate's side when she criticized him.

"Nate's not like you," she said softly. "He's cut from the same cloth as the rest of this family. They're all—"

"We're all dastardly sinners, bent on villainy!" Gerald declared, striding into the room.

He flopped into the chair beside Daisy, giving her a friendly peck on the cheek. Tatiana followed him in with two gormless-looking King Charles spaniels trotting at her heels.

"There's only so long you can look at a velocycle lounging in a stable," Gerald sighed. "I've tried to explain why I'm a scientific genius, but the audience only wanted to hear about the action. Without the star himself, they lost interest. Where's he gone to?"

Roberto pointed at the ceiling. "I'm to handle the Irish estates," he said glumly. "It's a brush-off, thank God. I'm sure he's going to get lumbered with the business in America."

"That'll go down well—"

Gerald was cut off by the snarl of an engine from outside. There came the sound of panicking horses and a door slammed against a wall. They all rushed to the French windows. Nathaniel was racing from the stables on the back of his velocycle, tearing along the cobbled road that led around to the front of the house. In seconds he had disappeared from sight, a light cloud of dust settling in his wake, and the roar of his mount fading into the distance.

"He took the news well, then," Daisy commented.

"My God," Gerald breathed. "He took off like the hounds of hell were at his heels."

"Well, he had been talking to the old man," Berto said.

"Where do you think he's going?" Daisy wondered aloud.

"If I were him," Berto replied, turning away from the window, "I'd go straight back to bloody Africa."

"He still hasn't given us our presents," Tatiana said.

Nathaniel squinted into the wind, urging Flash on ever faster. Gritting his teeth, he ached to put as much distance as possible between himself and his home. He would not become a slave to his father's wishes. If he had to leave Ireland and spend the rest of his life as a wanderer, then so be it. The velocycle reveled in its speed, its engine bellowing in the fresh morning air. They sped down from the hills, through the villages of Woodtown and Ballyboden, towards Rathfarnham, past dry-stone walls, cabins and country houses, overtaking coaches and wagons, and frightening horses. Mud spattered in their wake; young boys looked on, shouting and whooping. Men leaned on their shovels or against their carts, shaking their heads at the reckless, rich young scoundrel on his extravagant toy. Women tutted in disgusted fashion, and girls gazed on with a mixture of shock and wonder.

It was too much of a coincidence that he had come back on the same day that Marcus had been killed. Nobody would believe that he didn't have a hand in it. Memories of his brother sent a wave of bitterness through him and he leaned forward, the wind whipping the breath from his mouth.

Through Rathgar and Rathmines the rider and his mount raced, sending people running from their path, the machine cornering dangerously and accelerating so hard its front wheel lifted. And it reared as it rolled, roaring down the street on its back wheel.

He should have ignored Gerald's letter and stayed with Herne in Africa. He had been happier there than at any other time in his life. Maybe Roberto would have been given the business if he hadn't come back. If Daisy had been involved in the murder, had that been her plan all along? Had she counted on the fact that he wouldn't come home? The family had never been short of conniving women who achieved their ambitions through their menfolk; she certainly had Berto wrapped around her little finger.

At the Grand Canal they turned right, following it towards the river. They skirted past the horses drawing the barges of freight, turning left over the bridge at Grand Canal Quay and along by the feet of the factories and warehouses that lined the dock. They slowed here, struggling to get through the throng of stevedores unloading the barges. The men here were not the types to be intimidated by some young strip of a lad on a fancy engimal. Nate weaved carefully through the workers, around wagons and stacks of crates and barrels, and piles of coal.

Daisy was not the only one he suspected. The family was full of back-stabbing curs who would stop at nothing to advance their position. His Uncle Gideon, Edgar's only remaining brother, was one of the worst. He wanted control of the business so badly it drove him mad. He hated Marcus and had always been jealous of him. But Gideon was a coward at heart and Nate found it hard to believe he would dare to take on Edgar's eldest son . . . he was scared of Marcus and absolutely terrified of Edgar. The same went for Gideon's scheming wife. If they were involved, they couldn't have done it on their own.

Nathaniel and Flash followed a muddy alley through a fish market to the quays that lined the Liffey, where ships that came in from the sea along Dublin's river moored to disgorge their cargoes. Nate wrinkled his nose. The docks had lost none of their stink. He found it hard to believe anybody could work their whole lives here. There were a hundred smells; but above the pungent odor of fish, damp wood and fresh tar, there was the ever-present stench of the sewage-ridden river itself.

The cobbled streets in this part of town attracted all kinds. Businessmen checked their deliveries of freight while customs officers inspected their manifests; vagabond sailors drunk on beer or grog wandered from one brown-brick pub to the next, looking for work or looking to avoid it. Nate's velocycle drew attention wherever he went. He knew that they had never seen its like in this town. There were a few domestic engimals to be seen along the quays, but nothing compared to Flash. As he passed each ship, sailors and dock hands turned to gaze at him and his machine. Gulls and crows and other opportunistic birds circled overhead, hard shapes against a murky grey sky, waiting to pounce on scraps of fish or whatever else they could find.

The tarred-wood hulls of the boats creaked and groaned gently, and Nate could see men on the decks and in the rigging carrying out maintenance, changing ropes and repairing sails. But he knew most of the crews would be in the pubs here and in town, spending their hard-earned money as fast as they could before they set sail again.

The ship he was looking for was still in dock, as he knew it would be. The *Banshee* was a clipper; a square-rigged merchantman about 240 feet long, with three decks, three masts and a spread of canvas in full sail that was nearly a hundred feet wide. Owned by his father's company, this was the boat that had brought him home from Africa. The company had many of these kinds of ships, but he had grown to love this one. His heart lifted at the sight of it.

The crew were a motley lot, rough but thoroughly competent. It was strange to see so many foreign-looking faces here—he had grown used to a more exotic mix on his travels, but Dublin was still such a small, insular place. Here on the quays, however, you could find all sorts. Ships' crews were often made up of all manner of races—captains took good crewmen wherever they could get them. Sometimes by force, if necessary.

The *Banshee's* captain would be loyal to the family, but the ship's second mate had become a close friend and Nathaniel was sure the officer would hide him on board until they had sailed far enough out that they couldn't turn back. He could be gone before the family found him.

And yet as he gazed up at the ship, Nate knew he couldn't leave. There was something rotten in the heart of his family; his brother was dead and he had to find out why. If he had two months before he had to depart for America, then that would have to be long enough. He could still cut and run after that. He had loved Marcus, but he would not spend the rest of his years living his brother's life. And besides, there was one other thing to consider: if Nathaniel were to take his brother's place, whoever killed Marcus would be bound to come after him next.

VII

A GRAVE DISAGREEMENT ABOUT BONES

FRANCIE TOOK THE SHORTCUT through the graveyard, running across the carpet of soft grass past one monumental gravestone after another. The Wildensterns didn't do anything by halves, and their headstones were no exception. Giant stone crosses, door-sized slabs of intricately carved marble, looming sculptures of angels with their wings spread, all marked with Roman numerals or Celtic scrollwork or decoration from any period of the family's six-hundred-year history in Ireland.

The memorials cast long, gothic shadows over the grass in the clear morning sunlight, and Francie was struck by the thought that all the family's ancestors, lying there beneath his feet, were somehow watching him. Some frightened part of him wondered if they knew what he and his father were about. There had always been talk that the Wildensterns weren't natural. Their towering manor was often talked about in the hushed tones that might normally have been reserved for the likes of the Tower of London . . . or perhaps a haunted house.

He looked up just as he passed under the shadowy wings of a stone angel and its empty eyes filled him with dread. He ran faster, eager to be free of these menacing shapes. As he passed along the side of the small church—built especially by and for the family—he slowed and turned to look back. Each of these huge monuments could have paid for the kind of house his family inhabited in Dublin. But here they were instead, as if the dead had tried to keep hold of their money for as long as they could after their deaths. He remembered how his mother had told him stories of foreign kings from the East, who were buried with all their wealth and all their servants. To serve their masters again in the afterlife.

Francie climbed over the fence and hurried down the hill. Hennessy would notice he was missing sooner or later; he had to be quick. At the bottom of the hill he could see the messy spread of a building site. Through the middle of it, on a raised bank of earth and stone, ran the railway tracks that would carry the Wildensterns' private trains to and from the underground station beneath the house. The tracks disappeared into the mouth of a tunnel off to his right. There wasn't much activity here now; the tunnel was just about finished and the tracks were almost laid. Francie had been astonished how quickly the navvies had put down the rails. Once the ground had been prepared, the sleepers were laid and then the rails positioned on top of them. A man would walk the line, making sure the gauge was right—that the tracks were the correct distance apart—and then they were nailed in place by a skilled team of men with hammers beating to a scattered rhythm.

Waving to some of the men he knew, Francie trotted past the lines of workers with shovels, or pushing wheelbarrows full of earth, making his way to the arching, brown-brick mouth of the tunnel. The rails along the center of the gravel floor were shiny and new, gleaming in the sunlight. He followed them inside.

The daylight cut a lopsided semicircle into the darkness before giving way, and Francie carried on into the gloom. He found the man he was looking for about a hundred yards in, down a narrow side tunnel. His name was Ned O'Keefe and he was the foreman—a squat, tough, big-chested fellow with huge hands and iron-grey whiskers on a square, weathered face. He was standing with three other men around a trestle table and they were arguing over something. They were all dressed in the typical navvy get-up of double-canvas shirts, moleskin trousers and hobnail boots. The brawny men were cleaner than normal, suggesting that they had got little done that morning.

Francie moved closer, waiting to be noticed. He helped out with the horses down here when he could find the time, and the navvies had taken a liking to him. But Francie wasn't here for the horses today.

". . . I hear what yer sayin'," O'Keefe declared, "but yer talkin' through yer arse. There's no graves that deep. We've made sure o' that."

"The sniffer's never wrong, Keefo," another man put in. "And nobody's on for diggin' up the dead."

"I don't care what the sniffer says. The dead are all accounted for," O'Keefe retorted. "The family knows about every grave dug in this graveyard for almost the last six hundred years and they're all on this map. If they're not on the map, we don't worry about 'em. Now, yeh haven't done a tap all day, so yeh can get back on it quick as yeh like. Nobody's goin' on a randy tonight until this tunnel's broke through."

There were a few reluctant moans, but nobody was about to give O'Keefe any lip with the mood he was in. The foreman gave each of the other men a stony glare to reinforce his decision and then turned to find Francie standing near him.

"Francie! How's she cuttin'?"

"All right, Ned. What was all that about?"

"Ach, the sniffer's been actin' up. The lads're sayin' it's found human bone."

The sniffer was an engimal the size of a terrier that walked on stalk-like legs almost as long as Francie's. He had seen it at work and remained mystified by it. The creature could read the ground as if it were looking into glass.

One of the other men was putting it through its paces again and he watched carefully. The navvy gave its flank a light slap and it trotted off down the tunnel. Standing at the end, it stared at the wall of stone for a minute or two. Then it came back. There was a box sitting nearby and it stuck its nose into it. Francie had seen this bit before. There were different pieces of material in the box. O'Keefe stood in the middle of the narrow tunnel and the sniffer would lay out the materials that made up the ground that it had sniffed out. The closer the material to O'Keefe's feet, the more of it there was in the ground. Francie looked at the lumps that it had gathered. Closest was granite, then earth, then what looked like a lump of peat . . . and then a piece of bone.

"See?" the man said to Francie. "Bone—plain as yeh like. Talk some sense into 'im, Francie; he's as stubborn as a pregnant goat. There's bodies in that ground that we don't know about. It won't do to go disturbin' those at rest."

"I think you're all bleatin' like a flock of worried sheep," Francie told them, because he knew they liked a bit of cheek. "I'm here because my da wanted to know if you'll be workin' the day of the funeral. He's on for some cards."

The navvies were skilled laborers who had honed their expertise on the canals and railroads in Britain. There were many from Yorkshire and Lancashire, some from Scotland and Wales, but most of them were Irish; the Wildensterns had brought this company of men back from England to build this private railway. And the navvies had brought their wild ways with them. They were a law unto themselves and the scourge of the local villages; drinking till all hours, gambling and fighting and raising hell whenever they went on a "randy." They could win or lose a week's wages in one night of cards, and Francie's father, Shay, was known as a keen gambler.

"Sheep 'e calls us!" O'Keefe laughed. "Is this lad full o' ginger or wha'? Sheep!" He gave Francie a thump on the shoulder. "Tell yer oul' fella that there'll be no work that day. If it's cards he wants, it's cards he'll get—and we'll be happy to take his money off of 'im!"

"It's grand for some," Francie said. "I'll be workin' through for sure. What time are yez finishin' up the day before then? Is it a holiday like?"

"Finish at the usual time, I suppose," O'Keefe replied. "Assumin' we break through in this tunnel. Time enough to get dead drunk and sober by mornin'. We've to stand to like infantry when the coffin goes past. That young lord will be sent off like royalty."

Francie nodded. That was all his father needed to know. All the navvies would be up on the road to the graveyard on the day of the funeral. Which meant they wouldn't be down in this tunnel. That was settled then—the plan was on.

When Nate returned home, he was confronted by his irate little sister. Tatiana was demanding the ride on the monster that he had promised her, and the present she was due from Africa. She knew her rights. When it came to *her* turn to travel to far-off places, she informed him, he could be sure that he would not have to wait a *whole day* for his presents when *she* returned.

He told her to meet him in Gerald's rooms in an hour, and went to change. He was discovering that motorcycling could play havoc with one's wardrobe. It also left insects plastered to one's face in a most undignified way. After a quick bath, he donned a fresh outfit and made his way to his cousin's laboratory, presents in hand.

Gerald was his closest friend and Nate would have been forced to admit that one of the reasons for this was that Gerald was no threat to him. His cousin was thirteenth or fourteenth in line for the position of Patriarch, effectively putting him out of the running—barring some freak accident or a bloodthirsty act of mass murder that eliminated everyone in front of him.

But then Gerald had never been interested in money. He had simple needs: a minimum amount of food, some smart clothes, a steady supply of his favorite French cigarettes and, most of all, the means to indulge in whatever studies or experiments that took his fancy. And, like Nathaniel, he did feel the urge for an occasional bit of debauchery.

Gerald's rooms reflected his personality. His bedroom and living room were strewn with notes, books and unwashed clothes. His laboratory, which would have comfortably housed a university science class, was kept in a state of obsessive tidiness. Nate walked down past benches covered in tools and racks of test tubes, idly trying to guess the purpose of each arcane piece of experimental apparatus as he passed it.

Tatiana was at the far end of the room with their cousin. She was perched on a stool, peering intently at a rounded metal box that Gerald was probing with the tip of a scalpel. As he came closer, Nathaniel could see that the box had a stubby little leg at each corner and they were waving lazily, twitching every now and then as Gerald touched certain points with his blade. Nate put down his packages and leaned in.

"What have you got there then?" he asked.

They both looked up, Tatty with an air of expectation on her face as she saw the presents, Gerald looking slightly distracted.

"I'll show you," he replied. "I think you'll like this."

He turned the box over so that Nate could get a better look at the little engimal. Right side up, he could see it was about the size of a shoebox, with two slots on its back and a face that was little more than an eye and a vent at one end. Nate pointed to the shackle around one of its ankles and the chain that led to a ring in the wall.

"Why the chain?" he inquired.

"It's not house-trained yet," Gerald told him. "Keeps running off the table. Stupid thing just falls over the edge and smacks against the floor. Every time. More guts than sense." He glanced up at Nate. "A bit like you, really."

"Ha ha."

Gerald held up his finger and Tatiana clutched his sleeve.

"Oh! Can I do it? Please?" she begged, bouncing up and down on her stool.

"Of course you can, Princess. But don't tease it."

There was a loaf of bread on a breadboard behind Gerald, and Tatty reached over and cut a slice. She dangled the slice over one of the slots in the little engimal's back. The creature jiggled excitedly, trying to jump up and get the bread. Its chain clinked with each hop.

"It eats bread?" Nate grew more curious. He had never seen this before.

"No." Tatty shook her head. "Watch!"

She dropped the slice of bread into one of the slots. The engimal gave a sensual shudder and went still for moment. An orange glow emitted from the slot, along with a wisp of steam. Then the slice of bread popped back up and Tatiana snatched at it. She gasped, quickly passing it from one hand to the other, and then tossed it to Nate. He caught it, held it and yelped as heat burned his fingertips.

"It's toasted it!" he exclaimed, delighted.

"Instantly." Gerald smiled. "And it can heat muffins too. I haven't figured out if it has other talents, but we'll see soon enough. It'll all form part of my thesis: "A Demonstration of the Correlation Between Engimal Form, Nature and Function in Relation to *The Origin of Species.*" It's going to make me famous, don't you know."

"Not unless you shorten the title," Tatty sniffed.

Nate examined the toast, turning it over. "It's done both sides," he said in a disappointed voice.

"Barbaric, I know." Gerald shrugged, fondly petting the toast-maker. "But I'm sure it can be trained."

Nathaniel's stomach rumbled to remind him that he hadn't eaten since the previous afternoon. Tatiana's face reminded him that he had other duties to perform first.

"I suppose you'll want your presents then?" he sighed. "Gerald first, I think."

"You're so *mean!*" Tatty snapped, scowling and folding her arms.

Nathaniel handed his cousin the larger of the two packages, an oval shape wrapped in brown paper and twine. Gerald smiled and cut the string with his scalpel, carefully pulling off the brown paper.

"A shield," he murmured softly.

It was a piece of tanned skin stretched over a leaf-shaped wooden frame. There were two columns of symbols on its outer face.

"Bit flimsy for fighting," Gerald mused.

"It's a medicine shield," Nate informed him. "I got it from a witch-doctor. Thought you might find the story interesting. The skin is supposed to be that of an ancient medicine man who was flayed alive for offending the gods—"

"That's disgusting," Tatty burst out.

"The symbols were a decoration on his back. They are said to hold the secret key to a language only he understood," Nate continued. "Take a closer look."

"These look like mathaumaturgical symbols," Gerald muttered, running his fingertip down the column on the right.

Mathaumaturgy was a relatively new science that was attempting to explain magic and the supernatural—or even to determine whether they existed at all—through the use of mathematics.

"They're different, but close . . . But what are these?" Gerald went on, pointing at the column of over a hundred markings on the left. "They look like I's and O's."

"Or ones and noughts," Nate agreed. "I don't know. Thought you might be able to tell me."

"Could be nothing." Gerald held it up to the light from the tall windows. "Or it could be the key to the whole mathaumaturgical mystery. What did you trade for it?"

"A shaving mirror."

"A hard bargain." Gerald looked sideways at him.

"He wouldn't take "no" for an answer."

Tatiana looked fit to explode with impatience while Nate pretended to look at Gerald's shield for a while longer. Her eyes bulged at the other package.

"And I have something really special for you!" Nate smiled, finally handing it to her.

Tatty breathed again and then put on her best attempt at a reserved smile, clasping her hands together. The package was tall and round and wrapped in a more delicate, Oriental paper. Tatiana put it on the table and began to tentatively pull at the string that bound it. But her excitement got the better of her and she ended up tearing the paper to shreds to expose a large birdcage.

Sitting on the perch was the oddest bird she had ever seen. Like the toast-maker, it was an engimal but, unlike other engimals, it was actually shaped like a creature of flesh and blood. It was blue and silver, with a white breast, a copper-colored beak and bright orange eyes. It appeared to be made of a mixture of metal and some other, softer material.

"It's beautiful," Tatiana whispered. Oh, thank you, Nate. It's so beautiful. Can it fly?"

"Absolutely," he replied. "But don't let it out just yet. It has to bond with you first."

"Mm hmm." His sister's attention was firmly fixed on the creature, which was little bigger than her fist.

"Did you catch it?" she asked.

"No, I had to buy this one."

"Must've cost a bloody fortune," Gerald muttered under his breath.

Nate nodded grimly.

"Can it sing?" Tatiana turned to look up at him.

"Yes, it's trained to obey some key words," Nate said. He

leaned and whispered something in her ear. "But before you use it, I should warn you—"

"Songbird, sing!" Tatty cried, clapping her hands.

The petite little bird opened its beak, but instead of a melodic birdsong, a noise erupted from its tiny frame that had Tatty and Gerald recoiling in shock. A yowling cacophony like a quartet of hoarse violins trapped in the depths of hell carried across the room on a rolling, gyrating drumbeat. The bird flapped its wings happily as the deafening clamor bellowed from its beak.

Nate darted forward, cupped his hands around his mouth and shouted something to it. The bird fell silent again, looking slightly disappointed.

"Good God!" Gerald exclaimed. "What on earth was that racket?"

"It has an unusual repertoire," Nathaniel explained to his sister. "You have to learn how to use it. It took me a while . . . And you should have heard the abuse I got aboard ship until I got the hang of it."

Tatiana was wearing that mixed expression of horror and fascination peculiar to girls of a certain age. She didn't speak for a full minute, staring fixedly at the bird.

"If you'll excuse me," she said at last, "I think I'll take it to my room."

"By all means." Gerald waved her away. "Take the little menace as far away as you like."

Nathaniel waited until his sister had left before speaking again. Gerald was touching the side of his head tenderly.

"I've got a buzzing sound in my ears," he complained. "That thing could have deafened us all."

"I've got a favor to ask," Nate said to him.

"Well, ask it then."

"You're in . . . what—the third year of medical school?"

"I may jump up to fourth," Gerald said modestly. "The others are very slow."

Gerald was a genius; everyone who knew him knew that. He was less than two years older than Nate, but several years ahead in education and, as he delighted in pointing out, in evolutionary development.

"Have you done any autopsies yet?" Nate prompted him. "Anything like that? I want you to come and see Marcus's body before they finish fixing it up."

Gerald looked at him and sighed.

"Nate. Warburton's already examined it. He said there was no foul play."

"I want to see for myself . . . And I need you to help me," Nate pressed him. "You'll see things I won't. Please, Gerald. You know Warburton's half blind, and nobody's taking this seriously enough."

Gerald stroked the surface of the shield, avoiding his cousin's gaze.

"Maybe you should be thankful for that, Nate. If they did find something, you know who'd be first to be blamed. Berto's been sidelined—as we all knew he would be. You'll control the money when the old man's dead. The fingers will point at you. I mean, nobody would do anything about it, of course. That's the

Wildenstern way. But everybody's feelings are a bit raw at the moment. Maybe it's better left alone."

Nathaniel stared hard at him. He knew his face had turned red.

"You don't think I had anything to do with this, do you?" he asked quietly.

"Of course not, old chap," Gerald assured him, smiling slightly. "But maybe you shouldn't stir things up. After all, if you didn't do it, who did? Not Berto, that's for certain."

"No, not Berto," Nate said, shaking his head. "But what about his wife?"

Gerald looked skeptical for a moment, and then he frowned. None of them knew Daisy very well, but they were aware that she was ambitious and intelligent. And while she appeared to be fiercely loyal to Berto, she was nothing if not willful. If Berto ascended to the position of Patriarch, she would become one of the most powerful women in Europe—and Berto already consulted with her before making any major decisions. Gerald shook his head.

"I don't think she'd have the nerve, Nate," he said at last. "Don't get me wrong: she's a gold-digger, there's no doubt about that—take the shirt off your back if you gave her half a chance. But I just can't see her doing away with anybody. She's . . . Well, she's a *woman*, for God's sake."

"Will you come with me or not?"

"I don't think you should—"

"Somebody murdered him!" Nate shouted. "They killed my brother and I want to know who! He shouldn't have died like that—not in some stupid bloody fall off a bloody mountain."

Nathaniel was taken aback to find tears streaming down his face. His voice was cracking into sobs and his breath started to catch in his chest. "It's not right! It . . . it . . . You've got to help me find the vermin that did this, Gerald. Somebody's got to pay for this!"

His legs felt suddenly weak and he staggered over to a stool and sat down. He wanted to shout some more, but instead he found his pride stripped bare as he broke down in front of his cousin. Gerald left the room for a few minutes to spare his friend some embarrassment, and came back with a steaming cup of coffee once Nate's sobs had calmed down. Gerald often served himself when he was in the midst of delicate experiments. He found servants a terrible distraction at times. Nathaniel took the cup gratefully and sipped the hot, bitter contents.

"I've already seen the body," Gerald told him gently.

"You went without me?" Nate frowned, wiping his face with his handkerchief.

"Last night, after you'd gone to bed, I helped Warburton with the . . . the reconstruction," Gerald said. "I didn't find anything suspicious—but that doesn't mean you're wrong. I mean, maybe it *was* foul play. All I'm saying is . . . Look, he was in a bad way, all right? He fell from a height and his body was . . . it was horribly damaged, Nate. I thought it would be better if you waited until he'd been patched up a bit. It's not how you'd want to remember him."

Nate sniffed and blew his nose. He took another sip of the coffee and then put down the cup.

"I'll remember him how I like," he grated.

Slipping off the stool, he strode towards the door.

"You shouldn't have done it without me," he called over his shoulder before he left the room.

VIII

A MEETING IN A DARK CORRIDOR

DAISY HAD LONG AGO DISCOVERED that it was difficult to move discreetly in a voluminous crinoline dress; particularly one with heavy, embroidered binding on its tiered layers and flared over-sleeves that, rustled as one moved. There were more practical dresses she could have worn in order to stalk her husband, but there were issues of style to consider.

And she loved the exotic, Chinese-orange color.

Women in this day and age were not expected to be very mobile, but she was light enough on her feet as she kept a safe distance behind Roberto, letting him reach the next corner each time before she followed with quick, quiet steps.

Daisy glanced behind her, conscious that she was beginning to perspire. That would be a disaster. She tried to slow her pace, but Berto was tall and took long strides and would quickly outpace her if she gave him the chance. She nearly tripped on the hem of her dress and uttered an unladylike curse under her breath. Looking up, she was relieved to see Roberto had still not noticed her.

It was important that nobody else saw her either. Apart from being an undignified way for a lady to behave, the sight of her sneakily scurrying along after her husband would raise questions about their marriage. And she would not have that.

The servants were a different matter. Daisy passed a door and noticed a chambermaid pressed into the doorway, her face turned away. They were everywhere, like mice; busy but unnoticed. Whenever a member of the family approached, the junior house servants were trained to hide or turn their faces to the wall until the way was clear again. They had to be as unobtrusive as possible, but Daisy was not fooled. She remembered sneaking around her own house as a little girl, trying not to be seen and listening in on the adults. The servants heard and saw everything. But there was nothing she could do about that except count on their abject fear of being fired.

Roberto had been lying to her for some time; he was a woeful liar, so it hadn't required any great powers of deduction on her part to realize that he was hiding something from her. A secret that disturbed him so much that it had him tossing and turning in his sleep, and caused him to exhibit any number of other signs that any good wife would spot in her man. But she didn't think that anyone else had noticed, and if she had her way, they never would.

At one point they passed the hallway that led to Tatiana's room and Daisy was sure she heard some kind of horrible noise coming from that direction. Alarmed for her young sister-in-law, Daisy was about to give up her pursuit to check on her safety when she heard shrieks of laughter from Tatty's room. Reassured that her friend was not in mortal danger, Daisy continued on her way.

She turned another corner into a corridor that looked much like the others. It helped that the paintings appeared to be themed; this hallway lined with watercolors of naval battles, that one hung with romanticized oil paintings of the Irish countryside and its content peasantry. Even so, Berto was leading her a merry chase. Daisy had never been in this part of the house before and she was trying to map her way by remembering the décor. It didn't help that the whole house was stuffed full of baroque details that boggled the senses. Everything was adorned with ornate vine leaves or twisting animals or clever little curlicues. It was enough to drive a person blind. If Berto did become Patriarch, there was going to be some serious redecoration.

Her husband's agitation had grown steadily worse since Marcus's death, and Daisy was deathly afraid that Berto might somehow have been involved. He was not like the rest of the Wildensterns, of that she was sure—her husband was no killer. But deep in her heart, she had doubts. She knew he kept secrets from her, and like all the men in his family, he had been trained from childhood in the art of murder.

Berto was no killer, she told herself over and over again. This was a man who enraged his family by whirling servant girls around the dance floor at the summer balls or bringing beggars home for dinner. This was a man who caused havoc among the shooting parties, sending everyone running for cover by shooting over their heads, instead of at the "defenseless" pheasants. But normally he boasted of these exploits to her, delighting in his family's reaction. Whatever he was up to now, it was clear he did not even want his wife to know.

She paused at another corner, peering round the wall over the brass arm of a gas-lamp. Roberto had stopped by a tall grand-father clock that stood at the end of the hall. He took out his pocket watch and seemed to check the time against that of the clock.

Whatever he had done, Daisy was determined to find out and face it with him. She had promised to stand by him and so she would; be it guilt, disgrace, ridicule or damnation, they would face it together. Roberto had known about her father's looming ruin when she had agreed to marry him, but he had never ques-tioned her motives. He had trusted her and now she would repay his faith by being the loyal wife he so desperately needed.

Assuming, of course, that she could find her way back through this enormous bloody maze of a house.

Nathaniel strode along the hallway until he came to a trophy wall. It comprised the heads of deer and wild boar, all hanging from the mahogany paneling as if the wall had blocked off some deranged, multi-species stampede—each animal plunging through it up to their shoulders before being stopped dead. Literally.

There was a badger's head that hung in the middle of this stuffed menagerie, looking out of place among all the bigger animals. Looking around him to make sure that no one was watching, Nate stuck two fingers into the badger's gasping mouth and pushed down. There was a click, and the panel behind the black and white striped head popped outwards. Nathaniel pulled the secret door open and stepped into the space inside. There was a box of candles and some matches on a ledge beyond the door, and he put his hand on them before closing it behind him and cutting off the light.

He lit a candle and peered down the dusty passageway, illuminated for only a few yards by the flame's weak light. This was one of many secret routes through Wildenstern Hall. As children, they had been encouraged to play and explore through the massive building—often leading to frantic searches when one of the family's little darlings went missing in the sumptuous labyrinth. Part of their self-defense training had involved learning the secret ways of the house, its hidden doors and passageways, its safe rooms and booby traps.

This passage led to a number of different places in the house, including Warburton's surgery, where the good doctor was reconstructing Nathaniel's brother. Nate wanted to inspect the body for himself, but he didn't want to be seen doing it. He knew that he would be suspected if any evidence of foul play was found—but another thought had occurred to him. If Marcus had been murdered to advance somebody's position, then whoever had committed the act might not be finished. They might not have counted on Edgar's contempt for his next eldest son; Berto had always protested against his father's cold-hearted business methods and the family knew it. So the real power—the business in America—had been handed to Nathaniel. Which meant he could very well be the next target.

So now he needed to find out who was responsible, but he wanted to do it without tipping them off. The less they knew the better. He started off down the dark, musty corridor.

It was no mean feat to navigate these dark passageways; with each branch and junction, Nate struggled to remember the route. But all his training paid off and he became more confident as he recalled the games of catch and hide-and-seek they had played along these passages as children. He had almost reached the turn that would take him to Warburton's surgery when he heard a sound in the corridor ahead of him. He froze. Why would anybody else be using this passageway? Few enough people even knew of its existence; the closest family and a few trusted servants. Nate blew out the candle. Perhaps somebody else was trying to get into Warburton's quarters. Someone else with an interest in Marcus's corpse.

He stood still, not making a sound, and waited. A few feet away, a floorboard squeaked. And then another, squeaking again as the foot was lifted carefully from it. Nate held his breath. The darkness was like a mass of black wool around him, soft and yielding, yet smothering too. He ignored what his eyes were telling him, concentrating on his other senses. There came the barely detectable sound of tense, nervous breathing. There was a man here with him. Nathaniel could smell the faint whiff of tobacco smoke on his breath and the pomade in his hair.

Fingers suddenly brushed across Nate's face and he grabbed them, twisting the hand back to try and get an arm-lock. The other man reacted quickly, reversing the move and almost succeeding in wrenching Nate's arm up behind his back. Nathaniel turned to the side, pushed down sharply with his fist and then drove his elbow up into his opponent's chest. The air was driven out of the man's lungs. The wheezing exhalation gave him a target and Nate, too close to use his fists, swung his other elbow into the sound, catching his assailant across the cheek. He slammed his shoulder into the other man's midriff and they crashed against the wall. Nate caught a knee in the stomach and doubled over, but pulled aside before the edge of a hand could come down on the back of his neck. It hit his shoulder instead and he replied by bringing his head up abruptly under the man's chin.

There was a grunt of pain and he drove a couple of swift jabs into the man's stomach before twisting his opponent's arm up behind his back and shoving his face against the wall.

"Aaargh! Enough, for God's sake!" the man shouted.

Nate's grip loosened as he recognized the voice.

"Berto?"

"Nate?" came the incredulous reply. "What did you go attacking me for? That head-butt bloody hurt. I'm going to have a bruised chin from that . . . And what are you doing here?"

"I could ask you the same thing," Nate responded, letting go of his brother. "Why were you creeping around in the dark?"

"I heard you coming, thought it might be someone . . . you know, up to some mischief

"But why are you *here*?" Nate pressed him.

"I . . . I was going to have a look at Marcus's body," Berto said.

Nate knew he was lying as soon as he'd opened his mouth. Berto never could lie worth a damn. He wondered what his older brother was hiding.

"Why?" he asked. He lit his candle again, holding it up to see Roberto's face. "And why go in secret? You could just walk in and take a look."

"I wanted to do it in private," Berto said, sounding sheepish. He brushed his clothes down and took out his own candle. "Just so I wouldn't have the family telling me what was what. So I could see him for myself." He paused. "That's why you're here, isn't it? To find out if his fall really was an accident?"

Nate avoided his eyes, but nodded tersely.

"Can I pinch a light?" Berto held up his candle. Lighting it off Nathaniel's, he eyed the sputtering flame. "There was nothing to see. Warburton's already done a good job of fixing him up."

"I'm still going to take a look," Nate insisted.

"Suit yourself," Berto said, shrugging. "The undertaker's in there, but the old Cavalier painting with the eyeholes still overlooks the examining table. You can see the body through that— they won't even know you're there. God, these tunnels are dusty. Look at the state of my clothes! We'll have to get someone in here to clean up. Anyway, I'll leave you to your detective work; hope it gives you some peace of mind. Ta-ra!"

He seemed in a hurry to be off, so Nate let him go. Watching the glow of his brother's candle disappear off down the passage, he stood there, lost in thought.

"Pssst!" a voice hissed behind him.

Nate swung round, wax spraying from his candle.

"Who's there?" he demanded, dropping into a defensive stance.

A pale-faced figure in a coppery orange dress stepped into view from round a corner. It was Daisy.

"I'm sorry if I frightened you—" she began.

"As if you could!" he retorted, straightening up and trying to hide his frayed nerves. "What are *you* doing sneaking around in here?"

At first she hesitated, but she was in an impossible position and she knew it.

"I was following Berto," she confessed. "He's been acting strangely lately and I wanted to find out why."

"So you *followed* him?" Nate exclaimed, amazed at her nerve. Then he saw a way to take advantage of her indiscretion. "And what did you find out, exactly?"

"That's none of your business!" Daisy snapped.

"I'm making it my business," he barked back. "Unless you'd like me to tell my brother that his wife has been tracking him like a prize beagle!"

Her stare could have cut glass, but he returned it steadily.

"Nothing," she admitted at last. "I haven't discovered a thing. He entered this passage through a grandfather clock. Wherever he was going, he bumped into you before he got there. And now I'll never catch up with him . . . What was all that about anyway, that fighting? You were rolling around like a pair of piglets in the mud."

"It's how we show our brotherly love," Nate told her.

"There's such a thing as loving one's brother too much," she said with a disdainful expression. "But perhaps that's the

Wildenstern way. For Tatty's sake, I hope the same can't be said of your sisters."

Nate ground his teeth. The woman walked a thin line sometimes.

"So Berto didn't stop at Warburton's?" he asked her.

"I have no idea where one would find Doctor Warburton's surgery. But Roberto didn't stop anywhere until you *assaulted* him."

Nate sighed, gazing back up the passageway that Berto had taken.

"There's one other thing," Daisy added hesitantly. "He said he came in here to take a look at Marcus's body? But Gerald and Doctor Warburton worked through the night on Marcus; Berto knew that. He was down there this morning after they'd finished the reconstruction process—to discuss the funeral arrangements.

"Whatever Berto came in here to do, it had nothing to do with Marcus's corpse."

Nate nodded.

"I knew he was lying. All right then, it's one more thing to think about. If you find out anything else, I want to hear about it. I'll see you at dinner. You'd best go back the way you came."

Daisy didn't move. Glancing behind her, she gave him a reluctant smile.

"What?" he asked impatiently.

"I followed Berto in here," she explained. "I don't know the way out. I'm completely lost."

For just the briefest moment Nate considered running off and leaving her there, but his conscience got the better of him.

"Follow me," he said in a resigned tone.

It took more than ten minutes to find their way back through the twisting passageways to the wall of animal trophies where Nathaniel had come in. He checked through a spy hole to see that the way was clear and then opened the door. Stepping out, he brushed the dust from his clothes as Daisy negotiated her wide dress through the narrow doorway.

It wasn't until Nate had closed the door that he looked up to see Daisy put a hand to her mouth, and turned to find Gerald standing, his hands in his pockets, staring at them with his head tilted to one side.

"I know, I know," he said, giving them a lecherous smile as he took out his cigarette case. "There's a perfectly good explanation for this. But you'll excuse me if I prefer to let my imagination run riot."

IX

"SCREAMS IN THE NIGHT"

WILDENSTERN HALL DOMINATED THE HORIZON south of Dublin. For centuries it had remained one of the largest buildings in the country by expanding with each generation. The thirty-story tower that now formed the main body of the building had been completed some fifteen years before. From the steel frame that formed its skeleton, rooted deep in the bedrock, to the steam turbines that powered its mechanical lifts, the building was decades ahead of its time.

Its walls were lined with sculptured terracotta panels and at the top of the tower, arches and flying buttresses supported gothic turrets that jutted into the sky. Gargoyles gazed open-mouthed on the land beneath them, and as the sun set, the bats that nested in the eaves dropped from where they hung to take to the night sky and hunt.

ANCIENT APPETITES

Wildenstern Hall was a looming, menacing sight for those who lived around it. It had been designed that way. Its rooms and corridors had seen countless dramas and this night they were to witness another. It was not the first time that screams had echoed through the hallways of this house—but it hadn't happened for a while.

Daisy was sitting up late in her rooms, praying for patience as she waited for Roberto to come in and say goodnight, as he did without fail every evening before they both retired—like all good Christian gentry, she and her husband slept in separate rooms. He had disappeared again and she would not be able to sleep until she knew where he had gone—or at least, until he came back and gave her a half-convincing excuse. It wasn't jealousy so much as fear for his safety—that, and the unbearable thought that he was keeping some terrible secret from her. Well, perhaps there was a little jealousy too, but that was one of the deadly sins and she did her best not to harbor it.

She heard a screeching cry of pain.

There came another shriek as she pulled a dressing gown on over her nightdress and hurried out into the hall. Roberto was rushing up the hallway and Nathaniel was just opening his door.

"Did you hear that?" Berto asked them.

"You mean the awful, agonizing screams?" Nate waved in the general direction of the sound. "Yes, yes I did."

"Where's it coming from?" Daisy asked.

A gang of five footmen approaching from the other end of the corridor, all carrying pistols, looked intent on answering her question. Clancy was at their head and he stopped at a section of

— 107 —

wall halfway between the door to Nate's rooms and the elevator. Running his hands down the wall, he stopped at the dado rail and pressed something. A hidden door clicked open and a man in a footman's uniform collapsed out onto the floor, moaning and clutching his leg. Clancy examined him quickly, put his gun away and then looked to the other servants.

"A stretcher, quickly!" he barked. "And someone call for the doctor."

Two of them hurried back to the service elevator. Clancy noticed Daisy and the two brothers looking on; he stood up and strode towards them.

"A false alarm, sirs, ma'am," he reassured them. "McInerney there entered Lord Wildenstern's room without knocking, thinking it empty," he reassured them. Lord Wildenstern being the Duke's brother, Gideon. "McInerney was returning some shoes he had been polishing. His lordship was asleep at his desk, with the lights turned down; McInerney did not see him until it was too late. He surprised Lord Wildenstern, who thought the man was an attacker. His lordship pulled on a cord that opened a trap door under McInerney's feet. He fell from the floor above us into the compartment behind this wall."

"My God," Daisy exclaimed. "Is he hurt?"

"A broken ankle, I think, Miss Daisy. It could have been worse."

"Gideon has a trap door?" Berto blurted out. He turned to his brother. "I don't have a trap door. Do you have a trap door? And Gideon's being a little jumpy, isn't he? What's—?"

"What's he got to be so scared of?" Nate finished for him.

There was a long pause.

"His wife?" Berto suggested.

"Then perhaps he's not the only one," Daisy snapped. "But why resort to "wife" jokes when jokes about husbands are so much *easier*?"

"He's not joking," Nathaniel told her. "Eunice is obsessed with her children's place in the family. She'd do anything to help them get ahead. With Gideon gone, they'd all move up a rank."

"Dear God." Daisy sighed. "Is this whole family insane?"

"Just the lucky ones," Berto replied, moving closer to the injured man to get a better look. McInerney had fallen a good ten feet from the floor above, where Gideon and Eunice had their rooms. Nate felt a little put out that there was a booby trap beside his bedroom and he had never known about it. The servant was tall and athletic, with lean features and blond hair. His face was twisted in pain and his ankle was the size of a grapefruit.

The stretcher arrived and four of the servants carried the unfortunate man to the service elevator. Clancy took his leave of his master and went with them.

"Did you notice?" Daisy asked softly. "The injured man—he looked a bit like Nathaniel. Apart from being rather handsome, I mean."

"What do you mean? He's a *servant*," Nate retorted.

"No, she has a point." Berto shook his head. "He did look like you. If he walked into a dark room . . ."

"Someone might mistake him for you," Daisy concluded.

Nate was quiet for a moment.

"But why would Gideon set off a booby trap if he saw me coming into his room?"

"I can think of a couple of reasons," Berto said thoughtfully. "Either he thinks you bumped off Marcus and you're still looking to get rid of any competition . . ."

"Or *he* killed Marcus and thinks I might be out for revenge," Nate muttered.

"I wish you'd both stop finishing my sentences," Berto said sourly. "I'm more than capable of doing it myself."

Dr. Alexander Warburton was a small man whose narrow limbs contrasted greatly with his large potbelly. He wore well-cut suits to make up the difference. His half-inch-thick glasses were evidence of his failing eyesight and he was developing a habit of forgetting the names of his nearest relatives in the Wildenstern family, a sin whose grievousness was compounded when one considered that they also made up his entire list of patients. However, he still seemed very capable of spouting pompous strings of Latin whenever he felt he needed to impress someone with his expertise.

For this reason, Nate preferred to have Gerald around whenever he was dealing with the good doctor. Gerald's memory, in either English or Latin, was better than Warburton's and Gerald reveled in every chance to correct his former mentor. It made sure that Warburton stopped beating around the bush and got straight to the point. And when he was forced to think faster, Warburton was a useless liar.

". . . So, as I've already explained," the doctor concluded, "the tissue and bone damage to Marcus's body was extensive, in keeping with a fall. Not that I had any doubt on the matter, Nathaniel, because you will already know there were witnesses who actually saw it happen."

"But those injuries could have been caused by something other than a fall, right?" Nate persisted. "Or he could have been pushed or thrown off-—"

"I don't know what you're implying," Warburton protested, despite the fact that it was quite clear what Nate was implying. "Gerald will tell you, he saw the body before it was embalmed. Marcus was killed in a climbing accident. It's as simple as that."

He sighed and leaned back in his chair, putting his feet up on his polished walnut desk. Taking off his glasses, he started polishing them with a handkerchief while he gazed myopically at Nate and his cousin.

"All right, look, Nicholas . . . Nathan . . . er, Nathaniel . . . I know what you're afraid of—"

"I'm not *afraid* of anything—"

"You're afraid that this was an Act of Aggression, yes?" Warburton shook his head. "You think we're all covering it up and you're worried that whoever may have bumped off Martin . . . eh, Marcus . . . will come after you now that you're being groomed to take over the business in America, yes? It's perfectly understandable, Nich . . . Nathaniel it's just wrong, that's all."

"His nails," Gerald muttered.

"What?" Warburton frowned, putting on his spectacles.

"I didn't notice until Nate specifically asked me about them," Gerald said. "Marcus's fingernails were freshly manicured when he was brought in. Who gets a manicure before they go rock-climbing? And more to the point, how could his nails be in such perfect condition after he'd climbed a few hundred feet? There were no rope burns on his hands or arms either. He was harnessed up to a rope. You really think he fell and never even made a grab for it? You have to admit, Doctor, it all smells a bit off."

"No, it doesn't," Warburton snapped. "If it were an Act of Aggression, I'd tell you, all right? And when you've been around as long as I have, you learn a thing or two about spotting the difference between an accident and an assassination, thank you very much. Now if you'll excuse me, I have work to do!"

As they walked away from the doctor's office, Nate turned to his cousin with raised eyebrows.

"Well?"

"Oh, the old boy's lying, no doubt about it," Gerald snorted. "But then, that's his job, isn't it? He's the family doctor."

Nate nodded. That was how it worked. If somebody committed an Act of Aggression, it was immediately hushed up. If witnesses were needed, they would be ordered, bought or blackmailed into co-operating. Evidence would be manufactured. Warburton would have to do his best to ensure there was a presentable corpse, but as the family doctor, he was sworn to silence. Some day, it was assumed that Gerald would take over that particular role.

"So something's definitely up," Nate said, almost to himself, playing with the gold rings on his fingers, as he always did when he was nervous.

"Yes," Gerald grunted as he lit up a cigarette. "And if I were you, I'd sleep with the door booby-trapped, a pistol under the pillow and the lights on for a while."

"No change there, then," Nate replied. "It's good to be home."

Leaving Gerald back at his laboratory, he returned to his rooms alone. Nate sat in his living room, lost in thought. He had always quite liked Warburton. He remembered once, when he was a child, Edgar had insisted that his sons should join the fox hunt; Warburton had argued against it—Nathaniel was only six and barely able to ride. It was brave of the doctor to even try taking on the Duke, but Edgar was having none of it. Out in the countryside in the rain, Nate had been thrown from his horse and broken his leg. Warburton had stayed with him, accompanied by one of Edgar's Maasai servants, while some others went to fetch a brougham to carry him home. The Duke had carried on with the hunt.

Sheltering from the rain under a tree, the towering black footman had held the injured young boy in his arms and kept him warm. Nate had been fascinated by the man's dark skin, wanting to touch it and feel its warmth. To keep the child's mind off the pain, the footman had told him stories of Africa; of its wild animals and engimals, of the strange people and the incomparable beauty of its landscapes. Nate was in no doubt that he had become obsessed with Africa and its engimals because of that day.

He called to memory the Maasai he had met in Kenya. The men were magnificent fellows; they wore ochre on their bodies sometimes and had beads in their hair, and checked blankets flung over their shoulders. The warriors were known as *moran*, and their bravery was the stuff of legend; they fought with a heavy-balled club and used it to deadly effect. The tribes wandered the land with their cattle, living simple lives. Nate recalled how he had suffered pangs of jealousy when he had seen the closeness of their families.

He didn't know until much later that the Maasai servant who comforted him that day under the tree had been stolen from his own home as a child, and would have known little more about the Dark Continent than Nathaniel. The man must have read about it in books. Cradled in his arms, Nate had never even thought to ask the man his name. One rarely did with servants. But Dr. Warburton had reminded him to thank the servant and had shown his own appreciation with a curt nod—something the Duke would never have done.

A diffident knock on the door woke him from his daydreaming. Nate responded and Clancy stepped in.

"Winters is here with a message for you, sir. He says he was instructed to give it to you personally."

Nate sat up, his interest aroused. Winters was Marcus's manservant, and would already have been questioned about the circumstances surrounding his master's death, but Nate was determined to go over every detail again himself. This was as good a time as any.

"Show him in."

Clancy left without another word, leaving Nate alone with Winters. He could not have been more different from Clancy in appearance: tall and thin with refined good looks, he moved like a dancer. His face was expressionless; if Nate hadn't known, it would have been impossible to tell that the man had lost a beloved master only a few days before. That was how good a servant he was.

"Good afternoon, sir," he said softly, bowing his head. "Master Marcus asked me to give this to you in the event of his untimely death, sir."

He handed Nathaniel an envelope.

"And you're only giving it to me now?" Nate asked.

"My apologies, sir, but Master Marcus made it very clear that you were to receive it alone."

His heart pounding, Nate ushered the footman into his living room and tore open the envelope. There was a folded piece of notepaper inside. This was it, he was sure. The key to explaining Marcus's death. His eyes flicked down over it. Written on the paper in Marcus's neat, flowing script, were the words:

Find Babylon

He did not realize he was holding his breath until he let out a yell of frustration.

"That's it?! Those are his last words? What the bloody hell's Babylon got to do with anything?"

"I'm sure I wouldn't know, sir," Winters replied.

X

A VERY GRAND FUNERAL

DAISY WILDENSTERN WAS NO STRANGER TO DEATH. With all the new steam-driven machines, industrial accidents were becoming a new and increasingly common way for poorer people to pass on into the next world, while common illnesses and poor nutrition still claimed huge numbers of their children every year. The Grim Reaper showed a stubborn defiance of modern medicine, striking down even the noblest members of society with terrifying diseases such as typhoid, smallpox and tuberculosis. Funerals were a common sight in Victorian Ireland.

And they were expensive. Daisy's father was a self-made man, a former draper's assistant who had started with next to nothing and gone on to make his fortune. She remembered when one of her older sisters had died of influenza at the age of twelve, the family had nearly bankrupted itself to pay for a decent Christian funeral. Society judged people on how they buried their dead. Struggling families would often go hungry so they could put money aside in case their children should die. Anything to avoid the disgrace of a pauper's burial.

Perhaps it was because of her humble origins that Daisy felt uncomfortable sitting in the coach with her husband as it followed the hearse from the house to the family's church. Or perhaps it was the obscene, overwhelming pomp with which the Wildensterns were burying their favorite son.

For a start, the coaches for carrying the mourners were completely unnecessary. The road that wound round the hill from the house to the church was little more than a mile long—an easy walk, and one that Daisy did every Sunday unless there was inclement weather. She could have walked it faster too, but a more rapid procession would have given the spectators less to see. The lampposts that stood along the road were hung with wreaths and under them, standing along each side in orderly lines, were the workmen from the railroad—the "navvies," as they were called. They were a strange breed—a culture unto themselves, dressed in velveteen coats, their felt hats held to their chests as the funeral procession passed.

The hearse resembled some kind of devil's flowerbed, laden with elaborate wreaths and black velvet and dressed with a mass of black ostrich feathers. The horses too wore sprays of the bushy plumage. The coffin was barely visible through the glass sides, but Daisy knew it had cost more than most middle-class people made in a year. Attendants walked solemnly alongside the coaches, wearing long black tail coats, tall-crowned hats and black gloves. The whole procession was led by mutes dressed in gowns and carrying wands. Marcus was being laid to rest with all the ceremony of a state funeral. Daisy wondered if Queen Victoria—when she eventually gave up the ghost—would be treated with such honor.

There must have been a thousand people lining the road and around the church, come to pay their respects. Even the weather seemed to have submitted to the Wildensterns' grief, with swollen grey clouds hanging in a brooding sky. Daisy had been given an ostrich-feather fan with a tortoiseshell handle and she waved it in front of her. She wished for rain, if only to clear the muggy air.

Along the edges of the crowd were armed guards, and she knew there were more dressed in plain clothes among the spectators. Most of the important men of Ireland were gathered here today and many feared an attack by the new rebel organization that had emerged recently—the so-called "Fenians," named after the legendary Irish warriors, the *Fianna*. To her it seemed slightly absurd; the family had marginally less power than God in this country and the greatest threats to their safety were their own relatives. But she still found herself feeling nervous. If Marcus's death had not been an accident, whoever had done away with him might well have their sights set on Roberto.

She sat in the lead mourner's coach with her husband and Edgar. There were no horses drawing this vehicle; instead, four velocycles pulled at the harness, trained to move with their engines silenced. None were as impressive as Nathaniel's beast but the engimals still drew stares. Because of the Patriarch's great bulk, Nathaniel and Tatiana had been forced to take the second coach. The blinds were drawn and it was just as well, for Roberto could not contain himself; his body was racked with sobs, and tears streamed down his face. Daisy had never seen Edgar show any emotion other than a kind of muted pleasure or bursts of intimidating anger, but today he too was different. His face was impassive but his head was slumped on his chest and his breath heaved in and out like ocean waves. His sunken eyes were rimmed with red. She gazed through her veil at this implacable brute of a man and realized that he had truly loved his son.

They disembarked at the church and the coffin was lifted from the hearse and carried in on the shoulders of six footmen especially chosen for their uniform height and looks. Daisy took Roberto's arm and walked inside with him as he struggled to compose himself. Nathaniel and Tatiana followed them, and she could hear Tatty's shuddering breaths at her back. Edgar ignored them all completely, limping on his cane just behind the coffin.

Behind Nate and Tatty walked Edgar's brother Gideon with his wife, Eunice. Daisy hated them both with a passion. Even now they wore masses of gold jewelry when everybody else had dressed in sober colors, the women trading gold and silver for jet necklaces and brooches. Like the other Wildensterns, Gideon and Eunice believed that the precious metal had healing properties. But they took this belief to extraordinary lengths; clinging to the hope that draping themselves in gold would grant them long life despite their enormous appetites for rich foods and their sloth-like lifestyle. After them came their gaggle of obnoxious offspring—five sons who were the image of their father and reflected all of his worst qualities. Then there was Edgar's deaf sister, Elvira, a footman pushing her in her wheelchair while she tried to pick up snippets of conversation with her listening horn. Alongside her walked the Lord Lieutenant of Ireland—the Queen's representative, sometimes known as the Viceroy—and then, behind them, a great horde of other relatives Daisy still did not know. No doubt they were all wondering how Marcus's death would change their positions within the family.

She heard very little of the archbishop's sermon as she was kept busy throughout, comforting Tatiana on one side of her and Roberto on the other. Nathaniel sat motionless, staring at the coffin with an expression that was almost hostile. He looked more like a man who had been denied revenge than one grieving for his brother. The archbishop's voice droned on and on, echoing like the voice of God in the stone confines of the church, adding to the sense of menace that Daisy had been feeling for most of the day. It was as if the weight of the Wildensterns' brooding grief was crushing her in its attempts to gain release.

After the archbishop was finished, both Nathaniel and Roberto walked up to the pulpit to give eulogies. Nathaniel spoke briefly but touchingly of his brother in a distant voice, as if distracted by something. Then he eagerly surrendered his place to Roberto.

"I find myself unable to conjure the words to express my feelings," Berto said, his voice trembling with emotion. "So I have chosen instead to use the words of another. This is *When the Lamp Is Shattered*, by Percy Bysshe Shelley."

He paused to ensure he had everyone's complete attention for his performance. Then he began:

> "When the lamp is shattered,
> The light in the dust lies dead—
> When the cloud is scattered . . ."

Daisy saw Nate heave a weary breath. He was no fan of poetry; in fact, she knew he had earned himself beatings from Berto all through their childhood by running round shouting his elder brother's favorite poems, replacing key words with obscenities. Nathaniel rolled his eyes now as he listened, but suffered in silence.

The congregation, however, were deeply moved by the lament and were nodding tearfully in approval as Roberto returned to his seat. Daisy felt a rare moment of pride for her husband and clasped his hand as he sat down. Even Nathaniel gave him a soft pat on the back when he took his seat beside them. Daisy tilted her head back to gaze up into the arched ceiling. The late morning sun was shining through the center of one of the stained-glass windows. She recognized the biblical scene the window's image portrayed: it was the story of Lazarus, the man Jesus had raised from the dead.

Francie lay in the long grass beside his father, who was surveying the foot of the neighboring hill with a telescope.

"They'll have left a couple of guards wanderin' round the site to keep an eye on all the equipment," Shay said as he swung the eyeglass slowly from side to side. "We'll have to deal with those. Spud, Vinnie and Padraig aren't known to 'em, so they'll handle that part. Me an' Jimmy'll go on into the tunnel and find the spot. Francie, you'll keep watch outside while we do the job. Got it?"

"Aye."

Francie was nervous. He wiped sweat from his brow—it was a heavy day with grey, menacing clouds overhead and a feeling of tension in the air that might just be his imagination or might not. He had never been involved in one of his father's "jobs" before and it was only now beginning to dawn on him what he was doing. The other four men with them were hardened crooks; lads that Shay knew and trusted. Francie was the odd one out. He was also the only one who was supposed to be at the funeral that was taking place on the hillside below Wildenstern Hall; but he was confident that his absence would not be noticed among the crowds of servants in the cemetery.

Right now, the remains of Marcus Wildenstern were being loaded onto the back of the hearse and carried slowly from the house, where they had been lying in state, to the church. Francie and the other stable boys had been up most of the night cleaning and polishing the brass fittings on all the horses' tackle. He was dog-tired and nearly cross-eyed by the time they were finished, and he couldn't resist a yawn now as his da passed him the telescope to have a look.

The family's church was full to brimming and there was still a large crowd outside. It was hard to say if all those people were there because Master Marcus had been so popular, or if they were attending because they all lived under the influence of the

Wildensterns and were expected to show up if they knew what was good for them. What was important was that beyond the church the army of navvies lined the road like a guard of honor, dressed in their best duds.

"Any other day, there'd be more guards on the site with all that gear there," Shay muttered. "But they don't want to be seen to be disrespectful to the family today. Every man they can spare will be standing along that road, hat off and lookin' proper grief-stricken."

He took the telescope back off Francie and had one last searching look at the area of broken ground around the railroad.

"Right. Let's get on with it."

Navvies were tough to the core but Spud, Vinnie and Padraig knew their business. There were only two guards and they didn't stay in sight of each other. Shay's hard men took them one at a time, putting each one down with a few savage blows, then tying him up and pulling a sack over his head and shoulders. Once the unconscious men had been pulled out of sight behind a shed, Francie followed Shay and Jimmy towards the tunnel.

His heart was thudding against his ribs. Unable to decide if he was thrilled or terrified, he knew there was no turning back now. Even if the raid were successful, he would have to be back at the stables in an hour before the funeral crowd broke up. Shay had said the gang would have to go straight back to their normal lives after they pulled off the job, and keep their heads down for a few weeks to avoid any suspicion. As he ran into the darkness of the tunnel, Francie wondered how the hell he was going to live under the Wildensterns' roof after robbing them blind.

A light burst over him, dazzling him, and he stopped short with a terrified cry. It was over; they'd been had. They'd walked right into a trap. It would be prison for the lot of them. His da had stumbled to a halt in front of him.

"Jaysus, what the bloody hell is that?" Shay gasped.

Francie held up his hand to shield his eyes and then breathed a relieved sigh. "It's just the engimals, Da. They light the way."

"Frightened the bejaysus out of me is what they did," Shay growled.

There were two of the creatures, nestling at the entrance to the side tunnel where Francie had found O'Keefe and his men the other day. Waist-high, they had large heads—each face dominated by a single eye that shone brighter than any lantern. Their necks were hinged like arms and could fold and rotate in a full circle to tilt their heads at almost any angle. Francie stepped forward and petted one on the back of its dark-brown neck. Its leash was tied round a hook in the wall.

"They're bright-eyes, Da. They use 'em in the digs sometimes instead of candles and lanterns," he explained. "Cos they don't have any flames that could set off the black powder."

The black powder was used for blasting through rock in major digs such as this one. It was dangerous work, made worse by the unpredictable explosives. Two men had died building this very tunnel.

"Well now, that's just the thing we need, so." Shay grinned. "Here, hand us a lead there, Francie, and we'll take one with us. You go back and keep a lookout like I told you, there's a good lad."

Disappointed that he wasn't going to get to see the treasury, Francie untied one of the leads from the wall and passed it to his father. Shay took it and waved to Jimmy, heading off up the side tunnel with the bright-eye leading the way. It skittered along on four spiderlike legs protruding from a small but heavy body, mewing happily and eager for some exercise.

Francie undid the second engimal's leash and led it back to the mouth of the tunnel. He figured they could keep each other company. There was a bench near the entrance and he sat down for a minute or two. But he couldn't relax so he stood back up again. The bright-eye was restless too. It flashed its light on and off at him. He sniggered and did a little jig in front of it. The engimal tried to imitate the steps, dancing delicately on its spindly legs. Francie laughed, adding some more steps. Again the bright-eye copied the moves.

They danced around each other, the boy leading and the engimal following, dancing to imagined music. That was how the three remaining members of Shay's gang found them when they drove up with the horse and dray. Staring down from the flat-bedded cart, the men's faces wore expressions of disgust.

"This is our lookout, is it?" Padraig sneered, tying the horse to one of the rails. "We'll be right as rain so."

Francie blushed from his ears to his collar and pulled the engimal's lead up short.

"Less dancin' an' more lookin' an' listenin', yeh little git," Spud grunted at him. "Or yeh'll feel the back of my hand across yer head."

Feeling deeply ashamed, Francie sat down on the bench and

kept his eyes on the ground as Padraig led the horse past him. The other men grabbed a wheelbarrow each and followed the cart into the tunnel. They were right, of course; he was supposed to be keeping watch, and instead there he was dancing around like a ninny. Well, that was enough of that. He kept his eyes out on the yard beyond the tunnel and listened carefully for any sounds of approach.

But it was boring. He struggled to keep his attention from wandering, to keep from drifting into a daydream. His gaze passed over one of the trestle tables used for laying out plans, and fell on a large roll of paper. He strolled over to take a peek. Unrolling it, he saw it was a copy of the plan he had stolen the week before, showing the lowest level of the tower section of Wildenstern Hall. The railway tunnel was here, leading into what was to be the underground station. Along its left side was the access tunnel that O'Keefe and his men had been working in over the last few days. To the right of this tunnel was the treasury. Shay and his men would be using black powder to blast through the dividing wall. It was so far underground, the people in the funeral procession above wouldn't hear a thing.

Then they would load the wheelbarrows and fill the cart. If they played their cards right, they could all be rich men overnight.

Francie was smiling nervously to himself just thinking about it. No more polishing buckles or cleaning the manure out of the stalls. No more sleeping in that poky, damp, drafty, smelly attic. And good riddance to it all. His eyes followed the line of the tunnel to the treasure room. He frowned.

The word "Treasury" had been crossed out on this plan.

Underneath it, in a scrawling handwriting, were the words "Pow-der Store." Francie stared down at these words until the world around them seemed to fade into a haze. All he could see were those words: "Powder Store." He could hear his pulse in his ears. His breath caught in his chest . . . and then he started running.

Tearing up the tunnel as fast as his legs could carry him, he screamed to his father.

"Da! No! It's not the treasure! It's not the treasure!"

A figure appeared in the gloom ahead of him.

"What is it, Francie?" Shay called, hurrying towards him. "Keep your voice down, for the love of God! What's wrong?"

"It's not a treasure room, Da!" Francie panted desperately. "It's the p—"

Then an invisible brick wall slammed into them and they were hurled towards the mouth of the tunnel in an exploding cloud of dust and shattered masonry.

XI

AN UNFORGIVABLE INTERRUPTION

WHEN THE TIME CAME for the coffin to be carried on its bier out to the cemetery, Daisy suddenly found herself involved in a battle of the sexes as she arrived at the door of the church.

"Eunice, you mustn't create a fuss." Gideon was pleading with his wife. "It would be a breach of tradition for you to go to the mausoleum. Women don't attend the interment."

"I don't care if it's not tradition!" Eunice hissed. "I want to see him buried!"

Tatiana piped up in a petulant voice:

"If she's going, I'm going. I want to see him buried too. I don't see why women aren't allowed. Why shouldn't we be?"

She looked for support from Daisy, who closed her eyes for a moment and prayed for strength. Women did not accompany the coffin to the grave; it just wasn't the done thing. And though it was just one of the many injustices heaped upon women in this day and age, this wasn't the time or place to have the argument. She was painfully aware of the massive crowd watching curiously from the sidelines. All around her, men were staring impatiently, outraged at this act of female rebellion.

"Perhaps we could just see Marcus's remains taken as far as the mausoleum, Uncle Gideon," she said sweetly, "And then we can retire and leave the men to the interment."

"What a load of rot!" Eunice declared. "I'm watching the whole thing. Are you with us or not, Melancholy?"

Daisy bridled at the use of the name she hated so much. Edgar was standing off to one side in a posture that said he would take no part in this disgraceful discussion. That left Roberto as the next most senior man in the family. She hesitated, then turned on her husband, who was observing her with an expression of reluctant amusement.

"Roberto, we'd like to attend the interment."

"My darling—"

"Yes, dear?" She arched an eyebrow at him.

Berto did not want any friction with the family today, but he already knew the hell she could put him through if she did not get her way. He glanced again at that eyebrow, cloaked behind the gauzy veil—it rose another fraction of an inch. But it was the look on the face of his father that decided him.

"Perhaps we could break with tradition this once," he said in a loud voice, glaring defiantly at Edgar. "I think everyone should have the chance to say goodbye to Marcus."

Gideon wore an expression of disgust, Eunice one of triumph. Nathaniel was standing back with Gerald, both of them suppressing mocking grins. As the coffin continued on its way, Daisy spotted a man at the edge of the crowd pressing his thumb to the top of his head. But then his wife slapped the back of his neck and he sheepishly cut short the gesture.

In the end, as the men bristled with indignation, over a dozen women followed the casket into the cemetery. All the family's recent Patriarchs were interred in a huge, gothic marble mausoleum at the top end of the cemetery, near the church. Further down, the Heirs who had died before reaching the position were placed in another mausoleum; not quite as grand but mightily impressive nonetheless. The great iron door stood open. Above the columns framing the entrance, an eight-foot, white marble angel raised the tips of his wings straight up towards heaven.

The men filled the path on either side of the door, and Daisy found herself standing beside Eunice on the grass in the shadow of the angel. The archbishop started droning on again in his professionally mournful voice. The six footmen carried the coffin inside on its bier. She had to raise her head to see over the men's shoulders. Her shoes were not well suited for walking on grass and she could feel the high, narrow heels starting to sink into the soft ground. She leaned her weight onto the balls of her feet.

Looking at the other women in their black silk crêpe dresses, she was struck once more by the obscene amounts of money spent on funerals. These designer dresses would be used once and then thrown away; it was considered bad luck to keep funeral outfits in the home, even though most of these women would continue to wear black for months after the burial. This would be done partly because they were in mourning, but also out of fear of the dead. It was believed that dead souls clung to the living and that dressing in black hid the grieving family from the recently departed. As this unholy thought went through her mind, Daisy stared at the iron door of the mausoleum and a shiver ran down her spine. Born to a family like this, what kind of souls haunted that dark cavity?

"Bloody clergy, you can never shut them up," Eunice muttered. "I wish he'd get on and be done with it. These shoes are killing me—"

And then it seemed as if Judgment Day burst over them. The ground erupted with a cracking, deafening boom, muffling everything that followed with a whining silence as a shock wave lifted the people off their feet and cast them aside like leaves in the wind. Daisy found herself sliding across the flagstones of the path, yards from where she had been standing. She couldn't hear a thing and grit filled her eyes. Soil was falling from the sky.

She struggled against the confining folds of her unwieldy crinoline dress and staggered to her feet. Tearing off her veil, she rubbed her eyes, blinking rapidly to try and clear them. Bodies lay tossed and tangled all around her.

A coffin crashed to the ground—and then another, splitting open to spill out broken skeletons wrapped in shreds of cloth. Others fell in pieces. It rained splinters of wood and bone.

Nathaniel was near the door of the mausoleum, looking stunned and trying to stand up. His mouth was open and he had his hands over his ears. There was a long angel-shaped shadow on the ground around him and as Daisy watched, it moved. She looked up at the roof of the mausoleum. The marble angel above the entrance was teetering forward. Daisy screamed at him but he could not hear her.

For a second she froze—and then something crashed to the ground behind her and the fright it gave her started her running. She just managed to reach Nate before her foot caught on the hem of her dress and she stumbled, careering forward and shoving him aside. Daisy sprawled on the ground and before she could get up, the towering marble sculpture toppled from the roof and slammed down on top of her. Nathaniel experienced a moment of complete confusion. One second he was standing watching his brother's coffin being deposited in the mausoleum, the next he was conscious only of being hurled against the mausoleum wall by a huge and sudden force. Then he was falling forward onto the ground, winded and stunned. Reflex had him back on his feet almost immediately, but it had the effect of spinning the world around him in a most unsettling way. He wondered why he couldn't hear anything . . . and why the air was filled with dust and debris.

He was gaping in awe at a sky filled with smoke, earth and flying coffins when a second thrusting force threw him forwards onto his face, knocking what little air was left out of his lungs. His jarred senses gave up their valiant struggle and tipped him into unconsciousness.

When Nate came round, he was surrounded by a crisscross flicker of running legs. Lifting his head, he coughed up and spat out some crumbs of soil that he had somehow swallowed. His chest hurt, but not as much as his neck, head and shoulders. Getting stiffly to his feet, he looked around.

The cemetery was in ruins. Downhill and to his left yawned a massive crater of fresh earth. Tilted and broken gravestones formed angular black and white marks in the new carpet of fresh topsoil. Ruptured coffins lay scattered all around them, and in places a macabre snow of shattered bone had fallen with them. People were running everywhere; screaming, panicking, or making frantic efforts to help the injured.

As his hearing returned, Nate became aware of a voice behind him.

". . . Nate? Nathaniel!"

He turned and was astounded to find the marble angel from the mausoleum's roof standing on its head behind him. Its upraised wings were embedded into the ground almost to its shoulders and its square base jutted into the air. Lying trapped beneath it was his sister-in-law.

"Would you be so kind as to help me?" Daisy hissed through gritted teeth.

Nathaniel took time to assess the situation properly. It posed a fascinating problem. The statue had landed on its wings in such a way that its head was still clear of the earth; but the wings had nailed the folds of Daisy's wire-hooped crinoline dress firmly to the ground on either side of her. She must have been thrown forward at the time because the dress was up around her waist and was pinned so tightly that she could not move her body. A quick peek behind the sculpture confirmed that her frilly, white, ankle-length bloomers were clearly visible.

"Nathaniel!" she screeched. "Have you no decency?! Good God in Heaven, I'm in this position because I just saved your life!"

"I'm much obliged," Nate replied, thinking it highly unlikely that she was telling the truth.

"It's a decision I'm already beginning to regret. Are you going to help me or not?"

He regarded the upturned statue with great deliberation as she lay there fuming.

"I think," he said at last, "that it'll take a team of men to draw your new friend from his scabbard. I'll have to get help."

Daisy made a barely audible whimper, but maintained a dignified expression as she looked up at him from between the shoulders of the embedded sculpture.

"You will be discreet, won't you?"

"Of course," he assured her, taking his coat off and draping it over her exposed undergarments. "You can trust me."

"And don't take too long," she added.

"Don't worry," he called back to her as he walked away, "you'll be quite safe. After all . . . you have an angel watching over you."

Francie woke to find himself being carried through the settling cloud of dust. He coughed hoarsely, gagging on the grit in his throat. As his head lolled to one side, a nightmarish shape charged towards him and he heard snorting and panting breath over the rapid stomp of hooves. The drayhorse galloped past him, its eyes wide with panic, its flanks streaked with wounds. The remains of its cart clattered along on broken wheels behind it. In seconds it was lost from sight in the dusty fog.

Struggling feebly, Francie tried to get his feet under him. The strong arms holding him lowered him gently to the ground. He stood on shaky legs and rubbed his eyes. Shay gripped his shoulders and looked into his face.

"Are y'all right lad?" he asked.

Francie nodded slowly, but found he was crying.

"It's gone to pot, Francie," his father told him in a broken voice. "The whole place is blown to hell. The others are gone, d'yeh understand? They're gone. It's just us two. In a couple of minutes this place is goin' to be crawlin' with navvies so we have to skidaddle, d'yeh get me? Now listen, Francie, 'cos this is the hard bit." He pulled his son closer. "Yeh have to go back to work."

"*What?*" Francie frowned in bewilderment. "What're yeh on about?"

"If we run now, they'll know it were us." Shay shook him by the shoulders. "We have to act normal. They'll come after whoever done this and they'll be lookin' for anyone actin' like they shouldn't. Yeh have to go back to work . . . And don't ever let on you were here."

Francie was numb from shock. He couldn't grasp what his father was saying. The world had exploded around him and he was supposed to pretend it had never happened?

"Da, I—"

"Can yeh walk all right?"

"Yeah, but—"

"Then I have to leg it. Get back to the stables, son. Quick as yeh can now!"

With that, Shay was gone, running into the haze of dust that was settling around them. It was only as he was vanishing into the cloud that Francie noticed his father was carrying one of the bright-eyes from the tunnel. Francie didn't give it much thought. He could hear voices and he suddenly felt fear again. If they caught him here like this, he was finished. Starting off at an unsteady stagger, he quickly found his feet and bolted for the nearest bushes. He only just made it out of sight when the first of the workmen came bounding down the hill.

XII

"THE SITUATION IS WELL IN HAND"

THE CEMETERY WAS THRONGED WITH PEOPLE. A second, smaller explosion punched up through the ground nearby, followed by another two in quick succession. They did no damage but added to the panic. Most of the injured were making their feelings felt: screams and moans carried through the air. But some of those stretched out on the ground lay without moving, and made no sound at all.

Nathaniel strode through the chaos towards his father. Edgar was standing, leaning on his cane and smoking a cigar. His claw clicked in a steady rhythm. Coated in a layer of dirt, he dominated the scene like a battle-hardened general, barking orders to those around him:

"Warburton! Enlist the help of any other doctors we have on

hand. See to the most seriously wounded only—let the servants deal with the rest. Gideon, you and Roberto take some men and get these crowds back, damn it. It's like a bloody circus in here! O'Keefe, I want teams for heavy lifting for those who are trapped, and assign some men skilled in explosives to explore every inch of this area and make it safe.

"Eunice, supervise the women. See that brandy, blankets, smelling salts and bandages are brought out for those who need them and inform the housekeeper to make the West Hall ready for casualties. Where's the Viceroy? I want troops from the Royal Barracks here to secure the area within the hour. Gerald! Where's Gerald?"

"Here, Uncle Edgar."

The Patriarch turned to find his nephew standing behind him.

"Ah," he grunted. "You will assist Warburton for as long as he needs you, then I'm putting you in charge of the remains that this cataclysm has spewed out all over the cemetery. You will be responsible for uniting each corpse with its respective components and seeing that they are laid to rest once more in the state they enjoyed before they were so suddenly exhumed."

"Yes, Uncle Edgar."

"Now where the hell is Nath—?"

"I'm here, Father," Nate announced as he walked up.

"You will—"

"Melancholy is trapped, sir," Nathaniel cut in, taking some satisfaction in being able to interrupt his father. "I need some men to free her."

Edgar stared at his son with his one good eye for a moment

and then nodded. Reaching up with his claw, he took the cigar from his mouth.

"Then take them," he growled. "Take what men you need and make good use of them."

Daisy kept her eyes fixed on the ground, her cheeks blushing a stark crimson.

"You said you'd be *discreet*," she muttered between clenched teeth.

"I could have kept your situation to myself altogether," Nathaniel replied. "But some blackguard might have come along and taken advantage of you in your exposed condition."

"So you decided to set an example?" she hissed.

In fairness, he thought, I could have brought the whole crowd. He had called over the eight strongest-looking men he could find to help him lift God's messenger off his sister-in-law. The navvies were treating the situation as delicately as they could, doing their best to avert their eyes from her misfortune. But Nate knew that Daisy would be the talk of the town before the day was out. He took her hands and nodded to the man nearest him as the navvies gripped the angel's wings.

"One . . . two . . . three . . . Heeaave!"

The marble sculpture slowly came up, the stone sliding from the earth with a soft grating sound—but their strength failed and it slipped back down again with a slushy thud.

"And again!" Nate urged them. "On three!"

They all counted off once more and, with a concerted effort, hauled the statue up far enough to free the folds of Daisy's dress and allow Nate to pull her free. The sculpture toppled down onto its front as he helped her get to her feet. He was all ready with his next jibe when he saw Clancy walking towards them. The footman's face was as inscrutable as ever, but Nate felt suddenly ashamed of himself. Looking down into Daisy's face, he saw that it was taking all her strength to keep from bursting into tears. She had been dreadfully humiliated, and instead of trying to ease her distress, he had made fun of her.

He picked up his jacket and draped it over her shoulders. Clancy stopped just short of them, his eyes fixed on Nathaniel. The manservant glanced diffidently at Daisy, nodded towards the navvies and then looked pointedly back at his master. Nate got the message and felt even more embarrassed; as a gentleman, this was his situation to deal with. Clancy should not have to point out his duties. Nate glanced around; it appeared that no one else had noticed Daisy's plight.

"Ah, there you are, Clancy," he said. "Take these men up to the house. Give them five shillings apiece and a stiff drink. Note down their names so that they may be commended to their foreman . . . and thank them for their discretion."

"Thank . . . thank you very much, sir," one of the navvies stuttered.

The others mumbled their thanks, but they had received the warning loud and clear. If word got out about what had happened to Daisy, they would lose their jobs.

"Yes, sir," Clancy replied.

He didn't move an inch. Nathaniel was at a loss for a moment. Had he forgotten something? Clancy would never speak up in front of the workers, but—Nate could have kicked himself.

"I will escort Miss Daisy to the house myself," he added.

"Very good, sir."

Daisy clung onto his arm as the others walked away. Then he led her through the ruined graveyard towards the church.

"We should tell Roberto," he said softly to her. "He needs to know."

"He didn't come looking for me, did he?" she whispered back, her throat tense. "Anyway, it's probably just as well he wasn't there he'd only have got all melodramatic. You know what he's like. I'll tell him when I'm ready."

There were tears streaming down her face now. They both fell silent. He gave her his handkerchief, wishing he had done more to ease her embarrassment. His conscience always seemed to rear its head too late. As the two of them walked, their feet sank into the dark brown earth that had been sprayed over the grass by the explosion. The crowd of gawking onlookers stood behind a cordon of footmen, eager to see as much of what had happened as possible. They would be drinking on this for weeks.

Nathaniel noticed that the ground was covered with hats, caps and bonnets—all knocked off heads by the blast. He had lost his own, he realized. The carriages were gone: the horses and velocycles had obviously bolted. They would have to walk up to the house. It would probably do Daisy good to walk for a bit. His Aunt Eunice was moving to intercept them, some rolls of bandages in her arms.

"Daisy, my dear," she called. "This is no time to be a weeping willow. We've all had a shock. Chin up! You must *compose* yourself, young lady."

Nathaniel could see flecks of earth caught in his aunt's dentures. He felt a sudden contempt for this petty, overbearing woman.

"Wildenstern ladies must set an example, my dear," Eunice went on. "Stop your crying now. Stop it! You have to be made of stronger stuff than this!"

"You have soil in your teeth, Aunt Eunice," Nate said to her, and led Daisy straight past as the elderly woman dropped the bandages and hurriedly took out a compact mirror to examine her mouth.

"Don't pay her any mind," he said quietly to Daisy.

"No." Daisy stopped abruptly. "She's right—I should be helping."

She wiped the last of her tears away and took off Nathaniel's jacket, handing it to him.

"I'll be fine, thank you."

Roberto, who had been supervising the cordon with Hennessy, spotted Daisy and started to hurry across the lawn towards them, concern written all over his face. Before he reached them, Edgar appeared with his black servants looming behind him.

"Miss Melancholy." He bowed his head to her. "I trust your predicament was handled with sufficient propriety?"

"Yes, Father," she answered, glancing sidelong at Nathaniel, who swallowed nervously.

But Daisy had no wish to embarrass him here and now. She

fervently wished she could just escape the whole damned lot of them. She would get back at Nate in her own good time.

Nathaniel surveyed the chaotic scene around them. The damage would take weeks to repair. He shook his head in disbelief, flabbergasted by what had happened. Marcus's funeral had been *bombed*. The enormity of the situation was still sinking in. He found his entire body was shaking; his grief for his brother turning into a terrible rage.

"We have to find whoever did this," he growled through clenched teeth. "We have to find these rebels, these *curs* and . . . and . . . *destroy* them. There must be hell to pay for this."

"The perpetrators will be dealt with," Edgar told him in a matter-of-fact way. "The situation is well in hand."

The Patriarch turned to look round for a moment and Nate followed his gaze. Standing by the corner of the church was a broad-shouldered figure dressed in a suit and bowler hat. It was Slattery, the man Nate had met outside his father's office a few days before. He gave Nathaniel a friendly grin, showing off his gold teeth, and then disappeared round the corner: "The situation is well in hand," Edgar said again.

XIII

THE BOG BODIES

FOUR PEOPLE HAD BEEN KILLED in the funeral explosion. Dr. Warburton said it could have been much worse. The rebels who had perpetrated the attack had set off some explosives in the old treasury. The money and valuables had been cleared out so that the space could be used to store the black powder the engineers used for blasting out the tunnels. The entire stock of powder had exploded. It was pure chance that more people had not been standing on the ground over the store when it was detonated.

Two days later, Nathaniel was prowling the corridors of Wildenstern Hall, his mind seething with frustrated rage. The rebels had gone too far this time. Over the last few years there had been the odd revolt—raids on food stores or bands of resistance organized against evictions—but they had never attempted anything like this before.

The nearest comparison anyone could draw was the famous gunpowder plot of 1605, when Guy Fawkes and some English dissidents had tried to blow up the Houses of Parliament. To Nate, killing the King and a gaggle of politicians had some kind of logic to it. At least, if you were of the revolutionary persuasion. But who in their right minds would attack a funeral? A *funeral*, for God's sake!

He kept turning the event over and over in his mind, striding relentlessly down one hallway after another. On top of everything else, he was still no closer to finding Babylon, in spite of numerous inquiries. And even if he did, Marcus's cryptic message had given him no clue as to how a childhood plaything would help catch his killer.

Tired and dispirited, he eventually found himself near Gerald's quarters. Nate knew what he needed to do to ease his mind and he decided to try and convince his cousin to come along.

Gerald was standing in his laboratory, in the light of the tall windows. He was wearing an apron over his clothes and was gazing up at the overcast sky, lost in thought. On the tables around him were the remains of the corpses disinterred by the explosion. They were in various states of decomposition. Even the skeletons varied in age, some a stark yellow-white, others turning a dirty brown. Nate wrinkled his nose at the smell of old decay.

Gerald did not notice him until he was halfway across the room.

"Welcome to my mortuary," he said, turning round and blinking as if waking from a sleep.

"Enjoying the work?" Nate asked him.

"I am, actually," his cousin replied, gesturing towards the nearest table. "I was a bit irritated at having to put aside my work on engimal behavior, but this is pretty fascinating stuff. Fitting the skeletons back together was easy, where the bones are intact. But piecing together the fragmented bones is proving a little more difficult. A bit like a jigsaw in three dimensions. And I'm not sure if you're supposed to use *glue* on mortal remains or not."

"Probably sacrilege," Nate commented. "Still, you always did like puzzles."

"Mm." Gerald nodded. "But there's an even bigger puzzle. All the graves in this cemetery have been recorded and marked down on a map. The family has always been diligent about its record-keeping—it's one of the reasons we're so rich. And as far back as records on this graveyard go, we can account for all the people buried here. The explosion unearthed the graves of eighteen people. We know this for certain."

"So?" Nate asked.

"So why," Gerald continued, "do we have twenty-two bodies?"

Nate shrugged.

"The records must be wrong, or someone chucked an extra few bodies into the graves without telling anybody. That's no great mystery."

"I don't think so," Gerald said, shaking his head. "Have a gander at this."

He walked down to the end of the room, where two long

tables were draped in sheets. Lifting off the covers, he folded them carefully and laid them aside. Stretched out on the tables were four cadavers. Nathaniel leaned over, studying each one.

They were different from the rest of the corpses. The others were little more than skeletons, if that. These four were remarkably intact. Each one was caked in mud, but still had flesh on its bones. The skin was dark brown, tough and wrinkled like old leather, the teeth bared as if in a grimace. The bodies had a flattened appearance, as if they had been crushed and even folded in places. Hair and fingernails and even eyelashes were still visible, and their clothes had not fully rotted. There was metal around their necks and wrists that looked like the remains of jewelry. Two of them were unmistakably women, the other two men.

"They're bog bodies," Gerald told him. "This whole area was peat bog once, before it was drained and converted into farmland. And then the church and the cemetery were built here. But these people were buried before that . . . and without coffins. I haven't had time to clean them properly yet; it's delicate work. Bogs can preserve corpses from decay for millennia; that's why they look the way they do."

"Why are they flattened like that?" Nate asked.

"It's from the weight of the ground as it settled and built up around them," Gerald told him. "And the shifting over the centuries distorts their shapes too. Even so, I've never heard of a single body as well preserved as these—and to find *four* of them! We're looking at a piece of history here, Nate."

"How do you know so much about these things?"

"I read," Gerald replied.

He took out his cigarette case, drew one out and lit it up. His face was solemn as he regarded the leathery corpses. Nathaniel knew that this was the kind of intellectual challenge that his cousin thrived upon, and he was keen to interrupt Gerald's obsessive curiosity before it really took hold.

"I want to get drunk," he declared.

"So get drunk."

"No, I mean completely and utterly, unhealthily out-of-my-face drunk," Nate explained. "Let's go into town—we could go on the tear in Monto."

Gerald looked reluctant to give up his work. He eyed the bog bodies with a longing that Nate found a little disturbing. Pulling his watch from his waistcoat pocket, he checked the time. It was after five.

"You'll turn into a prig if you spend all your time in the lab," Nate persisted. "Come on, let's get buckled. It's how Marcus would have wanted it. And we can take Flash into town and show it off to the girls."

Gerald raised an eyebrow.

"Will you let me ride it?"

"I don't think it'd have you," Nate retorted. "Besides, I'm not that desperate for your company. I'll let you tell everyone the story of how we caught it, though—you can embellish your part in it if you wish. Look, we haven't hit the town together in over a year and a half; I need to know if you can still cut the mustard. Now are we getting drunk or what?"

"Well, since you asked so nicely"—Gerald slapped his thigh in mock jollity—"I suppose I could do with an evening of dolly-mops, booze and belly-timber. Besides, these old codgers won't be getting any deader tonight. Let's hit that town then!"

Monto was a sprawling neighborhood of ill repute in north Dublin, centered on Montgomery Street. Ireland had long been the most irritating thorn in the backside of the British Empire and it was reflected in the large numbers of troops stationed in the country's capital. There was good money to be had for supplying the kind of bawdy entertainment that all these soldiers demanded, and much of that money was made in the streets of Monto after sundown.

The pubs, clubs and opium dens that nestled in this pit of sin also offered noble young gentlemen—even some who were still in their teenage years—the chance to experience the seedier side of life with relative anonymity . . . if they were discreet about it. Nathaniel and Gerald were not. As they rode down the center of Montgomery Street on velocycles, their engines roaring with machismo, the two young gentlemen quickly became the center of attention. Their wealth had always given them a certain celebrity status, and velocycles were not unheard of among the rich and famous, but one look at Flash told the spectators they were seeing something special. Whispers drifted about that this was none other than the Beast of Glenmalure. The savage velocycle growled at the people on either side as it rolled down the street, overtaking hansom cabs and horse-drawn trams. The crowds made it nervous.

After riding up and down the street a few times to flaunt their machines to curious women and envious men, the two riders turned down a lane and pulled up at the door of a gentleman's club. A small crowd of admirers followed them at a safe distance. Whipping off their insect-flecked goggles, they carefully chained their mounts to a lamppost—both to stop them wandering and to prevent them from being stolen. Taking off his leather riding cap, each man opened a box on the back of his saddle and took out a fashionable top hat.

"Right," said Nathaniel, ignoring the people behind them. "A bottle of wine and a slap-up meal and then we go looking for some ladies to impress."

He took off his coat, which was spattered with mud.

"There'll be no *ladies* in these parts," Gerald told him.

"Then we'll just have to make do with whatever fillies we can find," Nate replied. "Come on, let's get buckled."

A racy waltz was being played inside the club and they could hear the sound of dancing feet on a wooden floor. They were welcomed in by the doorman, who was trained to recognize important faces and treat them accordingly. The social columns in the local papers had already announced Nathaniel's return. The doormen of Monto could earn some extra income by informing the gossipmongers which teenage playboys were out on the town, and what kind of mischief they created in the process.

But another set of eyes was watching Nathaniel and his cousin with a burning resentment. Shay Noonan peered out from a shadowed doorway as the two gentlemen entered the club. He had been about to walk out of the offices of a moneylender, having just paid off his debts, when he saw them arrive. Shay still had plenty of money left over and was intending to put some of it on a cock-fight in town. When he saw the velocycles, he decided to change his plans.

He had not slept for two nights and there were dark bags under his eyes. It was a close evening, and his collar and the band of his cap were damp with sweat. The word in town was that Slattery, the bailiff, and his men had been asking questions. Jimmy and the other lads involved in the disastrous heist were dead and they had already been reported missing. Anybody who knew Jimmy would be aware that he worked with Shay. The moneylender who had taken the engimal lamp off his hands for a tidy sum would keep his mouth shut, but sooner or later somebody would talk. Shay needed to get out of town. Everybody thought the explosion had been the work of the rebels. If Slattery's lads got hold of him, he was a dead man—if he was lucky.

But Shay couldn't stop thinking about his friends. All they'd wanted was to score some loot; to take some money from a family that had more than they could spend in a hundred lifetimes. Instead, his mates had been blown to pieces. The memory of it was like a physical pain to him.

This was the Wildensterns' doing—them and the whole system that had driven him into a life of crime. Watching these young lords cavort with careless ignorance of the poverty and misery around them made him sick to his stomach. He'd get out of town all right; but not before he'd pulled off one final job. Something that would hurt and humiliate the swells he despised so much.

Waiting for the group of spectators to depart, he checked that the doorman had gone back inside and crept up to the velocycles, looking them over. Their front legs were chained to the lamppost, but the lock would be easy for him to pick. Having seen the gentlemen riding them, he figured they were tame enough. The smaller of the two was obviously a little afraid of its companion. It was careful to keep the post between them. The big one was a beauty; easily worth ten times what the money-lender had paid for the bright-eye. It shone its eyes at him and growled quietly as he came closer, but he wasn't impressed. He admired its sweeping lines and powerful bulk.

"Right you are, then," Shay said softly. "You'll do nicely."

Stroking its head, he leaned over to take hold of the lock.

The engimal roared and pivoted to the side, slamming him up against the lamppost. Shay cried out as he felt some-thing crack in his chest. He staggered back but was caught as the machine bounced off its back wheel and hit him again, knocking him to the ground. In a moment he was back on his feet, stumbling away. The velocycle struck out once more with its rear wheel, spinning it at high speed as it kicked Shay up the backside. The racing wheel added to the force of the kick, and he was hurled across the laneway and spilled face-first into the mud.

The engimal pulled at its chain, snarling ferociously. The racket did not go unnoticed, but by the time the doorman came out to investigate, Shay had limped out of sight around a corner. He hurried away into the darker alleys of Monto. A clicking just over his heart told him he had broken a rib—one more point to the Wildensterns. But this wasn't the end of it, he swore to him-self . . . not by a long way.

•   •   •

It was the early hours of the morning when Nathaniel and Gerald, drunk and exhausted, made their unsteady way back down the laneway to their velocycles. They had gone from one venue to the next and tasted the best that Monto had to offer; now they wanted to go home. A drizzly rain was starting to fall and the air was swollen with the smell of an oncoming storm. The engimals' eyes lit up and they whined plaintively as their chains were undone, eager to go for a run.

". . . I don't care if she had a voice like a magpie," Gerald was saying. "I wasn't listening to her anyway. I was lost in the depths of her eyes."

They each took off their top hats, putting them in the boxes behind their saddles and taking out leather riding caps instead.

"It's wha' was coming ou' of the depths of 'er *throat* that had my attention," Nate retorted in a slurred voice, wrapping up his chain. "Was like listenin' to nails on a blackboard."

Flash was giving him a funny look. Nate patted its head and went to swing his leg over the saddle. The velocycle jerked to the side and Nate missed, his leg coming down so hard he lost his balance and nearly fell over.

"Whash got into you?" he asked the engimal.

He tried to mount the velocycle again, but again it twisted out his way. Nate tried for a third time and this time he did fall over, landing clumsily in the mud.

"F' Godsshakes!" he roared, flailing around as he tried to stand up again. "Stand still, damn you!"

"I don't think it wants . . . you riding it while . . . while you're drunk." Gerald chuckled as he swayed back and forth on the saddle of his own engimal, taking his goggles from his coat pocket.

"I'll ride it when and where I like!" Nate bellowed. "Oi'm in charge 'ere!"

"It looks it," Gerald snorted. "Get on the back here—I'll give you a lift. Otherwise you'll have to find a cab."

"Right!" Nate snapped, giving Flash a petulant kick. "You're in my bad books now. You'll just have to follow us home. And don't go chasing any bloody rabbits or the like. Stay right behind us, y'hear me?"

Flash looked subdued and a little hurt. It rubbed its front wheel up against Nate's leg.

"Don't start," Nathaniel said to it. "I'm really annoyed with you."

He climbed on behind Gerald and pulled on his goggles. They rolled out into the street with Flash trailing behind. The city was empty and dark at this hour and Gerald smacked the side of his beast hard with his riding crop, egging it on through the deserted streets. Neither rider was in a fit state to be in the saddle, and with each corner they came dangerously close to falling off. With no stirrups to steady himself, Nate hung onto Gerald's waist and tried to hug the velocycle with his thighs. Gerald shouted at his machine, his voice loud and raw in the quiet night air.

The wind rose and the rain began to fall more and more heavily, until it was cascading down in a wall of spray that turned the night scene to brushstrokes in the light of the engimals' eyes. They crossed the Grand Canal and raced up Rathmines Road.

Gerald leaned into a hard turn right on the muddy corner that led to Rathgar. The velocycle skidded, lost its footing and suddenly slid out from under them, sending them tumbling across the road.

It happened so fast that Nate barely had time to register he was falling before he found himself prostrate on the ground, the wind driven from his lungs. He sat up and winced, working his right shoulder, which felt as if it had been badly twisted. His coat sleeves were torn and the skin of his right palm was in ribbons, embedded with muck and small stones. His knees were in a similar state, visible through the rips in his trousers.

Gerald was on his knees, his hand to his mouth as if he were in danger of throwing up.

"Are you all right?" Nate asked him.

His cousin held up his other hand for a second.

"Got hit in the mouth by the handlebar," he said at last, spitting out some blood onto the wet ground. "Think I've lost a couple of teeth."

"Oh, bad luck," Nate said. "Front ones?"

"No, no." Gerald felt around the inside of his mouth with his tongue. "I'll keep my dashing good looks, thank God."

The engimal was lying on its side, groaning, but didn't appear to be too badly injured. Flash coasted up and stopped beside Nathaniel. It uttered a worried gurgle.

"Don't give me any of your sympathy," he exclaimed, pushing at the velocycle. "This is your fault and you know it."

XIV

A GASPING BREATH

WHEN THEY FINALLY GOT BACK to the house, tired, filthy, sore and disheveled, they went straight up to Gerald's rooms. He lit a couple of the gas-lamps and took some iodine and gauze out of a cupboard.

"We need to clean out your hand," he said, ushering Nathaniel to a stool at an empty table. "It could get infected. Are you hurt anywhere else?"

"Just a sore shoulder and some bruises. And I skinned my knees too. I'll put some coins on them before I go to bed."

Nate was gripping a handkerchief to his injured palm and when he opened his fingers, the linen was stained with blood. Laying his hand on the table, he bit his lip as Gerald poured iodine over the torn flesh—causing it to sting like a flash-burn—and started to use a gold-tipped tweezers to painstakingly pick out the stones and bits of grit.

"Are you sure you're sober enough to be doing this?" he asked.

"Not really, no."

Nathaniel looked around the room, searching for something to take his mind off his wounded hand. His eyes fell on the four shapes covered by sheets at the end of the room. The tweezers dug into his hand and he yelped.

"God Almighty! Can't you be a bit more careful?"

"Sorry."

Nate drew a hissed breath in through his teeth as he felt the metal tips probing his damaged palm. The wind blew rain against the windows and there was a distant rumble of thunder.

"Let's have another look at your bog bodies then," he said. "I need a good laugh."

"If you like."

Gerald finished cleaning the wound and told Nate to rinse it under the tap before putting on a bandage. Then they walked down the half-lit room to the tables where the leathery bodies lay. Lifting off the sheets, they gazed at the distorted, flattened forms in silence. The room flashed—lightning turning everything to black and white for an instant. A glint of metal caught Nate's eye and he leaned over one of the male bodies, examining the right hand.

"Look," he said. "That's gold."

On the ring finger of the hand was what appeared to be a misshapen signet ring. Nate took his bloodstained handkerchief and rubbed some of the dirt off it. He gasped at what he saw. The ring bore the Wildenstern crest. His father wore the same ring, given to him by his father before him. This corpse . . . this man, whoever he was, had been a Patriarch.

"Well, I'll be damned," Gerald breathed.

There was another flash of lightning, making them blink. Nate saw another glint of metal; this time it came from between the dead man's bared teeth. Squeamish about touching the cadaver with his bare hands, he pressed down the teeth of the lower jaw and reached into the mouth with his hankie.

"There's something in here," he whispered.

Sticking his fingers down into the throat, he felt a hard shape and pulled at it. It came away and he held it up, gripping it with his handkerchief. It was a grimy gold coin. They both exchanged looks and Nate peered into the mouth.

"There's more," he said.

Sliding his hand in again, he pulled a second and then a third coin from the throat. The dead man's gullet was full of gold coins.

"He didn't do this himself," Gerald muttered softly. "Somebody stuffed those in. It might even have been what killed him. Imagine that! Imagine how much somebody would have to have hated him to ram *gold* down his throat . . ."

"And not take it *out* again when he was dead," Nate finished for him.

Thunder cracked and rolled outside. Rain lashed against the glass, running down it in streams.

He could still see metal in there. Slipping his bare fingers between the teeth, he tried to reach it. The coin was far down in the throat, but he almost had it—

The jaw suddenly clamped shut on his hand. He let out a terrified scream and pulled his hand out. The grip was feeble and he freed himself easily, but he screeched again for good measure.

"Jesus!" he cried. "Jesus Bloody Christ! What the *bloody hell* . . .?"

Nate started hyperventilating, but Gerald was ignoring him completely. Seizing a small pair of tongs from another bench, he rushed over to the body and tipped back the crushed head. He reached down into the mouth with the tongs and pulled out the last coin. The leathery corpse coughed and drew a weak, ragged breath.

"Get me a bellows and the galvanizing apparatus from the cupboard over there!" Gerald yelled at his cousin.

"It . . . it bloody bit me, Gerald!"

"It was a gag reflex," Gerald barked at him. "He was trying to breathe."

He turned and stared at Nate with a strange light in his eyes, his face like that of a saint struck by a divine vision. Lightning shocked the room white again and thunder crashed against the windows.

"He's alive," Gerald said in a hoarse gasp. "It's impossible . . . completely impossible. But he's *alive*."

Nathaniel gazed in utter disbelief at his friend. For a moment he was sure that Gerald had lost his mind. But then he looked at his own hand and saw that it was bleeding again. The bog body took another wheezing breath and Nate saw the chest rise and fall almost imperceptibly. He and Gerald looked at each other. And then they turned to look at the other three corpses.

It was to be the longest night of their lives. As Gerald tried to resuscitate the reanimated man, Nathaniel probed the throats of the other three bodies. Each one was jammed with coins or gold jewelry. Moments after he had gingerly cleared each blockage, he heard the dry rasp of air from desiccated lungs. The butler, MacDonald, was summoned, along with Clancy and a small cadre of the most trusted servants. The entire floor of the building was sealed off and Edgar was informed.

The Patriarch limped down to the laboratory on his cane, wearing a dressing gown over his nightshirt and flanked by his Maasai footmen. Standing over the revived cadavers, he watched as servants used bellows to gently push air into the lungs of the bog bodies whenever they failed to breathe by themselves—but breathe they did. He listened dispassionately as Gerald explained what had happened.

"How is this possible?" he asked at last.

"I . . . I could only guess . . . theorize, sir," Gerald replied nervously. "Nothing like this has ever happened before. There is no precedent."

"Then *theorize,* damn it, man." Edgar scowled. "We have dead bodies drawing breath before our eyes! Tell me how this can be!"

"There must have been some kernel of life left in them," Gerald stammered, running his hand through his hair. "I don't know how, Uncle. Some animals hibernate for long periods—but they still need to breathe. Insects can be dormant, sometimes for years . . . but . . . I don't know. It's almost as if these preserved bodies are like the dried husk of a seed that can still sprout leaves. Clearly, *aurea sanitas* is at work here . . . but I . . . I've never ever heard of anything like this. It shouldn't be possible."

Edgar sniffed loudly, clearly unsatisfied with the explanation.

"Are they capable of recovering? Will they be able to speak—to walk?"

"I don't know, Uncle."

The Patriarch turned his attention back to the bog bodies.

"Will they be able to have children?"

Gerald shrugged helplessly, baffled by the question.

"We'll see if Warburton can tell us any more," Edgar grunted.

"If he can, then he'd be lying!" Gerald retorted, more aggressively than he'd meant to. Composing himself, he added: "There is nothing in the world of medicine to prepare someone for this situation, Uncle. Let me continue to work on them and see what can be done. Please! If I need assistance, I will be the first to say it."

Edgar stared at him for what seemed like an age . . . and then nodded. Turning to the room at large, he gestured to Gerald's four new patients.

"Not a whisper of what is happening here must go beyond these walls. Of the servants, only you here are to know of it. I do not need to tell you what will happen to you if you utter so much as a word of it. As for the family, we will include only those closest to me, and whatever scientific minds Gerald feels might be needed.

"Gerald, you will be responsible for their treatment and also for uncovering their past. If this man was a Patriarch, I want to know which one. There are too many questions unanswered here."

With that, he walked out of the room. Gerald looked over at Nathaniel and gave a tired but triumphant smile.

And so the work began. Gerald wrote out a list of the things he needed and men were dispatched to find them. Two footmen stood by each body, ready with a bellows in case their breathing failed. Using a stethoscope, Gerald discovered weak, thready and painfully slow heartbeats and listened to lungs that sounded like brittle paper bags. He inserted gold needles into key *aurea sanitas* points over each body and connected them via wires to a galvanizing apparatus that ran a low-voltage electrical current into the leathery flesh. This was a technique he had pioneered which had been proven to stimulate *aurea sanitas*'s recuperative properties.

Using an eyedropper, he dripped water into their throats, to see if they were capable of swallowing, and therefore rehydrating their bodies. Every breath, every waking moment seemed to require supreme effort for these preserved people, but eventually they began to drink. As his confidence in them grew, Gerald added sugar to the solution.

Nathaniel helped where he could, following Gerald's instructions, but he was working in a daze. He could not comprehend how any of this could be possible. Gazing down at the first man they had brought back to life after his centuries-long sleep, Nate wondered what kind of eyes lay beneath those sunken eyelids. As if parting the petals of a flower, he delicately pulled back one of the dark-brown eyelids to see. Deflated against the wall of the hollow socket, he found a shriveled yellow ball with a bleached pupil. Clancy was standing next to him and tilted his head to look closer.

"If they do wake up, do you think they'll be blind?" Nate asked quietly.

"I think that remains to be seen, sir," Clancy replied.

Gerald joined them, his fatigue starting to show through his zeal.

"There are other questions to ask, Master Nathaniel, if these extraordinary souls recover," Clancy added softly, careful not to let the other servants hear him. "It is clear that they were killed . . . or at least attacked and then buried in the belief that they were dead. This was an act of hateful vengeance. And to be buried in a peat bog as they were was a fate most often reserved for those who died in disgrace, or were being punished for the most serious of crimes. What kind of people were they to deserve such a death?

"But there is one more thing to consider," he went on. "Because if this man here was a Wildenstern Patriarch—though evidently not a *popular* one—and he regains his faculties, then he will be by far the oldest living male in the family line."

Clancy turned to look at Nate and Gerald. He could see that with everything that had gone on, they had not even considered this.

"He could claim the family," Nate said. "He could take over from Father."

Outside, dawn was starting to creep across the eastern sky.

• • •

Francie shifted around restlessly in the narrow bed, unable to settle. Beside him, his bedmate, Patrick, tugged angrily on the thin blanket.

"Francie, will yeh stop yer fiddlin'!" he muttered. "Some of us're tryin' to sleep, y'know!"

Heaving a frustrated sigh, Francie rolled out of bed and felt around in the dark for his clothes, which lay in an untidy pile on the floor. He was half dead with exhaustion but knew he was not going to sleep. He had been unable to doze for more than an hour at a time since the explosion. His nerves were raw, he felt sick and he was cold all the time. Memories of the disaster and the men who had died constantly forced their way into his thoughts. Guilt and fear washed over him in waves. This was the third night now and still he couldn't find peace.

It was still raining outside; the storm had been blowing for two nights and there had been less work to do. Normally he would have been happy about this, but now he found that work offered the only relief for his uneasy mind. He couldn't light the lamp with all the others asleep, and in his weary daze he managed to pull both braces onto one shoulder and put his hat on backwards before he straightened himself out.

Hugging his coat tightly around him against the night's chill, he crept down to the hay stalls at the far end of the long attic, opened the trap door and, hanging from the ledge, dropped down into the darkness and the pile of hay that lay below. Brushing himself down, he walked through the stable, listening to the breathing of the horses. Some of them were awake, moving nervously as the storm blustered overhead.

He had returned to the stables after the explosion looking as if he'd been buried alive. There was no way he would have been able to wash his clothes in time, and he only had a spare shift; no other trousers, boots or jacket. He had considered fleeing the grounds, but his father's words had stayed with him. They had to act normal. Francie had still been trying to come up with an excuse for the state of his clothes when Hennessy had walked in. The old man had taken one look at him, strode forward and wrapped his arms around him, hugging him tightly.

"Francie, little Francie," the old man had cried. "We thought yeh were dead when we couldn't find yeh. Thank God yer all right!"

That was when Francie had found out about what had happened at the cemetery. Hennessy—who, despite his gruff manner, was very protective of his lads—assumed that the stable boy was in a state because he had been in the wrong place in the graveyard when the ground erupted. And Francie let him go on thinking that.

His eyes were adjusting to the gloom and he ran his fingers along the wooden walls of the stalls. Being with the animals relaxed him a little and he whispered comforting words to some of them, reaching over to stroke their noses. He had been visiting the new engimal regularly and was making his way towards the velocycle's stall when a sound from ahead of him made him start. A tall figure had come from nowhere and was walking through the darkness towards him. The man had a candle in his hand, but the light had not yet reached Francie. Not wanting to explain why he was up and about, he carefully opened the nearest door and slipped in. A warm damp nose nuzzled his ear and he reached up to scratch the horse's chin.

The glow from the candle passed over his head and he heard the side door of the building open.

"There you are. You're late," a man said softly.

He spoke like a gentleman and Francie assumed it was one of the Wildensterns. He couldn't tell which one.

"Sorry, sor," Old Hennessy's voice replied. "There wuz a watchman out on the lawn."

"You don't have to call me "sir" here, when there's nobody around," the gentleman chided him warmly. "But you're right. All this new security's going to make things difficult. The place has turned into a bloody barracks since the attack on the funeral. The inside of the house is almost as bad, what with our efforts to raise the dead and all that. We'll just have to concoct an excuse for you to move around with more freedom. Leave it with me; I'll come up with something."

"Aye," Hennessy replied.

"And for God's sake, don't get caught by any of those thugs standing guard. They'll shoot on sight they're so on edge at the moment. Don't do anything to make them suspicious—we're taking enough chances as it is. The family will cover up my crimes, but they won't forgive you yours. Come on, let's get out of here . . ."

The door opened and the sound of the storm drowned out the rest of the conversation. The door closed quietly and the light disappeared. Francie peeked over the wall to check they were gone and then came out of the stall. His mind was filled with questions: Who was the stranger? What was Hennessy doing talking to him in the stable in the middle of the night? What were they up to? What did the stranger mean about raising the dead? But the question that was really nagging him was how the gentleman had got in. If he'd come in through the big double doors at the front, Francie was certain that he would have seen him. Creeping down to the front of the building, he felt the ground at the door. It was dry. The doors had not been opened.

He straightened up and looked around at the stone walls on either side. Some of the older lads said that Wildenstern Hall was riddled with secret passages. Francie wondered if it was true— and if one of those passages happened to lead to the stables.

XV

THE MATTER OF THE DEAF HORSE

NATHANIEL LAY AWAKE, staring at the ceiling. Even in the dark, he could see the coving around the edges and the oil painting that hung above his bed. It portrayed an eight-wheeled behemoth found in North America, now living in the Wildensterns' zoo. Gazing at it upside down, he remembered the excitement of seeing it when it had first arrived, tugging at its chains, steaming belligerently and snarling at everyone. He was thirteen and it had been the scariest, most exciting thing he had ever experienced.

Until the night a corpse had bitten his hand. The graze from the velocycle accident had almost fully healed, but he could still feel the brush of those teeth over his raw flesh. He was unable to get the bog bodies off his mind.

And he still was no closer to finding that goddamned, bloody

Babylon either. Thinking the message might have been a code, he had broken the letters up and tried re-form them into other words, but it did not seem to be an anagram—nor, for that matter, was it a numerical code or any other system of encryption that he or Gerald could think of. But then, how could they tell without some kind of key?

He had questioned Winters at length, but with no satisfaction. The footman was telling the same story as everyone else. It could be the truth, or it could be Edgar forcing the servants to maintain a cover-up according to the Rules of Ascension. Nate's father didn't trust him enough yet to share those kinds of responsibilities.

But Nate was sure now that the message wasn't a code. Babylon was not where it should have been and he had several servants trying to find out what had happened to it. And anyway, what did the message *mean*? If he found Babylon, how would it lead him to Marcus's killer? Was the little scamp carrying another note? Was the murderer to be found in the same place? Did it even have anything to do with the murder at all?

Nate let out a yell of frustration and thumped his head against his pillow.

Climbing out of bed, he pulled on a dressing gown and made his way down to the laboratory. As the elevator doors slid open on the floor where Gerald had his rooms, Nate heard a low moaning sound. Three voices were softly wailing in a haunted chorus of pain. He hurried along the hallway. It could only be the bog people, and this was the first time he had heard their voices.

He was not surprised to find Gerald awake. The four ravaged

figures were breathing unaided and his cousin was watching them as if hypnotized. The bodies were covered by blankets and a fire burned fiercely in the fireplace, but still they shivered uncontrollably. There were still gold needles visible, sticking out of their flesh, but the electrical wires had been removed. They had Gerald's complete attention now: all the other bones and corpses unearthed by the explosion were gone; reassembled and returned to their graves. He was spending every waking hour assisting them in their recovery. He looked up with a start and greeted Nate with a nod.

"How long have they been making that racket?" Nate asked.

"Started about an hour ago," Gerald replied. "They're still not conscious—it's as if they're in a delirious state. Well, three of them anyway; this fourth one hasn't made a sound."

He indicated the taller of the two males. The man's body was in the worst state of all of them, and at nearly seven feet tall, was easily the largest. They had found wounds all over his body and it was clear that he had not been buried without a struggle.

"Quite the brute, isn't he?" Gerald muttered. "Doesn't seem to be much fight in him now. Not like the others."

The moaning filled the room, an aching, sorrowful noise. Nate found the sound deeply disturbing.

"It's bloody awful," he breathed.

"You've been hurt enough times yourself . . . and you've had to heal," Gerald said quietly. "Think about it. You know what it's like to have a wound close up, or have a broken bone knit itself back together. It's painful. Sharp pain eventually subsides to a throbbing, then the itching and discomfort of healing, the feeling of being fragile . . . *mortal*. Their bodies are just starting to feel again after hundreds of years. Their entire physiologies are rebuilding themselves; their organs are beginning to function again, their nerve endings are growing back. Ever come back inside on a freezing cold day and felt the pain in your hands as they started to thaw out?"

Nathaniel nodded.

"These people are coming back from the *dead*," Gerald whispered. "And every inch of their bodies is in absolute agony . . ."

Nate leaned over to take a closer look at one of the women. She lay on the table with blankets tucked up to her chin, her feeble jaw opened as wide as it could, moving slightly as she groaned. The woman had the remains of black hair and a set of what must once have been good teeth. Gold needles stuck out of her cheeks and jaw, and he could see that her flesh was paler and already seemed to be filling out. Her body had lost some of its flattened appearance. Her eyelids did not look as sunken as before. When he touched the skin it was still cold, but it no longer had that dead, leathery quality.

The other woman had red hair and a misshapen face, which had been crushed crooked by the ground that had buried her. As she moaned, her shivering body gave sudden twitches. When she was found, one of her legs had been folded back across her body at an impossible angle; Nate noticed that it had been straightened out.

"The bones are regaining their original shapes?" he asked.

"Yes." Gerald nodded. "Don't ask me how. I've been resetting where I could, but it wouldn't be possible if their limbs kept the shape the ground had forced upon them. It's the same with their skulls and their teeth too—they're recovering their original forms. It's another mystery to be solved."

Nate looked at the shapes stretched out under the thick blankets. For the first time he began to see them as people, rather than archaeological oddities.

"We should put them into beds," he said.

Gerald straightened up.

"You're right, of course," he agreed. "I wasn't thinking. We should try and make them as comfortable as we can."

While Nate examined each of the patients more closely, his cousin gave some instructions to a servant standing unobtrusively in a corner. The man bowed and left the room. Nate looked at his own hand, thinking about the wound on his palm that had almost healed. Normal people's injuries did not disappear in a couple of days. He and these strange bodies shared a link he could not comprehend. Where had this unearthly power come from?

"I don't understand," he said at last.

"Nor do I." Gerald chuckled, coming up beside him. "But I *will*."

The wailing moans grew louder, as if the reanimated bodies sought to share their suffering.

Nathaniel snapped awake, roused by the sound of moving furniture. They were bringing beds into the laboratory next door. He was sitting on the sofa in Gerald's living room. History books and scribbled notes littered the floor; Gerald was still trying to trace the ancestors' past. Clancy was standing by the door and Nate had the impression that he had been there for some time.

"Clancy . . ."

"Master Nathaniel." The manservant dipped his head in a modest bow.

Nate rubbed his eyes and yawned. He had come in here to sit down and must have dozed off. The melancholy moans were still going on. He felt as if they had seeped into his being; he was feeling thoroughly depressed and in need of escape from the bodies and their unbearable pain. His thoughts turned to Marcus and his heart felt as if it were made of lead.

"I'm sorry to disturb you, sir," Clancy said to him. "But the Duke has requested your company at your earliest convenience."

Nate scowled. He very much doubted that his father had used the word "request." Realizing he was still in his nightshirt and dressing gown, he stood up and yawned again. He couldn't face his father in a dressing gown. Not only was it improper; he needed as much armor as he could get.

"What time is it?"

"Just before nine, sir."

"That late? I must have been asleep for hours. I need to get dressed."

"I took the liberty of bringing some clothes down for you, sir," Clancy said, gesturing to a grey suit hanging on a shelf by the door. "The Duke indicated that your prompt arrival would be appreciated."

Nate drew a hissed breath through his teeth. There was to

be no delaying then. He had hoped for a cup of tea first at least, while he chose the right outfit.

"I see I have no excuse for being late. Thank you, Clancy."

"Your convenience is my reason for living, sir."

Nate experienced the usual butterflies in his belly as he approached the door to his father's study. Knocking diffidently, he waited until he was summoned into the imposing room. Edgar sat behind his desk, and standing on the near side of the slab of teak was Slattery, the bailiff. He gave Nathaniel a welcoming smile, a gold tooth glinting in the morning light.

"You're late," Edgar grunted.

"Sorry, Father."

The two Maasai servants stood in the corners, looking for all the world like a pair of ebony statues. Nate didn't know if these were the same two who'd been here last time. One of them might have been the one who had comforted him when his leg was broken; he couldn't be sure. There were four altogether, all brothers, and he sometimes had trouble telling them apart. By their very nature, servants were supposed to be unnoticeable. The three bull mastiffs were asleep near Edgar's feet.

"It is time you involved yourself in the family business," his father said to him. "You will start by overseeing the investigation into the rebel attack. Slattery here will brief you on the progress to date."

Nate nodded. He still had no interest in business, family or otherwise, but he was determined to play his part in helping find the vermin who had attacked his family. He sat down in an armchair and looked to Slattery, who bowed his head respectfully.

"Master Nathaniel. This is what we've dug up so far," he said, facing the younger man with an upright stance, his hands clasped behind his back. As he talked, he began to pace back and forth. "We know the attack was pulled off by a gang; at least three men and possibly four or more. We believe that some of them may have been killed in the explosion. But there were definitely some who survived.

"One of the men involved was a small-time thief by the name of James McCord. He's not known to have rebel sympathies so we don't think he was the ringleader, but we're sure he was part of the gang."

"Why are you so sure?" Nate asked.

"Because his horse was found wandering not far from the estate, sir," Slattery replied. "It was dragging the broken wreck of a dray cart . . . and it was stone deaf."

"Deaf?"

"Aye, sir. Deaf as a post—couldn't hear a thing. It was caught in the explosion, see? Had shrapnel wounds all over it too. It didn't take long to find out whose it was, once we'd asked around. People round here knew McCord; he hired out his cart from time to time."

"Ah."

"Anyway, now we've figured out who he is, it won't take long to suss out who his mates were and then we'll be in business."

"And what will you do then?" Nate inquired, his interest sparked by the ease with which Slattery seemed to get results.

"Then we'll pick them up, sir." Slattery rubbed his knuckles. "We'll take them someplace quiet. And we'll ask them questions in such a way as they won't refuse us an answer."

Nate nodded but didn't say anything. He knew he should have a problem with this. These matters were supposed to be handled by the law, not some hired thugs. But the prospect of his family's enemies suffering a little abuse gave him no qualms at all.

Slattery studied him for a moment and seemed to find what he was looking for. He gave a grim smile.

"But that's not all, sir," he added. "You see, this had to be an inside job. The rebels knew where the powder store was and wasted no time getting in there. They knew it was below the cemetery and they knew what time the funeral procession would reach the mausoleum. All this took incredible coordination. They'd have needed the schedule for the funeral so they'd know when and where the mourners would be gathered, a series of lookouts at key points around the hill and, most importantly, they would have needed a map of the railway tunnel showing the powder store."

"My God," Nate muttered. "I hadn't really thought it through. You're right; one of the staff must have been in on this. Someone has betrayed us."

"They will be found and they will be dealt with," Edgar rumbled. "But there is a more pressing matter before us. Consider the resources the rebels have been able to muster: they were able to plan and organize this complex plot in an extraordinarily short time. They had only a few days between Marcus's death and his funeral to execute the most telling blow against the governing powers of this land. It was one of the very few occasions when such a collection of influential figures would be gathered in one place—an ideal opportunity for an assault . . . *but the rebels had no way of knowing it would happen.*"

Nate found the two men looking expectantly at him. For a moment he was at a loss and then, with a growing sense of horror, he saw the light.

"You mean . . .?" he began and then paused, struck by the enormity of what they were implying. "You mean the only way they could have known the funeral would happen was if they *made* it happen?"

"Indeed," his father said through gritted teeth, the hate in his voice tinged with what sounded like admiration. "We are facing an enemy with immense cunning. For this plot to be carried out as it was, the only conceivable way it was possible was for them to *create* the opportunity."

Edgar stood up and leaned forward over the desk, staring at his son with his one good eye.

"The rebels had to kill Marcus."

Nathaniel came out of the meeting with his father and the bailiff with his head spinning. The scale of the plot against them had been huge. And they could only assume that their enemy would try and strike again. Until the mastermind behind this attack was found, no one in the family was safe.

Standing in the mechanical lift, he watched the needle arc counter-clockwise around the numbers before it finally settled on the ground floor, where the breakfast room was located. He badly needed some tea and toast. He thanked the boy perched at the control lever and stepped out to find Tatiana standing in front of him wearing a petulant expression, flanked by her two black-and-white spaniels.

"You said I could have a ride on the monster!" she declared. "It's been almost a week and still nothing!"

The spaniels looked at him with large, reproachful eyes. He sighed. It had been a rash promise and he had been regretting it ever since.

"I know, Tatty, and I'm sorry. It's just that— "

"It's just that what?"

"It's just that I can't let you ride it on your own—the creature is still a little . . . unpredictable. And you can't ride behind me because . . . Well, you know why."

Women rode horses side-saddle—with both legs on the same side of the horse—to avoid being placed in the scandalous position of having their large and complicated skirts lifted at the front. No respectable lady could ride with a normal saddle and no man would be caught dead trying to sit on the front of a side-saddle.

"So you lied to me, is that it?" Tatiana looked close to tears. "You went and raised my hopes and now you've dashed them like a doomed ship on the rocks."

It occurred to Nate that his sister had been reading too many maudlin romance novels. But he still hated to disappoint her. Perhaps he could just lead her round the lawn on Flash's back— the engimal would probably behave itself.

And then he had a thought. A smile crept across his face, and when Tatiana saw it, the corners of her mouth curled up slightly.

"What are you thinking?" she asked.

"There might be a way for you to get your ride after all," he told her, grinning down at her. "But we're going to have to do something really shocking."

"Oh, good!" she exclaimed, clapping her hands.

He took her arm and they walked down to the breakfast room with the spaniels at their heels.

XVI

A YOUNG LADY'S CURIOSITY

IT WAS LATE IN THE EVENING when Nathaniel strolled down to the stables and took Flash out. Hennessy saddled up the velocycle and Nate clicked his heels against the engimal's sides and rode around to the side of the enormous house. Tatiana sneaked out of a clump of bushes with an exaggerated tiptoed walk, her face alight with nervous excitement. She was dressed in some of Nate's old clothes: some trousers, a shirt, a jacket and a leather velocycle hat strapped under her chin that hid her bundled-up hair. Clancy had dug out the garments, but not before he had dropped ominous hints of the consequences of Tatiana being caught dressed up as a boy. There was every possibility that she was putting her future marital prospects in jeopardy.

This had only thrilled her all the more.

Climbing onto the saddle behind her brother, she put her arms around his waist and gave him a tight squeeze. Flash did not seem to object to the new rider, but Nate was determined to keep a close watch on the contrary velocycle all the same.

"So this is what it's like to wear trousers," Tatiana observed. "It's the oddest feeling, not like bloomers at all—"

"I really don't need to hear my sister talk about her undergarments," Nate interrupted her. "Hold on tight, we're going to go very fast."

He tapped his heels and she squealed with delight as they took off down the drive. Actually, they rolled along at quite a leisurely pace, but to Tatty it seemed as if they were riding the wind itself.

Nathaniel got off the main road as soon as he could, following the farm roads and country tracks that would keep them out of the way of curious onlookers. In the fading light they rode along the grassy trails beside the dry-stone walls that threaded through the countryside. It was almost nine o'clock and anyone who worked the land would be settling down to sleep—if they weren't in bed already. Work would start not long after dawn; there would be cows to be milked and brought to pasture, ground to be weeded, walls repaired.

As he thought about it, Nate realized that he knew very little about farming. And yet all the farmland around them belonged to their family. When he had been in Africa, he had spent time with the Boers, the Dutch settlers. In those few months he had seen more of their farming than he had ever seen on his own land. Such menial work had never meant enough to him to spark his interest.

It was growing steadily darker and Flash's eyes grew brighter to compensate, lighting the way ahead of them. They passed a clachan—a group of peasants' cabins—with their turf walls and thatched roofs. They were miserable hovels for the most part, and Nate saw no reason to spare them more than a passing glance. If the steady growl of Flash's engine roused any sleeping souls, there was no sign of them at the windows.

Behind him, Tatiana made appreciative noises and gaped in wonder at how the world looked when seen from the back of a speeding monster.

"I've decided what I'm going to do with my life," she called to him over his shoulder.

He slowed the velocycle down to quiet it.

"Are you going to find a suitable husband, marry well and have a crowd of children?" he asked hopefully.

"There is more to the life of a modern woman than marriage, Nathaniel," she chided him. "Women today must have a purpose. I made up my mind after the explosion. I am going to educate myself in medicine and set up hospitals, like Florence Nightingale or Mary Seacole."

"Oh?"

"Yes. I'm going to bring health to the common people."

"That's very decent of you," he said to her. "God knows they need it."

"That's what I thought," she went on. "I see them sometimes

at the side of the road on the way to town or when we're out riding. Some of them don't look very well at all."

They were coming to what looked like the end of the track. Flash's bright eyes picked out a pile of rubble. As they drew closer, Nate saw it was the remains of a cottage. The turf cabin had been demolished by some terrible force. There were tracks on the ground around the wreckage and he drew in a sharp breath. He was about to turn round and head back down the trail when Tatiana looked over his shoulder.

"What's that?" she asked.

There would be no pleasing her now until she had seen all there was to see. He pulled Flash to a halt and let her get off. She looked taller somehow, in her boy's clothes. Wandering around the tumbled turf blocks and the broken wooden beams of the roof, she kicked some straw thatch over to see what lay beneath. Nate was gazing grimly at the twin sets of serrated tracks that crisscrossed the area around them, each track more than two feet wide and each pair more than two yards apart. He knew these feet. Nothing had feet like Trom. He looked over to where the ridges of potato plants should have been; the staple diet for peasants. The family's potato plot had been churned up and crushed by the massive engimal.

"This was a house," said Tatiana. "I've seen these before, but I've never stood in one. I never realized how small they were."

She pushed a beam out of the way and paced the length of the whitewashed wall.

"It's smaller than my bedroom," she remarked. "I wonder where they put all their things."

"They probably didn't have a lot of things," he told her.

"But still—it's so *small*," she persisted. "And it's been flattened. What do you think happened?"

"An engimal came through here," Nate said to her. "A really big one."

"My God, people could have been hurt. Shouldn't someone try and catch it before it does any more damage?"

"Someone already has," he muttered. Then, raising his voice, he said: "Look, we need to go, Tatty."

"I'm coming, I'm coming. It's just as well; these trousers are starting to rub between—"

"I don't need to know, Tatty," he said, cutting her off.

"What happened to the people, do you think?" she went on. "I expect they've moved into one of their other houses."

"I doubt they had another house, Tatty. Somebody will have taken them in, I suppose. If not, they'll have gone to the poorhouse . . . Although most people would rather die than end up there."

"Really? Why? What's so bad about it?"

He thought about it for a moment. He knew very little about the poorhouses.

"I don't know."

"I can't see how they can be *that* bad—I mean, they're there to look after people, aren't they? Although Charlie Parnell says people die in there all the time. He says he heard that they take children away from their parents."

"Oh? And how long has Charlie Parnell been trying his luck?"

"Nate, don't be crude," she giggled, blushing. "Anyway, how

can somebody be so poor that they live in this poky little shed of a thing when there's so much work to do around here? Don't they want to work? Father's always saying there's so much to do. Why don't we pay poor people to do it? They wouldn't be poor any more if we did that, would they? Then everybody could live in proper houses."

"I don't know, Tatty . . ."

"I think it's terrible," she went on. "Look, they don't even have room for a piano. There doesn't even seem to be a sink or a bath. How did they keep clean?"

"I don't *know*."

"It doesn't really seem fair—us being so rich when they're so poor, does it?" she mused.

"Our wealth is good for the country," Nate said. "If we weren't rich, things would be a lot worse. We create jobs, we pay wages and buy goods, and all that money we spend here trickles down to the poor, you see? It's all for the best."

Tatiana nodded slowly. Then, looking at the wrecked cottage, she added:

"Perhaps it should trickle a little quicker?"

"Come on, let's get out of here," he urged her impatiently.

"Maybe I'll set up a hospital right here." She climbed onto the saddle behind him.

"That would be very noble," he said, growing more and more exasperated.

Turning Flash round, he found that some wire from the wreckage had become tangled in the velocycle's front wheel. He reached down and pulled it free, wrenching at it with unnecessary force and making the engimal flinch. It was time to head back to the house, he decided. Seeing Trom's tracks had spoiled his good mood. He had loved the huge engimal as a child—the great, dull, clumsy brute had been a constant source of wonder for him . . . until he had found out what it was used for.

Tatiana leaned her chin on his shoulder.

"Nate, do you remember the Famine?" she asked over the sound of Flash's engine.

"A little bit," he replied. "I was very young."

"What was it like?"

He found himself thinking of the bog bodies that lay a few miles away in Gerald's laboratory and he shuddered slightly. They reminded him of the nightmarish things he had seen as a child.

"I don't remember a lot," he said. "It didn't affect our lives much. But sometimes we'd take a coach into town and Mother would pull the blinds to stop me from seeing what was outside. That just made me curious, of course, so I peeked out whenever I could.

"It was as if the dead had risen from their graves. People who were little more than skeletons wandered the roads, their clothes hanging on them like ragged curtains. I saw starving children with swollen bellies; it was the oddest sight—fat bellies on bodies that were little more than skin and bone. Gerald told me later that it's a side effect of hunger that can be caused by gas or water retention. The oddest sight. It's hard to describe a starving persons face . . . It's . . . It's like they've died, but their soul hasn't left their body. And they have a horrible look of despair. I heard there were rotting corpses in the roads and the ditches and lying out in fields in the middle of nowhere. You could smell them when you passed them—there's nothing as bad as the stench of decaying flesh. If the poor didn't die of hunger, they were killed by disease. It was everywhere. I remember Mother being terrified that we would catch the fever. A lot of children did. You didn't have to be poor to fall sick, and it was a horrible way to die."

He fell silent, his eyes on the rough road that would lead them back to the house. He remembered being appalled at the way people had lived in some of the tribal villages along the Congo River. It had seemed unbelievable that human beings could still live in such squalor in this day and age—in this Age of Enlightenment. The sooner the Industrial Revolution reached Africa the better. But now, seeing through Tatiana's eyes the poverty that surrounded them here at home, he realized that industry was doing nothing for his own people. Peasants here lived in worse conditions than anything he had seen in the Congo or in the shanty towns on the Cape. It was no wonder so many of them were getting worked up about it. Not that it gave them an excuse to go around murdering people.

It was like Tatiana said: there was plenty of work to do. Anybody who wanted to improve their lot only needed to put their backs into it. And if the rebels thought they were going to change things by attacking his family, they had another think coming.

"Nathaniel," his sister said into his ear, "how much of this land is ours?"

"All of it," he told her. "Everything you see."

• • •

It was Francie's day off and he normally spent it with some of the other lads from the stables if he could. He got one day off a month and Dublin was too far away for him to visit his family unless he could get a lift there and back. But his father had sent him a message to meet him in a pub near the estate, so once he had finished his chores for the morning, he cleaned himself up and got ready to go out.

On the way out he stopped in to look at the big velocycle, as he so often did. He had managed to touch it a couple of times now. and he thought it might be starting to trust him. He dreamed of being allowed to take it out for a walk . . . or a roll, or whatever.

It appeared to be in a bad mood when he looked over the wall at it. It was twitching and rubbing its front wheel against the wall, making frustrated grunts. Francie knew the signs. Something was irritating it, and it was fidgeting like a horse with a stone in its hoof. He licked his lips, thinking about how much trouble he could get into if he interfered with an engimal. But after helping to blow up a crowded cemetery, the risk of trying to ease an expensive machine's discomfort was small potatoes. He slowly climbed over the wall and lowered himself into the stall. The engimal turned to look at him.

"There y'are, Flashy old thing," Francie said in a sympathetic tone. "I'm not goin' to hurt yeh. And yer not goin' to hurt me either, are yeh, Flash? No, yer not. I'm just goin' to get in here and see what's up with yeh. And then we'll make it all better for yeh. How's that sound, eh?"

He edged closer, nervously noticing how the velocycle had

bunched up as if ready to lunge forward. Stretching out his hand, he kept making soothing noises.

"Sssh," he told it. "There y'are now. That's it, Flash. Let's see what's wrong."

Going down on one knee, he gently stroked the engimal's front wheel, sliding his fingers up to its right front leg, which it had been rubbing against the wall. Flash trembled with tension but made no move to stop him. He realized it wasn't just being aggressive. It was afraid. He knew then that it must be in pain. Feeling around the metal muscles of its leg, Francie's fingers found their way down to where its ankle joint held the wheel. Something jagged and sharp was caught there and the engimal flinched when he touched it.

"That's it, isn't it, boy?" he said softly. "Let's just have a look and see what yev got there."

It was a piece of rusty wire, wrapped around the axle joint where it met the wheel. It had probably got caught up out on the road somewhere. He tugged carefully and Flash flinched again and growled.

"It's all right there, lad," Francie reassured it. "'S just a bit o' wire. Not to worry—we'll have it out in no time."

Getting a better grip, he pulled the end out and, with tender movements, unwound the rusted wire. He could see where it had chafed against the engimal's metal skin. The last tangled length of wire grated against the wheel and Flash let out a sudden snarl, slamming Francie back against the wall. The boy winced as the back of his head whacked off the wood, but he didn't panic as the wheel crushed his torso against the wall. The wire had cut the crook of his index finger and he sucked on it, eyeing the machine. There were flecks of rust in the cut, and he stretched over and washed the finger in the water trough. He took his time doing it, determined to show he wasn't afraid of the engimal.

Flash did not release him, but it didn't lean any harder either. With its weight, it could have crushed his chest like a matchbox. Stroking the wheel that was pressed against his ribcage, he reached in and finished unwinding the offending wire, pulling it free.

"I'm sorry, I'm sorry. There now," he said at last. "How's that for yeh?"

The velocycle hesitated for a moment and then backed away. It made a noise that sounded like a mixture of apology and grudging appreciation. Francie stared at the magnificent machine with a hint of a smile on his face.

"You 'n' me," he said breathlessly. "We're goin' to be friends . . . aren't we?"

XVII

A GRADUAL RESURRECTION

FRANCIE MET HIS FATHER in the smoky atmosphere of McAuley's, a pub not far from the Wildenstern estate. This was the first time Shay had ever come up here to meet him. Francie sat on a stool at a rough wooden table beside his father, sipping on a pint of warm stout and wiping away the foamy moustache it left on his top lip.

"There'll be no more robbin' from nibbles and clodhoppers," Shay was saying to him in a lowered voice. "It's rich folk and nothin' else for me from now on. Absolutely deffiney—no more small-time. What's the point in robbin' from them as don't have a ha'penny worth takin', Francie? Sure it's these toffs' fault that we're thieves in the first place, yeh know what I mean? I wouldn't be such a gouger if I hadn't been oppressed since I was born."

Francie listened quietly, wondering what his father wanted. He didn't point out that his mother had been born into the same circumstances as Shay, and was as saintly as any woman alive. Being poor didn't make you a thief. His ma had never stolen a thing in her life and she'd tried to teach Francie to be the same. There wasn't a hope of that with Shay around.

"We're goin' to be like that English fella from the stories," his father was saying. "Yeh know . . . the one who lived in the woods and robbed the rich to give to the poor. Wha' was 'is name?"

"King Arthur?" Francie suggested.

"Tha's the fella. King Arthur. Anyway, we're turnin' over a new leaf. From now on, we're goin' to be like him."

"So are we goin' to be givin' to the poor, then, Da?" Francie asked skeptically.

"One leaf at a time, Francie." Shay gave him a sly look. "One leaf at a time."

He was about to go on when an old man came over to them with a glass of stout in his hand. Placing it in front of Shay, the man slapped his shoulder and gave him a nod.

"Good on yer, son," he muttered. "Have one on me. It's about time the swells got what was comin' to 'em!"

Without another word, he turned and walked back to a group of men who were leaning against the worn wood of the bar. They looked over in Shay's direction and there were a few winks and some of the sideways nods of the heads that passed for a salute in this part of the country. Giving his son a smug look, Shay raised the glass to them. They raised theirs in return.

"What was all that about?" Francie asked.

"It's been goin' on for a few days," Shay replied under his breath. "Word must've got about in Fenian circles that I was in on the explosion in the cemetery. They think I'm startin' a revolution or somethin'. My arse! Still, it's good for a few pints, wha'?"

Francie felt the hairs rise on the back of his neck. First his father blows a Wildenstern funeral to smithereens; now he was trying to pull the wool over the eyes of the Fenians. They wouldn't take kindly to being fooled—and there'd be hell to pay if any of them ended up in Kilmainham Gaol or the cellars of Dublin Castle because of his da's explosive cock-up. And then Shay leaned over, slipped an envelope into Francie's hand and explained what he wanted his son to do.

That was when Francie finally decided that his father was completely off his head.

Nathaniel hit the floor hard, landing on his back with Clancy gripping his arm and shoulder. Nate kicked the older man in the chest before the arm-lock came on, and wrenched his arm free, flipping back onto his feet and putting some distance between them. He was breathing hard, but Clancy was panting in short bursts and Nate knew there wasn't much left in him.

"You're losing your touch, old man," he taunted his manservant.

"It's not lost just yet, sir."

The servant closed on him again, jabbing with his left and then aiming a front kick at Nate's groin. Nate pivoted around it and landed a spectacular double roundhouse kick, striking Clancy's calf and then his ribs, winning a grunt of pain from his opponent. He had little time to enjoy it—as his foot pulled away, Clancy caught the ankle and rammed the heel of his hand into his master's sternum. The blow stopped Nate long enough for Clancy to sweep his other leg out from under him and send him crashing to the floor again.

"You've got to watch those high kicks, sir," Clancy told him, bending forward and wincing as he rubbed his bruised ribs. "You don't want to be standing on one foot for too long."

They were in the family's gymnasium, sparring on the wooden floor, dressed only in loose trousers and undershirts. It was a room about the size of two tennis courts, with a high ceiling and small square windows along the very tops of the longer walls. Motes of dust floated in the shafts of late afternoon light that painted oblongs across the floor. Around the edges of the room was a wide range of training equipment for gymnastics, as well as for fencing and other fighting arts. A large selection of weapons lined the wall at one end.

"I'll have you winded before long," Nate retorted.

"Not much good if you keep ending up on the floor, Master Nathaniel."

Nate had sparred with Clancy since he was a boy, and he relaxed the master-servant formalities while they were fighting. It was no fun having an opponent who did whatever he was told. They had both outgrown their various instructors and Clancy had proved himself useful as an all-around coach. Indentured into the service of the Wildensterns as a child, the footman had been training in these skills for most of his life.

"I'm out of practice," Nate breathed as he got to his feet. "Didn't get much while I was away. One more round?"

"I am at your disposal, sir." Clancy took up a defensive stance.

They were about to go at it again when Silas walked through the door. With his thin frame, his mop of dark hair and his pale skin, he was an older, less flamboyant version of his brother Gerald. Silas shared much of his little brother's intellect, but none of his imagination. It made him the perfect choice for the position of Edgar's private secretary and one of the family's chief accountants.

"Nate, you were supposed to be up in my office half an hour ago," he said stiffly. "Your father told me to run over the books with you."

"I don't want to run over the bloody books," Nathaniel answered back, relaxing his stance for a minute. "The books can take a flying bloody leap for all I care."

"And what should I tell the Duke?" Silas regarded him with an expectant expression. "He'll doubtless want to know why the accounts are taking a flying leap. You know how he pays attention to these things."

Nathaniel swore under his breath. He glanced at his manservant.

"What?" he snapped. "I know you were going to say something."

"I wouldn't presume to comment on your affairs, sir," Clancy said.

Nate made to turn away, but the footman continued:

"After all, this is *your* business, sir. And I'm sure you'd want to keep it that way—seeing as you are so determined to be your own master, sir."

There was a barely perceptible raise of his eyebrow. Nate stared back at him, grinding his teeth. There were times when he could swear his manservant was attempting some kind of hypnosis with these coded messages of his. Sometimes it wasn't clear who was really in charge.

"Tomorrow," he said, turning to Silas at last. "I'll take a look at the books tomorrow . . . after breakfast. How's that?"

"Splendid," Silas replied. "I'll have them waiting."

He strode back out, closing the door behind him. Nate sighed, picturing the pile of leather-bound ledgers with their columns upon columns of figures. If there was a hell on Earth, he was sure that accountancy was involved somehow. Bouncing on his toes, he raised his guard and nodded to Clancy.

"Right, now I'm really going to trounce you."

Neither had time to land a blow before Gerald burst through the door, sweating and disheveled.

"They—!" he gasped, then ran out of breath and started coughing, holding up his hand for them to wait for him to finish.

Nate and his footman stood there as Gerald got over his coughing fit and tried to catch his breath.

"Couldn't wait. . . . for the . . . elevator," he explained in panting breaths. "Ran down . . . the stairs."

Nate worked it out. His cousin had obviously run full-tilt down fourteen flights of stairs and crossed from the other side of the huge building. No wonder he was out of breath.

"They're awake!" Gerald managed at last. "They're talking!"

He didn't need to say who.

"Well, then," Nate replied, picking up his shirt. "Let's go meet the ancestors."

He charged out of the door, dragging Gerald with him, and together they ran back up to the laboratory.

By the time they reached it, Gerald was staggering forward on rubbery legs, wheezing like an old woman. Nate didn't care what the doctors claimed, there was no way smoking could be good for the heart or lungs. They pushed through the door to find the room shrouded in a gloomy light, the sun having passed to the far side of the building. The lamps had yet to be lit. Sitting on a bed in the corner was a hunched figure, being supported by an uneasy-looking young footman. The figure looked frail and cold; shivering despite the blankets wrapped round his shoulders. With an achingly stiff movement, the man turned his head to look at them.

Nathaniel found himself staring into the grey, filmy eyes of a man who had once been a corpse.

"My God!" he whispered.

Gerald pushed him forward and together they approached the huddled old man. Despite his frail state, he looked extraordinarily well. His skin was dry and creased with wrinkles, but it was no longer the color of the peat bog; blue veins were visible beneath, and bone and muscle had redeveloped to the point where he could move by himself to a small degree. His eyes were clearly working—they moved about, trying to focus on the faces around him; however, Nate doubted that the old man could see very well. It was a noble-looking face; long, with high cheekbones and a prominent brow over a narrow, hooked nose. His hair was a bleached brown, but there was an inch of black at the roots. His original hair color was growing back.

"He said his name is Hugo," Gerald said in a low voice. "I haven't been able to get much sense out of him though. He's very confused—as you'd expect from someone who's been dead for centuries. The two women are awake too, but they've just been lying there babbling so far."

Nate looked over at them, lying in their beds. He could see that their eyes were open and their lips were moving, their heads rolling weakly from side to side. The second man still lay unconscious, the slight rise and fall of his chest the only sign that he too was alive.

"Elizabeth," the old man said abruptly in a feeble rasping voice, reaching out for the black-haired woman in the bed next to his. "Oh, what have they done to thee? What have the beasts done?"

Nate caught him before he fell forward and gently pushed him upright. The woman turned her head and looked in the direction of the voice, mumbling incoherently.

"Do you know who this is?" Nate asked him.

"It is Elizabeth, my sister." Hugo gestured to her with his hand. "Is she dying?"

"Quite the opposite, in fact," Gerald told him. "She is . . . You are *all* making miraculous recoveries. There are four of you altogether. Can you tell us anything about the others? Can you tell us what happened to you?"

Hugo looked round at the other beds, his underdeveloped eyes squinting at the shapes.

"There is a red-haired woman and another man . . . a huge man," Nate prompted him.

"Brunhilde . . . my younger sister," Hugo gasped. "And Brutus, my brother. Ahhh, Brutus . . . they hated him most of all. What a warrior he was! He fought like a lion before he was overcome! He must have cut down a dozen of the vermin—no . . . more. He was like a mighty lion."

It was the longest speech he had uttered so far and it seemed to leave him exhausted. Gerald and Nathaniel looked at each other.

"Can you remember who attacked you?" Nate pressed the ancient man. "You were found with gold stuffed down your throat. Can you tell us what happened?"

"Peasants," Hugo spat, his face screwing up with hatred. "Heretic peasants led by a mad monk. We were betrayed by our guards and by our servants. They came in the night like rats and took us in our beds."

"Some things never change," Gerald quipped, taking out his cigarette case.

Hugo's hand went to his throat as he struggled to remember. "I . . . I fought, but the cowards had taken my sword. I was held down . . . Some of them wanted to burn us. Then the monk . . ." His voice drifted off. "The monk said we should go into the ground. But not before they had made us suffer."

He went quiet for a moment, tired and out of breath. His head hung as if his mind was lost in the moment of his death, centuries ago.

"We all cursed them; we showed no fear of the vermin," he continued in his weak rasp. "Brunhilde bit the nose off one of them, and we laughed at them then! But they hurt us . . . for days they put us through pain." He paused, lifting his head. "And then they threw us into deep holes and tossed soil on our faces." He went silent again. "And now we are alive again. Truly we have been blessed with a miracle. Only God himself could have done such a thing."

"You were wearing this when we found you." Gerald held up the gold signet ring, which had been carefully cleaned. "Do you know what this is?"

"Of course I know. Do you take me for a fool?" Hugo grunted. "It is *my* ring, passed down to me by my father and by his father before him. I am *Wildenstern*."

Nate and Gerald shared another look.

"I think it's time we got Father down here," Nate said.

XVIII

"A RIGHT CAN OF WORMS"

BY THE TIME THE DUKE ARRIVED, with his brother Gideon and Dr. Warburton in tow, Hugo had lapsed back into a weary daze; muttering nonsensically and gazing with his weak eyes at the floor. Edgar waited for a few minutes to see if there would be any further developments and then, after a few words with Gerald, he left again.

Nathaniel and Gerald struggled for the rest of the afternoon to get any more sense out of the newly awakened patients, but with no success. As evening fell, the women became more alert and stopped their mumbling, lying still instead and looking around them. Hugo asked for food and was given milk and broth, as he was still unable to chew. A servant helped spoon-feed him until he was able to manage by himself. His appetite proved to be immense and he ate bowl after bowl of the soup, washing it down with warm, sweetened milk. Soon the women were able to eat too, and with equal hunger. But they still did not say a word. There was no sign yet of Brutus regaining consciousness and Hugo often looked at him with sorrowful concern.

Nate finally went to bed and lay awake for hours, his head full of unanswered questions. When he arose the following morning, feeling drowsy and numb, he made his way straight down to the laboratory, where he found his ancestors asleep. Gerald sat by them, with dark rings around his eyes, and told his cousin that they had been sleeping for a few minutes at a time through the night, and eating with supernatural appetites.

Then they awoke again. And they began to eat once more. Nate left them and went down to breakfast. He trudged through the morning in a weary daze, only half aware of the goings-on around him. There was a new tension in the house and everybody knew its source. Those who knew of the ancestors' existence (and there were more and more of them as the gossip increased) had heard about Hugo's claim. He had the gold signet ring with the family's coat of arms as proof . . . and there could be no doubt that he was blessed with *aurea sanitas.* He even bore a resemblance to some of the portraits of old Patriarchs that hung in the main hall.

And if he was who he said he was, then the family was faced with an unprecedented problem. By right, everything around them belonged to him.

"For God's sake, nobody say anything to him," Gideon spluttered over breakfast, spitting bits of kipper through his dyed-black beard, over his fat belly and onto his lap. He waved his heavily ringed hands about. "We've opened a right can of worms here, and I won't have everything we've worked for being upset by some throwback turning up out of the blue like this and laying claim to our fortune. I won't have it, by the Lord Harry!"

Edgar refused to be drawn on the subject, which just made things worse. He merely sat there eating and took no part in the chatter. Nate watched him and wondered what was going through his mind.

He also tried to avoid looking at Daisy. She had been especially cool towards him since having her dress pinioned at the funeral, and he knew that she had not forgotten his insensitivity. He had been waiting for her to get her revenge and it was at this moment that she chose to strike. And she did so with dastardly cunning.

"It seems to me, Father," she addressed the Duke with a thoughtful air, "that what we must do is ensure that Hugo and his sisters are kept occupied with *civilized* pursuits. They have a lot to learn about our world, and the more we fill their time with less martial and more . . . *contemplative* matters, the better it will be for all concerned.

"There is so much they must be taught about our history, politics and the new geography of our world, not to mention all the ins and outs of the family business. And we could lighten the academic load by supplementing their tuition with pleasurable occupations such as botany, music, painting. I think *poetry* would be most beneficial. All things that would keep their minds off thoughts of advancing their positions.

"But this tuition would have to be carried out by someone whose position—and character—would hold Hugo's respect. Someone whose education and worldly experience are up to the task."

She paused before delivering her masterstroke.

"Someone like . . . Nathaniel, for instance."

Nate sat frozen for a moment, but then stammered a defense:

"I . . . I have far too much to do with learning the business in America without—"

"It will give you an excellent sense of perspective," Edgar cut him off. "The prospect of teaching a subject can be an effective way to motivate learning it. A capital idea, Melancholy. Thank you."

Nate's nails clawed the underside of the table as that conniving, calculating cow gave him her sweetest smile.

The thirty family members who had attended breakfast broke up into various factions afterwards and went their separate ways.

Nate was finishing a second round of toast after everyone had gone when a footman came in holding an envelope on a silver platter. Nate opened it and found a note inside, written by someone with an obvious fondness for capital letters. It read:

Master Nathaniel,

We have Found a man We Believe is Connected with the Assault on the Funeral. We will have him in Custody by Lunchtime and We would be Greatly Obliged if You would Elect to Join us Below Stairs in the South Wing at Your Earliest Convenience.

    Yours Respectfully,
    Patrick Slattery

Nate felt his pulse quicken. They had found one of the bombers. He read the note again in puzzlement. He did not understand where he was supposed to meet the bailiff—there were no servants' quarters in the south wing. Then he realized what he was reading—Slattery did not mean the servants' quarters. He meant the dungeons.

In spite of the unbearable curiosity he was feeling about Slattery's exploits, Nathaniel kept his promise and showed up at Silas's office at around eleven. Just as he feared, the accountant had a pile of ledgers sitting on his desk, in a room filled with more ledgers, books, folders and filing cabinets. Every piece of information regarding the Wildenstern empire was diligently laid out; categorized, alphabetized and, where applicable, filed in numeric or chronological order. Nate regarded the large room with a growing sense of dread.

"Good morning," Silas said, beckoning him in.

The slight young man always gave the impression of being ill-at-ease around people and this morning was no exception. He spoke very quickly, avoided eye contact and his hands fidgeted constantly.

"We'll just go over the basics today, to give you an overview of the various businesses. I'll try and keep it simple, as I know you'll have very little grasp of financial matters. Despite the fact that we're one of the wealthiest families in the world, I've found most of the family members know little or nothing about money."

"What makes you say that?" Nate retorted. "I know plenty about money. I spend it all the time."

"Really?" Silas asked. "Then perhaps you can tell me how much you'd pay for a pint of milk?"

Nate hesitated for a moment and then shrugged, shaking his head.

"A loaf of bread?"

Another shrug.

"A horse?" Silas persisted. "A decent hat? A pound of sugar? A pistol? A pint of beer—"

"You can get a pint of beer for as little as a penny," Nate told him. "But it's worth paying more for the good stuff."

"Yes, well . . ." Silas sighed. "Let's see if we can expand your horizons a bit, shall we?"

And so it began. Nate reluctantly sat down beside Silas at the desk and together they began to pour through the books of figures. It was true, he discovered: he knew next to nothing about the family business. As the Heir, Marcus had taken on so much responsibility so readily that Nathaniel and Roberto had not been trusted with any at all. Nor had they looked for it. They had been happy to live their lives and indulge their passions without any thought to where their money was coming from.

The scale of the Wildenstern business was astounding, and as he listened, he understood for the first time the kind of power the family could wield . . . and why some members were so bloodthirsty in their attempts to control it. Silas droned on, his hands restlessly flicking through the pages. But Nate's mind was already running along a different track, trying to piece together the puzzle of his brother's death. He was still skeptical about the idea of a Fenian mastermind cooking up diabolical schemes against them. It seemed hard to believe the rebels could have pulled off such a subtle murder. But his family were *trained* to do this kind of thing.

". . . We are the single biggest owner of property in Ireland, of course," Silas was saying, "as well as retaining several large estates on mainland Britain. But the income from all these pale in comparison to our profits from the North America Trading Company . . ."

Different relatives controlled different areas of the Company, Nate knew. But Marcus was in effective command, and with his death, everyone would change rank. Many of them would move up a notch. There were dozens of people with a reason to kill him.

". . . Up until the American War of Independence we controlled all the trade with the United States," Silas went on. "After that, we lost our monopoly unfortunately, but we still ran all the major shipyards and a majority of the ports, so many of the Atlantic trade routes are still under our control. The North America Trading Company ships everything from maize to cotton, horses to fashion items, as well as doing a healthy trade in coffee and tobacco . . ."

But anybody who tried to kill Marcus and failed would be faced with a powerful and resourceful young man who would waste no time in taking his revenge. It would have to have been someone who could afford to take the risk and also someone who would get the greatest benefit. Nate began to list off the suspects in his mind: himself, obviously, then Roberto and Daisy, and after them, Gideon and Eunice. And after them, it could be any of their children—most of whom Nate despised and would have suspected on principle anyway. For the sake of argument, he included Gerald and Silas—although their positions would hardly change at all—and also Tatiana, because he hated to leave her out of anything. And then there was the possibility it had been one of the servants . . . His mind went back to what Hugo had said. They had been betrayed by their servants. And Slattery believed there was a spy in the house—he was reminded of the bailiff's note. Perhaps they would soon find out who that spy was. His eyes fell on one of the books on the desk. It was the wage record for the house staff.

". . . America is a veritable treasure trove of resources," Silas was explaining. "And then there's the cheap labor, of course. As you know, slavery was abolished in the British Empire in 1833. But it is still alive and well in America—particularly the South, where most of our estates and factories are located. There has been talk of a civil war over the whole slavery business, but your father thinks it's all balderdash. I'm inclined to agree. Americans talk a lot of rot sometimes."

Now that he thought about it, Nate realized it would be all too easy to get a spy into the Wildenstern home. They had a staff of over a hundred; he couldn't say exactly how many. He knew hardly any of their names, and he was on better terms with many of the servants than most of the other family members. These people guarded them, fed them, dressed them and made their beds for them. The senior servants like Clancy and McDonald the butler were trained from childhood, but for the lower-level positions . . . well, as long as they had good references and did their work properly they could move around the house without suspicion. There was no way of telling if they were rebel sympathizers or not.

"To protect our business out on the seas, the Company has the power to commandeer vessels of the Royal Navy," Silas continued. "But this is rarely necessary—most of our ships are extremely well armed. We can also draft in armies here in Ireland to deal with any insurrection. Although I suspect Irish soldiers would be more trouble than they're worth —which is why we have so many British troops at our disposal . . ."

There could be dozens of assassins in the house and we might never know, Nate was thinking. They could murder us all in our beds.

". . . Not that the British government is completely on our side either," Silas added, speaking too quickly now as he grew more animated, still unaware that Nate was hardly listening. "They are constantly trying to place limits on our power, and there is a new and disturbing wave of liberal thought sweeping through Britain, a growing movement of bleeding-heart lawmakers who think we would have less of a problem with the rebels if we did more to raise the poor out of their "misery." As if you can reason with bloodthirsty *lunatics* . . ."

"They could kill us all," Nathaniel said aloud.

"I'm sure they would, given the chance," Silas agreed.

XIX

CONSIDERATION, RESPECT AND DIFFIDENCE

NATHANIEL LEFT SILAS'S OFFICE as early as he could, taking the mechanical lift to the ground floor. He walked outside with Slattery's note clutched in his hand. Careful to check that he wasn't observed, he made his way round to the south wing, the oldest section of Wildenstern Hall, built nearly three hundred years ago. The door he was looking for was below ground level, at the foot of a flight of stone steps. It was solid oak, reinforced with iron bands, and he was surprised to find the hinges well-oiled and the lock in good working order.

He pushed on it, but it didn't budge. Looking back up the steps, he found he was nervous, unsure of what to do. He knocked tentatively and then again, harder this time, annoyed with himself for being so hesitant. Wildenstern Hall was his home, after all.

There came the sound of footsteps and he heard a key in the lock. The door opened slightly and a face peered through the crack.

"Ah, there y'are, sir. We was expectin' yeh to come through the passage. We don't use this door so much."

So there was another way in, Nathaniel noted. Strange that he didn't know it. The man opened the door and ushered him in, taking a quick, furtive look outside before closing it again. There was only a hint of daylight now, from around the door. Nate found himself in a long dark stone tunnel. The air down here was cool and a little damp, and there were heavy wooden doors at regular intervals on either side of the corridor.

"Not been down here before, sir?" the man asked. "Better let me lead so. Roof's a bit low and the floor's uneven, so yeh have to watch yerself. McHugh's my name, sir. Pleased to meet you."

The man had a candle in his hand and it cast a fluttering light as they walked along. Nate noticed that McHugh was wearing a leather apron over his shirt and trousers. He was a short man, with a stocky body, large arms and short legs; short red hair circled a growing bald spot. The roof was very low in places and Nate found himself catching his toes on the worn and cracked flagstones. He had a dozen questions he wanted to ask about the place, but he couldn't bear to sound so ignorant of his own home. He supposed there were places all over the house that the servants knew better than their masters.

The tunnel took them to a door at the end where lantern light shone from round a corner. Going through the doorway,

McHugh stepped aside and let Nate walk past. He wasn't prepared for what he saw and his breath caught in his throat.

There were three men in the large, chilly room apart from
McHugh. Slattery was on the far side, leaning over a table
wearing only an apron over his bare upper torso, and washing
his hands in a wooden basin. Its water was red with blood. The
second man was obviously another of Slattery's thugs, a giant of a
fellow with matted hair on his bare forearms and tufts of it sticking up from under his collar. He too wore an apron.

But it was the flabby, middle-aged man in the chair who
seized Nate's attention. His wrists and ankles were shackled to
the sturdy chair. He was naked to the waist and blood was spattered all over his chest, most of it seeming to come from his nose
and mouth. His head hung limply forwards, but Nate could still
see that his face had been badly beaten and some of his teeth
were broken or missing.

There was a bottle of whiskey on the table and Slattery
poured a little onto his hands, rubbing them together before
rinsing them in the basin.

"Good afternoon, Mr. Wildenstern, sir." He nodded. "Be with
you in a moment." Seeing Nathaniel look at the whiskey bottle, he
smiled. "It's good for cleaning a person's smell from your hands, sir.
In this line of work I find myself continually covered with the stench
of others. And though I like the smell of whiskey, I never let a drop
pass my lips—or those of my men when they're in my company. I
believe that alcohol is the root of all sin and will be the ruin of this
nation. It makes us lose control . . . and that is a terrible thing."

He finished washing his hands and, picking up the basin with

one hand, came over to his battered victim. He threw the bloody
water into the man's face. There was no reaction. Grabbing him
by his greying hair, Slattery lifted the limp head and stared into
the unresponsive face.

"We are despised, my lads and I," the bailiff declared softly,
letting the man's head drop back onto his chest. "It's not how we
would like things—we're not *evil* men. We'd like to be treated
with the consideration, respect and diffidence that normal people expect, but it's us as has to do the hard things that need to be
done to keep order. The unpopular things.

"Information, Mr. Wildenstern, is the key to control," he
continued. "Your father—if you don't mind me sayin' so—is a
great believer in it. Know what's going on, know who's doing
what and, above all, know who knows what you don't." He indicated his senseless prisoner. "This man's name is Eoin Duffy.
He's a moneylender and a trader in stolen goods. A few days
ago we received a tip-off that an engimal—one of those known
as "bright-eyes"—that belonged to the company building the
railway tunnel for the Wildensterns had been bought by a local
collector. We retrieved the engimal from the collector and per-
suaded him to tell us where he had bought the creature. He gave
us Mr. Duffy's name."

McHugh tossed Slattery a rag and he dried his hands. Nathaniel was torn between being riveted and repulsed by the sight of
the tortured man.

"Mr. Duffy here has been very helpful," Slattery went on,
taking down his shirt from a coat hanger that hung from a hook
on the stone wall. "He gave us a name: Séamus Noonan. Noonan

is a known associate of the late James McCord, the former owner of the deafened horse. Again, he's not known to be a rebel sympathizer, but Duffy here is, aren't you, Mr. Duffy?" The unconscious man did not reply. Slattery grinned. "Noonan gave him the engimal to pay off the money he owed Duffy and make a little more on top—they're worth a lot of ochre, these things."

Pulling on his shirt, he did up his tie and donned his waistcoat and jacket.

"So we can put McCord and Noonan at the site of the explosion and connect them to the Fenians through our friend here. Duffy says their relationship was just business, but we're not swallowin' that. We still don't know who the spy in the house is, or who's runnin' the show. Chances are, he doesn't know; it would make sense for the boss to keep his lackeys in the dark. Duffy's not a strong man and he's probably told us all he can. We'll give him some time to pull himself together and then we'll work on him some more—just to see what else he can give us."

Nate gulped down a lump in his throat. He had grown up in an environment that had prepared him for violence. And this was not the first time he had witnessed grievous injuries; he had even seen men killed on the hunts in Africa. But what he saw here turned his stomach.

"That's enough," he said hoarsely. "I want you to clean this man up, treat his injuries and take him down to the police office. This is a matter for the magistrate now."

Slattery's expression went flat for a moment and Nate felt a chill go down his spine.

"People of . . . tender years, like yourself, sir, are often disturbed by these harsh realities, sir," Slattery began. "But your father—"

"My father put me in charge of this matter," Nate interrupted him, "despite my "tender years"—and you will do as I bloody tell you! Take this man to the magistrate! He will be tried properly and given the sentence he deserves. Do you understand me?"

Slattery gazed at him with dead eyes. His two henchmen were on either side of Nathaniel and he felt his skin crawl as they looked to their boss for his reaction. The moment seemed to last an age. Then Slattery smiled and held his hands up in a friendly gesture.

"As you like, Mr. Wildenstern, sir," he said at last. "After all, we should have involved the police in our investigation from the start. I suppose my enthusiasm for being an amateur sleuth got the better of me. My apologies, sir. Mr. Duffy will be delivered to the magistrate as you've instructed. If you don't mind, we'll follow up on the information we've received thus far and keep you—and the police, of course— informed of developments. Thank you, sir."

And then Slattery said no more. The three men stood staring at Nate, none of them moving. He looked from one to the next and eventually just nodded and walked out of the room. Stumbling along the dark corridor, he had reached the door before he realized he didn't have the key. With a start, he turned to find McHugh standing behind him, without his candle. The man hadn't made a sound. Reaching past Nathaniel, he unlocked the door.

"Yeh'll be wantin' to get out, I expect, sir," McHugh said to him, and then added in a softer voice, "Not to worry. This is a messy business and not to everyone's taste—least of all a gentleman like y'self. But these toerags'll get their comeuppance, you can count on that. They'll regret the day they crossed the Wildensterns."

Nate nodded to him and stepped through the door. It was a bright day outside and he was taken aback by the sunshine. For some reason he had been expecting it to be late evening.

"Take care, sir," McHugh muttered, and then closed the door.

Nathaniel climbed the steps and hurried away, trembling.

Hugo and his sisters continued their recovery. It took little more than a day before they were able to eat solid food, which they put away with appetites that Gerald said must surely defy the laws of physics. They became insatiable, eating until they were fit to burst and then stopping only long enough to sleep for an hour or two and let their meals settle. When they finally started using the toilet—needing help at first, but soon walking down the corridor on their own—there was little about them that resembled the bodies that had been blown from the ground not so long ago. The women were talking now too, but only to their brother.

Hugo had the appearance of a man in his fifties; he was still weak and sickly, but growing steadily stronger. His hair was black at the roots and he was cultivating a moustache and triangular goatee. The two women looked even younger, but in different ways. Brunhilde was a nervous, twitching mass of energy; her shrewish face constantly twisted into various aggressive expressions. She often appeared confused or suspicious of those around her. Elizabeth was more placid and far easier on the eye. She moved around with demure grace, seeming to find so many things that interested and amused her. Unlike her defensive sister, her fragility gave her the appearance of a delicate flower. But there was an air of calculation about her too, and as with Hugo, there was a keen intelligence evident behind those eyes.

Their skin had stretched and become smooth, marred only by the pattern of wrinkles that were all that remained of their leather-like appearance, like a sheet of paper that had been crumpled and ironed out again. Proper clothes had been found for them, and books for them to read—they took a particular interest in history books and spent much time reading the King James Bible. But still, the sisters' would speak to no one but Hugo, and Gerald became convinced that one of the reasons they were so shy was that none of them had woken with complete memories. They were still in a state of confusion.

Their other brother, Brutus, continued to lie in his perpetual sleep.

Two days after they became conscious, Edgar demanded an audience with Hugo. Nathaniel volunteered to take his ancestor upstairs. When they reached the elevator, Hugo looked suspiciously at the small room that lay past the open doors.

"What is this?" he asked, frowning at Nate. "You wish to imprison me?"

"It's a mechanical lift," Nate informed him. "It will take us to the top floor. Cables . . . ropes attached to a winch and counterweights pull this . . . this room up through the floors. It's very clever. You'll see."

He gently guided the old man inside and nodded to the boy

at the lever. When the floor lifted under their feet, Hugo gave a start and stared down fearfully. He was uncomfortable for the ride up and obviously uneasy about being in a confined space. Considering the man's history, Nate thought that was entirely understandable.

When the doors opened, Hugo gasped in shock at finding himself in a different corridor to the one they had just left. He lunged out of the lift to look around and then stepped back in again, gazing warily at his new surroundings.

"What magic is this?!" he exclaimed.

"It's—" Nate began, then stopped himself. "Hugo, there's a lot about our world you're going to find . . . different. We'll try and explain things as we go. But Father is waiting and he's not the most patient of men."

Leading the old man down to his father's study, he knocked on the door and they were summoned inside. Edgar was waiting in front of his desk. For the first time in Nate's memory, neither his father's servants nor his dogs were present. Hugo eyed the Duke with interest and then looked around at the huge room.

"This is Edgar Wildenstern, Duke of Leinster and our Patriarch," Nate said to him. "Father, I give you Lord Hugo Wildenstern."

"Welcome to my home, sir," Edgar told the man. "Nathaniel, if you will excuse us. I will have someone escort our esteemed relative down when we are finished."

Nate nodded and stepped back through the door, closing it behind him. He was desperately disappointed at having to leave. That was going to be one hell of a conversation.

Instead, he had another session with Silas to look forward to, learning how the accounts worked. The elevators doors opened on the accounting floor and, with a sigh of resignation, he walked out and down to Silas's office. He was surprised to find Roberto there, talking to their cousin. Berto looked up and a look of relief came over him.

"There you are, thank God," he said. "I need your help."

"And I need you here to go through some business," Silas reminded Nate in an irritated voice. "You go to America in a matter of weeks and we have too much to do as it is. Your father expects you to cooperate."

Nate gritted his teeth, resisting the urge to plant his fist in Silas's peevish face. He did not need reminding about his father's wishes.

"I have to *evict* someone, Nate," Berto told him in a sickened voice. "Father said I have to go with Slattery and watch it done. They're harnessing up Trom! I don't want to do this on my own, Nate—I just *can't*. Why don't you come along? Wouldn't you like to take a ride in the country?"

"What do you need me for?"

"You're meaner than I am. You can offer moral support while I drive people out of their homes."

Nate took one look at Silas and then slapped his brother on the shoulder.

"Anything for my brother! Of course I'll come. I'm sure the books can wait for another day," he said, smiling.

XX

AN UNPLEASANT DUTY

DAISY HAD NEVER SEEN TROM up close before. It was kept in an island paddock with a moat crossed by a massive drawbridge to keep it from wandering, but unlike the engimals in the Wildensterns' zoo, she had never been tempted to go and look at it. Now she couldn't take her eyes off it.

It was the size of a large locomotive; a broad, squat shape with a hide of grey, banded in places with zigzagging yellow and black stripes. Its skin was marked all over with scars, including the near-indestructible shovel that jutted out in front of its head like a massive metal jawbone. Like many engimals, it had wheels for feet, but Trom was one of a breed known as bull-razers; creatures that could use their shovel to ram through anything in their path. Bull-razers had thick, hinged belts that rotated round their wheels like a caterpillar, which gave them incredible traction. There was little that could stand in their path once they went on the rampage.

"I don't know about you," Roberto muttered beside her, "but that thing gives me the willies."

The Wildensterns used Trom for evictions, and Daisy was accompanying her husband to oversee the first one under his stewardship. As she rode with Roberto in an open-topped coach behind the bull-razer, Daisy felt a sick fear at what they were about to do. It wasn't a very cold day, but there was a chill in the wind and the sun was hidden behind a ceiling of pale cloud.

The engimal rolled ahead of them, its dull brain following commands from Slattery, who stood with a couple of his men in a sunken area on its back, holding its reins. Even sitting up in the coach, she could feel the vibrations from the ground caused by the movement of the engimal's huge mass. Berto sat beside her, gripping her hand and looking very queasy, his free hand playing with the buttons of his waistcoat. Nathaniel rode alongside them on his own beast. It was impossible to tell what he was thinking; his face was a careful mask of indifference. It was a mask that many gentlemen wore when they ventured out into the less fortunate world. Behind them came a wagon filled with Slattery's men, in case extra muscle should be needed.

Daisy smoothed out the folds of her peacock-blue dress as she wrestled with the conflicting emotions over what was about to happen. The tenants of three of these cottages had not paid their rent for months and so they had to be evicted. She had run a business and knew that there were times when you had to make hard decisions in order to maintain your profits. When her father had run his factories into the ground, she had been the one who had made the decision to shut some of the factories so that the rest could be spared. She had laid off loyal workers—many with families—to save a business that might still provide for many others.

If someone was not paying their rent, then they had to make way for someone who would. You couldn't have something for nothing—not in this life. But Daisy knew it wasn't that simple. Most of the Wildensterns' tenants did not pay their rent with money; they paid with labor. These people were allowed to live on the land as long as they used it to produce enough crops or livestock for their landlords every year to cover the cost of their rent. In return, they could build a stone or turf cabin and keep a small patch of the land for themselves, on which they grew the nutritious potatoes that formed the main part of their meager diet. If they could manage to grow enough to sell on the side, they were lucky. Then, along with the potatoes they might enjoy some milk, cabbage and sometimes butter or even a bit of bacon.

Trom rumbled and clanked along the road, crushing the verge on either side under its rolling feet. There were few roads in the country that could accommodate its tremendous size. It snorted steam, grunting and growling with each pull on its reins. The sound of it brought people out of their houses to watch it pass. Everyone knew what it meant and everyone hoped the engimal wasn't coming for them. Slattery snapped the reins to lift the creature's head and gave the onlookers a gracious wave. Daisy looked away in distaste.

All the food the peasants grew for their masters on the fertile land—the corn, wheat, beef, poultry and any number of other things—was sold in the cities or exported. As people grew more discontented and rebel raids on farm stores increased, armed soldiers were being used to guard goods being transported to the docks.

The Wildensterns had been demanding more and more from their tenants, leaving them with less land and less time to grow their own food. Hungry people did not work well and many were failing to meet their landlords' demands. Evictions were increasing. People were getting angry. Daisy shook her head as she gazed out on the countryside. It was bad business—you couldn't keep squeezing your workers dry. Sooner or later, something would have to give.

And using creatures like Trom and men like Slattery could only make things worse. The strange caravan of vehicles had traveled a few miles west from Wildenstern Hall and came to a stop near a clachan of five thatched cabins huddled together off a narrow road on a low hillside. Slattery handed the reins to McHugh and climbed down from the engimal's back. Striding over to the carriage, he took off his hat and bowed his head to Roberto.

"This won't take long, sir," he said. "Once their houses have been tumbled, they'll get the message."

He looked over and waved to McHugh, who turned the engimal off the road and urged it up the hill. The bull-razer pushed through a dry-stone wall as if it wasn't there, crushing the stones into the earth. Its treads churned up the soil as it climbed the sloping field towards the small group of houses. Slattery shook his head in disdain as people appeared from inside, shouting frantically to others, their voices high with shock and fear.

"There's always a few as'll put up a fight," the bailiff told his young master, an eager smile flashing his gold teeth. "We used to burn the roofs off the hovels. But we find this makes more of an impression. Everyone gets out sharpish when they see Trom coming."

The stone cabins looked like tiny, fragile constructions before the might of the huge engimal. It would be on them in seconds. It was absurd—this behemoth could smash through the legs of a railway bridge and here they were, sending it to demolish a few tiny cottages. Daisy could see some men standing in its path, waving at it to stop. McHugh paid them no attention. Slattery chuckled, shaking his head dismissively.

"I'll thank you not to laugh, Mr. Slattery," Berto said curtly.

"Yes, sir." Slattery's face immediately adopted an expression of utmost solemnity, which only made his men grin more widely.

Daisy watched them sourly. Her husband rarely chose to exercise his authority and, as a result, he had not earned the respect of these hard men.

"Roberto, somebody could be hurt," she whispered. "There must be another way of doing this."

She saw Nathaniel glance at her, but he said nothing. Berto did not take his eyes off the bull-razer. She knew he was horrified by what he was seeing. His hand was clutching hers so tightly her fingers were going numb.

"Bugger this," he hissed. "They can keep the bloody houses.

What do we care? We have a thousand more like them. What does it matter if we give away a few hovels and a patch of land? They can keep 'em! That'll give the old man the hump."

"No!" said Daisy. "Your father's given you power, so *use* it! Do you want him to think he can't even trust you to collect some rent? How can you help anybody then? Come up with another way for them to pay, but first stop this madness before somebody gets killed!"

Two men dived out of the engimal's way moments before its shovel slammed into the first house, driving through it as if it were a pile of leaves, tossing roof beams and straw thatch into the air and crushing stones and furniture underfoot. Daisy caught her breath. There might have been people still in there. A woman was running down the road towards them.

"Please!" she cried. "Please, my mother is in our house. She can't be moved. She has the fever and she can't be moved. For the love of God, please call off your animal!"

The woman was dressed in a worn skirt and blouse; a tattered headscarf hung down her back, where it had fallen as she ran. She made it as far as the door of the carriage, seizing Roberto's hand before Slattery dragged her away.

"Don't mind her, sir," he said as he pulled her back. "If the woman's old, she's dead anyway. We'd be doing her a mercy. The fever'll finish her off whether she's outside or in."

"Take your hands off that woman!" Roberto snapped at the bailiff. "Let her speak!"

With a barely concealed scowl, Slattery released the woman, who darted back to the side of the carriage. She was about to speak when Trom swiveled and lunged out of the ruins of the first cabin, crashing straight into the second one. The woman let out a whimper.

"My mother, sir." She addressed Roberto. "She's in bed with the fever in the middle house there. If we move her, it could kill her. No one else will take her in—not in the state she's in! They'd be puttin' their own at risk and I wouldn't ask it of 'em. Please, sir. Don't take our home!"

She pressed her cheek, wet with tears, against Berto's hand.

"Don't take our home! It's all we've got! We'll work harder for yeh. We'll make more than ever for yeh next year . . . just don't take our home!"

Berto withdrew his hand, self-consciously wiping it against his jacket. He looked sickened, but Daisy could see the resolve setting on his face. McHugh was steering the bull-razer across the yard towards the middle house.

"Slattery!" Berto said in a clear voice. "Call off your man."

"That's not a good idea, sir," the bailiff told him. Roberto started to interrupt, but Slattery talked over him. The Patriarch had warned the bailiff about his errant son. "It'll set a bad example. Take it from me, sir. They've all got sob stories if you stop to listen to 'em. Give them half a chance and they'll have the bloody parish priest out here screamin' blue murder. Don't go givin' them the idea they can—"

"My brother gave you an order, Mr. Slattery!" Nate barked. "Now do as you're bloody told!"

They all turned to look at him. His command hung there for a moment, and for that instant Daisy saw a look of his father about him. The air of a man who would not be defied. And Slattery saw it too. He pulled a whistle from his pocket and blew hard on it. McHugh did not hear it and Slattery blew again, twice more. Trom's driver glanced over to see his boss waving him back. He hauled in on the engimal's reins just before it ploughed into the third house. McHugh looked at them in confusion and then pulled the engimal round and headed back down the field towards them.

Daisy leaned over and whispered something in Berto's ear. He nodded and beckoned to the peasant woman.

"This is not an act of charity, madam—" he began.

"I wouldn't ask for your charity, sir," she cut in hurriedly. "Just a fair chance to earn our keep—and for you not to send great big beasts tramplin' through our house."

"Yes . . . yes, exactly." Berto nodded, still a little unsure of himself. "We'll send someone to, eh . . . to renegotiate the . . . the terms of your rent. We'll work this out . . ."

As he spoke to the woman, Daisy turned to watch Slattery walk away. The bailiff was shaking his head and she was sure she could hear him cursing to himself. He threw a glance back at her and she shuddered, putting a hand to her breast. She had never had anyone glare at her with such a expression of hatred. Not even Nathaniel.

"He's an animal, that man," Berto said softly from behind her, and she could tell he was watching Slattery too. "And he's really only loyal to Father. He despises the rest of us. Marcus had to hit him once, to pull him into line. You should have seen the look in Slattery's eyes then—I'd say there are few men who could strike Patrick Slattery and live to tell about it. I think Marcus would have fired the brute if he could, but Father wouldn't have it."

"Marcus hit him?" Nate asked. "Why? When did that happen?"

"It was a few years ago, when Marcus ran the Irish estates," Berto told him. "They had an argument while they were watching an eviction. Slattery said something about me being a soft-hearted wastrel—Heaven knows why. Marcus lost his temper and lashed out. You should have seen the look Slattery gave him after he was hit. It turned me cold."

The peasant woman was hurrying back to her cabin. Slattery was climbing onto Trom's back. Taking the reins, he steered for home without waiting for further instructions. Neither he nor his men looked back at the carriage.

"I don't think Mr. Slattery likes people who get in his way," Nate observed.

He didn't say any more, but Daisy knew what he was thinking. He was wondering if Marcus had been one of those people.

Nathaniel stood in front of his father's desk, his eyes lowered towards the old man's favorite pen, which sat on the blotter. The afternoon's outing with Trom was still fresh in his mind and it occurred to him that despite all his family's fears of armed rebels and stealthy assassins, that pen could affect the lives of more people in a stroke than any act of violence. Edgar picked up the pen, dipped it in a bottle of ink and scrawled his signature on a contract, changing some more lives. The Patriarch closed the ledger he had been reading and put it and the new contract to one side, wiping the powerful pen clean again.

"What news is there of Hugo's recumbent brother?" he asked, finally looking up at his son.

"Still no sign of Brutus recovering, sir," Nate replied. "Gerald is concerned about him. He says the wounds the man suffered before his . . . death are still open and some have become infected. He has found the beginnings of gangrene in some of them, and thinks he may need to operate . . ."

"Hmph," Edgar grunted. "Does Hugo know this?"

"Not yet, sir. Gerald wanted to tell you first."

"Tell Gerald to do whatever he needs to do to keep Brutus alive," the old man said. "But now to the real business at hand. You have a few more weeks before you leave for America. When you are not working with Silas, I want you to act as Hugo's tutor. He is ignorant of the world around him, so you will educate him in how we live. He has been given rooms to himself, as have his sisters. Eunice and Miss Melancholy will take care of the women; Hugo is your responsibility."

"Yes, Father," Nate replied reluctantly.

He had no wish to be anybody's nanny. He was still no closer to finding out the truth about Marcus's death, and with little time left before his departure, he had been planning a trip up to the Mourne Mountains to see where his brother had died. Now he would have to cart that ancient relic up there with him.

"Father, can I ask something?"

"What is it?"

"If Hugo really was a Patriarch, isn't he . . . couldn't he—?"

Nate's nerve failed him for a moment, but then he tried again: "Why did you let him live?"

His father exhaled noisily, staring down at the top of the desk for a few moments.

"That is none of your concern, boy."

Nate ground his teeth, struggling to contain his temper. Here he was, taking on the responsibilities of the Heir, and still he was being treated like a child.

"You will teach our honored ancestor everything he needs to know to pass for a modern man," Edgar went on. "And bring him up to date on the history of the family. However . . . I do not want him knowing the full extent of the family's wealth just yet.

"He and his sisters hail from more turbulent times, when life was lived by the sword and empires were built by kings rather than trading companies. There may come a time when I choose to give him a role in our business, but first he must learn to understand modern politics and economics. Silas can assist you with whatever learning is beyond your limited expertise. But Hugo *must* be given a thorough introduction to the Age of Reason. He can know about our estates in Britain and Ireland, but the Americas were unknown in his time and I would prefer if he remained ignorant of them—and our business with them—for the time being. And that must be communicated to the other members of the family.

"Do you understand what I am telling you?"

"Yes, Father," Nate answered with the hint of a smile on his face. "You're saying that Hugo must not discover America."

XXI

A POISONING OF THE BLOOD

BRUTUS'S RECOVERY WAS FALTERING. Nate entered Gerald's laboratory to find his cousin cleaning his surgical instruments with alcohol. Hugo was kneeling by his brother's bed, crying and clutching Brutus's right hand and offering prayers in Latin.

"The hand has to come off or he'll die," Gerald told their ancestor, and Nate got the impression that he had been telling the old man this for some time now. "The flesh of his hand is dead and the decay is producing toxins that are poisoning his blood. It is only because of your brother's extraordinary powers of healing that he is not dead already. But that will not last. The same flesh that can manage such a remarkable recovery is also producing a remarkably powerful toxin. The hand must come off."

Nate took his place at Gerald's side. He had aided his cousin in minor operations before, but never something so drastic. They waited at Brutus's bedside for Hugo to finish.

"If it must be done, then so be it," Hugo said at last, in a choked voice. "I can only hope that he will forgive me for allowing him to be crippled so. This sword-arm was the most feared in Ireland."

He wiped his eyes and stood back, a look of abject misery on his face. Gerald waved to four waiting servants, and together they lifted the giant over onto the operating table. Hugo watched Gerald set out a number of blades on a side table.

"Don't worry," Gerald reassured him, his attention already focused on the job at hand. "He won't feel a thing."

A bottle of laudanum stood on the side table, in case Brutus should suddenly wake up. Gerald placed a bone-saw beside the other blades. Hugo put a hand to his mouth and hurried out of the room.

"It's true, what he said," Gerald muttered to Nate as he tied a tourniquet around Brutus's arm. "I finally found a mention of them—in just one book, a rare family journal from our own library. But our dear old ancestors were hard to find—almost as if they had been erased from history. They were a mongrel breed who came over with the Normans in eleven seventy to try and help Dermot MacMurrough—that disgraced King of Leinster— to win back his lands. In return, he promised them land of their own." He swabbed Brutus's wrist with alcohol. "MacMurrough couldn't deliver, but the Normans took what they could by force of arms anyway.

"The Wildensterns were among them. Brutus is said to have

killed nearly a hundred men in one day of battle. He was unstoppable. They seized land south of Dublin and held onto it by sheer ferocity. Hugo was a master strategist, apparently; but he was merciless—a complete bloody tyrant. Anyone who spoke out against him had their tongue cut out. The same went for any other body parts that offended him. Nearly forty years after he moved in, some fanatical monk convinced everyone that Hugo was the devil himself and led the people in an uprising against him and his family. They tortured the four of them for days, buried them alive and then tried to destroy every trace of their existence. Nearly managed it too, by the looks of it. I've always thought the Wildensterns didn't get here for decades after that. The ancestors we know about must just have followed these valiant pioneers. It seems we have Hugo to thank for starting the family on the road to greatness."

Gerald picked up a scalpel and prepared to make a cut just above Brutus's right hand.

"Oh, I almost forgot," he said to Nate. "Take a syringe and go and ask Hugo if we can take some of his blood. Our mighty friend here is going to lose quite a bit and hopefully we can use Hugo's to replace some of it."

As Nate picked up a syringe, he watched Gerald press the scalpel into Brutus's flesh, drawing the first blood.

"I wouldn't want to be around when he wakes up and finds someone's chopped his hand off," he observed.

"These are extraordinary times," Gerald replied. "Who knows? Perhaps it'll grow back."

•   •   •

Hugo's education began the following morning. Nathaniel's new charge wanted some sword practice and Nate, who was fast becoming convinced that the house was full of rebel spies, was happy to oblige. It was clear that he would need to stay on his toes if he was to survive long enough to make his trip to America— or rather, to solve Marcus's murder and then flee to wherever he could escape his father's influence. Hugo would hardly be a challenging opponent, old and decrepit as he was, but every bit of practice helped. And besides, it was more fun than teaching history or politics.

Nate led the old man to the gymnasium, noticing that Hugo was steadier on his feet than he had been the day before. His movements were becoming more and more confident as time passed.

The first argument started over which swords they were going to use. Hugo immediately chose a hefty long-sword, the weapon of his time. Nate refused, on the basis that the old man was far too weak to be swinging four and a half pounds of metal around. It would also require the use of a buckler—a small shield—and Nate doubted that Hugo would be able to even lift a long-sword with one hand, let alone swing one.

The old Patriarch persisted in demanding a heavy sword, pointing first at a Scottish claymore, then a cleaver-like falchion, and then finally a six-foot two-handed sword, which sent Nathaniel into fits of laughter. He could barely hold that one up himself. Instead, Nate took down a pair of épées; light and blunt and ideal for training. He handed one to Hugo, who looked at the flimsy sword in disdain.

"Do people commonly fight with knitting needles in this new age?" he grunted.

"It's built to develop speed, not to chop horses in half," Nate replied. "Let's see what you remember."

Clancy, who was standing nearby, invisible as all good servants should be, helped the two gentlemen into their padded jackets, gauntlets and wire-mesh helmets and then stood aside to watch.

Nate raised his blade in front of him in salute, then took up the *en garde* stance, blade extended, his free hand above his shoulder. He nodded to Hugo, eager to see what his opponent would do. The Normans were masters of the battlefield in their day and he had no doubt Hugo was a seasoned warrior. The old man nodded back and held his sword horizontally at head-height in a pose that Nate recognized from medieval fighting manuals. Nate gave a resigned sigh; his opponent was determined to learn the hard way. Nate lunged in with an attack.

At this point all pretense at formality went out of the window.

Nate scored two strikes while Hugo was still making his first swing. The older man had clearly used a sword before, but he made big, sweeping moves that telegraphed his intentions and left him wide open. He wasn't used to the tighter, quicker style of modern fencing.

"Stop using it like a big sword," Nate told him. "Small movements . . . short and quick!"

He deflected Hugo's blade again and thrust the point of his sword into his opponent's chest. Hugo snarled and stamped on Nate's toe.

"Aagh!" Nate yelped.

Hugo pinned Nate's foot down long enough to smack him on the side of the helmet with his blade. Nate gave a curse and pulled free. He parried the next blow and jammed his point into the protective pad on Hugo's chest again. Hugo grabbed the blunt blade with his free hand and kicked Nate in the shin. Nate was so surprised, the old man managed to get two more kicks in with the other foot before swinging his sword so hard against the younger man's side that the blade bent.

Nate grunted in pain. He should have called a halt to it there and then, but his temper flared and he swept Hugo's sword aside and jabbed his point into the man's mask. Hugo staggered back and Nate followed, lunging after him to whip the thin blade across the man's unprotected thigh—going for pain rather than points. Hugo let out a scream and jerked away, lashing wildly with his crooked sword.

They both came forward, clashing again, and Nate scored several more strikes as Hugo fought like a whirling dervish, his frantic efforts all the more comical because of his pathetically weak limbs. Nate would have laughed, but the old man was taking it so seriously. Nate leaned onto his back leg as Hugo came at him again, avoiding the thrusting point, and with a neat spiraling motion, whipped the blade right out of Hugo's hand.

That should have been the end of it, but even as he was disarmed, Hugo grabbed Nate's wrist. Wrenching his mask off, he whacked Nate over the head with it and then sank his teeth into the young man's arm, provoking another yell of pain. Only the material of Nate's sleeve saved him from broken flesh.

They pulled apart, breathing heavily. Hugo was wheezing

through gritted teeth, clutching his chest, looking frighteningly absurd as he snatched his sword from the floor and tensed up his weak, aged frame, raising his bent weapon in a guard position.

"This is not how we practice fighting," Nate growled. "You have to use more control."

"Any warrior knows you gain control by winning," the old man panted. "Perhaps you should *practice* less and *fight* more?"

He charged forward to make another sweeping attack with his sword. But Nate had run out of patience; if the old relic wanted to play dirty, that was his own lookout. With a flick of his wrist, Nathaniel parried the clumsy strike and stepped aside to let Hugo's momentum carry him past. Nate brought his knee up sharply into the other man's ribs, doubling him over and sending him crumpling to the floor.

"I'm a great believer in practice myself," Nathaniel breathed, relishing the adrenaline rushing through his body. "It's *how* I win."

Hugo lay on the floor, struggling to get his wind back, the ache in his side etched in lines across his face.

"Indeed," he gasped. Then, looking up at his opponent with a grimacing smile, he added: "So . . . same time tomorrow?"

XXII

ETIQUETTE AND THE RULES OF ASCENSION

DAISY POURED THE TEA under the judgmental eye of her Aunt Eunice. Elizabeth and Brunhilde sat on a sofa on the other side of the small table, one a picture of absolute stillness, the other chewing her thumbnails down to the quick, her eyes darting suspiciously around the spacious drawing room. Daisy knew that her conversation skills were about to be tested to the limit.

"You won't have had tea before," she said. "Might I suggest a little sugar and milk?"

Neither woman answered, so Daisy decided for them, handing their cups across the table before serving herself and Eunice.

"Daisy and I have been asked to introduce you to life in the modern world," Eunice began, pressing a hand to her ample bosom; a gesture that implied that she was the only one they need listen to. "I was thinking we might begin by telling you about the prominent members of our family."

Brunhilde picked up her cup of tea, sniffed it curiously and then took a large gulp.

"Oh, mind that!" Daisy exclaimed. "It's very ho—!"

There was an explosion of tea across the table as Brunhilde spat out the burning liquid, spattering some of it over Eunice, who was unfortunate enough to be sitting opposite her. A maid, who had been standing unobtrusively in a corner, scurried forward to clean up the mess. Brunhilde wiped her mouth with her sleeve and glared furiously at the offending cup. Elizabeth cast a concerned glance towards her sister but did not move. Eunice let the maid finish and then waved her away. She examined her dress and checked her makeup and decided both were still in a fit state for them to carry on with the proceedings.

"Yes, perhaps we should start instead with some simple dining etiquette . . ." she muttered stiffly.

"Perhaps they could tell us about *their* world first," Daisy suggested. "We could—"

"All in good time, dear." Eunice put a heavily ringed hand on her niece's knee. "All in good time."

And so Eunice launched into a tedious lecture about how to behave at the Modern Dinner Table. Daisy sat fuming with impatience. These two women were from *another century*; there was so much that could be learned from them, and yet this biddy wanted to talk about which fork to use for your salad. Any time Daisy tried to interject, Eunice either cut her off or just ignored her completely. The old bag was intolerant of anyone interrupting while she was listening to the sound of her own voice.

". . . and of course, one should *never* put one's elbows on the table—"

"Is this a God-fearing house?" Elizabeth asked suddenly.

There was complete silence for a moment as Eunice sat with her mouth open. These were the first words heard uttered by either of the ancient women. Brunhilde leaned forward and slurped some tea. She dug her fingers into the sugar bowl and added several more lumps.

"Y—yes, of course." Eunice gave a faltering smile. "Why, we have helped finance the building of three churches in Ireland in the last ten years alone! We have our own chapel on the grounds of the estate."

Elizabeth seemed to be digesting this, looking towards the window with a distant expression. Eunice was about to expand on the family's religious credentials, but was interrupted again.

"Do women have power in this new world?" Elizabeth inquired, turning to hold Eunice's gaze.

The question was gentle but insistent, and Daisy noted that the woman had a smooth, sonorous voice.

Eunice struggled to answer.

"Well, there is Queen Victoria, of course, although she must abide by the will of the government. Women are responsible for the home, and . . . and . . . and play a great part in the culture of—"

"Under British law, women are controlled by their husbands or fathers," Daisy said sharply. "We cannot own businesses or property, we cannot vote and we can play no part in government. But we're working on changing that."

Elizabeth nodded her thanks but said no more. Brunhilde continued to slurp her tea. Eunice struggled to find a subject on which she could lecture her uninformed ancestors.

"There are many women's movements—" she began.

"Are you ruled by this Queen . . . Victoria?" Elizabeth spoke again.

"Edgar has a poor view of the Queen unfortunately," Eunice said apologetically. "He knows her personally, you see, and we are distantly related . . . His position is that we are Irish first and British second, but above all we are *Wildensterns*—"

"And the British Empire, can go hang if it thinks it can tell him what to do," Daisy finished for her.

Elizabeth nodded approvingly.

"And what rank will Hugo hold now, in this family?"

Daisy hesitated. They needed to be careful here. It would be very easy to say the wrong thing.

"Let me explain," Eunice said, smiling. "There has never been a situation like this . . . ever. So there are still a lot of matters to be worked out. You can be assured that you are welcome here . . . but . . . well, the family has a firm structure and it is governed by some very strict rules. Edgar . . . the Duke is the Patriarch and will be until his death. He will decide what Hugo's position shall be."

"And his will is never questioned?" Elizabeth asked innocently.

"By the time one becomes Patriarch," Eunice told her, "one will have earned the right to govern. Of course, I'm forgetting—you didn't have the Rules of Ascension in your day, did you?"

"Aunt Eunice . . ." Daisy said softly.

Elizabeth raised her eyebrows and shook her head, leaning forward slightly.

"Ah," said Eunice. "Then I shall enlighten you, so that you can understand our . . . special arrangements."

"Aunt Eunice . . ."

"It's all right, Daisy dear. I have this well in hand," Eunice assured her. She sat up straighter and readied herself for her recital. "Now, Elizabeth, Brunhilde. With the intention of encouraging the qualities of aggression, strength and ambition, the family will sanction the act of assassination of one family member by another, under eight strict conditions—the Rules of Ascension. They are as follows:

"Number One: The Act of Aggression must be committed by the Aggressor himself and not by any agent or servant.

"Number Two: The Act must only be committed against a man over the age of sixteen who holds a superior rank in the family to the Aggressor.

"Number Three: The Act must only be committed for the purpose of advancing one's position and not out of spite, or because of insult or offence given, or to satisfy a need for revenge for an insult or injury given to a third party.

"Number Four: All efforts should be made to avoid the deaths of servants while committing the Act. Good servants are hard to find.

"Number Five: The Target of the Aggression can use any and

all means to defend themselves, and is under an obligation to do so for the good of the family.

"Number Six: Retribution against the Aggressor can only be carried out after the Act has been committed. Should the Aggressor fail in his attempt, and subsequently escape to remain at large for a full day, only the Target of the Aggression and no other person will be permitted to take Retribution.

"Number Seven: No Act of Aggression or Retribution must be witnessed or reported by any member of the public. All family matters must be kept confidential.

"Number Eight: Any bodies resulting from the Act must be given a proper burial in a cemetery, crypt, catacomb or funeral pyre approved by the family."

Eunice nodded and sat back, looking pleased with herself. Daisy was covering her face with her hand. Roberto had been made to recite these rules from the age of ten. This family was insane, and she had been mad to marry into it.

"And rank in the family is decided by bloodline?" Elizabeth pressed her tutor.

"Of course," Eunice said. "So Roberto is the Heir, as the Duke's eldest remaining son. Then Nathaniel and after him Gideon, as Edgar's eldest remaining brother."

"I'm curious to know then," Elizabeth went on, "why the Duke allowed Hugo to live?"

"Oh, heavens," Eunice tittered, her bosom quivering with incredulous mirth. "You've only just come back from the dead—we can't go sending you off again! It's not like your brother's a *threat*, now, is he?" Her laughter faltered. "Is he?"

Elizabeth gave her a demure smile.

"My brother is just happy to be alive, as are we. We are born again, through some miracle of God, and our efforts will be devoted to praising Him, living worthwhile lives with this new time He has given us, and praying for the awakening of our brother Brutus. You have nothing to fear from us."

"Of course not, dear," Eunice sighed, patting the woman's knee.

But Daisy listened to Elizabeth's words with a faint feeling of dread. The woman had been very deliberate in her questioning for somebody who just wanted to live a "worthwhile life." They all lapsed into an awkward silence, and as Brunhilde started to shove sugar lumps into her mouth, Eunice suggested they have some more tea.

With everything that had been going on, Nate had neglected his investigation into Marcus's death and he had made up his mind to get to the bottom of it all. There was something about the idea of rebels killing his brother in order to attack his funeral that just didn't ring true. The rebels had never shown that kind of cunning in the past. They tended more towards near-suicidal assaults on public buildings, goods shipments or the occasional army barracks.

The one thing that they all had in common was that they invariably failed—but they had always acted with a rough kind of honor too. There was no honor in blowing up a funeral, and it was bound to cost them much support in a country where the dead were often held in higher regard than the living. If the family really was dealing with the Fenians, then these were a new breed, and Slattery was obviously no closer to tracking down the culprits.

Nate was certain that the answers lay in the Mourne Mountains, where Marcus was supposed to have fallen. He would go and see the spot for himself—climb the same route up the cliff if need be—and question everyone who was there.

But first he was determined to find out just why his brother had left the mysterious message about finding Babylon. If Marcus had wanted to leave a clue to the truth about his death, he could have provided something more helpful.

Marcus's rooms took up a whole floor of the tower, and since Roberto and Daisy had not asked to move into them, they had not yet been disturbed. Nate had already been up here since the funeral, but if there were any clues to find, so far they had eluded him. He paused before the door into the living room and then opened it hesitantly.

Marcus had style; everything from the carpet to the plasterwork on the ceiling was evidence of his modern but refined tastes. There were numerous artifacts from his travels too: Japanese swords and armor, Chinese fans, Russian furs and even a Mongolian saddle. There was a clutter of alien objects that Nate had always delighted in. He ran his fingers over a buffalo hide from the North American plains that hung on the wall. Marcus had bagged the animal himself—he had been a keen hunter. Nate had always been more fascinated by engimals than flesh-and-blood animals. And there was far more to be gained by capturing them alive.

He had asked Winters to join him. The manservant was being transferred to the service of one of Nate's cousins, but Nate had pulled rank so that the man could help him in his search. There was no dust anywhere; the rooms were still immaculately clean—the servants kept them that way—and yet they felt stale without his brother's presence.

He was surprised to find Marcus's climbing gear had been brought back and placed in its cupboard—it had not come back with the corpse and Warburton had told him it had been destroyed. It was slightly surreal to see all the ropes and bags of pitons hanging up, knowing Marcus had died using them. Nate examined everything carefully. It all looked intact, but he was struck by the fact that the crampons were still attached to the boots. In fact, he wondered why the ill-fated equipment had been brought back at all, seeing that everyone seemed so eager to brush the whole affair under the carpet.

Over the next two hours they slowly and methodically pulled the place apart. Winters was uneasy about disturbing his master's things, but Nate was merciless. They pulled out furniture, over-turned mattresses, emptied wardrobes, cupboards and drawers, lifted up rugs and pulled back the edges of the carpets. All the secret panels were opened and examined, the entrances to secret passages exposed and the passageways searched. Nate went through Marcus's papers, reading the most significant and putting the rest aside for closer analysis later. By the time they were finished, his older brother's home looked as if it had been hit by a typhoon; and they were no closer to solving the mystery of

Babylon. Nate flopped into an armchair and let out a frustrated curse, rubbing his face with his hands.

"What the hell did he mean?" he burst out. "What the bloody hell has *Babylon* got to do with anything? What kind of stupid . . . stupid . . .? Oh, for God's sake!"

He threw up his hands in exasperation and then sat in silence for a few minutes, playing with the rings on his fingers. Winters stood nearby, his face carefully neutral. Nate's gaze fell on the cupboard that held Marcus's climbing gear. He wondered about the crampons on the boots again.

"Winters," Nate said at last, "when you went with Marcus to the Mournes, you said you didn't climb with him?"

"That's correct, sir."

"But you prepared his gear, yes? He never let anyone else do it."

"Of course, sir."

"You're lying to me, Winters," Nate hissed, his lips drawn tightly across his teeth, his fingers gripping the armchair. "And I've had enough of everyone's lies. Now, you're going to tell me what Marcus was doing in the Mournes, or I promise you I will make your future a living hell."

"Sir! I assure you . . . I . . . I wouldn't . . ."

The servant's composure was starting to crack, but whether it was out of loyalty to his dead master or fear of disobeying the Rules of Ascension, he was still holding back what he knew. Nate stood up and strode over to him.

Overcome with a sudden anger, he grabbed the footman by his collar and shoved him back against the wall. "Who packed up his climbing gear, Winters? There are crampons on the boots. Crampons are for climbing on *ice!* There's no ice in the Mournes at this time of year. Marcus wasn't climbing, so where the hell was he? What was he doing in the Mournes? Talk to me, man!"

Winters folded visibly, his face a picture of resigned relief.

"Master Marcus had come back to Ireland against the Duke's wishes, sir," he said. "The Duke felt that with the way things were with the civil unrest in the United States, it was no time to be taking a holiday. But Master Marcus was adamant; he . . . he was certain that the Duke's brother was formulating plans to get hold of the business and that he would have to remove Master Marcus himself, as well as yourself and Master Roberto from his path to succeed. Master Marcus decided that the Duke wasn't doing enough to stop him."

This did not surprise Nate in the least.

"So if he was so concerned about an assassination attempt, why did he go gallivanting off to the mountains?" he asked again.

"Master Marcus went to the Mournes to give himself an alibi," Winters admitted quietly. "He meant to come back to the house in secret, and assassinate the Duke's brother before himself, Master Roberto or you could be hurt.

"I was to follow early the following morning in the coach and make it appear that I was traveling with Master Marcus. He would come back up to meet me on the road and arrive in the coach that morning, so it would appear as if he had been en route when Lord Wildenstern was killed."

Nate nodded to himself. Marcus was ranked above Gideon in the family, so the Rules of Ascension forbade him from killing his uncle in anything other than self-defense. But Marcus had not been prepared to wait for Gideon to hatch his plans and had taken matters into his own hands. And without the family's sanction, it would be straightforward murder, so he could not afford to be caught. Pretending he was out of the house would also mean that Gideon would be easier to catch off-guard.

"I reached the place where Master Marcus had told me to wait," Winters went on. "The coach driver and I waited for a whole day. It was terrible, sir; just waiting like that with no way of knowing what was happening. In the end I decided to continue to the house and pretend I had been sent there on an errand. Master Marcus's . . ." The footman's breath caught in his throat. "Master Marcus's body had already been found . . . in one of the secret passageways. It was the Duke who ordered that his son's death should be covered up by saying it was a climbing accident. The witnesses were all arranged accordingly . . ."

Nate released the manservant's collar and trudged back to his chair, slumping into it. So the family had done what it did so well; it had made an accident out of a killing. Gideon, possibly with the help of his sons, had beaten Marcus. Nate had known them all his life and found the idea of Marcus being outwitted by their buffoon of an uncle hard to stomach; Gideon and his sons were backstabbing curs with no shortage of ambition, but they had little courage and more of an animal cunning than any real intelligence. They should not have been able to better Marcus. Still, anyone could get lucky.

Nate rubbed his chin, overwhelmed by exhaustion. It seemed he had found the answer he was looking for and yet he was wholly unsatisfied. Why had Marcus spent his last words urging him to find Babylon? Nate was convinced there were still answers left to find. Then, when he was absolutely certain of Gideon's guilt, he would decide on how he would have his revenge.

The ancestors joined the family for dinner that evening. Despite having the kind of appetite expected of someone in their late teens, Nathaniel had long ago learned not to eat everything that was put in front of him. There was a massive quantity and variety of food, and to try some of every dish would render a person obese in a matter of months. Each dish was served in a single bowl or platter placed along the middle of the enormous table and the servants then dealt out food to each diner. Apart from reasons of presentation, the shared dishes meant that it would be very difficult for any family member to poison one rival without putting half the family to death.

It was largely traditional, however, and their *aurea sanitas* gave the family a formidable resistance to poisoning anyway.

Hugo had been given the place of honor at the table, at Edgars right hand—normally the Heir's position—facing Gideon and Eunice. Elizabeth and Brunhilde sat alongside the husband and wife, facing Roberto and Daisy. Nate sat beside them. Beyond this clique sat the rest of the immediate family, over thirty in all. This included Gideon's five sons, all younger versions of their father, their stocky, muscular bodies already a trifle overfed. The Gideonettes, Nate called them, and he regarded them now with barely concealed hatred. They tended to speak in short, barking sentences and wear truculent expressions. Each expressed his individualism by sporting his black facial hair in a different style. All the most up-to-date cuts of moustache and goatee were represented there that day.

At the other end of the table, furthest from the important elders, were the younger members of the family, including Tatiana. Responsibility for their good behavior was entrusted to Aunt Elvira, an endearing old harridan with bad legs and worse hearing, who listened to everything with a horn extending from her ear and shouted *"What?"* down the table at regular intervals.

"Moors?" Hugo muttered in disbelief as he gestured to the Duke's two black servants, who stood at the wall behind their master. "You allow blackamoors inside your walls?"

"I judge my servants on their ability and their loyalty, not on their race," Edgar retorted. "They and their brothers provide the most expert service."

"Just wait until they find out slavery's been abolished," Daisy said under her breath.

Nate gave her a hard look, but he was the only one who heard.

Hugo and his sisters spent some time taking in the majestic dining hall with its magnificent stucco moldings and the painting of a heavenly feast on the ceiling. Tapestries of hunts and battles hung on the walls and there were six doorways and numerous alcoves where the servants could conceal themselves from the family's view. The ancestors then turned their attention to the bewildering array of silver cutlery before them.

"Start on the outside and work your way in," Daisy whispered to them. "We'll explain the more complicated bits later."

The first course was brought in, consisting of turtle soup,

ANCIENT APPETITES

bread, chicken, plovers' eggs, various salads and numerous other
delicacies. The gorging began. The three ancestors had still said
very little about their previous lives, and some of the family tried
to engage them in conversation by asking about meals in their
times. Hugo and his sisters said little or nothing in response and
soon the questions dried up. The ancients clearly did not want to
be bothered while they ate. And eat they did, greedily sampling
one dish after another with insatiable appetites.

Nate found Elizabeth staring at him as she ate. He fumbled
with his knife and fork, suddenly nervous without knowing why.
She looked no older than thirty-five or -six now, and while her
face was beautiful in a cold, proud way, her eyes were so intense
he couldn't meet her gaze. They fixed on him now as she bit into
a small tomato and a single drop of juice ran down the side of
her mouth. His knife skidded across his plate with a loud squeak.

The second course was served: steaming platters of venison,
beef, pork, sturgeon, salmon, lobster and more, with heaps of
vegetables, butter and more bread. MacDonald, the butler, was
reaching across to carve slices from the breast of a roast goose,
but Hugo couldn't wait. He lunged out and grabbed a drumstick.
MacDonald pulled back, but not in time to avoid Hugo's impul-
sive lunge, and the razor-sharp edge of the carving knife caught
the ancestor across the back of his hand.

"Aargh!" Hugo roared. "You clumsy swine! Look what you've
done!"

A hairline cut across his knuckles started to bead with blood.

"I'm dreadfully sorry, sir!" MacDonald exclaimed. "It was an
accident—I'll fetch a bandage for you imm—"

It was as far as he got. Hugo snatched the hand with the knife and wrenched it towards him. He pulled the knife from Mac-Donald's fingers and pressed the servant's hand flat on the table.

"Hugo!" Edgar barked. "That's enough!"

Hugo raised the knife high and brought it down hard . . . slamming the point deep into the table between the butler's thumb and forefinger, just missing his flesh. MacDonald yelped in fright and then gave a gasp of relief as he realized he had not been hurt. Panting a little, he gave Hugo an ingratiating smile and tried to take his hand off the table.

And that was when Hugo grabbed the butler's middle finger with his free hand. In a vicious movement he bent it back—back at an awful, impossible angle until there was a snap and Mac-Donald screamed. Hugo released him and let him stumble backwards, clutching his broken finger.

"You'll be more careful in future, you dolt," he hissed, pressing a napkin to his own wound.

A couple of the footmen rushed forward to help MacDonald, escorting him out of the room. Daisy had her napkin up to her mouth. Elizabeth let out a patient sigh and Brunhilde uttered a little giggle.

"That wasn't necessary—" Nate began, but Edgar cut in.

"Hugo," he rumbled, "we do not indulge in summary punishment of our servants in this house and we certainly do not tolerate it from our guests. There are protocols to follow for disciplining any member of staff. In future, you should direct any grievance to Nathaniel, who will deal with it in the appropriate manner."

"I will discipline servants as I see fit!" Hugo snarled. "And I will not be commanded by any man."

"You will be commanded by me, while you are under my roof and eating at my table," the Duke told him in a low voice like stone grating across stone. "Have no doubt about it."

They stared at each other for what seemed like the longest time . . . and then Hugo dropped his eyes. He nodded truculently and, taking the knife that he had snatched from MacDonald, he cut some meat off the goose. He did not look at the Patriarch again.

Nate found that he was gripping his own knife tightly and his hands were shaking. He took them off the table and pressed them against his thighs. For the briefest instant he had been sure that the two old men were about to have a go at each other. The idea thrilled him, but he knew it would not have been a fair contest. Hugo did not know how close he had come to being seriously hurt. Nate exhaled slowly and started eating again.

"Ha!" Brunhilde blurted out. Baring her teeth to those around her, she grinned and chewed with her mouth wide open. "Fresh meat! Eat, everyone eat!"

Not knowing how else to react, they obeyed.

XXIII

AN EVENING OF CONFESSION AND DISCOVERY

SHAY NOONAN BURST into the damp, grotty room that he shared with his wife and slammed the door behind him. He didn't dare light a candle, but there was enough light from the night sky shining through the window for him to see. Cathy was already waking up, looking up from the mattress on the floor as he grabbed her and shook her shoulders.

"We have to get out of here, Cathy!" he whispered hoarsely to her. "Up into the attic, quick!"

"What?" she asked dully. "What're yeh talkin' about, Shay? What ungodly hour is this to be wakin' me up?"

"Forget the bloody hour, woman! Slattery's men are outside and they're lookin' for me. If they find either one of us, they'll have our guts for garters. Now get up out of that bed and get yer dressing gown on. We have to go out by the roof."

"I'm not going out on any roof!" Cathy retorted. "I'll catch me death o' cold!"

He seized her up roughly and shoved her threadbare dressing gown into her arms.

"You'll catch yer death of Patrick Slattery if he finds us here. Now come on!"

He pulled over a chair and stood on it, pushing open the trap door to the attic. Then he took hold of the rim and pulled himself up. Cathy stepped up onto the chair, wobbling slightly as she was still drowsy, and held up her hands for her husband to grasp. With a grunt of effort, he heaved her up through the opening. He lowered the hatch and stood up, taking a stub of a candle from his pocket. He lit it and held it up. There were no windows or doors out to the roof, but over by the corner he saw what he was looking for: the glow of the night sky through a hole in the gabled roof.

Guiding his wife across the rafters, he made his way towards the corner, stepping carefully from one board to the next. If either of them put a foot wrong, they could fall through the plaster ceiling into the room below. They ducked as the roof sloped down and finally reached the hole. It was small, but it was enough for Shay to reach through and push aside some of the slate roof tiles. It only took a minute for him to make it big enough to fit through.

Ignoring Cathy's whispered protests, he climbed out and pressed himself down against the slates.

"Come on!" he hissed impatiently.

She struggled clumsily through the hole and let out a moan of terror as she looked down at the ground, four stories below.

"Don't make a bloody sound!" he warned her.

They heard the muffled voices of Slattery and his men through the floor of the attic. Shay looked around frantically for some way off the roof, but there was nothing. He heard the attic hatch being opened and quickly laid his body across the hole to block out the light inside. Every move he made seemed to cause the loose slates to shift, and he closed his eyes and lay still. A light was held up into the attic, he could see it shine through the gaps on either side of his body. He could hear Cathy's teeth chattering and his own heart beating like a drum.

The light disappeared and he took a deep breath before daring to peek inside.

"They're gone," he said at last. "But they might have left someone behind down below to wait for us to come back. We'll give it a while and then come down by one of the other hatches."

"Séamas Noonan, you tell me what's going on this instant or I swear to Almighty God—"

"All right, all right, woman!" he rasped, covering her mouth in exasperation. "Keep yer voice down! Me 'n' Francie stole somethin' from the Wildensterns, and I fenced it through Duffy in town. That's how I paid off what we owed on the rent. But Slattery must have got to Duffy, 'cos now he's on our trail. And because of what we stole, he thinks we were in on the explosion at the funeral, all right? If we're caught, we're dead. It's as simple as that."

Cathy stared at him, aghast. For a minute she seemed lost for words—a rare event indeed. Leaning back against the slate slope, her feet flat against the tiles, she gazed out on the roofs of Dublin around them. It was a clear night and she could see as far as the river; she had never seen her city from this angle before and it was a beautiful sight. The air was clearer too this evening. There was less of the gritty smog that thousands of coal fires and factory smokestacks churned into the sky each day. She looked on her city with new eyes.

"And what about Francis?" she asked at last. "He's still at the house, isn't he? How long before they figure out who he is and sling him into Kilmainham Gaol for the rest of his life?"

"None of us will live to see gaol if we're caught," Shay muttered. "But we've got to warn Francie. He's supposed to be doin' a job for me tonight. It was goin' to set us up for life, Cathy. But we'd have to leave the country. I had our escape planned—I've got a boat set to take us to England and everything; you, me, Francie and the girls. It's all sorted. But we've got to hide up now until it's ready to leave and we've got to get Francie out of that house—"

"I don't want to go to England!" Cathy exclaimed, close to tears.

"Keep yer voice down, for God's sake! They could hear us!"

"We can't just pick up and leave like that! I can't . . . This . . . This is the last straw, Séamas; I've had enough of living with you and yer sins. Yeh'll go up to that house and get Francie out before they realize his part in this. I've prayed for yer soul every night since our marriage, but the devil can have it now for all I care, yeh miserable guttersnipe yeh!" Her face creased into a mask of rage as she grabbed his collar. "But yeh're not takin' our little boy with yeh! I want you to pray for him now, Shay. Pray for all yeh're worth!"

"Get yer hands off me, I'm not prayin' for nothin'!"

Cathy smacked him hard across the face, nearly knocking him loose from his perch. He scrabbled for a grip on the tiles, sliding down before he caught himself. Staring in shock at his wife, he opened his mouth to curse her name but she slapped him again.

"Yeh'll pray, Séamas Noonan, or I'll knock us both off this roof!"

With disbelief written all over his face, Shay gaped at his wife. He had never seen her like this, but the look in her eyes convinced him she was serious. Bowing his head, he closed his eyes, and Cathy glared at him for a minute longer before joining him. And clinging there to that slate roof, they prayed for the life of their son.

Most of the stable boys went to bed not long after nightfall. Their work was hard and they had to rise early in the morning, so only the diehards stayed up that night to play cards around the top of a crate by the light of a candle. Francie played until the last hand, and then waited impatiently for the others to go to bed. He said he was going out for a walk; it was forbidden by Old Hennessy, but most of the lads did it now and then. It was almost time to pull off the job of his life, but he needed the others to be asleep before he set about it.

He made his way down to the stables, slipping quietly through the door and stroking the noses of some of the horses, which whickered softly when they caught his smell. He liked being here, just standing among the animals when he had no work to do. It gave him a sense of peace. Walking slowly down past the stalls, he came to Flash's door. He let himself in and crouched down by the engimal's front wheel, running his hand over its front legs. It leaned against his hand, enjoying the contact. There was no reticence now; they had become friends at last.

"Tonight's goin' to be a big night for you 'n' me," Francie whispered to it. "Life's about to change for the both of us."

At that moment he heard a noise at the end of the stables. Pressing himself up against the low wall that looked out onto the stable, he pushed the engimal away from him and held his breath. There came the sound of footsteps, and the flickering light of a candle passed the stall and carried on down towards the other end of the building. There had been no sound of the stable door opening. It must be the mysterious gentleman again. Francie was about to come out of hiding when he heard more footsteps. He ducked back down again and peered through a gap between the boards. His eyes had adjusted to the bad light and he saw that it was a short, slender man in ill-fitting clothes. Francie got a brief look at his face but didn't recognize him. The stranger had come from the same end of the building, but was not carrying a light. Francie wondered if he was following the first person.

But where had they come in?

When he was sure the stranger was gone, he darted out through the door and crept down to the end of the stables.

They had not come in by the big double doors; he was sure of it. Somehow, they were getting into the stables at the house end and sneaking through to go out of the side door, which couldn't be seen from the house.

He turned to look at the wall to his left and was just in time to see a section of it swinging shut. Lunging forward, he stuck his foot in the gap and held the door open. The stones on the front of the door were real, but it was balanced so perfectly it swung easily, and with hardly any sound at all. Pushing one of the smaller stones operated a latch, and he closed the door and opened it again. When it was closed, its shape was hidden amongst the stones of the wall. He marveled at the clever engineering. Peering inside, he saw there was a stack of candles just inside the door, and a box of matches. A stone-walled passage disappeared into the darkness beyond.

Francie was itching to explore it, but there was no point. It was a pity that this was to be his last day in Wildenstern Hall. He would have loved to follow the passage and see where it went; he wondered what secrets he could uncover. But he had a job to do and this wasn't it. He swung the door shut and heard the latch click home. He would wait a little while longer to give the lads upstairs time to fall asleep, and then he'd make a start.

Daisy crept through the stables, careful not to let Roberto see her following him. She waited until he had gone out of the side door before letting go of the secret door in the stone wall and hurrying past the stalls to the other end of the building. She reached the side door and opened it cautiously, peering out.

He was not going to get away from her this time. After hearing about Tatiana's velocycle ride, she had decided that she too would dress for adventure. She hitched up her trousers for the umpteenth time that evening, unable to get the braces tight enough. Wearing a man's clothes was an alien and exciting sensation. It solved the problem of trying to negotiate one of her cumbersome dresses through the narrow hidden passageways, and if she were spotted, a man would attract less attention walking around at this time of night than a woman alone. Assuming one of the trigger-happy sentries didn't shoot her, of course.

Making sure her long hair was still piled up under her flat cap, she ventured outside and was just in time to see her husband making his way down towards the end of the huge lawn, staying close to the hedge to avoid attracting attention. She had deliberately taken some of his less flamboyantly colored clothes for this task and was able to meld into the darkness behind him with relative ease.

He was headed for the woods that bordered the southeast edge of the grounds. A lazy rain was beginning to fall, but there was still enough light from the sky to allow her to trail behind him at a distance. Roberto was normally a graceful mover but tonight he walked with a dogged purpose. Daisy almost had to run to keep up. They entered the woods along a path she did not know, the airy beech trees still allowing in enough of a glow from the moon to see where she was going, but it became harder to keep Roberto in sight in the fragmented light, as she had to watch where she put her feet to avoid tripping on the roots and undergrowth. The jacket she wore was not heavy enough and the rain was starting to soak through. It fell from the branches above her, no longer a light spray now, collecting instead in large drops that spattered on her head and shoulders and dripped down the back of her neck.

There should have been sentries somewhere in these woods, she knew. The gamekeepers were normally out on the lookout for the poachers who came looking for deer or pheasants that were bred on the Wildensterns' estate for hunting, but more armed guards had been posted around the perimeter since the attack on the cemetery. She wondered if Roberto had somehow found a way to divert them from this area.

They followed the narrow, snaking path for nearly fifteen minutes before coming to a road. Roberto stopped here and Daisy took up a position behind a tree to see what would happen next.

They were not waiting long. The sound of cantering hooves carried down the road towards them and a rider came into sight. Daisy recognized the stooped shape by the easy way in which he handled the horse. It was Hennessy, the head groom. He reined the horse in and climbed down. Roberto stepped out onto the road to greet him, shaking his hand as if he were an equal.

"I thought you might not make it," he said to the older man.

"The guards were gone, like you said, sor," Hennessy told him. "Came out here ahead of you so as we wouldn't be seen together."

"You always have my interests at heart," Berto said gratefully, still gripping the other man's hand. "Well, I suppose we'd better get on with it."

He released his grip and reached into his pocket, taking out a wad of pound notes, which he thrust into Hennessy's hand.

"This ought to be enough," he sighed. "At least for now. God, it's a frightful business."

"Life isnae always fair, sor," Hennessy declared. "We all have our crosses to bear."

"Indeed," Berto replied. "You'd better go. I've sent the guards off—told them I wanted them to spy on the navvies, but I doubt they believed me. Probably thought I wanted to go off gallivanting with some woman, knowing the way they think. They'll return in a couple of hours, so if you can't be back by then, stay at your brother's for the night."

"Aye, sir." Hennessy nodded and made to get back on the horse.

Before he could, Roberto grabbed him roughly and spun him round. What Daisy saw next made her recoil in horror. Stifling a sob, she stumbled away from the tree, turned and ran frantically back along the path with tears streaming down her face.

Francie heaved in a breath and nodded to himself. It was time.

He had been standing there thinking about it long enough. It would be all too easy to stand there all night and wait for the perfect moment—that moment would be when he had the balls to go ahead and do it. Unbolting the door to the stall, he led Flash out. He had been speaking to the velocycle in a low voice for the last hour, calming it and putting it at ease so that it would make as little noise as possible when he walked it out of the stable. It worked. The engimal's motor made hardly a murmur as they crept carefully towards the side door and the lights of its eyes were dull and sleepy.

Francie's imagination taunted him with his fears. If anybody saw them—either the lads or Hennessy or any of the sentries—he was done for. He had to escape with Flash into the night without being seen by a soul, and meet his father by the broken oak on the crossroads in the woods. It was possible to get under the wall that circled the estate and, hopefully, past the sentries by following a stream through a culvert under the stonework. It was deep in the woods and overgrown with bushes and brambles, so he was sure it had long been forgotten about. Flash should just fit through.

When the theft was discovered, there would be no place to hide—they had to be out of the country by morning. But it was worth it all for the prize; his father would get enough money for this engimal to make them all rich. Francie had thought the oul' fella was mad for thinking of it, but things had changed now that Francie and the engimal had made friends.

Francie felt in his pocket for the envelope Shay had given him. He had given it serious consideration and had decided to disobey his father on this one. It was bad enough that they were stealing Nathaniel Wildenstern's pride and joy; there was no need to rub salt in the wound. The letter would be staying in his pocket until he had a quiet moment to get rid of it safely.

Francie stopped before the door just long enough to fit Flash's saddle and then lifted the latch. The door was well oiled and opened without a squeak. He peered out into the darkness. The sky was cloudy and there was a light rain falling, but he could see well enough. Flash tucked in its horns to get through the door, and together they made their way slowly along the hedge towards the woods.

As they reached the edge of the trees, Francie heard heavy breathing, what could almost have been sobbing, coming towards them. Looking around desperately, he pulled Flash towards some bushes and quickly but gently coaxed the machine to lie down behind them. His heart racing, he watched through the foliage until he saw a figure run past. It was the second man he had seen sneaking through the stable. Francie could swear the fellow was crying. There was no time to wonder what it was all about. If the man was out here without clearance and was spotted by the guards, they'd be all over this place like a rash. Francie had to get out of here as soon as he could.

Pulling Flash onto its feet, he looked into its face.

"Now listen up, lad," he whispered. "We're going to ride out of here now, but I need yeh to be quiet. D'yeh understand? And I need yeh to keep yer eyes dull, Flash. No lights, d'yeh get me?"

The engimal rubbed its head against his hand and he took that to mean it understood him. They would find out soon enough. Climbing into the saddle, he patted the velocycle's head and tapped his heels against its side. It rolled quietly through the wet undergrowth to the path and turned down it, its engine making no more sound than that of rustling grass, its eyes showing only the faintest flicker of light.

Francie knew the path well, having walked down here many times. It was twisting and narrow but was relatively clear of low-hanging branches, and Flash gradually picked up speed,

obviously having no problem seeing its way in the dark. Francie
leaned forward between the engimals horns, feeling the wind on
his face. The dripping trees blurred past him on either side, the
ends of branches snagging his jacket and trousers, threatening to
whip off his cap.

He had left the stable with only what he had on him but it
was all he would need. There would be no more mucking out
the stalls, no more polishing tack or taking lip from the grooms.
No more knuckling his forehead to every swell who said a word
to him. He was free! The exultation rushed through him—he
wanted to scream with joy, to let it out into the forest around him.

It was just at that moment that they swerved round a high
bank of thick foliage and Francie's breath caught in his throat.
Standing right in their path was a man, his head hung low, lost in
thought. They were going too fast to stop on the wet path. Flash
reared and let out a bark of surprise as they slammed into the
man, throwing him off his feet. He had time to scream before
his body fell under the wheels of the velocycle. The jolt bounced
Francie out of the stirrups just as Flash came down hard on its
front wheel, its back wheel striking the man's torso and bucking
the boy forward over the handlebars. Francie crashed into a bank
of ferns and soft earth, the impact knocking the wind out of him
and leaving him stunned.

Getting up onto his knees, he bent forward, trying to get his
breath back. There came the sound of shouting in the distance,
off to one side. The guards had heard the noise. They were
coming. Francie looked around for the velocycle. Flash was
standing on the path, looking from Francie to the fallen man and

back again. Francie waved to it, his chest still too constricted to call the engimal, but it backed away warily, turned and scuttled off back towards the house.

"No!" Francie wheezed. "Come back, yeh blackguard!"

But it was no use, the velocycle was gone. The man lying on the path moaned in pain, barely conscious. Francie wondered if he should try and help him, but what could he do? The voices were getting closer; he couldn't tell where they were coming from. There was nothing to be heard from the direction of the house—it seemed like the only way left to him. Francie stood up shakily and started running, weakly at first but then faster and faster until it seemed as if his feet were hardly touching the ground. Terror gave him wings and he raced back to the edge of the woods and up the lawn along the shadow of the hedge. The alarm had not yet been raised in the house; there were still few lights to be seen in the huge edifice. He had time to make it back before all hell broke loose.

He staggered to a halt in amazement. Flash was standing nervously by the side door, as if waiting to be let in. Francie shook his head and walked the last few yards, his legs suddenly feeling stiff and heavy. Opening the door, he ushered the velocycle in, stopping only to give it a sound kick up its arse as it slipped past him.

"I never figured yeh for a coward!" he hissed softly. "Look at yeh! The size o' yeh and yeh run like a mouse when yer startled!"

Flash looked suitably cowed, hovering by the door of its stall. It made an apologetic grunt but Francie opened the door and shoved it inside, muttering curses under his breath. Once the velocycle was put away, he sneaked back out to the rear of the stables and climbed the stairs to the loft. Wincing at the creaking floorboards, he found his way through to his bed in the darkness. Wiping the sweat from his forehead, he sat there feeling utterly drained. He was wearily pulling off his clothes when Patrick rolled over and squinted up at him.

"What are yeh gettin' up for, Francie? It's a bit early yet, isn't it?"

Francie hesitated in the middle of unbuttoning his shirt. He carefully started buttoning it back up again, and pulled his braces onto his shoulders before answering.

"Somethin's goin' on outside," he said to his friend. "It woke me up. Thought I'd go and see what the story is."

"Jaysus, I'll go with yeh," Patrick declared. "'S bin a while since we had a bit o' drama."

Francie nodded and tried to look enthusiastic. He'd had his fill of drama for one night. Standing up, he grabbed his cap and jacket and waited for Patrick to get dressed. He was standing with his hands in his pockets when he realized he should have been able to feel the letter his father had given him. He checked the pockets of his jacket but he already knew he wouldn't find it. He had dropped it somewhere out in the woods. Sitting down on the edge of the bed with his back to Patrick, he tried not to cry.

XXIV

AN UNJUSTIFIED ACCUSATION

IT WAS AFTER THREE IN THE MORNING when Clancy woke Nate to tell him he had been summoned to the main drawing room. Roberto had been attacked. Stopping only to pull on a pair of slacks, shoes and his dressing gown, Nate rushed down to see his brother.

He arrived, out of breath, to find Roberto stretched out on a divan, looking pale and uncharacteristically disheveled and muddy, his waistcoat open and his shirt torn. He was holding a damp folded cloth to the side of his face. Sitting in armchairs on either side of him were the Duke and Gideon, and Nate was surprised to see Hugo there as well. Standing by the Duke's chair was Slattery, a strange smile playing on the corners of his mouth.

"What happened?" Nate demanded.

"Your brother was attacked in the woods," Edgar growled.

"By whom?" Nate asked, then he frowned and added to his brother, "And what were you doing in the woods at this time of night?"

"I was taking a walk," Berto replied defensively. "I can still take a walk when I like, can't I? I couldn't sleep."

"Are you hurt?"

"The good doctor says I've cracked some ribs, but apart from that and some bruises and a rotter of a headache, I'm fine . . . apparently," Berto said in a skeptical tone. "I don't *feel* fine. I feel bloody awful."

"Someone riding an engimal, most probably a velocycle, ambushed him and almost killed him," Edgar said. "This, in an area surrounded by armed guards. We do not know if it was an opportunistic attack, or whether somebody was deliberately targeting the Wildenstern Heir. If so, it was a bold and extraordinary act of aggression."

"Well, that's not likely, is it?" Nate stuck his hands in the pockets of his robe. "Who could have known Berto was going to take it into his head to go for a walk in the middle of the night? Or *where* he'd walk? It must have been an accident. And you said they used an engimal? That doesn't sound like rebels or poachers—more like someone from the family."

Both Hugo and Gideon were following what was being said very closely, but said nothing.

"Sit down, Nathaniel," Edgar said quietly.

Nate felt the hairs rise on the back of his neck. He was missing something here. Something was badly wrong. He reached for an armchair and pulled it closer, sitting down clumsily.

Slattery stepped out into the middle of the floor and gave him a little bow.

"Good morning, sir," he began, his cold eyes locking onto Nate's. "I'm pleased to say that my men and I have already investigated the scene of the attack and have reached some early conclusions based on the evidence collected thus far."

The bailiff started to pace back and forth across the floor, delivering his speech with a dramatic air.

"You are right in supposing that it would take a great act of foresight to anticipate Master Roberto's spontaneous and ill-fated walk in the woods. So I would speculate that either our villain had the remarkable luck to find the Heir alone in the forest entirely by chance . . . or he followed him there with a view to instigating his attack."

Slattery stopped pacing for a moment to draw a long breath.

"Given that Master Roberto walked from the *house* and that said attack was carried out using a large enginal—an unlikely weapon for a rebel, as you rightly pointed out, Master Nathaniel—and given that the perimeter was being patrolled by armed men, it would be fair to assume that the culprit could have also come from Wildenstern Hall. I am aware that members of the family do indulge in the occasional act of . . . aggression, in order to . . . well, to get ahead, shall we say? I could not rule out the fact that this might be just such an act.

"But then we found *this*," he said abruptly, flourishing a cheap-looking brown envelope. "And things got a lot more interesting!"

"Get on with it," Edgar grunted, his enginal claw clicking restlessly.

Slattery nodded respectfully to the Duke. Taking out the piece of notepaper contained in the envelope, he unfolded it and handed it to Nathaniel. Nate took it and held it up to the light to read it:

A message for the Willdensterns,
Yor days of grynding good working people under yor hele are numbered. Take this, as a worning that there is no place to hyde from us. We can reach past yor walls and yor gards and strike wher you leest espect it.
Releese yor grip on the poor people of Ireland or sufer the connsequenses.
Yors faithfully
The Irish Liberty Brigade

"Looks to me like their spelling is no better than their assassinating," Nate quipped. "I've never heard of them. 'The Irish Liberty Brigade?' Where did they spring from?"

"We'll find out," Slattery assured him. "But since this was left for us to find, it suggests that the person who followed Master Roberto from the house is in league with this group. Perhaps someone who is working with the rebels in order to advance their position within the family."

Nate nodded, but thought it unlikely. It was only then that he noticed somebody was missing.

"Where's Daisy?" he asked. "Shouldn't she be here?"

"She's vanished," Berto muttered sourly from behind the cloth. "Nobody can find her."

"I bloody knew it," Nate said through gritted teeth.

"Daisy was not the attacker," Edgar declared. "Although her complicity has not been ruled out. Carry on, Slattery."

"Yes, sir." Slattery took center stage again. "As you'll know from your experience in tracking, Master Nathaniel, every engimal leaves a unique footprint, by which they can be identified. We were fortunate enough to be left with a perfect imprint of the offending velocycle's feet."

He snapped his fingers and a footman brought forward a jacket. Roberto's jacket. Slattery held it up for all to see, clearly marked in a diagonal line of mud across the front, the track left by the attacker's engimal. Nate caught his breath. He recognized it instantly.

"Naturally, we checked it against all the velocycles in the stables first," the bailiff told him. "We nearly forgot one, as it was being kept in a spare stall with the horses." His eyes held Nate in their unswerving gaze. "It was *your* velocycle, Master Nathaniel, and its feet matched the print perfectly."

"This is absurd! It can't be . . . I . . ." Nate began. "I haven't left the house all night! Someone must have stolen Flash and—"

"But the damned machine won't let anyone else ride it, Nate," Roberto pointed out, looking utterly miserable. "Nobody else can even sit on the cursed thing. I mean . . . I'd understand if it was an accident, you know? If that's all it was—"

"It wasn't me!" Nate shouted.

But from the expressions on the faces around him, it was clear that nobody believed him. He stared helplessly at his brother, unable to fathom how Roberto, of all people, could suspect him.

They had always trusted each other completely, and that trust was one of the few things in his family life that Nate had always thought he could count on. And as that was shaken, so too was everything he believed in.

"I can't say which surprises me more," Edgar rumbled. "That you had the nerve to finally attempt an act of aggression, or that you managed to cock it up despite a lifetime of training."

That remark seemed to bring Roberto's misery to a head and tears welled up in his eyes. Mortally embarrassed, he struggled up off the divan and hurried towards the door, wiping his face with the cloth. Nate stood up, trying to reach his brother one last time, but as Berto passed him, he stopped and glared at Nate with bitter hatred.

"What about Marcus?" Berto asked. "Was that you too?"

Nate turned away.

"Go to hell," he hissed.

As Roberto left the room, Nate faced the four remaining men.

"If I did this thing, do you really think I'd carry it out with the one engimal that could identify me? I know a hundred ways of killing a man—including half a dozen that don't leave a trace—and you think I'd try and run my brother down with a *velocycle?* Do you think I'd leave a bloody note that linked me to some stupid bloody Fenians and risk everything I was trying to kill him for? And as for the *letter* . . . My God! Do you seriously think I'd hand on a note with that many spelling mistakes? *Have you all lost your bloody minds?!*"

"Perhaps it was a rash act, perhaps you planned too hastily," Edgar replied. "Perhaps you hoped to make it look like an accident but when you realized you hadn't killed him, your nerve failed you and you fled back to the house. Perhaps you left the note to throw us off the trail and avoid the emotional repercussions from the family. Perhaps you faked the handwriting and spelling mistakes to make it look as if it were written by an uneducated hand. We do not know these things yet. And until we do, you will not leave this house.

"Slattery tells me you ordered the release of the moneylender, Duffy."

Nate gave the bailiff a hostile look.

"They beat the man to a pulp, Father."

"If they did so, then it was only because it was necessary," Edgar assured his son. He went on in a dispassionate tone, "You see, Nathaniel, if you had simply attacked Roberto, the Rules of Ascension would apply to protect you. But when I hear that you have taken pity on a known rebel sympathizer, and then this letter is found at the scene of your brothers assault, I am forced to re-evaluate your position." His voice was lower now, and grating with menace. "For we know that there is a traitor in this house, and if I find out that the betrayal is yours, I promise you the most dire consequences."

He paused to let those words sink in.

"That is all. You are dismissed."

The whole room waited in silence for Nathaniel to leave. He gritted his teeth and stood there for as long as he could bear his father's piercing stare.

"It wasn't me," he managed at last—but it sounded weak and insubstantial after his father's declaration.

He spun on his heel and left the room, trying not to show his hurt. He had taken enough from the old man—from the whole family. His face burned with rage and shame, his hands were clenched into fists. The gas-lamps were turned down in the empty corridors, only every one in four glowing; he took the dimly lit stairs all the way up to his floor, savoring the darkness and quiet, letting his anger smolder away as he worked his legs up one staircase after another. The exercise helped, and his feelings had subsided by the time he reached his rooms. He was able to think more clearly.

There was one good thing to come out of this at least: it was unlikely that Edgar would hand his business on to a suspected traitor, so it looked like his move to America was off. Now all he had to do was plan his departure from this damned house.

He threw off his dressing gown and climbed into bed, stacking the pillows up behind him so that he could sit up—there was no chance of him getting back to sleep. Wrapping the blankets around him, he lifted the cap on the speaking tube and asked Clancy—who he knew would still be awake—to bring him some cocoa and two slices of hot buttered toast.

Once his late-night snack was delivered on its tray, Nate sank into a miserable mood, brooding about how unbearable his life had become. He had intended to maintain this sulk until he drifted off to sleep, but it turned out that he was to be denied even this pleasure. There was a knock on the living-room door, and he knew at once that it wasn't Clancy.

Muttering under his breath, he set the tray aside and climbed out of bed, pulling on his dressing gown once more. He strode out into the living room and disarmed the booby traps on the hall door by pressing a series of levers on the underside of his writing desk. Then he grabbed the door handle and swung the door open, ready to unleash a string of abuse at whoever was standing on the other side.

Instead, he found himself speechless. Hunched in a thoroughly despondent posture in the hallway was his sister-in-law, dressed in one of Roberto's old suits. Nate's mouth opened and closed a few times, but nothing came out. Daisy didn't wait to be invited in. Brushing past him, she stumbled into the living room, flung herself on the sofa and burst into tears.

Deciding that everyone in the house had gone completely off their rockers, Nathaniel sighed, closed the door and went and sat down beside her, looking at her in bemusement. Unsure of what to do to comfort her, he thought it best to get straight to the point.

"So what's wrong?" he inquired.

"Roberto's having an affair!" Daisy cried.

"Ah. I see."

"No, you don't!" she sobbed. "He's in love with another *man!* I saw them kissing!"

Nate sighed again. He had known about Roberto's tastes for a few years now; since before the marriage. He had spent enough time in boarding school to meet boys with all sorts of strange hobbies so it didn't bother him much. Homosexuality could land you in prison, although it was unlikely anyone would try and prosecute a man of Roberto's power. But not only had he betrayed his wife; if word got out, she would face the worst kind of humiliation.

OISÍN McGANN

"So who's the other man?" he asked.

Daisy glared at him, feeling that she wasn't getting the comfort that was due to a woman in her situation.

"Hennessy, the head groom," she told him.

"Hennessy? Really?" Nate gaped. "A *servant?* You're sure it's love? Besides, Hennessy's a bit old, isn't he? I knew Berto like the company of older men, but I always assumed it was because Father hated him and he needed some kind of . . . foster father. Hennessy's a salt-of-the-earth type, but he's hardly the most handsome man in the world, is he?"

"How should I know what he finds attractive?!" Daisy screeched at him. Pulling out a well-used handkerchief, she blew her nose. "My husband's in love with a *man!* How should I know what he likes any more? I saw them kissing! It was the most awful thing. He's never kissed me like that. Never! I've tried to be a good wife—I tried so hard to do everything right. Men control every aspect of my life and now *this!* What can I do?"

She grabbed him by the scruff of the neck.

"How am I supposed to compete with a man for my husband's love?"

Nate regarded her with sympathy, bunched up in her ill-fitting suit, damp dark ringlets of hair hanging from under her flat cap.

"I don't know, Daisy. But you might well be wearing the right clothes for the job."

She stared at him blankly for a moment and then burst into sobs again. Not knowing what else to do, he handed her a fresh handkerchief. He felt stupid now for saying that. Clancy would never have said it. Clancy would have known what to do with this distraught woman. Nate considered calling him for advice, but thought the better of it. For Daisy's sake, the fewer people who knew about this the better.

Instead, he put his arm around her shoulders and pulled her close. It seemed to be what she needed; she laid her head on his shoulder and put her arms around his neck and stayed there until the sobs subsided. It was an extremely compromising position for a young man to be in with his sister-in-law at this time of night, but it didn't seem as if much else could go wrong, so he didn't care.

When she had finally composed herself, she lifted her head and dabbed her eyes. There was a damp patch on his shoulder, but Nate said nothing. His mind was already on another track.

"Where did you see them at it?" he asked, and realized too late that he was being insensitive. So be it.

"In the forest on the south side of the hill," she replied, heaving in a breath. "I was following him again—that's why I'm wearing these clothes; I got the idea from Tatty." She gave him a hard look. "He met Hennessy on the road and gave him some money . . . and . . . and sent him on some job or other. I don't know what."

"Knowing Berto, he was probably sending money to help those people pay their rent and rebuild their houses," Nate mused. "You know, the ones Trom rolled over. Berto's been doing that kind of thing for years—partly out of some misplaced sense of charity, but also because it's another way to have a dig at Father. I don't suppose you saw anyone else? Someone on a velocycle?"

"No," she said. "Just bloody Hennessy and his bloody horse. I ran off when I saw them . . . saw them kiss . . . and came back through the hidden passageways, but I got lost. I've been wandering around in there for hours. Why?"

"You do know Berto was attacked tonight, don't you?"

"What?" Daisy was visibly shocked.

"Someone ran over him with a velocycle. Everyone thinks it was me."

"And was it?" she asked bluntly.

"What? No! Of course not!"

She didn't spare him another word. Jumping to her feet, she ran to the door. As she threw it open and hurried out, Nathaniel went after her.

"Put on a bloody dress before you go to him, for God's sake," he called. "He'll have a fit if he sees you like that!" He slammed the door and headed back to his bedroom, adding to himself, "And if he doesn't, maybe you should dress like that from now on."

XXV

THE WONDER OF INTELLIGENT PARTICLES

NATE STARTED THE MORNING with another madcap sparring match with Hugo. The old man was growing stronger and quicker by the day, but still seemed unable to grasp even the simplest rules of modern fencing. Nate came away from the bout with a bruised arm and sore shins, but strangely elated by the sheer excitement of fighting such an unpredictable opponent. The frantic combat stopped him from thinking about his situation.

He was supposed to go and see Silas after training, but he decided that if he was to be branded a traitor, he was no longer under any obligation to obey his father's wishes. It had been a while since he had seen Gerald, so he made for the laboratory instead. Hugo went with him to check on Brutus's progress.

Gerald was working on his toast-maker, which was sitting

quietly as he poked around inside one of its slots with a screw-
driver. The ancient giant was still showing no sign of waking up.
Hugo knelt by his brother's bedside and, clasping his hands, lowered his head to pray.

"That's being very well behaved," Nate said, nodding at the
toast-maker. "You get it trained then?"

Gerald shook his head but didn't look round. He got like this
when he was absorbed in his work—as if the outside world no
longer existed for him. Lifting his head at last, he looked at Nate
with a feverish excitement in his eyes. Nate noticed the weari-
ness in his face and wondered if his cousin was sleeping at all
these days.

"I've made some incredible discoveries," Gerald said softly, as
if he didn't want Hugo to hear. "Incredible. Look here."

He gestured towards a microscope and Nate looked down
through the eyepiece. Through the lens, he could see some kind
of blood cells.

"What am I looking at?" he asked.

"Some of Hugo's blood," Gerald whispered, looking warily
over at the old man kneeling by the bed on the other side of the
room. "Now watch."

He lifted the top slide and used a needle to deposit a drop
of something on the bottom piece of glass, then he replaced the
slide.

"Bacteria," Gerald said. "Watch it attack the blood."

Nate kept looking and saw the small, spiky cells of the bacteria attach themselves to the concave blood cells. They didn't last
long. A kind of haze spread out from the blood cells and coated

the bacteria. Nate watched as the attacking organism was eaten up by the strange mist. In less than a minute the bacteria had been destroyed.

"I can't see properly," he complained. "What's the misty stuff? Can you make the magnification stronger?"

"It's on its strongest setting," Gerald told him. "That's all I've been able to see too, so far. But I've done other tests. This haze, whatever it is, reacts differently to different threats. And that's not all; it doesn't just destroy—it can *rebuild*. I think it may even have intelligence."

He checked again to see that Hugo was not listening.

"We've never been able to observe *aurea sanitas* at work, other than seeing the results of the accelerated healing our family enjoys, but I think this is it. This mist in Hugo's blood is a cloud of particles that's thick enough to be seen. We don't have so many, so we've never been able to spot them before. Hugo and his brother and sisters are loaded with the little beggars."

"Particles smaller than cells?" Nate asked incredulously. "Intelligent particles? Is that possible?"

"Our ancestors rebuilt their bodies from scant remains," Gerald replied, with something like awe in his voice. "Something kept the seeds of life in them even after their corpses were mummified. Their brains were dead, but some part of them remembered . . . like drawing the plans of a machine or a building, so their physical forms could be recovered. Their own memories are not complete; but even so, the fact that Hugo and his siblings can move and speak after six hundred years . . . I think it was these particles. Something about the quality of gold acts as a stimulus or fuel for them, and using it, they have the power to regenerate life, almost to the point of granting immortality. But I don't think they are a *part* of life. I think we're looking at mathaumaturgy here—once upon a time, someone actually *made* these things and put them in our blood. I think this is evidence of a science beyond our understanding.

"You see, this isn't the only place I've seen this kind of healing action," he went on. "We've always wondered how the engimals healed. After all, they're made of inorganic compounds—metals and other elements. They have no lymph or circulatory systems, no capacity for producing new cells because they have none to begin with. And yet they can heal. I think they use the same mathaumaturgical particles to rebuild themselves.

"Just on a whim, I decided to see if these marvelous little mites were interchangeable; whether I could create a link with an engimal using the particles in my blood. That's the whole basis of my theory, after all—that they were created to serve. Normally it takes days or even weeks of work to bond with an engimal. I put a single drop of my blood in the toast-maker's drinking water and all of a sudden it obeyed my every word! Do you understand what I'm telling you?"

Nate understood completely, but he wasn't sure he believed it. Gerald giggled, as if he were on the edge of hysterics.

"Once a link is created with a master, they appear to be instantly obedient. Forget all this nonsense about breaking them in—this can override all that. And it proves once and for all that they were designed and built to serve by a race whose science was far beyond our own. I'll have to carry out experiments on some of our other engimals to get a better idea of how it all works.

"Imagine if we could find some way to *communicate* with them, Nate—perhaps with mathematics or some long-lost language. Imagine that!" He ran his hand through his dark mop of lank hair. "I must write to Charles Darwin and involve him in this. I think these particles are the key to discovering who was responsible for creating the engimals. Darwin's theories on evolution are only the tip of the iceberg; if I'm right, Hugo and the others could be proof that—"

"We are proof of God's mercy!" Hugo's voice cut in.

They turned to find him standing right behind them.

"God returned us to this world to do His Work," he announced.

"Yeeesss, that's all very well," Gerald said carefully. "But I'm interested in how He pulled it off."

"He is the Almighty God! His Will shall be done."

"Hugo," Gerald began, "a lot of things have changed since you've been away—"

"Gerald, I don't think this is the time," Nate muttered.

"Modern science has debunked many of the old superstitions," Gerald continued, ignoring his cousin. "And while I would not be one to deny the existence of God—I think the whole question of God is a philosophical, rather than a scientific one—our perception of the world has come a long way. Mankind has chosen to rely on reason rather than faith, and it's about time too—"

"Gerald," Nate hissed, his eyes fixed on Hugo's face.

"Frankly we've developed somewhat since we came down

from the trees and I'm eager that we keep going. And to do that, we must use our brains."

"What do you mean, 'came down from the trees?'" Hugo asked.

"The latest theories suggest we are descended from apes," Gerald replied.

"Apes? What are apes?"

"Like monkeys."

Hugo looked as if he had just been struck. Gerald helpfully pointed to a drawing on the wall next to him, which showed the progression of man's development from crouching ape, with his long arms and jutting brow, through his various stages to the civilized, upright posture of modern man.

"What is this heresy?" Hugo exclaimed. "There are no animals in *my* family! I was made by God in His image!"

"Well, there lies the rub. We've no idea where God came from," Gerald replied, looking fondly at the drawing. "Who's to say He didn't start off as a monkey?"

The back of Hugo's hand caught him across the face at startling speed; Gerald's head whipped to the side and he was thrown to the floor by the force of the blow. Jumping to his feet, he clenched one fist, the other hand clutching his burning cheek. He looked at Hugo with a cold rage.

"Out of respect for your advanced years, I'm going to let that go," he said in a tense voice. "But if you ever touch me again—"

"Go back to your studies, boy," Hugo snorted. "I don't converse with animals."

And with that, he left. Gerald swore softly to himself and sat down on a stool, shaking his head and blinking rapidly.

"He nearly took my bloody head off," he said. "The old bugger's stronger than he looks."

"And he's getting stronger all the time," Nate added.

"Intelligent particles," Gerald observed with admiration, rubbing his swelling cheek. "When I figure out what's making him tick, I'm going to change the world."

Nate hung around the laboratory for a while longer, but Gerald was too intent on his work to pay him much attention. Nathaniel had no desire to face the rest of his family in the drawing room or out on the grounds, certain that the gossipmongers would already be spreading the suspicions of his treachery to the rest of the house. So he sought out the only other person he knew would never believe the lies, and who might go some way towards cheering him up.

He took the stairs up three floors to Tatiana's room, and as he approached her door, he heard a thunderous noise emitting from within. It had a throbbing African beat to it, which was accompanied by the sound of stringed instruments being slashed to pieces with a machete. He opened the door to find Tatiana jumping on her bed, her hair loose and flying wildly about her head, her yellow crinoline dress flapping up and down around her bloomers. The songbird engimal he had given her was out of its cage and flew around her in circles, its beak open as it sang its ear-shattering tune. For a moment he was convinced that she had been possessed by some kind of demon, but then she looked over and waved at him.

"Nate!" she screamed over the music. "Come and . . . jump on the . . . bed with me! It's a new . . . invention! It has . . . *springs* in it! It's one of the . . . first ever!"

"I think my bed-jumping days may be over!" he yelled back.

"Don't talk . . . rubbish! Get up here and . . . jump about . . . Take your shoes off first!"

She continued to bounce on the mattress in time to the beat. A smile spread across Nate's face as he watched her. She was always able to make him smile. Kicking off his shoes, he climbed onto the bed and began jumping around with her. At first it didn't work because his greater weight made the mattress buck under her, which would throw her off her feet, but soon they managed to get a rhythm, and Tatty started flying up towards the ceiling as Nate's feet hit the mattress. They laughed and whooped and got the giggles and laughed again until they were out of breath and then they jumped even harder on the bed.

That was how Daisy found them when she walked in, looking for comfort, her face like that of a lost child.

Tatty waved her up to join them, but then lost her timing and ended up being thrown against Nate, knocking him off the end of the bed. He landed on the floor with a crash, buckled over with hysterical giggles.

"Jump on . . . the bed!" Tatty screeched over the bird's bestial song.

"Tatiana, this is hardly a fitting way for a lady to behave," Daisy scolded, trying to hide a smile at the same time.

"Never mind . . . that! Jump on . . . the bed!"

She was not to be defied, so Daisy gave a reluctant grin and took off her shoes. Tatty stopped jumping long enough for her sister-in-law to get onto the bed and then they started bouncing together. Daisy was hesitant at first, missing the beat and trying to maintain her dignity, but soon she gave in and was hopping around like a wild thing, in desperate danger of having her wire-hooped skirt flip up around her waist. Nate recovered himself and joined them, and the jumping grew increasingly chaotic until, with a creaking surrender, the bed collapsed beneath them, the mattress folded in the middle and they all tumbled into the fold in a tangled mess of limbs, tears of laughter streaming down their faces.

They lay there for a while, exhausted. Then set about untangling themselves; Tatiana told the bird to hush, and it did. As the noise faded, she announced:

"I've decided I'm going to be a teacher."

"Really?" Nate raised his eyebrows. "I thought you were going to set up hospitals?"

"I might do that later . . . if there's a war or something," she said thoughtfully. "But I've decided that the common people need schools, so I'm going to set up some of those instead. Poor people need an education so that they can get better jobs. Did you know that most of them can't even speak French?"

"I had no idea," Nate replied. "Perhaps they don't have any need for it."

"They would if more people spoke it," Tatty pointed out.

"Impeccable logic," Daisy chuckled as they all sat up on the edge of the broken bed. "So what made you decide to teach?"

"I think I'd be good at it," Tatiana told her. "I've been teaching Elizabeth . . . and even Brunhilde . . . a bit. Although I suspect she's a little . . . dotty. Anyway, Elizabeth said they were learning a lot from me, so I think I'd make a good teacher. Or at least, I could *train* teachers—I don't think ladies are supposed to become teachers themselves."

"And what kinds of things have you been teaching them?" Daisy asked, glancing at Nathaniel.

"Oh, all sorts of things," Tatty replied. "Lots of family history—particularly about the Rules of Ascension. They're really interested in those—things weren't as civilized in their day; people just bumped each other off without any rules at all. They think we're so much more sensible; they feel much safer than they used to. And they've been asking all about the members of the family, so they can get to know them, now that we're their new relatives. They love all the stories about Father—especially the bits about all the fights he won in the olden days." She lowered her voice in a conspiratorial whisper. "I think they're a bit bloodthirsty. They always want to hear the gory details!"

"So did I," Nate said, nodding to himself. "I listened to all the stories when I was young—I thought they would help me learn to fight like him." He paused for a moment. "I think I'd better go and have a word with him."

"Do that," Daisy said to him. "Everyone seems so intent on keeping Hugo in his place, and yet his two sisters are free to spend their time diligently gathering all sorts of valuable information. You men need to pay more attention to all the women in this house.

"And while you're speaking to your good father, ask him why he's been telling his impressionable young daughter all those horrible stories."

XXVI

A MESSAGE FROM BEYOND THE GRAVE

EDGAR WOULD NOT GRANT Nathaniel an audience, nor would he accept any messages from him. The Duke seemed to have made his mind up that his son was a traitor, and was going to have nothing more to do with him until his punishment had been decided.

Nate spent the rest of the day with Tatiana and Daisy, who seemed to be avoiding her husband. She had still not challenged Roberto about Hennessy and was unsure if she even wanted to—and she was thankfully reluctant to discuss it in front of Tatty. Nate felt his sister was still a little young to be dealing with the harsh realities of a marriage in crisis. Better that she spend a while longer believing in the kind of life portrayed in her romance novels.

It would have helped if Daisy could have brought herself to

cheer up a bit. With her pale face, glassy stare and the bags under her eyes, she looked awful. Tatty kept asking if she was ill.

The three of them walked in the gardens and went riding in the early evening; leaping their horses over gates and hedges galloping across the countryside until the animals were lathered and panting and eager to return home.

Whenever Nate passed any of his other relatives during the day, he caught their suspicious glances—the way they avoided contact with him if they could. He decided not to take dinner in the dining room, eating in his rooms instead, with only Clancy for company. He asked his manservant to sit with him and have some tea; something he had never done before. It was a strange thing to be alienated in your own home, to be lonely with your entire family around you. The fear of what his father might do to him for his supposed treachery was beginning to set in too. The Duke was a master of cruel and unusual punishments. As they sat there together, Clancy related amusing stories of Nate's childhood, and Nate was grateful for the small comfort he got from them.

He retired early, weary from his low mood. This could not go on; he would have to talk to his father tomorrow—he would force his way into the old man's office if need be. This misunderstanding had to be sorted out. He found peace in this resolve to take action and drifted off to sleep . . .

A soft knocking on the hall door woke him and he lay there for a moment in the dark, his fears playing on his mind, wondering if the Duke had finally made up his mind to dole out his punishment. But it was more likely to be Daisy again, fretting over Roberto's nighttime habits. He climbed out of bed and pulled his dressing gown on over his nightshirt. The knock came again. Out in the living room, he disarmed the booby traps and, after some hesitation, took a six-shot revolver from the drawer of the writing desk. If these were his punishers coming to pounce on him in the night, they were going to get a right bloody shock.

Opening the door, he stood there speechless for the second time in as many nights. In the dim light of the corridor, Elizabeth was waiting, dressed only in a white nightgown. Her long dark hair hung down over her shoulders and her feet were bare.

"I'm sorry for waking you, Nathaniel," she said softly. "But I think we need to talk, you and I."

Nate remained frozen there for a moment, and then decided that it would be slightly less scandalous to let her into his living room than to leave her standing out in the corridor. Waving her in, he immediately went to the speaking tube to summon Clancy to escort her back to her room.

"If you are uncomfortable with my being here," Elizabeth told him as she sat down on the sofa, "I won't take up much of your time. Sit here next to me, so we can talk quietly."

Nate drew in a breath and closed the tube, sitting down at the far end of the sofa.

"What do you want?" he asked warily.

"I need to ask you, Nathaniel, if you are guilty of the treachery of which you are accused."

"No," he retorted. "No, I'm not bloody guilty. You came here in the middle of the night to ask me that?"

Elizabeth regarded him for what seemed like the longest time and then nodded to herself.

"I believe you," she said. "Hugo and I both think you were wrongly accused. That is why I am here. We want to ask for your help. We are hoping that the Duke will soon recognize us as being full members of this family, and when he does, we intend to take on our share of the responsibilities. Hugo has paid great attention to what has been happening in this house since God chose to resurrect us, and he has great fears for this family."

She moved closer, and Nate became aware of her scent: clean skin and a faint perfume. The way she turned her head towards him accentuated the line of her throat and her elegant neck and shoulders. There were still the faintest lines on the skin of her face from the leathery wrinkles that had once covered it, and he had to remind himself that this woman was more than six hundred years old. He tried not to meet her eyes; they had a mesmerizing fervor to them he found disturbing, so he watched her lips instead as she spoke.

"Hugo feels that all your modern science—all these marvelous comforts with which you surround yourselves—are making the family weak and vulnerable to attack. Your fighting arts are used only for sport; your armory is too far from your living quarters. Your windows are too large to prevent missiles from being hurled through them. You have no keep to speak of—the walls around your boundaries are low and would be impossible to defend."

Nate gave her an incredulous look, not knowing whether to laugh or not. She did not seem to notice, continuing to list the family's faults.

"None of you wear armor when you leave the castle, and you often travel far afield without an armed escort. Your older men have grown fat, anchored to their chairs by their huge backsides. This cannot go on!"

Elizabeth moved closer still, until he could feel her breath on his skin.

"Hugo believes that this is why we were brought back from the dead," she whispered huskily. "To save this family from its sloth and gluttony and weakness. And save it we will! But we will need strong, moral men to help us in our struggle—men like you." She took his hand. "Is this all you want from your life: spending your days playing with toys, your nights dallying with chambermaids or drinking to excess? Let Jesus Christ, Our Savior, give meaning to your life, Nathaniel.

"We are only beginning to understand how powerful this family is, but it is clear that decisions here affect the entire land; how you choose to live causes ripples across its people. Don't let sin bury your family, Nathaniel. Work with us, be a warrior for our Lord God and do His work on this earth. Join us, and we can promise you Paradise!"

And as he hesitated, shaken by what he was hearing, she leaned forward and pressed her mouth against his.

Nathaniel had Clancy start packing the next morning. He wanted to get away from this house and everything in it. Elizabeth's shameless attempt to seduce him into betraying his father had reminded him why he had fled to Africa nearly two years ago. This way of life was unbearable; being surrounded by people who were bred to believe that success was more important than loyalty, or love or even plain, common decency. He needed to find some space, some time to himself. His revenge on Gideon and his brood would just have to wait.

The fact that he was under house arrest meant nothing to him—let anyone try and stop him from leaving. He would wait out the day and make his escape in the early hours of the morning. There was the small matter of Hugo's impending betrayal to deal with, but Nate would corner his father at dinner and warn him then. He wasn't sure how great a threat Hugo could be, but he was still in no position to oust the Duke.

There were a couple of hours before dinner, and he decided to spend them going through the papers he had taken from Marcus's desk. He was not the studious type and had put it off long enough. Besides, he didn't want to have to take them with him— he would have enough baggage as it was.

The business documents threatened to put him to sleep, but he combed through the texts, searching for anything that might relate to his brother's death. But he didn't know enough about the business to determine if anything was incriminating or not. He decided to hand them on to Silas before he left.

Then there were the letters Marcus had kept with him wherever he went: the peach-colored, scented envelopes of letters that Tatiana had sent to her big brother in America; the flowing script of Roberto's lyrical prose and the spidery scrawls of Nate's observations from Africa. Nate clutched them so hard they crumpled between his fingers and he found himself close to tears. With all the scheming, all the conspiracies, it took these simple pieces of writing to remind him how much he missed his brother.

He was stuffing the letters back into their envelopes with unnecessary roughness when his eyes fell on his most recent letter, which Marcus must have received only just before he left America for Ireland. Drawn on it in hasty lines was a map of what looked like streets. No, he corrected himself—not streets, corridors. It was like the maps they had made as children when they played games in the hidden passageways; but if it was on this envelope, it meant Marcus had been doing some exploring in the week before his death. It appeared to be a route marked in paces . . . and it started in Marcus's living room. The route ended at a point marked with the words: *"panel next to fireplace."* Seconds later, Nate was rushing down the corridor towards the elevator.

He knew the doorway behind the bookcase in Marcus's living room and wasted no time in pushing the worn copy of Poe's *The Fall of the House of Usher* to open the door. Inside, he found a candle and matches and started along the narrow corridor, ignoring the dust and the insects and spiders that had made the dark place their home.

The route on the map took him deep into the house, through passageways he hadn't known existed. Finally, he reached a ladder extending up through the ceiling and down through the floor. Reading the map with a frown, he took hold of the ladder, gripping the candle as best he could, and started climbing upwards.

The ladder led him up to another corridor, and it was twenty paces along this passageway that the map ended. In front of him was another door, with the compulsory box of candles and matches on a shelf to one side. Blowing out his candle, Nate peered through the tiny peephole in the door. His heart sank as the room he saw beyond confirmed his fears. His hate for his family became absolute.

Nate moved away from the door and lit his candle once more, following the map's directions back to his dead brother's living room. Something rustled in the dark near his feet as he made to open the door and he kicked out at it, presuming it was a rat or mouse.

As he opened the bookcase in front of him, a flash of red darted out between his feet, shot along the skirting board and disappeared behind a chest of drawers. He heard it skitter away out of sight. Getting down on his hands and knees, he started crawling around, looking under the tables, desks and chairs. The little creature dashed out from under a divan and into Marcus's trophy room. Nate crawled in after it. The room's walls were lined with the heads and hides of other animals his brother had valiantly shot dead. There were glass cases for the smaller trophies. Nate crawled back and forth, searching under the bottoms of the cases.

A maid barged in at one point, found him on his hands and knees on the floor, and quickly excused herself, blushing violently. He sighed and continued his search.

He saw a skittering movement under the curtains and lunged after it, but the creature was as small as a mouse and moved almost as fast. It scooted under a case and he scrambled over the floor in pursuit, reaching in to grab it and nearly knocking the case over. The creature evaded him again, but this time he saw where it was going and, jumping to his feet, bounded over and slammed the living-room door shut to stop it escaping. The little creature changed direction, teasing him to come after it again.

"Enough playing," Nate panted, grabbing a polar bear skin off the wall. "Your master is dead."

He threw the heavy hide over the engimal before it could run again. It was slowed down long enough for him to pin the skin over it and force it out into his hand. It was bright red, with black spots like a ladybird, and was a similar shape. It ran on a single ball tucked into its belly.

The creature's large, single amber eye looked up at him and it gurgled some gibberish at him. Marcus had bought this little mite a few years ago and Nate had always been fond of it. He wasn't surprised that Marcus wanted him to have it. It must have gone wandering not long before Marcus left for the Mournes. Like Tatiana's songbird, it could make a wide range of sounds, but most of them were in the form of human voices. None of them made any sense, and if they were in any language at all, it was one that nobody in this world understood. That was why Marcus had named it as he did. Because it babbled on and on.

"Hello, Babylon," he said softly.

"Hello, Nate," the engimal replied, and Nate nearly dropped it as he recognized Marcus's voice. "Hope you're well, old bean. Unfortunately, if you're listening to this, I must be dead."

Nate clutched the creature in trembling hands, hardly able to believe what he was hearing.

"As you've no doubt realized," Marcus's voice continued with a slight underlying hiss, "Babylon has the capacity for recording speech. I only found out myself a few months ago. He can also follow simple instructions; such as giving you this message— when you are alone and you call him by name. Dashed clever, isn't he? But that's another conversation for another day. Perhaps in the afterlife, eh? Let me get to the point."

Nate drew in a sharp breath. The thing spoke *exactly* like Marcus. He had heard of these "mimic messengers" before, but had never come across one. Hearing Marcus speak to him from beyond the grave like this was downright spooky.

"For some time now," the voice went on, "I've had my eye on the throne. You know I've always been ambitious, and I finally came to the conclusion that I could do Father's job better than he could. I wanted control of the family. It was what I was brought up to do, after all, and I thought it was about time. And, well . . . You know what that meant.

"I had to murder our father, Nate. I found a secret way into his bedroom and I intended to kill him in his sleep. Now, you might think it's a bit extreme, but I also know you won't be too upset either—you always hated the arrogant blackguard even more than I did. But since you're hearing this message, I can only assume that I have failed in my attempt and he has snuffed me out instead. What a confounded bore this whole business is! I hope I made a handsome corpse.

"So consider this a warning, old chum. You and Berto were never cut out for this life; I've done some pretty horrendous things since I started work and I'm certain that neither of you would have the stomach for them. And you're definitely not ready to take on Gideon and all the other coves who are going to come at you now that I'm gone. They won't play fair and they're more ruthless and vindictive than you'll ever know. Take my advice: go into exile—take Daisy and Tatty and go to the far side of the world. For God's sake, Nate, get the hell out of that house.

"Father won't protect you; it's not his way. He always said you and Berto were too weak to be Wildensterns . . . and you are, I suppose. You've no taste for blood—and that's what the world is built on. Other people's blood. Don't let them spill any of yours, Nate. Take what money you can and run. I don't want you joining me just yet.

"Ta-ra, old bean. Look after yourself."

And with that, Marcus fell silent for the last time. Nathaniel put his fingers to his cheek and found it wet with tears. He remained sitting there for another hour.

Daisy was in the church, praying for guidance. Judging by her continuing state of bewildered distress, her prayers seemed to be falling on deaf ears. She had still said nothing to Berto about his affair with Hennessy, but she had spent more time horse riding, using it as an opportunity to speak to the head groom, to find out what kind of man he was. To her disappointment, Hennessy did not appear to be the devil himself, but was instead a quiet, simple man from Donegal, with a wry sense of humor and the kind of humble dignity often found among those in service.

It made her despise him all the more.

But now Daisy had something else to worry about. Elizabeth's maid, Mary, had come to her earlier in the day, her eyes red and raw from crying. Her hair was hanging down over one side of her neck, which came as a surprise because Mary was a conscientious girl, who was always very careful about her appearance around the family. Then Mary showed her why her hair was hanging down. The maid had gone with Elizabeth to meet Hugo in the conservatory. Hugo had started "givin' 'er the eye," as Mary put it, and Elizabeth, who had been watching her brother, had contrived to leave him alone with her maid. Once his sister had left, Hugo had turned on the charm—or so he seemed to think—and after a momentary courtship, had tried for a kiss.

Mary was "havin' none of it, but couldn't rightly say so to his lordship," so she had tried to be coy and turn away. That was when Hugo had pulled her against him and bitten her neck. His bruised teeth-marks were still clearly visible on the skin just above her shoulder. He had even broken the flesh in a couple of places.

That was what she got for "being a tease," he'd said.

Daisy had walked her right up to the Duke's study and demanded that Hugo be forced to apologize. The Duke had assured her that no apology would be forthcoming, nor was it the policy for members of the family to apologize to servants.

Now, Daisy knelt in the church and prayed for guidance. She did not care much for this church. It was cold, which was not unusual for churches, but it had a menacing air about it too, and there was too much gold ornamentation for her tastes. It seemed to be everywhere. It was positively gaudy. It was disturbing how fond this family was of its gold.

Someone else was coming up the aisle. She could hear soft footsteps on the mosaic floor, but she did not look up. She wanted to be alone, and as long as she kept her eyes closed and the conversation remained between herself and God, she probably wouldn't be interrupted.

The wooden pew on which she was kneeling creaked and she felt the weight of another's knees bow it slightly. Daisy resisted the urge to open her eyes and see who it was.

"You are a devout woman, Melancholy," a voice said quietly, shockingly close to her ear.

She looked up to find Hugo kneeling right beside her. Daisy was overcome with a sudden rage.

"Don't you dare open your mouth to me!" she hissed at him.

"But I feel compelled to, my dear," he crooned. "After all that *your* mouth has been saying about me. It seems my mouth has been uppermost in your mind."

"Only when it bites into the necks of servant girls!" she snapped. "What kind of savage are you?"

"I confess, my appetites get the better of me sometimes," he said airily, his hand coming to rest on hers where it lay on the back of the pew in front of them. "I am a passionate man, used to taking whatever he wants. But you must understand: I am from a harsher time and I know I can be overly sharp. I am a sword in need of a sheath."

"It's less your sharpness, but more the danger of infection from your rust that I fear," Daisy retorted, getting to her feet. "Like so many men, sir, you are a weapon with no sense of direction. If you'll excuse me, I think I should remove myself from the range of your sword before it seeks a scabbard it cannot hope to fill."

And with that, she left.

XXVII

WELCOMED INTO THE FAMILY

DINNER WAS ESPECIALLY LAVISH that evening, and the Duke was slightly less truculent than normal, failing to insult a single relative throughout the first course. He pointedly ignored his youngest son, but Nate hardly noticed. Sitting between Daisy and Gideon, Nate avoided conversation and picked at his food. He had no appetite. Elizabeth sat across from him and attempted to attract his attention several times, constantly trying to make eye contact. He rarely looked up from his plate.

Marcus's last message haunted him. His brother had tried to murder his father and had been killed in return. The thought made him physically ill. He was sick of it all—all the talk of conspiracies and threats and murders. It had surrounded him all his life so that he had grown up thinking it normal. Now he was jaded, worn out from the constant tension, the fear that had been instilled in him from birth that someone somewhere was out to get him. How could he have spent his whole life like this? How could he ever have thought this was a normal way to live?

Under the table, Elizabeth's foot touched his shin and he moved it away, avoiding her gaze as she forked meat into her mouth. He had made no attempt to tell his father about Hugo's plotting. He wanted no more part in any of this.

The second course was served, and there was much wondering over the reason for the Duke's uncommonly good mood. As the steaming platters of duck, pork, beef, pheasant and heaps of buttered vegetables and bread were all laid on the table, Edgar stood up and cleared his throat. There was immediate silence.

"We are faced with challenging times," he declared. "And now, more than ever, we must face adversity with all the strength we can command. I am happy, therefore, to welcome into our family four noble individuals whom God has seen fit to bring back from oblivion, and from whom much of our strength might originally have been drawn.

"Hugo, Elizabeth and Brunhilde . . .and let us not forget your unfortunate brother, Brutus." He raised his wine glass and everyone hurriedly stood up and did the same. "You are Wildensterns—you must consider this house your own, and all those within it as your kin. Welcome home!"

"Welcome home!" the family cried dutifully and drank the toast.

Hugo and his sisters stayed standing after everyone else sat down. They were at the head of the table on either side of the

Patriarch; they had tears in their eyes and looked deeply moved. Elizabeth and Brunhilde hurried to Edgar's sides and knelt to kiss his hands, Brunhilde on his left and Elizabeth pressing her lips to the claw on his right. Nate lifted his head, looking first at Hugo then at his father, his blood going cold. It couldn't be. Not yet. Hugo bowed to the Duke.

"I have hoped for this moment since the hour of my awakening. Sir, you honor us!"

And as his sisters gripped Edgar's arms, Hugo snatched up a carving knife and plunged it into the Duke's chest.

The room erupted into furious motion; some of the women screamed, men shouted, chairs were kicked back and hands grabbed for any weapon within reach. Nate reacted on reflex, his hatred for his father forgotten. In an instant he was up out of his chair, a steak knife in his hand as he leaped onto the table and bounded down to the end of it. Edgar had fallen back over his chair, but if the blade had pierced his heart it appeared he had little use for the organ. A throwing knife appeared as if by magic in his left hand and he slashed at Brunhilde's abdomen, breaking Elizabeth's grip at the same time and seizing her by the throat with his claw. Hugo pulled his knife out and drove it in again and then a third time before Nate crashed into him, hurling him to the floor. The four Maasai servants were already there, leaping to their master's aid, two of them drawing pistols. But a gunshot rang out from the other end of the table and then three more in quick succession, and two of the black servants crumpled to the floor. Nate turned in shock to see Gideon and his sons charging into the fray, also armed with pistols. Gideon

stopped and aimed, firing off a fifth shot that spun another of the
Maasai round before a final bullet caught the servant through the
head. Hugo used the distraction to elbow Nate in the face and
lunged at the remaining bodyguard, who struck the ancestor's
wrist with the edge of one hand, knocking the knife away, before
delivering a stunning blow to the back of Hugo's neck. Gideon
took aim again, but Nate kicked the gun aside, only to be pummeled into the floor by two of Gideon's burly sons. He saw Berto
hit the floor beside him, fighting like a berserker against three
more of their cousins.

The cold ring of a gun barrel was pressed against Nate's forehead and he froze, a growl rising from his throat. Out of the
corner of his eye he saw his father struggling to regain his feet,
blood spurting from one of the wounds in his chest and making
the floor slippery beneath him. Gideon drew a short sword from
under his jacket and strode towards the Patriarch.

"No!" Nate screamed. "Don't you bloody dare, you—"

The barrel of the gun pulled away and slammed across the
side of his head. As his vision swam, he rolled over, trying to
crawl free, but too many strong arms held him. He watched
helplessly as Gideon seized Edgar by the hair and pulled him
into a kneeling position. Edgar roared, punching his claw up
into Gideon's groin. Gideon howled and collapsed to the floor,
dropping the sword and clutching his injured privates.

"You always were . . . an embarrassment . . . you . . . treacherous cur," Edgar snarled at his younger brother, blood gurgling in
his throat.

Hugo picked up the blade. Edgar glared up at him, his

left hand vainly trying to stem the lifeblood bubbling from his chest.

"Get on with it then," he grunted.

Hugo nodded solemnly and cut the Duke's head off with a single powerful blow.

The head landed on the tiles with a thump and bounced once and rolled, finishing up on its side. His expression was no less belligerent in death than it had been in life. An unnatural calm settled over the room and for a few moments nobody moved.

The room had divided into three groups: there were those who had joined Hugo's conspiracy—mostly Gideon's family and allies. They had come armed and ready, and had positioned themselves to block those who had risen to the Duke's defense—his sons, some of the servants, Gerald, Silas and Daisy. The rest stood motionless, waiting to see which way the tide would turn. For those few moments after the beheading, nobody breathed.

Then Edgar's lifeless body slumped forwards and fell over and Hugo gave an audible sigh. Dropping the bloodstained sword by the corpse, he righted the chair at the head of the table and sat down. Taking up Edgar's fork, he began to eat from the Patriarch's plate. After a few mouthfuls he sat back and gazed at the stunned faces around him.

"Be seated," he told them. "Let us offer thanks to God for the food he has provided for us."

Nobody moved. Still charged up with the fury of battle, their hands and legs shaking, their weapons clutched tightly, they did not know what to make of this. Some of them exchanged bewildered glances. Brunhilde, still clutching the wound in her abdomen, sat down at her brother's side and began to eat with one bloodied hand.

"Praise be to God," Elizabeth exclaimed.

She sat down next to her brother and smiled beatifically at her new family, beckoning them to sit down. One by one, they obliged. All the uninjured servants returned to their positions at the edge of the hall. Eventually only Nathaniel, Roberto, Daisy and Tatiana remained standing. Nate did not look at Gerald; he knew his cousin was playing the game. It would be wiser to feign loyalty and bide their time, but Nate had no stomach for it.

"If you are not with me, you are against me," Hugo said without looking at them.

"If you think that, you have a lot to learn about this family," Nate replied coldly.

With that, he turned his back on the new Patriarch and, leaving his father's remains where they lay, led the others out of the room.

Nate's mind was racing as he stood in the elevator, watching the arrow turn around the dial. How much time did they have? Would they even make it out of the house? The bell chimed, and the boy dressed in smart livery sitting by the levers tipped his hat as the doors opened onto Tatiana's floor.

"You have fifteen minutes," Nate told his sister. "Pack a couple of changes of clothes—only what you need to travel. Don't dither."

"There's nothing to dither about," Tatty replied tartly as she strode towards her room.

He was amazed at her composure. She seemed to be taking their father's murder in her stride. He suspected the sheer scale of what had happened would not hit her for a while yet and he intended to use that time.

"We stick together," he said to Berto and Daisy. "We gather what we need and we leave. Don't trust your servants—do everything yourself. We don't know who's loyal to whom."

Even as he said it, Patrick Slattery walked round the corner. He gave a gold-plated grin and leaned his head back round the corner.

"They're here!" he bellowed.

"Berto," Nate said quietly. "I'll handle this. Get them to safety."

"I'm not leaving you—"

"I can take care of myself. You need to protect them," Nate told him.

Berto nodded. Taking Tatty and Daisy by the hand, he led them at a run to the end of the corridor and disappeared round the corner.

"I've been waiting to settle with you for some time," Slattery grunted, taking off his jacket. "No more Mr. High 'n' Mighty any more. Just two fellas and their fists. I'm goin' to break that stuck-up nose o' yours and then I'm goin' to break the rest o' yeh."

He carefully hung the jacket on the ornate brass of a gas-lamp and cracked his knuckles. Nate was afraid. For all his training, he had never been in a serious fight until today. He was still untested. Slattery, on the other hand, did this for a living.

"You're just a thug, Slattery," Nate said in a tight voice. "Always letting your gang do your work for you. Let's see how you do in a fair fight."

"Who said anything about fair?" The bailiff laughed and suddenly there was a switchblade open in his right hand as he lunged at Nathaniel.

Nate stepped to one side and swept the knife-hand to the other with the back of his own hand. Slattery whipped it in and slashed backhand at him, forcing him to jump away. The bailiff kept coming, jabbing and slashing, changing the knife from blade up to blade down and back again with practiced ease. Each time, Nate was driven backwards. Sooner or later he was going to run out of hallway.

Slattery thrust the knife at his belly and Nate sidestepped it, but this time he caught the bailiff's wrist. Before Slattery could pull it back, Nate swung it round and up and smashed it into the glass of the gas-lamp beside him. The flame guttered, but not before it had scorched Slattery's hand. The man snarled, dropping the knife but then swinging his left fist at Nate's face. Nate ducked and drove one elbow into the other man's ribs and then the other one up under Slattery's chin. The bailiff's head snapped up and he fell flat on his back. Nate managed to stamp on his knee and then on his groin before two of Slattery's men piled into him, bringing him to the floor. He grabbed the switchblade and jammed it into one man's thigh and was rewarded with a scream of pain, but the second man's fist caught him across the cheek and then scored another blow against his jaw. He tasted blood. He jammed his knuckle into the nerve cluster in the man's armpit, making him jerk away in shock, but his opponent did not let go.

"Hold him!" Slattery roared as he wrenched the knife from his man's leg. "I'm goin' to cut the little guttersnipe's face!"

The injured man grabbed Nate's arms and the other bailiff held his legs. Nate shrieked defiance at them, thrashing to get free. Slattery limped up and stood astride him, leaning down, the knife held loosely between fingers and thumb.

"You got me a good one in the gonads there, lad," he hissed. "I'll take my time thankin' you for that."

There came the sound of something bouncing down the hall-way and they all turned towards it. A metal sphere about the size of a cricket ball rolled towards them, trailing a thin stream of smoke.

"Grenade!" Slattery shouted.

It exploded before it reached them, but there was no blast, only a billowing spiral of smoke. It enveloped them, blinding them and filling their nostrils and throats with acrid fumes. Nate coughed, struggling to free his hands so that he could cover his nose. There was a thump and the man at his head toppled forward. Nate pushed him aside as Slattery plunged into the smoke to tackle a dimly visible figure rushing towards them.

Everything was grey. Nate gagged as the smoke caught in the back of his throat. His lungs burned. Somebody got behind the remaining bailiff and brought a wooden club down on the top of his head. Nate shoved with his feet and the stunned man collapsed back against the wall. Even with his irritated eyes filled with tears, Nate could recognize the man with the club. It was one of the Maasai. A second servant helped him to his feet and he stumbled with his rescuers through the dissipating fumes. A third Maasai, his arm in a sling and a pistol in his good hand, waved them forward. All the rescue party had wet cloths across their noses and mouths. Slattery was lying semiconscious on the floor, with a gash in his forehead. He lifted his head as he saw Nathaniel passing him.

"Wait . . . wait," Nate muttered.

Swinging back his foot, he gave the bailiff a sound kick to the head.

"You can thank me for that one later!" he called as they hurried away.

XXVIII

MEMORIES OF THE DARK CONTINENT

NATE TOOK ANOTHER SIP OF THE WATER and blinked his swollen red eyelids. He was sitting in a small room on the top floor of the tower that connected to his father's rooms through a number of hidden doors. This was the living quarters of the Maasai. The room could not have been more than twelve feet square, but their entire private lives were contained within it. Nate had seen Clancy's room a few times and was surprised that Edgar have given his servants less space than those of his children. The Maasai had made up for the lack of space by cluttering it with the focus of their passion. Africa.

The room had no windows and was lit by a small lamp. A speaking tube by the door allowed the Maasai's master to summon them any time of the day or night from anywhere in the house. Maps hung on the walls, along with an old sword, an assegai spear and a shield. Nate was sitting on the bottom bunk and could see a beaded necklace adorning the narrow headboard of the top bunk facing him. On a shelf was a modest collection of books on the Dark Continent, and various other tourist souvenirs lay scattered around. But these servants had never been back to their homeland since being taken from it as children. He was quite sure they had never been out of the house unless they were accompanying the Duke. Nate wondered how they had managed to collect all this junk.

"People have been kind to us, sir," the man opposite him said, as if reading his mind. He spoke with the cultured tone of an Oxford graduate. "It is our dream to visit our homeland again some day."

Nate nodded, but he knew there would be no chance of that now.

"You saved my life," he said. "I'm in your debt. I'm sorry . . . but I don't . . . I don't know which of you is which."

"When we do our jobs properly, sir, people should not notice us at all," the man said, smiling. "I am Abraham. The one with the wounded shoulder is Isaiah and the one with the bandage on his arm is Jacob. Our brother, Joshua, was shot dead in the dining room."

"I'm sorry," Nate said again. "Servants are supposed to be protected by the Rules of Ascension."

"It is the one rule the family does not follow to the letter," Abraham told him. "They will justify it to themselves later. Are you feeling better, sir? Isaiah has gone to fetch Mr. Clancy; they will be here soon."

"I'm fine, thank you," Nate replied. "I have to get out of here and find my brother and sisters. At least we bought them some time to escape."

"I'm afraid not, sir," Abraham said mournfully. "They were caught moments after they rounded the corner by the Duke's brother and his sons. We chose to aid *you* . . . we had a greater chance of success and you were in the more imminent danger. I'm afraid Master Roberto and the ladies are in the hands of the enemy, sir."

Nate cursed under his breath and put his head in his hands.

"They will not kill the ladies, nor your brother while you still live, sir," Abraham told him. "Jacob is following them by the secret ways to see where they are being held. We will free them, but the enemy will not rest until they have found you. You must flee the house—stay alive and find more allies."

He leaned forward, his eyes lowered, careful not to meet Nathaniel's gaze out of respect for his position.

"We have no purpose but to serve the rightful Heir . . . and his brother, Master Nathaniel," he said in a low voice. "We failed our master, but we won't fail you. Let us be your vengeance."

"This isn't your fight," Nate said gently.

"The enemy took our master. The Duke was a hard man, but he was the sun around which our earth revolved. If you will forgive me for saying it, sir, he was like a father to us."

"That's more than he was to me." Nate snorted at the irony of the remark. "You can have your own vengeance, Abraham; I need none of it. I want to get out of here and take my brother and sisters with me. And that's all I want."

"So be it," Abraham said, and his eyes hardened. "When Mr. Clancy arrives and Jacob returns, we will go and free the hostages." He made it sound so simple. "Then you must go your way, sir, and leave us to do our duty."

Nate thought he detected a rebuke in the man's tone. Looking around the room, he realized that without their master, these men had no identity, no purpose. Not like Clancy; Clancy was his own man. They had been plucked from their home and, as black men, would never be fully accepted by the other servants here. They dreamed of going back to Africa, but after a life in an Irish manor house, they would never be accepted by their own people either. Abraham saw him staring at the books on the shelf.

"You have been to Kenya, sir?" he asked eagerly. "Did you encounter the Maasai? Please tell me about them."

"I didn't see much of them—I wasn't there for very long," Nate replied, relieved to talk about something other than conspiracy. "They are a proud people; tall, like you—even the women! I remember their loud laughs and booming voices. The tribes wander with their cattle . . . They treat their cattle with the utmost care. They mourn when one is slaughtered." He racked his brain to remember more. It seemed to mean so much to the footman. "The warrior class call themselves *moran* and they are known throughout Africa for their bravery and ferocity."

They were also notorious among farmers for being cattle thieves, but Nate saw no need to mention that. Abraham continued to listen in fascination.

"They form bonds for life with the other men their age in the tribe—I think they even get circumcised together!" He paused, embarrassed, realizing that was hardly a suitable subject to discuss with servants. "And of course, to prove his manhood, a Maasai warrior must kill a lion—"

Even as he said it, Nate knew he had made a mistake. Abraham's face fell. Nate tried to come up with some way to cover up his blunder, but he couldn't. Abraham and his brothers were in their forties and had never even seen a lion in the flesh. There was a long and awkward silence.

"I will go to Africa," the servant said solemnly, "and I will kill a lion."

Nathaniel was saved from answering by the sound of someone in the passage outside. Abraham aimed his pistol at the door, but two sharp knocks followed by two more put him at ease. Isaiah walked in with Clancy behind him.

"I think it's time to get you out of here, sir," Clancy declared.

"We need to free the others first," Nate said.

"Hugo and Gideon will count on your doing that, Master Nathaniel," Clancy replied. "They will be waiting to trap you. You must leave and gather allies—perhaps in the south, or in England—and then come back in force. If you are taken, they will kill you and your brother both. But they won't dispatch him until they have you, sir—not while they can use him as leverage against you."

Nate knew he was right, but he couldn't admit it out loud. He would have to leave his brother and sisters to their fate. His fists clenched so tight they turned pale and the muscles knotted around his jaw. The choice was almost more than he could bear. There had to be another way. There *had* to be.

"Goddamn it to hell!" he burst out, thumping the wall. "I can't just leave them!"

"You must, sir," Clancy said simply. "And you must do it now."

There was nothing for it but to go. Nate allowed himself to be led along the secret passageways back to his room. He needed some ready money and the weapons he kept there. Clancy assured him that the Duke's servants were the best men to have on their side in the house. They had been taught every hidden path and doorway and were extremely capable. Nate hardly listened—he should not have been relying on servants to save his kin. His face burned with shame.

The passageway did not go all the way to Nate's room, opening instead through an eight-foot-tall oil painting of the Duke at the end of the corridor. They closed the painting behind them and walked quietly up the hallway.

"I left the room protected, sir," Clancy told him. "They might expect you to come back here."

Nate was deep in thought, wondering where he could go. They had cousins in Cork and Galway, and some in Belfast too. He knew there were a few he might count on. But Gideon would already be contacting them by the houses telegraph, warning them that Nathaniel was no longer to be trusted. Nate was engrossed in plans of escape and rescue when he reached his door, carelessly grasping the handle.

"Sir!" Clancy barked.

But it was too late. Nate flung open the door and walked through without pressing the safety catch in the handle. The next thing he knew, Clancy was slamming him against the door frame and he felt a sharp pain in his chest.

"*Agh!*" he yelled. "What the bloody hell's got into you?"

He pushed the footman away, clutching his chest. That was when he saw the metal point sticking out of the breast of Clancy's jacket. Clancy collapsed against the opposite door frame and slid down to the floor, groaning. The tail of the cross-bow bolt sticking out of his back clacked against the floor. It had been shot from a crossbow mounted in the base of the sofa on the other side of the room; a booby trap meant to protect Nate . . . and he had walked right into it. It was the tip of the bolt he'd felt digging into his own chest, after it had embedded itself in his servant's body.

"Oh God," he whimpered breathlessly. "Oh God, no. Not you. Oh God, I'm sorry."

He pulled his handkerchief from his pocket and tried to stem the bleeding. Clancy struggled to sit up. "Stay down, man!" Nate urged him, his voice cracking into a sob. "I'll get help. I'm so sorry. Gerald . . . Gerald can help you—"

"I'm dying," Clancy replied with wet noises in his throat. "There's no one can help that."

He sounded furious. Nate caught his breath and wiped tears from his eyes. He couldn't bear to have the man angry at him now, when they had so little time left.

"Hush," he said. "I'll get help."

"Shut up and listen, boy," Clancy growled, his Limerick accent suddenly stronger, all trace of civility gone from his voice. He seized the collar of Nate's jacket. "Shut up! Listen to me. You can't let them take what's yours, y'hear me? Don't . . . don't let those bloody snakes take over. This is your family . . . you must claim it back!" He choked on something, coughing.

"Don't worry about me now," Nate told him. "We need to—"

"This isn't about *you,* you little whelp!" Clancy snarled again. "There's more at stake here than your privileged little life . . ." He ran out of breath, growing steadily weaker. "Your father didn't want you or Roberto taking charge, y'understand? You don't have his greed and he sees that as weakness. It takes an appetite for . . . for money . . . for power to run this family the way he wants and you don't have it, y'understand? The Duke's seed was gone, he could have no more children. And Gideon is a coward . . . and . . . and stupid to boot. The Duke needed a new Heir . . . That's . . ." He took a shaky breath. "That's why he let Hugo and the others live. Because the Duke needed to seed a ruthless new generation."

He went quiet for a moment, struggling to breathe. Blood pooled under him, despite Nate's attempts to cover the wounds.

"This wealth isn't theirs to take," Clancy managed at last. "Nor is it yours . . . for that matter. You never earned it—none of you did. But . . . but you can spend the rest of your life making good. Be a just master . . . You have a duty . . . Don't disappoint me . . . Nathaniel."

He slumped down, barely conscious, letting out short, loud, wet panting groans. Nate pulled him up and heaved his servant onto his shoulder. Hurrying back to the painting at the end of the corridor, he entered, lit a candle, and slammed the Duke's portrait closed behind him.

"Where is he?" Gideon demanded. "We'll find him anyway, you know."

"Then why bother asking?" Roberto said through broken teeth.

Gideon and his stocky brood of five sons with their thick black pelts and various facial hair arrangements wrestled their captives along the hallway towards the Duke's study. Daisy had tried to hold them up so that she could tend her husband's injuries, but they would have none of it. Berto had put up a fight and had paid the cost. The fingers of one hand were dislocated and Daisy was sure he had fractures in his ribs or arm from the way he walked. His face was badly bruised.

Holding Tatiana's hand, she walked as quickly as her dress would allow, shaking her arm free when one of the Gideonettes tried to drag her ever faster. They reached the door of the study and Gideon threw it open, two of his sons becoming jammed in the doorway behind him in their efforts to be next through. The rest of the party managed to enter with a little more dignity. Berto was thrown to the floor in front of the desk, with three men holding him, his face pressed into the carpet.

"The prodigal children return!" Hugo greeted them with a grim smile as he stood up from behind the desk. "I trust you have recovered from your pampered tantrums and are ready to behave with a little more decorum?"

They stared for a moment, struck by the strange sight of a man wearing a dress suit, but with a vest of chain mail over his shirt. It must have come from one of the antique costumes the family kept. The steel links glittered in the light under his black suit jacket. A purple cravat covered a stout leather collar protecting his neck. He saw them looking.

"Old habits die hard," he said, gesturing at the armor. "Best to be careful until I know where everyone stands, eh?"

He came round the desk to face them, glancing at Roberto for just a moment before fixing his gaze on Daisy. Taking her hand, he kissed her knuckles, his waxed goatee brushing against her fingers. She wrinkled her face in disgust at his touch, but she was not going to give him the satisfaction of showing her fear. There was nothing left to her but her dignity.

"This family has bathed in sin long enough," he said softly. "It is time to accept Christ into your hearts. I have been chosen to save you all from your sins that we might spread His Word across this benighted land."

Daisy threw him a contemptuous look.

"The problem with people who think they've been chosen by God is that all too often they haven't," she said to him. "But they enthusiastically proceed in committing all manner of atrocities, safe in the belief that anything they do is God's Will. Don't mistake your motives for His. I'm quite sure Christ is not in the business of stabbing his host at the dinner table."

"I am Christ's Sword," Hugo said solemnly. "And I will do His Bidding."

"I don't remember Jesus using a sword, or any other weapon for that matter. Perhaps it's someone else's voice you're hearing?"

Hugo flinched, but then laughed and opened his arms wide.

"By Jove, you've got spirit!" he roared. "You are a woman of substance and no mistake. My sisters and I are going on a visit to the zoo. Will you join us, ma'am?"

"I'd rather you just let us leave," Daisy retorted.

"Hah! No," said Hugo, his smile changing to a regretful expression. "I'm afraid a trip to the zoo is the best we can do for you at the moment."

XXIX

A NIGHTTIME VISIT TO THE ZOO

NATHANIEL MADE HIS WAY DOWN through the labyrinth of wooden and stone-walled passages, the light of the candle throwing a bobbing glow ahead of him that would announce his approach to anyone lying in ambush. He turned every corner with care, pistol raised. Clancy had still been alive when they reached Gerald's laboratory. Gerald did not offer much hope, but had begun operating immediately. Nate had been forced to leave his footman in his cousin's hands; they would all be in danger if Nate was discovered there.

Every step he took felt like a betrayal. Tatty, Berto and Daisy were all behind him and he was deserting them to save himself. It would be days, if not weeks, before he could return with allies from the family in Cork, and anything could happen in that time.

OISÍN McGANN

And by then, Hugo would have secured his position in the house. Nate would return to find a fortress waiting for him.

But there was nothing for it; he couldn't defeat Hugo on his own. Clancy's last words grated at him. The family's power was not his responsibility—it never had been. He just wanted to get the others out safely. Descending a narrow staircase, he followed a twisting corridor to a door made of stones mounted in an oak frame. Blowing out the candle, he peeped through the spy hole in one of the cracks to see that the way was clear and then gently unlatched the door and swung it open. He was in the east wing of the stables.

It was dark, but not the pitch black of the passage behind him. He could smell the horses and their hay and the oiled leather of the tack hanging up on the wall beside him. The quiet was disturbed only by the animals shifting position or snorting softly, and the creaking of the grooms and stable boys moving about in the attic above. Letting his eyes adjust to the gloom, he walked through the stable until he reached Flash's stall.

As he opened the door to the stall, he was surprised to find the velocycle was not alone. One of the stable boys was asleep next to it, hugging its front wheel. Flash greeted Nate with a friendly grunt and turned towards him, waking the lad. Blinking his encrusted eyes, the boy took a moment to register Nathaniel's presence. He gaped in shock, jumped to his feet and whipped off his hat, knuckling his forehead.

"I'm sorry, sir!" he blurted out. "I was just—"

"Shhh!" Nate whispered, holding up his hand, forgetting that he was still holding his firearm.

The boy started to shake. Nate looked at the gun and then put it in his pocket.

"It's all right, I'm not going to hurt you," he reassured the lad. "I need you to be quiet though, you understand me? You're . . . I've never seen anyone so comfortable with this beast. You must be good with engimals. What's your name?"

"Francie, sir. I mean . . . Francis Noonan, sir."

Noonan. Nate tried to remember where he had heard that name before—and then it came to him.

"You're related to Séamas Noonan?"

The boy didn't answer at first, but his hesitation was enough to give him away.

"He's me father," he admitted at last.

Nate leaned back against the door. Suddenly, things started to make a little more sense.

"Saddle it up . . . quietly," he said, gesturing at Flash. "I'm leaving here and I don't want anyone to know it. And you're coming with me. You're going to take me to your rebel friends."

It did not surprise Nate that Francie knew how to lead Flash with its eyes dimmed, without making any noise, and that he knew the path through the woods to the forest road. After all, he had stolen the velocycle once before. What did surprise him was that the rebels would recruit such a young agent. They must be a cold-blooded lot indeed. But once Francie knew the game was up, he wasted no time in telling the full story, in a desperate attempt to convince this gent that Shay Noonan was neither a rebel nor a murderer.

"You blew up the cemetery because you were trying to *rob* us?" Nate asked in a low voice, his disbelief evident.

"They were just tryin' to blow through the wall," Francie explained. "They thought there was a treasury on the other side. They didn't know about the powder store."

So much for the Duke's theories about a criminal mastermind, Nate thought.

"But what about your attack on my brother? You left a bloody note!"

"I was just nickin' the engimal, sir!" Francie protested softly. "Da just wrote the note to put the wind up yez. I wasn't even goin' to leave it except I ran into Master Roberto and dropped it by mistake when I fell off."

"Bloody hell," Nate sighed. "All this mayhem because a few petty thieves were trying to steal some gold. So you're definitely not rebels?"

Francie shook his head vigorously, his eyes ever watchful for a chance to make a break for it. He wasn't sure why Nathaniel was being so sneaky about wandering around his own grounds, but there could be no doubt that Francie was well and truly scuppered. He was probably too young to be hanged, but there was plenty of space in Kilmainham Gaol for the likes of him.

When they were a little way into the forest, Nate climbed into Flash's saddle and had Francie get on behind. With Flash still suppressing the sound of its engine, they rode through the forest towards the wall that surrounded the estate. Francie felt the thrill of the ride again, relishing the engimal's raw power.

It took less than ten minutes to reach the wall, and then they stopped.

"There's a culvert off to the right," Francie said. "You'd have to get wet, sir, and Flash would have to be pushed through on its side—"

"Nonsense," Nate declared. "We're going to jump it."

He steered the velocycle round until they were about thirty yards back from a grass bank that lay in front of the wall. Nate knew his beast's agility could make a ramp of that hillock and the ground on the other side was clear enough for a landing.

"I don't know if this is such a good idea, sir," Francie whispered nervously. "This thing's a contrary craythur at the best of times."

"Just hold on," Nate told him, and kicked his heels into the velocycle's sides.

Flash reared and its eyes flashed bright, its engine raised in a roar. They hurtled forward, gathering speed at a tremendous rate. The beams of Flash's eyes picked out the stone wall and then the ramp . . .and then the wall again. Nate felt the engine falter.

"No—" he managed, before Flash slowed as they hit the ramp and then came to an abrupt halt, hurling the two riders over the wall.

The ground struck with a shocking suddenness in the darkness. Nate found himself sprawled in the long grass, unable to see where he was and in too much pain to find out. He could hear Francie giving wheezing cries a few feet away. And then he heard someone else shouting.

Sentries had been alerted by the noise and the lights. Did they know there had been a change in power? Were they Hugo's men now? There was no way to be sure. Nate heard two voices, possibly three. He lay still in the grass, trying to discern where they were coming from. Turning his face to the ground, he detected running feet approaching from his right. He felt for his pistol, still in his jacket. Falling on it had left a nasty bruise under his ribs, and he winced as he drew it from his pocket. A man came hurrying through the grass and was almost on top of him when Nate sprang up and whipped the butt of the gun across the side of his head. The man flipped onto his back and hit the ground with barely a grunt.

Grabbing Francie's arm, Nate pulled him onto his feet.

"Come on," he hissed. "That blasted beast has shafted us good and proper. We have to get out of here."

"But . . . but why are yeh runnin' from yer own family?" Francie gasped as he hobbled after Nate on wobbly legs.

"That's a bloody good question," Nate replied.

The zoological gardens where the Wildensterns kept their menagerie of exotic wildlife—including their collection of untamable engimals—was a bizarre place in daylight, but at nighttime it was positively eerie.

Some footmen had gone ahead to light the gas-lamps along the walkway, but the place had not been built to visit at night and the widely spaced lamps gave a meager light; they still needed two of the footmen to guide the way with lanterns. The enclosures loomed over them in all shapes and sizes, from closed-off sheds to fenced pens to ridiculously ornate cages. Daisy let herself be led on Hugo's arm, willing to play along until an opportunity to escape presented itself. And if one didn't, she was determined to concoct one.

They were accompanied by Elizabeth, Brunhilde and Gideon. As they stepped through the tall east-iron gates of the zoo, Elizabeth gasped in delight at the shadowy beasts around them. Brunhilde began scurrying from one to the next, chattering, grunting and panting as if she were trying to communicate with the creatures. The woman had no class whatsoever.

"The smaller creatures are kept here," Gideon explained as they strolled down the walkway. "Wild mowers, a few breeds of snake-chain, some miniature cranes . . . you get the idea. Down by the canal are the larger engimals, including the ones that require moats, like Trom. Although none of them have been tamed like Trom, of course."

"Let us see the most magnificent first," Hugo said.

Gideon nodded and led them through the avenue of dark buildings. They heard an array of noises emitted by the restless engimals: clanking, clacking, whirring, ticking, whistling and any number of other faint sounds. Hugo and his sisters listened with interest. They must have seen enough engimals in their time, but Daisy knew there would have been nothing like the Wildenstern Zoological Gardens in their century.

But they could see very little without lighting each enclosure individually, so they walked on as Hugo had requested, to see the most magnificent first. As they strolled arm in arm, Hugo would rub Daisy's arm against his side and she could feel the hard links of the chain mail beneath his jacket. Sometimes he stroked her fingers. His touch made her skin crawl and she was glad that the diameter of her crinoline kept him a good two feet away. Every now and then he gave her a smile that she supposed was meant to be charming, but merely made him look like the depraved old man that he was.

As they moved along the path, they passed an enormous bronze birdcage. There was a faint white glow emitting from it. Elizabeth stopped to peer inside and even Daisy turned to look. She hadn't seen the leaf-lights in darkness for some time. Roberto had taken her here at night, during their first year of marriage, for one of his well-orchestrated romantic evenings.

Daisy wondered bitterly if he had ever taken Old Hennessy to the zoo.

There was a thick pane of glass between each intricately shaped bar of the cage, forming a solid dome.

"I saw creatures like these once," Elizabeth whispered in a sensuous voice. "On a campaign in France. Do you remember, Hugo? They flew past my tent one night when we camped in a forest."

The leaf-lights lay on the floor of the cage. It appeared as if someone had taken a ream of paper—of sheets about six inches square—and cast them across the boards. But these sheets of paper glowed, and as the people approached the glass, the creatures floated up into the air and fluttered in a rustling cloud towards their visitors.

Elizabeth put her hand to the glass, but it was the servants holding the lanterns who interested the engimals. They drank light; during the day they basked in the sun and in the evening they took to the sky in wild and meaningless dances. They danced now, whirling in a dizzying display of agility. Elizabeth clapped her hands and Brunhilde pointed and laughed.

"We didn't come here to look for toys," Hugo said after a few minutes.

"Yes," Gideon replied, making a big hand gesture so that his rings caught the light. "You wanted something *magnificent*. Come this way. I don't think you'll be disappointed."

The most magnificent engimal was a behemoth even larger than Trom. It was an eight-wheeled juggernaut, brought all the way from North America, where it had roamed the endless plains of the Midwest. Now it was held in an enclosure of little more than three acres; it would spend days and nights rolling around the perimeter one way and then the other, tirelessly searching for a way out. Its body was black, gold and purple, with a narrow sloping tail and a huge muscular torso shaped like a tightly clasped fist with two thumbs. It was scarred along its front and sides from territorial battles. But its fighting days were over. Now it stood listlessly at its water trough, sucking up water.

"This is Colossus," Gideon announced proudly as they stopped at the railing to peer across the moat at the gloomy scene. "It is the mightiest, most untamable monster this side of the world. You would have to go to Africa, or even Asia to find its match."

"Indeed." Hugo stared across the moat with a faint smile on his face.

There was a raised pier that ran out over the stonewalled moat, so that visitors could look down on the engimal from

above. Hugo let go of Daisy's arm and ran up the steps and along
the length of the walkway to the end. He stood there, his tall,
upright figure silhouetted against the sky, the lanterns casting a
faint light from below. The others followed him up more slowly,
and Daisy felt a sense of foreboding come over her as she came
up the last few steps and saw the new Patriarch leaning over the
railing, a look of wonder on his face;

There was a knife in his right hand, and as they watched, he
pressed the tip into his left palm. Blood welled forth, looking
almost black in the dim light. Hugo held his wounded hand out
over the railing and squeezed it into a fist. Daisy reached the
rail and looked over in time to see a few drops of blood fall into
the darkness below. She could just see the outline of the water
trough below the brow of Colossus. Hugo was feeding the creature his blood. The engimal stopped drinking and sniffed. Steam
drifted up from its nostrils. Then its eyes blazed with a blue light
and it backed away from the trough, snorting warily.

"Untamable, you say?" Hugo asked Gideon.

"Irredeemably savage," Gideon replied. "We would all be
dead were it not for this moat."

Hugo jumped over the rail and dropped the twenty feet to the
ground in front of the juggernaut, landing with the grace of an
acrobat. It towered over him and he stared back at it, shielding
his eyes against its light.

It could have crushed him like an insect, but instead it rocked
back and forth like a shy child being introduced to a stranger.
Hugo held up his bloodied hand, fingers splayed, and the juggernaut edged forward. The wound closed up, the edges knitting

together, leaving only the bloodstain. With a timid movement, the machine the size of a house leaned forward and nudged his outstretched fingertips.

"My God!" Gideon exclaimed.

"My brother." Elizabeth corrected him with a smile.

XXX

"SORRY FOR YOUR TROUBLES"

IT WAS OVER TWO HOURS LATER when the party of four returned from the zoo. Daisy, already disturbed by what she had seen there, was shocked at the change in her husband. Roberto seemed to have aged and he looked ridiculously relieved to see her walk through the door. She felt a mix of feelings at his reaction. Even though she could not bring herself to forgive him for cheating on her, she still had hope that she could win him back. But that could all come later. First she needed him to be strong—to protect herself and their sister like a good husband should, instead of letting his emotions get the better of him.

They could not allow themselves to be intimidated. With a shudder, she thought about the macabre acts she had just witnessed at the zoo. They could not allow themselves to be *seen* to be intimidated, at least.

Berto was in an armchair by one of the tall windows, flanked by two of his treacherous cousins, both of whom held revolvers. The curtains were open and she knew he had been watching for their return. Tatiana was sitting on a stool beside him, holding his hand. She looked less bothered by their situation than by the effect it was having on her brother. He smiled like a puppy at Daisy, who stared back sternly at him, urging him to show a bit more backbone.

"Nathaniel has escaped," one of the Gideonettes informed them as they walked in. "He got his velocycle as far as the wall, but had to abandon it, so we know he's on foot. Slattery has gone after him. The bailiff knows his business—we should have our little outcast by daybreak."

Hugo nodded, taking his seat behind the desk. Stroking his goatee, he stared with empty eyes at Roberto. He chewed the inside of his mouth, a pensive expression on his face.

"If he still intends to vanquish me and return to Wildenstern Hall, he won't seek help from outside the family," he mused. "We must discredit him, so there will be no help available to him. Spread word that it was he who shot that wretch of a blackamoor we killed at dinner. Say it was over some petty breach of etiquette or other. Make him into a murderer.

"We will not speak of Edgar's death and there will be no funeral yet. The body will be kept until a more convenient occasion arises. Instead, we will say that he has been struck down by the fever and is at death's door. Needless to say, he is highly infectious and is not receiving visitors."

"And then what?" Daisy asked. "What are you going to do with us?"

"Our two errant young boys will be kept alive only for as long as they are useful," Hugo replied. "And I don't anticipate that being very long at all. You and Tatiana will be spared . . . But you will spend the rest of your days within these walls. The family needs good breeding stock."

"You can't do that," Daisy said in a tight voice. "The Rules don't allow for Aggression against women."

"They don't have to, my dear Melancholy," Hugo said with a solemn smile. "You are women in a man's world. The late Duke, God rest his soul, kept his last wife trapped in the attic for years. Even her children didn't know she was still alive. I hear she was completely out of her mind by the time she finally succumbed to a merciful death." An edge of menace crept into his voice. "And unless your behavior pleases me, you can look forward to the same fate."

Elizabeth crossed the floor to where Berto and Tatiana were sitting. She was wearing a new cloak; a strange white affair with a patchwork effect and a high collar. It moved as she did, with a lightness that belied the weight of the material.

"Come, Tatiana," she said, holding out her hand. "It is long past your bedtime and it has been a terrible, traumatic day. Let us retire and leave these grown-ups to their bickering."

"I'm not going anywhere," Tatiana retorted.

"Now," Berto said through gritted teeth. "Now, Tatty!"

"*Harsh—loud!*" Tatty cried, and lifted her skirts to reveal her ankles.

Her shameful act of exposure took the others by surprise—but it was nothing compared to their reaction as her pet engimal burst from beneath her dress and erupted into a deafening cacophony of metallic drumbeats accompanying what sounded like giant church bells crashing to the ground from a great height. Everyone gasped in pain and covered their ears—except Roberto. Launching himself out of his chair, he jabbed his rigid fingers into the windpipe of the nearest Gideonette, seizing the pistol from his cousin's hand and kicking him in the stomach, knocking him back against the wall. Elizabeth had her back turned and did not hear Hugo's warning over the ear-splitting noise. Berto swung his arm round her neck and pressed the gun against her temple, yelling something nobody could hear.

"Hush," said Tatiana, and the bird went quiet, fluttering down to settle on her wrist.

"—*moves and I'll shoot this slattern!*" Roberto finished shrieking.

Every other pistol in the room was now pointing at him, and Daisy carefully moved out of their line of fire, searching for a weapon of her own. She picked up a poker from the fireplace, concealing it in the folds of her skirt. Berto had fooled her and everyone else; his simpering had just been an act—and it had worked.

"We're walking out of here and you're not going to stop us," Berto was saying.

"No, I don't think you're going anywhere," Hugo replied.

Berto tightened his grip on Elizabeth's neck and pointed the gun at Hugo, firing off a shot. The bullet hit the wall over Hugo's shoulder.

"I only need one hostage," Berto warned him. "The next shot will take you between the eyes."

Hugo spared his sister a glance and she managed a strained smile as she gasped for breath. His eyes flicked back to Berto's.

"You're not a killer, Roberto," he said. "You show your weakness in every move that you make, every word that you say. Your father said you always lacked nerve. You won't hurt my sister."

"The hell I won't!" Berto yelled, his voice a little too shrill.

Even from beyond the grave, it seemed that Edgar was undermining his sons. Daisy gripped the handle of the poker, sidling up behind Gideon, whose attention was fixed on the hostage situation. If anyone made a move towards her husband, Gideon was going to get it over the back of the head.

"Give me the weapon, Roberto," Hugo said gently, holding out his hand. "You don't want it to go like this. Think of your sister. She could get hurt."

"I can look after myself," Tatiana informed him tartly.

"We're getting out of here," Berto said tightly, but he sounded less confident now.

He went to move, but Elizabeth would not walk and he nearly tripped over her.

"Move!" he cried.

Elizabeth looked to her brother. His face was expressionless. He gave a barely perceptible nod. Her cloak let out a rising hum and then burst into pieces. Dozens of leaf-lights, each one no heavier than the page of a book, swept back over Berto, their paper-thin edges cutting gashes into his skin and clothes. Elizabeth knocked his gun-hand aside and stepped away, making a pushing motion with her other hand. The leaf-lights obeyed, whirling in a loop and coming at him again. He disappeared in a blizzard of blinding white movement, letting out a panicked cry as he was carried backwards and thrown through the window with a great crash of glass and wood.

He tumbled backwards, screaming into empty space, thirty stories above the ground.

Daisy gave a gasp, dropping the poker and rushing towards the window. Hugo stepped into her path, catching hold of her and pulling her to his chest.

"It's best you don't look, child," he said in a soothing tone. "Best that you don't look."

She shrieked like an animal at him, clawing at his face, but he was too strong. Grabbing her wrists, he gripped them in one hand as he used the other to press her face against his shoulder, and she burst out into helpless sobs.

"Shhh. It's all over now," he whispered.

It was. She had no more fight left in her. She didn't even have her dignity left. Collapsing against him, her body shook as she cried for her dead husband, her best friend.

The others crowded towards the window, but Tatiana reached it first. From somewhere below the window came a long, fearful moan.

"He's not dead!" Tatty exclaimed.

Daisy caught her breath. She felt Hugo's grip relax as he looked over in surprise and she pushed away from him, rushing to the window. Elbowing her way through the Gideonettes, she leaned out through the broken glass. In the light of the windows two stories down, she could see Roberto suspended out in the darkness as if by magic.

But then she saw what had saved him. He was bent backwards over the broad neck of a gargoyle and was hanging on precariously to one of its horns.

"Hold on, my love!" she called to him. "We're coming for you!"

He was obviously in severe pain and could only answer with another moan. She tried to get out past Gideon and his sons, intent on making for the stairs. They held her, turning to Hugo for instructions. He grinned, tugging at his moustache.

"Let us save the young whelp," he laughed. "This is the most entertaining night I've had in centuries!"

Despite the hindrance of their hooped skirts, Daisy and Tatiana were first to the door and led the charge down the stairs to Roberto's floor. Only Brunhilde stayed to watch from above. Leaning her hands on the glass-strewn windowsill, she stuck the top half of her body out of the window and opened her mouth wide, letting a thread of spittle drip from her tongue. Then she became completely still. Roberto stared up at her in bewilderment until he realized what she was doing. She was pretending to be a gargoyle.

Nathaniel knew that Slattery would be coming after them, so he led Francie cross-country, winding through the fields and narrow lanes, stumbling over the rough ground in the dim light from the sky. He couldn't stop thinking about Clancy, sure that his manservant must be dead by now. Gerald had taken one look at the wound and shaken his head, but Nate had urged him to do everything he could. Nate nearly tripped on a rabbit hole in the middle of the field and was brought back to his own predicament. He and Francie had been on the move for nearly two hours, but as the sky began to brighten, any hope of making the train station at Kingstown before dawn slowly faded with the darkness. From there he could catch a train to the south and seek refuge with some relatives in Cork.

They were descending a grassy hill, wet and muddied from their flight through the countryside. They could see lights in the windows of one building on the road. It was a pub, and Nate turned towards it, hoping he could borrow or buy a horse from someone within.

As they drew closer, they could hear the sounds of singing voices, fiddles, tin whistles and the beat of bodhráns. There appeared to be a party going on within.

"Must be a wake, to be goin' on at this hour," Francie said. "I wonder who for? I know this pub—it's Hanratty's. We're near Stepaside."

"Hanratty's. That's a Fenian pub, isn't it?" Nate asked.

"Aye, I don't think yeh'll be too welcome there, sir."

"We'll see about that," Nate declared, striding ahead.

Francie hurried after him.

"Sir, you can't just walk in. It'll all be just family and friends in there. They won't take kindly to strangers bargin' in."

They reached the end of the field and climbed over a stile.

OISÍN McGANN

Once on the road, they found it was only a couple of minutes' walk to the front door of the pub, a small stone building with a thatched roof. Nate, who was not accustomed to being refused entrance to drinking establishments, opened the door and stepped inside. Francie followed him reluctantly.

If Nate had hoped to be discreet, he was sorely disappointed. The music faltered and stopped, and every face in the room turned to stare at him. For a moment he didn't know what to do . . . so he just stared.

Most of the musicians, about six or seven of them, sat in one corner of the room. More than sixty other people were squeezed in among the tables, either sitting on beaten-up benches or stools or standing against the wall. The air was thick with pipe smoke and the smell of stout and whisky. The scent of drink made Nate realize how thirsty he was himself. Most of the people were peasants, dressed in their paltry Sunday best for the funeral, now looking all the more worse for wear after an all-night drinking session. There were a few of the middle classes there too, their clothes and hair of a better cut.

Some of the people stood up when they saw that Nathaniel was a gentleman; perhaps they even recognized him. Others stayed in their seats. Some of them glared at him in open hostility. In the center of the room, resting on two tables, was a cheap coffin. It was closed. He had never been to a wake before, but he had heard that it wasn't uncommon to have the box open so that the corpse could take part in the proceedings. He wondered if there was a reason the lid had been kept on. Sitting on the lid was glass of whisky, presumably for the corpse, should he want it.

— 346 —

"What . . . What can we do for you, sir?" a small, mousy-haired man with spectacles asked.

He was standing with a tray of drinks in his hands, obviously in the middle of serving. Nate felt everyone's eyes upon him.

"Pardon my intrusion," he said, only just remembering his manners. He should show some sensitivity to the mourners before trying to wangle a horse out of them. "What is the name of the deceased?"

"Duffy," the landlord replied. "Eoin Duffy."

Nate drew in a sharp breath and his face dropped. Off to one side, Francie went pale.

"The moneylender?" Nate asked.

"He had a number of businesses," another man in a grey tweed suit answered him. "I'm his brother, Eamon. May I ask why you are interested, sir?"

Slattery had disobeyed him. Nathaniel had walked out of the dungeon and the bailiffs had completely ignored his instructions to release the moneylender. And now the man was dead. Nate put a hand to his brow and closed his eyes for a moment. He seemed to be surrounded by death, and he was sick to the pit of his stomach with it all. Looking up at the unfriendly faces around him, a thought occurred to him. He had no intention of obeying the Rules of Ascension any more . . . or any other laws for that matter. He just wanted to rescue Tatty, Berto and Daisy. Gideon and the rest of the older generation had too much influence with the British for Nate to trust the authorities, but the Fenians hated his family almost as much as he did. Perhaps his enemy's enemy could be his friend.

"How did your brother die?" Nate asked, ignoring Duffy's question.

"He was murdered," the man told him. "He was found floating in the Dodder River with the guts hanging out of him. Now what can we do for you, sir?"

His tone was polite but insistent. He was a square-built man with a stern face and grey hair flecked with black. A silver watch chain hung from his waistcoat pocket. He stood taller than Nate and with the confidence of a self-made man. It was clear he was a figure of authority in this room.

"He was killed by Patrick Slattery," Nate told them, watching for their reaction. There was precious little. A few of the women exchanged puzzled glances, but nothing more. Everyone's expression seemed frozen in place.

"We know," said Duffy. "And it's a strange admission coming from you, Mr. Wildenstern, seeing as it's Slattery who does your father's dirty work."

"My father is dead," Nate replied. "And Slattery is working for his murderer. If there are men here who will aid me in my fight against the traitor, I will give you Slattery in return."

That caused a stir. A wave of mumbling carried around the room. Duffy held up his hand and there was quiet again.

"Slattery will pay for his crimes—come hell or high water, he'll get his," Duffy said. "But why would we want to help you? Your family can simply hire a dozen more like him. Nothing will have changed."

Nate bridled at the man's stubborn attitude. It sometimes seemed to him that the Irish peasant cared more for the dead than for the living. Perhaps that was the reason why so many of them seemed so apathetic about their lot in life.

"This is in your own interests!" he appealed to the people in the room. "There have been some terrible changes in my family over this last night. The man who has taken over our estates is a fiend of the worst kind. He has taken my sister and sister-in-law as hostages and I am sure he means to kill my brother. They are all I care about. I can get you past the guards and into the house, do you understand? You can strike a telling blow for your cause by assassinating him and anyone who defends him. It's in your own interests. This man will make life a misery for all those beneath him. He has no conscience and his greed knows no bounds—he will *bleed you dry!* If this tyrant is allowed to gain control of our businesses, you will all be reduced to living in misery!"

His plea was met with a brooding silence. Then a woman's voice piped up from the far end of the room.

"Sure, the British will protect us!"

The crowd burst into a roar of raucous, drunken laughter. Even Francie was trying to suppress a smile. Nate stood there helplessly as the hysterics lasted nearly a full minute before everyone settled down and wiped their eyes. Duffy rubbed his red, sweating face with a handkerchief and gave a final chuckle, followed by a sigh.

"It doesn't sound to me like anything will change at all, Mr. Wildenstern," he said. "Not a thing. Your family have always gone about your bloodthirsty ways and the rest of us have endured one tyrant after another for centuries. Another change won't mean anything to us."

"I know . . . I know that my father was not always fair," Nate pleaded with them, to a chorus of snorts and stifled laughs. "But whatever you think you've endured before, this will be much worse. This man is a fiend, I tell you. An absolute monster. You have to help me!"

"We have to do no such thing." Duffy shook his head. "Now if you'll excuse us, sir—"

"I understand that life is hard here," Nate cut him off. "But I—"

"You understand *nothing*," Duffy snapped at him. "What do you know? You think because you've seen a ruined cottage or two on your rides through the country, or taken a tour through the inside of a factory, that you know what life is like on your estates? You have no idea." His face twisted in a grimace of hatred. "You— who takes his sugar in lumps and each meal in a different room, and has his footman take the warming pan to his bed-sheets before retiring for the night, and has a freshly pressed change of clothes laid out for him every morning. What do you know—?"

He was interrupted by the sound of horses' hooves clattering across the ground outside. The landlord peered out of the window.

"It's Slattery and two of his louts!" Hanratty growled. "One of 'ems goin' round to the back door."

Nate pulled the revolver from his jacket pocket.

"Help me or stand back," he said, his jaw tight with tension. "I'm going to put an end to the bloody cur right now."

But Duffy stood up and gently pushed the gun towards the floor.

"Show some respect for the dead," he said sternly. "Hanratty here'll hide you. We'll see them off, don't you worry. But there'll be no shooting here this morning."

Francie melted into the crowd as Nate allowed himself to be led to a door behind the bar that opened into a storeroom. It had only one tiny window that offered no escape. Hanratty closed the door behind him, just as Slattery strode into the pub. Nate knelt down and peered through the keyhole.

"Well, if it isn't Eamon Duffy and his mob," Slattery declared as he stood, looking around the room. Nate observed with some satisfaction that the bailiff was still walking stiffly. "And who's in the box, then?"

"My brother, as if you didn't know," Duffy replied coolly.

The man who came in with Slattery walked past the bar and stepped in behind it to open the back door and look out. He was only a few feet from the storeroom door. Nate could feel the floorboards settle under the man's weight.

"I'm sorry for your troubles," Slattery said, without a hint of sincerity. "I'm looking for a tall blond gentleman about eighteen years old. The young Master Nathaniel Wildenstern. Has anyone seen him?"

"Aye, I've seen 'im," a man said from the other side of the room. "Up yer arse, pickin' daisies."

There was some nervous laughter. Nate couldn't see the bailiffs expression through the narrow hole, but his tone told him all he needed to hear.

"That's Charlie Fitzpatrick, isn't it?" Slattery retorted. "Sure, I never knew you were such a sparklin' wit, Charlie. Maybe you can spare some more of it when I come to collect your rent this Tuesday? You do have the rent money, don't you, Charlie?"

There seemed to be no more wit forthcoming. Slattery was silent for a moment, and Nate could guess that he was giving the crowd the evil eye. The man at the back door closed it and walked in behind the bar. Nate gripped his pistol, wincing as he pulled back the hammer as quietly as he could.

"Get on with your drinkin'," Slattery said at last, throwing some money on a table. "Drink away your troubles. Drink away your worries and drink away your sad little lives an' all. The more you all drink, the easier my job is, so have a round on me. And put some into poor dead Eoin there as well, why don't you? Don't want him meetin' the Almighty without drink on his breath. Give the Irish a bad name."

And with a shuffle of boots on the wooden floor, they were gone. Nate eased the hammer home on his pistol and let out long breath. Slumping down with his back against the door, he stared up at the light coming through the tiny window.

Listening to the sounds of the men mounting their horses, he felt as if he were in a daze.

"Master Wildenstern?" Hanratty's voice called through the door. "It's all right, they're gone now."

Nate did not hear the landlord. This latest turn of events had finally overwhelmed him. He had never known the dead man, and yet the news of Eoin Duffy's death had been more than he could cope with after everything that had happened. He had thought that all he had to do was get away from the family—go to some far-flung corner of the world where he and the others could stay out of the way of the Wildensterns and live their lives in peace. But it could never be that simple.

"He's not answerin'," Hanratty said to somebody else. "Do y'think he's all right?"

"Maybe he's fallen asleep—he looked knackered," somebody suggested. "You should have a look in and see."

Now Nate had a man's death on his hands because he hadn't cared enough to ensure his instructions were carried out. Servants were never permitted to think for themselves, but people like Slattery were given more slack. It meant the family could wash its hands of any inhuman acts that he committed.

"I'm not stickin' me head in there," Hanratty exclaimed. "He was bit jumpy with that pistol if y'ask me. If I woke him up, he might get a fright and start squirtin' lead all over the place."

"Best leave him to wake up on his own, so," the other voice concluded helpfully.

Nate had known how his family worked even as he stood in that dungeon looking at the battered face of Eoin Duffy. And yet he had turned his back and walked away. And Clancy too was probably dead by now, because Nate had been stupid and careless, and because he lived in fear. Sitting in that tiny storeroom, he swore to himself that was about to change. He understood now what Clancy had been trying to tell him. He had been born into a privileged position . . . now he had to earn it. It was time to claim his inheritance.

His eyes wandered around the little room with its shelves of boxes, cans and paper parcels. It was nothing like the huge cellars at home, with their massive stores of fine food and drink. A milk churn sat in one corner, with a bag of potatoes leaning against it, some of them already sprouting shoots out of their brown skin. The whole room had a musty smell of vegetables on the edge of decay. In another corner was a small meat-safe, a cupboard with a wire gauze front used for storing meat. The Wildensterns were one of the only households in the country with the modern refrigerators. On top of the meat-safe lay a few sheets of paper and a pencil. Somebody had been doing the accounts. They were very small numbers.

Standing up, Nate picked up the pencil and a blank sheet and wrote out a short message on it. Then he opened the door. The crowd of mourners were looking on in interest.

"Francie," he said. "I need you to take this to the nearest telegraph office and send it immediately. Wake them up if you have to—tell them it's a matter of life and death."

Francie looked at the message in confusion.

"But—"

"I need you to send it exactly as it is, do you hear me?" Nate insisted.

Francie nodded. Handing the note and some coins to the boy, Nate turned to Eamon Duffy.

"Sir, we need two horses. I can pay well."

"We'll loan you the horses," said the man, holding up two glasses of whisky. "All I ask, Master Wildenstern, is that you drink to my brother."

"It's the least I could do," Nate replied, taking the glass and holding it up. "May he be in Heaven an hour before the devil knows he's dead."

"Amen to that," the dead man's brother answered.

And so Nate rode away from the pub with the taste of whisky burning his parched throat. Like the bitterness of Eoin Duffy's death, it would take a long time to fade.

XXXI

A NEED FOR DESPERATE MEASURES

AT DAISY'S URGING, Roberto was carried on a stretcher down to Gerald's laboratory. She did not trust Dr. Warburton's loyalties; it felt as if the whole house was against them now. Hugo had come down with them—accompanied by Elizabeth and a couple of the Gideonettes—and was looking thoroughly amused by the whole affair. They found Gerald up and dressed, stitching up a wound in the chest of Nathaniel's man-servant, Clancy. Daisy wondered which of the family's lunatics had caused that injury.

"You have a new patient," Hugo announced, looking disdain-fully down at the unconscious servant as they came through the door. "Someone more deserving of your attention . . . Though for how much longer, I couldn't say."

Gerald looked up, his exhaustion evident on his face. His eyes closed for a moment in dismay as he saw Berto on the stretcher.

"He can't feel his legs," Daisy told him tearfully, still holding Roberto's right hand. "And his left arm is numb. We think his back is broken."

"Put him on the table there," Gerald said, pointing. He quickly washed his hands and then wiped them with a cloth. "Lay him on his front."

The two servants did as they were told. Gerald took some scissors and cut up the back of Berto's waistcoat and shirt. The trousers were soiled, but he made no mention of it. He ran his fingers up his cousin's spine, pressing gently in places.

"Here," he said finally, touching a spot halfway up the back. "A broken vertebra, maybe two or three. I . . .I'm sorry, Berto. It's a grievous injury. I don't know if there's anything that can be done."

Roberto stifled a sob. Daisy pressed her hand to his cheek and kissed him, crying for him.

"I can't live like this," Roberto gasped hoarsely. "I can't face being a confounded cripple. If you can't fix me then *end* me, Gerald. I won't live like this!"

"Don't say that!" Daisy said softly to her husband. "You'll be all right. You'll be fine. Won't he, Gerald?"

Gerald said nothing, avoiding her eyes. Hugo looked on with a bored expression, fiddling with his cufflinks.

"Is this ready?" he asked, nodding towards another body lying on the table nearby.

It was Edgar's naked corpse, its decapitated head stitched

back on. The claw was missing from the right arm. At Hugo's insistence, Gerald had used the engimal limb to replace Brutus's missing hand.

"Yes, the servants can take it to the refrigerators," Gerald replied. "The collar of a dress suit will hide the stitches . . . whenever you decide to hold a proper funeral."

"Excellent," Hugo grunted. "You are a talented boy. What of Brutus?"

"His recovery proceeds," Gerald said coolly. "Your blood has helped. There's no movement yet, but his breathing and color are better."

Hugo went over to stand by his brother's bed. His face softened and he knelt by the bedside. Gold needles were visible, protruding from Brutus's arms and neck, but they had been removed from his face. He had recovered much of his muscular bulk and now looked as if he were just sleeping. Hugo tenderly placed a hand on the huge man's brow.

"Not long now, my brother," he whispered. "Our prayers are with you. We will be together soon; it is God's will."

"I seriously doubt it," Daisy muttered under her breath.

Gerald took her elbow and led her aside. She felt a cold cylinder of glass and steel being pressed into her hand.

"Hugo likes you," he said to her in a hushed voice. "We can use that against him—you can win his confidence . . . get close to him. He's damned near invulnerable; I don't think we could kill him with bullets alone—perhaps with explosives or the right kind of blade . . . who knows? And now he's wearing bloody chain mail too . . . But this syringe contains a poison that can kill him if you can get close enough to stick it into his heart."

Daisy gave him a sharp look, checking to ensure that Hugo was still intent on Brutus's unconscious face. The others were on the far side of the room, looking at Edgar's corpse. She eyed the hypodermic syringe in her hand. It was filled with a dull, greenish liquid and had a rubber cap on the needle.

"Aren't the Wildensterns immune to poisons?"

"This is different," Gerald whispered. "It's made from the toxins produced by the dead flesh in Brutus's hand—gangrene, you understand? Now that their bodies are revived, their own dead flesh can infect their blood, I'm sure of it."

"I . . . I'm not like all of you," she said. "I don't know if I could kill someone. And besides, I can't leave Berto now."

"Do you want to spend the rest of your days living under a man who thinks the world is flat and his brain is in his chest? Because I cannot!" Gerald hissed. "What would you do to save Berto's life? Hold his hand or kill his enemy?"

She didn't answer, but she could feel her resolve growing. Elizabeth was looking over at them now and Daisy's heart started to beat faster.

"Why don't you do it, if you're so sure it'll work?" she retorted.

"Because *I'm* not the one he's making eyes at, woman!" Gerald said, almost too loud. "You need to get him alone . . . get him to take off that bloody armor and drop his guard. But you have to stick the needle in his *heart.* Anywhere else and he could take hours, even days to die. You understand what I'm telling you?"

Daisy hesitated, and then nodded. If she tried to kill Hugo

and failed, his revenge would be terrible. Clutching the syringe in the folds of her dress, she edged towards the Patriarch. Elizabeth's watchful eyes followed her, the leaf-light cloak giving off the faintest glow in the low light at that end of the room. Daisy glanced over at Roberto for a moment, and then touched Hugo gently on the shoulder. He looked round and up at her.

"My lord," she said haltingly. "Gerald tells me that . . . that if Roberto is to survive, he will need expensive medicine and surgery and . . . and a long convalescence. I realize that you two have had your differences, but . . ." She paused to compose herself, keeping her gaze lowered. "I wonder if I . . . if we could speak in private? Perhaps I could convince you to overlook his disloyalty and see that he gets the help he needs?"

"What are you doing?" Berto growled, trying to raise himself from the table on which he lay. "Daisy? What's going on?"

Elizabeth's eyes narrowed in suspicion, but Hugo stood up and gave a lascivious smile.

"Daisy?" Berto asked again plaintively.

It hurt her like a wound to ignore him, but she did. Instead, she fixed Hugo with a pleading, wide-eyed expression. He opened his arms in a generous gesture.

"Every great leader knows when to show mercy," he said. "Come, my dear. Let us retire to more comfortable surroundings and see if your beauty is matched by your persuasive powers."

Taking her arm, he led her from the room without a second glance at Roberto. As they passed Elizabeth, the two women locked eyes.

If there's anything left of this poison when I'm done, Daisy thought, I'm going to drive the rest of it into your rotten heart, you witch.

Gerald watched them leave. He instructed his footman to fetch a nightshirt, dressing gown and some more blankets for Berto and then waited until he was alone with his injured cousin. Then, taking a clean syringe, he strode over to Brutus's inert form and inserted it into the ancient warrior's arm. Berto watched as the young doctor drew blood into the syringe.

"What's that for?" he asked.

"It's for you," Gerald told him. "I've already given some to Clancy. His wounds were so serious I was at my wits' end. I would have given up on him, but Nate wouldn't have it. So I decided to see if our ancestor's blood could do anything. Thought it would finish him off, to be honest—he's a commoner, so he has no *aurea sanitas* of course." He pulled out the needle. "But it didn't. He may well make it after all. And if it can help him . . ."

He walked over to Berto and wiped the crook of his cousin's arm with some cotton wool and alcohol.

"I have to say, I think I'm getting the hang of this miracle business—"

"Gerald," Berto said in a choked voice. "Look."

Gerald turned round in time to see movement by Brutus's bed. The fingers of the giant's left hand were twitching.

"Oh, bloody hell," he said.

Nate left the horse tied to a gate, where it would be picked up by Duffy's people later that morning. In the first misty glow of dawn, he was able to slip by the guards patrolling the wall of the estate and climb over, making his way through the forest towards Wildenstern Hall. Dew dripped from the trees and strands of mist lay in the undergrowth, wetting his clothes and shoes, the cold making him shiver as his fatigue began to catch up with him. It wasn't fear that made him tremble, he was sure of that. For the first time in his life he was doing what he had been bred to do.

A bizarre sight awaited him on the lawn as he came to the edge of the forest. Standing on the grass not far from the house were two enormous shapes, their feet shrouded in mist. At first the light of the low morning sun made their shapes indistinct against the grey walls of the house, but as his eyes adjusted, Nate recognized Trom and Colossus, the juggernaut. They stood perfectly still, as if awaiting orders. He gaped at the sight in amazement.

Trom could never be left alone like that without wandering and Colossus . . . Colossus was too wild—too *insane* to be let out of its enclosure. Nate stared, bewildered, until he remembered what Gerald had told him. One drop of blood in an engimal's water and they were yours to command. He had found it hard to believe it would work on the simple mind of a toast-maker, never mind the tortured brain of the juggernaut.

He was under no illusions as to who was in command of the huge engimals. Creeping up along the hedge to the stables, he was careful not to attract their attention. Their eyes were dimmed, but he was sure they could come alert at any second. Unlatching the side door of the stables, he stepped inside and closed it after him. The stable boys were already up; he could hear them moving around upstairs. He knew the grooms would be here any minute too, to start feeding and exercising the horses.

He had to be quick. He needed his velocycle, and then he had to find Abraham and his brothers. There was a plan to be hatched.

Flash was in its stall and looked up timidly as he leaned over the door. It whimpered and turned its face to the wall.

"Bloody right, you should be ashamed," he snarled at the velocycle as he opened the door. "You're a downright liability . . . But I need you now, so you're getting one more chance."

Looking down at the beast's water trough, he thought about adding some of his blood to the mix. And yet there was something about Flash's cantankerous spirit that he loved. Even though it meant taking the chance the velocycle might disobey him again, he preferred to leave it with a will of its own. He knelt down to look into the engimal's eyes.

"We have to save my family today, Flash," he said softly. "We have to save the people I love. I could feed you my blood and make you my slave, but I won't. I need a friend now, not a servant . . . But if you let me down this time, I'll have your bloody wheels cut off, you understand?"

Daisy sat on one of the sofas in Hugo's private living room, with one hand resting on the secret pocket which held Gerald's syringe. The curtains had been drawn to hide the morning light, and instead, candles burned in silver holders around the room. The late Duke had indulged his morbid taste in décor with oil paintings and tapestries of gruesome Old Testament scenes in ornate frames, and had equipped the room with outlandishly carved ebony furniture that might have pleased the devil himself, upholstered in blood-red velvet.

She had freshened herself up and changed into a scarlet taffeta gown with a low-cut bodice and suggestive embroidery. It was one of her most provocative dresses and had the added bonus of a hidden pocket in the folds that she normally used for a compact or a handkerchief. It served just as well for concealing a syringe full of gangrenous poison.

As she waited for Hugo to appear, her hands shook, her stomach knotted up and her teeth chattered. She had never been so scared in all her life. Even now, she wasn't sure if she could go through with this. Daisy did not want to kill and she certainly didn't want to die. Left sitting there alone, images flashed through her mind of what Hugo would do to her if she tried to attack him and failed. She found it difficult to breathe. This was no good; if she was to fool him into thinking she was attracted to him, she had to—

"My dear!" he cried. "Sorry to keep you waiting."

He was standing at the door of the hallway that led to his bedroom. Dressed in a burgundy smoking jacket, he had his hair oiled and curled, and a cigarette in a holder in his left hand. The leather collar and chain mail were gone. It seemed she was to have her chance. Stroking his goatee with the fingers of his right hand, he glided across the room and sat down on her left side.

"So, what's your scheme?" he asked, smiling.

"I'm sorry?" she replied, her right hand unconsciously brushing over the syringe.

"Oh, come on," he chided her. "You don't fool me. You're no more devoted to that wastrel of a husband than I am. You're a conniving wench if ever I saw one . . . and I've seen a few, I can tell you. But don't be put off, dear. I like a woman who knows what she wants and will do anything to get it. God helps those who help themselves—and I believe in helping myself to everything I can get my hands on."

Daisy dropped her gaze. She knew she was perspiring, but hoped it would not give her away. Her hands were still now and her jaw had stopped its trembling, but her heart was still racing.

"You see through me, my lord," she said shyly, looking up at him again with her doe-like eyes. "I confess, I married Roberto for what he was, not who he was. And now I fear he is no longer the man I married . . . in so many ways. I am a resourceful woman, my lord. But I am loyal to my master . . . for as long as he lives. The same cannot be said for some of this family. I fear Gideon, for instance, will betray you at the first opportunity."

"Yes, he's a back-stabber, that one," Hugo agreed, sitting back, his arm casually draping across the back of the sofa behind her. "But a coward too. I know where I stand with cowards; they can always be trusted to fold under pressure."

"Men think only of themselves. You need a strong woman by your side," Daisy told him.

"But I have two," he said, pretending not to understand her, and leaning closer to her as if that would help. He placed the burning cigarette in an ashtray on the table in front of them and put his free hand on her knee. "Two women who would die for me if need be."

Daisy's fingers slipped into the pocket and closed around the syringe. His face was inches from hers and she could smell the smoke on his breath. His jacket hung open, with just his shirt and waistcoat covering his chest. She wouldn't get a better chance than this. Her breathing quickened. Gripping the glass cylinder, she pushed the rubber cap off the needle with her thumb.

"It wasn't the role of a sister that I had in mind," she said, staring at the point on his chest, just right of the sternum, where she would have to strike.

"Ah," he sighed, with a raise of his eyebrows. "You hope to steal my heart."

"Not exactly," she said, pulling the syringe from her pocket.

But just as she did so, there was a sharp knock on the door and then Gideon burst in. Daisy pulled the hypodermic back out of sight before it could be seen. Hugo was already on his feet.

"I told you I didn't want to be disturbed!" he roared.

"I wouldn't . . . except . . . I . . ." Gideon stammered.

He stepped aside to reveal a grey-haired, middle-aged man with a ramrod-straight back, dressed in a fine suit. Daisy recognized him immediately. It was the Lord Lieutenant—the Viceroy, the Queen's representative in Ireland.

"What is the meaning of this?" the Viceroy demanded, holding up what looked like a telegram. "Who the blazes are you, sir? Where is the Duke?"

"What is that?" Hugo asked, ignoring the questions and pointing at the piece of paper.

"I received this an hour ago," the Viceroy snapped, holding it up. "Let me read it to you. 'MY BROTHER HAS BEEN MURDERED STOP AN IMPOSTOR HAS TAKEN THE FAMILY HOSTAGE STOP SEND HELP IMMEDIATELY

AND COME IN FORCE STOP GIDEON WILDENSTERN STOP.'"

Gideon looked stunned. Hugo looked ready to spit venom, and would have aimed most of it at Gideon.

"I'm afraid you've been the victim of a prank, sir," the Patriarch said smoothly, managing a pained smile. "The Duke is bedridden with typhus—highly contagious —and as the brother next in line, it has fallen to me to take the reins until he recovers. His sons are not taking it well and have quite lost the run of themselves. It's clear that they sent this message in a fit of pique, hoping to embarrass me . . ."

He gently ushered the two men out of the room, closing the door behind him. Daisy let out a shuddering breath and put her head in her hands. She couldn't take much more of this. Beyond the door she could just hear the men's voices:

"You're the Duke's brother?" the Viceroy exclaimed incredulously. "How have we never met? He's never even spoken of you!"

"A family tiff that has lasted years, I'm afraid," Hugo informed him. "He called for me when he fell ill . . ."

Daisy lifted her head and gave a start as she found a tall black man standing in front of her. She stared up at him for a moment, wondering how he had got there.

"Abraham, isn't it?" she said. "What are you doing here?"

"It's time to leave, ma'am," he replied. "Master Nathaniel has asked us to take you to safety. The chief groom has a carriage waiting for you and your husband at the back entrance. Your husband assures us Mr. Hennessy can be trusted."

"Oh, I'm sure he does," she said acidly.

XXXII

TOO WELL-ARMED FOR TEA

TATIANA PEERED OUT OF HER BEDROOM WINDOW at the company of British cavalry, complete with a behemoth war engimal, approaching the front of the house. They were being led by the Lord Lieutenant's carriage. Striding across the room, she swung the door open and confronted the two Gideonettes standing guard outside.

"Why is the British Army coming up the driveway?" she demanded.

They hurried to the window and looked out. She was pleased to see that they appeared concerned by what they saw.

"It's nothing," one said in an unconvincing voice.

"Just a social visit," the other said, swallowing audibly.

"They seem to me to be a bit too well-armed for morning tea," Tatty observed.

That was when they heard the sound. It was like an angry bee at first, then deeper, like the growling of a big cat. And it was getting louder. Her two cousins drew their pistols and held them up. Tatty cocked her head to one side, listening intently. She recognized the sound.

"It's Nathaniel's velocycle," one of her guards said. "He's in the house; come to save his precious little sister at last. We'll have him now. Must be in the hidden passageways somewhere."

"It can't be." The other shook his head. "A beast that size could never fit in the passages. How could it turn the corners?"

"It's the velocycle, I tell you," the first one insisted. "He's going to try and just charge in and take her, the confounded fool!"

They leaned out into the corridor, revolvers at the ready. Tatty walked behind a screen in her room and started to undress, peeking through the cracks in the hinges to keep a weather eye on her two sentries.

"My big brother's coming!" she called to them as she shrugged the dress off her shoulders. "You're in trouble now!"

"Shut up!" one of them shouted back; then to his own brother, "There! Behind the oak panels—he's in the south passage!"

They sprinted down the corridor, following the sound of Flash's engine. Near the end of a row of oak panels, they pressed a knot and a secret door sprang open. The engine sounds grew suddenly louder. With their guns raised, they made ready to fire at the figure within.

"Thank God!" Gerald cried out. "I thought I'd be lost in there for days!"

That was when Nathaniel came out of the room behind them

and, with vicious speed, struck each one over the back of the head with his revolver. Gerald stepped out and handed the small engimal with the ladybird spots to Nate, who quieted it with a word. The engine sounds stopped.

"A marvelous contraption," Gerald remarked. "You'll have to let me dissect it some day."

"You have no soul," Nate sniped back. "I'd never let you get your grubby mitts on Babylon."

"I should hope not!"

They turned to find Tatiana standing waiting for them, dressed once again in Nate's old clothes. Nate smiled proudly.

"Good God," said Gerald.

"This whole sorry affair has opened my eyes," Tatiana informed them as she handed them some curtain cord. "I've decided I want to devote my life to the furthering of women's rights."

"This," said Gerald, "is what comes of letting women wear trousers."

Using the curtain cord, they quickly bound and gagged the Gideonettes and threw them into a cupboard where they would not be found for some time. Then they made their way through the hidden passageway down to Gerald's rooms. Roberto had already been stolen away by Abraham and his brothers and Edgar's corpse had been taken to the refrigerators. Only Clancy and Brutus remained. The giant ancestor lay there in his bed, the occasional twitch in his face and hands showing the slow surfacing of his consciousness.

Standing near the door was Flash, and tied up next to it was the boy who worked the elevator.

"I wouldn't've squealed," he protested.

"Sorry, we couldn't take the chance," Nate told him, urging Tatty to get on the velocycle. "Ger, you sure you want to stay? It's going to get a bit hairy."

"I want to make sure Clancy is stable before I move him; and besides, I need to pack up a few things," Gerald replied. "My work's too important to leave in the hands of these luddites."

"Right, then," Nate said, shaking his cousin's hand. "Good luck."

"And you, old chum."

Nate climbed into the saddle and tapped the engimal's sides with his heels. The velocycle purred quietly as they rolled out of the door and down towards the elevator halfway down the corridor. The doors had been jammed open to keep the lift car where it was, but as they crept down the hallway towards it, Brunhilde came round the corner at the far end of the corridor with three footmen. They were all armed with pistols and double-barreled shotguns.

"Bugger," Nate swore, seeing that they couldn't make it to the elevator without being shot. "We'll have to take the stairs."

There was no need to be quiet any longer. Swinging Flash round in a circle, Nate steered his mount down a side corridor, Tatty clinging on tightly as the velocycle's engine rose into a joyous roar. Leaping forward, they covered the twenty yards to the end of the hallway in seconds, swerving at the top of the landing between the staircases and plunging down the steps towards the next floor. Flash made the tight turn, swinging its back wheel round with a deft flick of its hips, and down again they went, the two riders rattled by the bouncing of Flash's wheels over the steps. The noise of its engine was loud in the stairwell, but Nate reveled in the sheer power of it and roared in unison.

They made it down two more flights before a shotgun blast nearly caught them, taking chunks out of the wall above their heads. Brunhilde had taken the elevator to a floor below them and was coming up the stairs towards them with some of her men.

"Shed light on their insides!" she screamed, opening the smoking gun to reload.

Nate wondered momentarily where she had learned to use a scattergun, but he was already turning the velocycle, its spinning wheels burning scars across the carpet as they skidded off the landing and down the hallway.

"We need to make it to the stairs on the other side!" he yelled to his sister over the bellowing engine. "I think we can take a shortcut through the dining room!"

Tatty nodded in agreement as Nate turned in a wide doorway and through an anteroom into the massive dining room. Footmen were running down towards them on either side of the long dining table, but Nate jumped Flash up onto the tabletop, knocking candlesticks and vases of flowers flying as they raced down its length and flew off the end, leaving a trail of burned French polish. As soon as its feet touched the floor, Flash was turned out of another door, on through an unused hall to the corridor beyond, which led to the stairs on the other side of the tower.

Rattling down another few flights, they found their way blocked by a barricade of furniture, and Nate only just lifted the front wheel in time before they careered straight into it. Flash half rammed, half climbed over the pile of wood, sending the defending footmen running for cover. But as it landed, Nate was unable to turn his engimal in time, and they spun into a suit of armor in a corner of the landing with a crash of metal, sending pieces of it everywhere. Seizing the arrowhead-shaped shield—a gauntlet still dangling from it—Nate got Flash back on its feet and only barely deflected the pistol shots fired at them as they took off down the corridor.

"The other side again?" Tatty asked expectantly.

"I suppose so," he sighed, throwing the shield away.

They passed through one deserted hall after another, cutting across the building. Every now and then Nate slowed and looked out of the windows, hoping for another exit.

"I had no idea so much of the house was unused," Tatty noted. "It seems such a waste."

"Perhaps we'll deal with that when we come back," Nate replied, steering them down another corridor.

The family would be using the speaking tubes and elevators to pen them in. The servants would be converging on them from top and bottom. They had to get out of the house . . . quickly. Two more flights of stairs brought them to the fourth floor. Nate skidded to a halt, breathing hard and thinking fast. Turning a corner, he saw a window at the end of the corridor. He pulled off his jacket and threw it over Tatiana's head and shoulders. He hoped it would be enough.

"Keep your head down and hold on tight," he said to her. Then, to Flash, he added. "This is it . . . Don't fail me now."

The velocycle responded with a thrilled growl and they accelerated forward, the carpet wrinkling under the grip of the wheels as they drove the beast on. Nate lowered his head and screamed as Flash hurled them through the window.

Broken wood and glass cut gashes in his face, neck and hands as they exploded out of the building. They landed with a brittle thud on one side of the gabled roof of the south wing, sloughing slate tiles away beneath their spinning wheels as they slid down the slope, the old roof barely supporting the velocycle's weight. They were going too fast to stop and they hurtled towards the edge . . . Nate pulling back to lift Flash's front wheel as they slipped off in a shower of slate and glass and splintered wood, falling, falling, until they hit the roof of the stables and Flash's back wheel punched through, jarring the two riders to the bone as they came to an abrupt stop.

"Come on, come on!" Nate screeched, struggling to free the velocycle.

Tatiana pushed down with her feet too but it was useless. The roof collapsed inwards, sending them tumbling into the building. They plunged through the hay store on the first floor, which slowed their fall before the boards gave way under Flash's plummeting weight and they crashed through to the ground. Tatiana screamed as she landed heavily on her side. Nate had the breath knocked out of him and hit his head against a broken rafter.

The grooms hurried to the scene, standing uncertainly, reluctant to lay hands on this man who had once been one of their masters. Nate rose from the wreckage of wood and hay, bloodied and covered in dust.

"Get out of my way," he snarled. And they did.

Pulling the velocycle onto its feet, he picked up his sister and helped her onto the saddle behind him. The engimal shook itself and snorted steam and then it reared, its back wheel grinding smoke off the ground. They lunged forward, out of the stable doors and round the house towards the front gate. The speeding shape raced across the grass, through the company of cavalry, startling horses and raising angry shouts from their riders. The war engimal, a navy-skinned creature the size of a large coach, with six wheels and a triangular head jutting with tusks, looked on dispassionately. It did not move without orders.

It turned to watch the velocycle skid onto the cobbled drive-way, sprint down between the two rows of poplar trees and disappear out of the gate. When it turned back to face the front, what it saw caused it to rise up on its hind wheels with a frightened squeal, throwing its rider. The fearsome war engimal staggered back, swiveled and bolted for the forest at the side of the house. The horses followed it with wide, panicked eyes.

From around the other side of the house, crushing the cobbles beneath their feet, the ground shaking beneath their great weight, came Trom and Colossus. On the back of the bull-razer, holding the reins, was Slattery, with Elizabeth beside him. Hugo and Brunhilde rode the juggernaut, and from the top of each behemoth, lengths of snake-chain coiled and reached out at the will of their master. And Hugo, wearing his chain mail once more with his suit and top hat, screamed an exultant battle cry as his monsters chased down their prey.

XXXIII

THE IMPORTANCE OF BEING PUNCTUAL

NATE LOOKED BACK, but could see no signs of pursuit. He wondered how long it would take Hugo to get clear of the Viceroy's soldiers, marshal his own forces and come after the fugitives. Nate just needed time to reach the train station in Kingstown. Abraham would meet him there with Daisy and Roberto so they could make their escape together. He squeezed Tatty's hand where it clung to his waist. He was hoping the British would delay Hugo for a while, but the first moves had been made, at least. He had to time this right. The timing was crucial.

They had covered more than three miles and were scrambling up a narrow sloping lane when the flock of leaf-lights struck silently and without warning. They swooped into Flash's path and swept across Nate and Tatty, their sharp edges cutting like a hail of glass shards. Thrown out of the saddle, brother and sister landed hard on the ground in a sprawling heap. Nate rolled up onto his feet, then dropped into a crouch to shield Tatty, pulling his jacket over her head again as the engimals came in once more, sweeping over him, raking their blades across his shoulders and back. He cried out, as much in anger as in pain. There seemed no way to fight these elusive creatures. Pulling out his revolver, he fired at them, over and over again, knocking two or three from the air, but there were dozens more and now his gun was empty. He frantically tried to reload before they came back in again, fumbling rounds into the chambers.

But they were changing tactics. The leaf-lights rolled together as they dived, wrapping into a single long spear-shaped formation that picked up speed as it solidified. Nate dived out of its way at the last moment, only to face it again seconds later as it spun and came at him from the opposite direction. It was only feet from him when Flash reared up on one side, blasting a jet of steam from its nostrils. The leaf-light javelin shot through the gushing, boiling-hot steam, and there was a high-pitched buzzing as the projectile burst into its component parts. The leaf-lights swirled in confused pain. Nate seized his jacket and swung it over them, gathering as many as he could in the material and bunching them together before swinging the thrashing bundle hard against the ground, over and over again until it went still. He jumped on it a few times for good measure.

The few remaining engimals fluttered up into the air, out of his reach. But just four or five of them could offer no threat. Nate heaved in deep breaths, wincing at the pain from a hundred small cuts. He noted with satisfaction that the older ones were already closing up. His inherited defenses were kicking in, his healing accelerated by the adrenaline coursing through his body. His muscles felt charged up from the rush, and despite the pain, a smile split his blood-stained face.

"That wasn't the act of a slave!" he said fondly to Flash, slapping its side. "You roasted them! By God, I'll make a warhorse out of you yet!"

"You're enjoying this," Tatiana said miserably.

He didn't answer, picking her up instead and getting into the saddle before helping her on behind him. No sooner had Flash started forward than they heard a sound like a cattle stampede and the ground started to tremble. Smashing through the trees behind him came Colossus, with Hugo and Elizabeth riding on its back. Trom rumbled along not far behind. They could not match Flash's speed, but whereas the velocycle had to work its way round the landscape, the behemoths could trample a line straight through it. Elizabeth's leaf-lights had bought them all the time they needed to catch up.

High hedges barred the way on either side, so Flash was forced to go uphill. Colossus was driving through walls and hedges to cut them off, while Trom lumbered up from behind. Flash brushed past only an instant before Colossus charged across the laneway. A chain snaked out, its link mouth catching onto Flash's right rear leg and starting to pull the velocycle back. Nate drew his pistol and shot the snake-chain twice in the head, severing it. But another was already locking onto the saddle behind Tatty. It yanked them back as Colossus turned and threatened to pull them under the juggernaut's wheels. Nate couldn't reach round to aim at the chain's head.

"Hang on!" he yelled.

There was slight slope on the huge enginal's head—enough for Nate to spin Flash round and, with its wheels spinning wildly, ride the velocycle right up onto the juggernaut's shoulders and over its back. Nate kicked Hugo out of his way, shooting the chain where its tail anchored it to the juggernaut's carapace. Still dragging the rest of the snake-chain after him, he rode down Colossus's tail . . . and straight out in front of Trom.

Nate jinked right and the slow-witted enginal followed him, its shovel-shaped jaw digging into the ground and throwing up earth like a sea wave, bearing down on the velocycle and its riders. Nate rode Flash up, tilted almost horizontal along the wave, bursting out at the end of it as Trom's enormous jaw rammed straight into the side of the juggernaut, bringing both behemoths to a juddering halt, chains slapping against their armor like tentacles.

The behemoth's riders had no chance to use their firearms before Flash and its riders disappeared over the crest of the hill. The snake-chain that was still hanging onto their saddle now coiled up and swung its three yards of tail over the front of the velocycle, wrapping around the riders like a constricting snake, trying to crush the life out of them. Tatty took the pistol from Nate's hand and calmly shot the thing in the head.

The two fugitives and their mount made it to the small, red-brick train station by the sea with time to spare. The train was still there, its barrel-shaped iron locomotive seeping steam as it sat waiting to depart. They were a strange sight to behold: the Beast of Glenmalure, being ridden along the platform by two bedraggled, bloodstained members of the gentry—one a young woman in men's clothes. Daisy and Abraham, who had been anxiously watching out for them by the door of their train compartment, ran up to greet them.

Nate and Tatiana dismounted stiffly, sore and tired. The thrill of the chase had left them and now they were feeling the aftereffects. Daisy hugged Tatty, examining her wounds with concern. Nate and Abraham shook hands, no longer master and servant, but still unable to be equal. Abraham handed Nate a rapier in its scabbard and Nate drew it out a few inches to check the sharpness of the blade.

"They're coming," he said at last, looking up at a single leaf-light that floated in the air above the roof of the station building. "We have a few minutes at most."

"Could the train outrun them?" Daisy asked.

"An engine like this can do nearly sixty miles per hour, ma'am," Abraham told her. "More than Trom could manage, I'm sure. I'm not certain about the juggernaut."

"It'll be all right," Nate said confidently.

"You're sure this will work? That Roberto won't be put at any risk?" Daisy persisted.

"All aboard!" the train's guard bellowed, blowing on his whistle and moving along the train to close any open doors.

"No," Nate replied, looking her in the eye. "I'm not sure of anything. We can only try."

"I suppose we can," she sighed, nodding. "All right, then. Let's do this. And may God go with us."

"Any help at all would be appreciated," Nate said as he helped her up into the carriage.

He turned to shake hands again with Abraham.

"This is where we part ways," he said. "I hope I'll see you and your brothers again soon. Good luck."

"I think you will need the luck more than we will," Abraham told him with a grim smile. "God-speed, Master Nathaniel."

"And to you," Nate responded, gripping the other man's hand tightly.

And for the first time in years, Nathaniel offered up a heart-felt prayer; just in case there was anyone up there still listening.

The locomotive started out of the station, southbound. Heaving and hissing, its pistons pushing the central driving wheels, which stood taller than a grown man, it gradually picked up speed in a cloud of smoke and soot and steam. It breathed like an asthmatic buffalo, but there the similarity with a living beast ended. This marvel of the Victorian Age had little in common with any animal, particularly the vigorous, fluid and tireless movements of engimals. But it had changed the landscape of this century in a way that they never could, and the iron engine moved now with seemingly unstoppable momentum, steadily gaining speed.

Its puffing grew louder and faster as they left Kingstown behind them and carried on along the rails and down the coast. The driver looked out from under the arched roof, through the round window of the cab at the track ahead, as the other engineman shoveled coal into the firebox and watched the boiler's gauge with an experienced eye. The engine panted quickly now; traveling at speed, it passed through pastoral land, which dropped away to the sea on its left; fields dotted with clachans and villages on its right.

Suddenly the man looking out of the window let out a cry of warning, reaching for the controls. The engine's brakes squealed, quickly followed by the brakes in the guard's van behind the carriages, but these trains could slow down no quicker than they could accelerate. There was a shriek of metal sliding against metal as the wheels scraped sparks off the rails. The enginemen blew the whistle in alarm, the train skidding inexorably towards its doom. The carriages' buffers impacted against one another as they were slowed suddenly from either end, and inside, people were thrown from their seats. Panic ensued.

And then the massive bull-razer the driver had seen careering towards them on a collision course crashed into the side of the locomotive, smashing the twenty-five tons of iron off its rails and sending it toppling over on its side. The six-wheeled tender tumbled after it, carpeting the ground with lumps of coal before it was pummeled aside by the carriages slamming into it from behind. Half the train followed the locomotive off the rails . . . and then, with a deafening crunch, the juggernaut rammed the guard's car, sending it over on its side and pulling the rest of the carriages with it.

Hugo stood up and gazed out on the devastation and saw that it was good. From the back of Colossus he could see the entire train lying on its side in ruin. Steam billowed up from the split boiler in the locomotive and smoke gushed from the twisted, punctured smokestack. People were starting to emerge, climbing out through the doors and shattered windows. Slattery blasted the roof of the train twice with his shotgun and there was more screaming.

"We're looking for four people!" he roared, casually reloading the weapon. "Two ladies, a young gentleman and his cripple of a brother. They are all we want. The rest of you may flee in safety!"

He jumped down from Trom and strode over to the wreck, climbing onto the first carriage. Elizabeth stayed on the bull-razer's back to keep watch in case any of their prey tried to escape. Hugo and Brunhilde climbed onto the side of the overturned train at the other end and started to walk down its length, each armed with a pistol and a sword. Brunhilde still wore a smart crinoline dress, and she held the hoops up with one hand as she climbed, revealing her bloomers in a most undignified manner, looking like an uncouth little girl determined to join in the boys' games.

The three met towards the rear end of the first-class carriage. Looking down through the remains of the glass in the windows, they found what they were looking for: Daisy, Tatiana and Roberto lay semiconscious in a sprawling heap on the internal wall of the compartment.

"Where's the other one?" Hugo hissed.

Elizabeth saw her brother's posture change and immediately knew something was wrong. She had regained her leaf-light cloak, looking a little worse for wear but otherwise undamaged. She raised her hand, ready to gesture the little engimals into attack. Instinct made her look round at that moment and Nate's fist caught her square across the cheekbone and knocked her flying. She fell off the far side of Trom's back, landing head-first on the dry turf. Nate dropped down and glared at her as she lay there, seeing the jagged angle of her neck. She wasn't dead, but she was close enough to it for now. The leaf-lights continued to wait patiently for instructions from their silent mistress.

On the carriage, Daisy had been pulled up through the door, and now Brunhilde was gripping her by the hair and banging her head against the wooden wall of the carriage.

"Where's the delicious one?" the gibbering woman asked, yanking on Daisy's hair to bring their faces nose to nose.

"You'll see soon enough!" Daisy snapped back, tears in her eyes.

Her hand found the pocket hiding the syringe and felt that it was still intact. Brunhilde smacked her head against the wall again and Daisy let out a cry. Her body was already racked with pain and each impact shot bolts of it through her skull. Hugo leaned in through the window.

Tatty was struggling to get to her feet and Roberto looked in terrible shape, lying unconscious on twisted limbs, his stretcher fallen on top of him.

"He wasn't on the train," Hugo said softly Then he bellowed it. *"He wasn't on the bloody train!"*

Flash's engine came upon them in a sudden roar and Nate leaped from the engimal's back as it piled into Slattery in a high-speed charge that hurled them both off the side of the carriage and over onto the ground below. Flash got back on its feet. Slattery did not.

Nate came to a running stop as he drew his sword and almost managed to drive the point of it into Hugo's unprotected thigh, but the Patriarch drew his cutlass with blurring speed and parried the strike. They pulled apart, swords in the guard position.

"You used your own *family* as bait to draw us out," Hugo remarked with a mixture of disgust and admiration. "Have you no conscience?"

"To be honest, I didn't think you'd actually crash the train," Nate admitted. "I thought you'd just block its path."

In fact, the ferocity of Hugo's assault had wrecked Nate's plans, and the sight of all the dead and injured had shaken him to the core. But it was too late to do anything about it now.

"You still have much to learn about the use of force," Hugo told him, and lunged in with an attack.

Nate swept it aside, cutting inside Hugo's guard at his torso, but the Patriarch's chain mail saved him. He came back at Nate in a repost that nearly drove the point of the cutlass into Nate's belly. Nate beat it down and twisted his own blade around it as it came back up, binding it and sweeping it aside once more. He struck out with a kick to Hugo's solar plexus, throwing the older man backwards and following him, blade driving forward. Hugo dodged the strike, flipped back onto his feet and came at his younger opponent again with a bewildering series of jabs and thrusts. Nate was astounded by the old man's strength and speed. With skills honed during years of medieval battles, Hugo began to drive him steadily backwards.

•　•　•

Brunhilde rose up, taking her pistol and drawing a bead on
Nathaniel as the two men fought with a frantic clashing of steel.
Daisy seized her chance and, pulling the syringe from her pocket,
went to jab at Brunhilde's side—only to find her wrist caught in
a crushing grip. Brunhilde's hand had moved impossibly fast and
without her even looking, and now she was forcing the needle
back. She turned on Daisy, her mouth open in a shrill battle cry,
the gun raised not to shoot, but to beat her victim to death in an
animal frenzy.

Daisy's thumb jammed the hypodermic's plunger home,
spraying the poison into the mad woman's face. Brunhilde yelped,
knocking the syringe from Daisy's hand so that it smashed against
the wall of the carriage. She staggered up onto her feet, letting
out little cries, rubbing her eyes as if they were burning. She
gagged on the toxins in her mouth.

Daisy looked in despair at the shattered syringe. Her chance
was gone. Half blind, Brunhilde snatched up her great Claymore sword and, raising it over her head, rushed towards Daisy.
A small, dainty hand reached up from inside the compartment
and grabbed the hem of her dress as she charged, catching her
feet and sending her face-first down onto the carriage wall. Her
sword clattered out of her hands and Daisy seized it, the weight
of it nearly pulling her over as she swung it back over her shoulder. Brunhilde scrambled to her feet and Daisy swung the blade
with all her might. With her eyes shut. She screamed as she felt
the sword catch something in mid-swing before flying from her
hands. Opening her eyes, she stared into the fierce glare of the
warrior woman.

Brunhilde's expression was so savage that it took Daisy a moment to realize that the woman's head was slipping from her neck. The head dropped into the carriage compartment below her, and her decapitated body collapsed over on its side. Tatiana sidestepped the falling head as it bounced against the lower wall and climbed up out of the compartment, looking from Daisy to the dead body and back in wonder.

"I always . . . always told her not to run in . . . in that dress," Daisy panted.

"No breeding," Tatiana agreed, before wrapping her arms around her sister-in-law's trembling body and holding her close.

Further down the train, Nate was losing his fight. He was being forced back, ever closer to the end of the carriages, to where the jagged wreckage of the tender lay between them and the ruined locomotive. Every thrust he made was met with the ringing of steel as Hugo answered and bettered his move, attacking viciously in return. Hugo caught him, the cutlass blade opening the flesh of his sword-arm just above the wrist. Nate flinched back in reflex and Hugo cut him again below the ribs of his right side. It was all Nate could do to keep his guard up. He bled from a dozen wounds, his movements uncoordinated and awkward, slower and slower as he weakened under Hugo's barrage. But Hugo was not unscathed. Despite his chain mail and protective collar, he bled too. For every dirty move that Hugo tried, Nate had two—drawn from a lifetime of training in the fighting arts, from both East and West. He attacked with punches and kicks and knees and leg sweeps, keeping Hugo at bay with an array of moves unknown to a medieval knight. They fought like demons—every limb a weapon, every drop of blood spilled dearly. But Hugo's experience and superhuman strength were beginning to tell.

Nate stumbled back, stopping just short of the edge of the carriage, nothing behind him but the torn iron of the tender and, beyond it, the wreck of the locomotive, flames coughing fiercely from its firebox and starting to spread across the spilled piles of coal. The air over the hellish scene was full of gritty, choking smoke. He nearly lost his balance, and his arms went out to regain it . . . leaving him wide open. Hugo drove his sword into Nate's side. Nate screamed, dropping his own blade. As Hugo made to pull back for another thrust, Nate clasped his hands around his ancestor's and lunged backwards, still impaled on the sword. Hugo was thrown forwards, tumbling over Nate's head as they fell into the pile of coal in the wreck of the tender. A sharp, white-hot pain shot through Nate as he landed, and the sword twisted in the wound, making him cry out again. Hugo got to his knees; jamming one foot against Nate's hip, he wrenched the bloodied blade out and raised it for a killing blow. But just as he did so, three figures rose up from beneath the coal, seizing his arms and legs in wrestling holds. He fought like a berserker to break free, but the Maasai were too strong, too well-trained, their hearts too set on vengeance.

"Unhand me, you blasted blackamoors!" Hugo shrieked, thrashing vainly against their iron grip. "What are you doing? What is this?!"

"This," said Abraham in a deep, calm voice, "is your personal Hell, Hugo Wildenstern. And we are here to deliver you to it."

"You can't do this!" Hugo screamed at Nathaniel. "You would let *servants* do your killing for you?!"

"They are free men now. What they do with you is their business," Nate retorted, sitting up with a grunt and pressing his hands against the wound. Not wanting to show how badly he was hurt, he got unsteadily to his feet and turned his back on his ancestor. Then he added: "I never wanted you dead—I just wanted you out of my house."

And with that, he walked away to join his family.

XXXIV

BRUTUS

GERALD LEANED BACK AGAINST THE WORKBENCH, smoking a cigarette and staring at Brutus. With all the family conflict going on around him, there had been little time to consider how recent events were going to affect his work. Now that he had a moment to think about it, it dawned on him that if Nate's plans succeeded, the ancestors' extraordinary bodies could be lost to science.

And Nate had to succeed—the prospect of these throwbacks taking control of the family was unthinkable. But while Gerald would have been the first to admit that the four ancients were abominations of the highest order (even for Wildensterns), he despaired at the thought of losing the greatest chance of discovering the true nature of the intelligent particles. If a transfusion of Hugo's blood could help Clancy recover from a mortal wound, understanding those particles could change the course of medicine for ever.

So Gerald made a decision there and then. He would take Brutus's inert body down to the cellars, where he could tell Nate he had incinerated it in the huge boilers that heated the house. There were forgotten rooms down in the foundations of Wildenstern Hall where Gerald stored some of his equipment, as well as more illicit materials he wanted to keep from prying eyes. He would keep Brutus there, where he could carry on his experiments in secrecy.

Gerald had enormous faith in his cousin. Nate had yet to realize his full potential in the family but Gerald knew what a formidable opponent he could be. If he succeeded in defeating Hugo and his sisters, for the sake of science it was imperative that at least one of the ancestors be kept alive.

The moral implications of what he was doing did not particularly bother Gerald—he considered himself a servant to a higher cause that could override all other considerations. Anything was justified to advance along the path of science.

On the off-chance that Nate *failed,* Gerald could always tell Hugo that he had been trying to save Brutus's life. That part at least would be true.

There wasn't a moment to lose, but there was still the problem of moving a man of Brutus's size without the help of too many loose-lipped servants. Gerald stepped over to the sleeping giant and put a hand on his brow—then he jerked back as the monster let out a trembling moan.

•   •   •

Brutus awoke. His consciousness returned gradually and he lay still with his eyes closed and let it come. As his awareness of his body stretched out along his limbs, a terrible pain in his right arm told him he had been wounded in the fight. He could remember a mighty struggle, hands grabbing him, blades cutting him. He tried to flex the fingers of his right hand, and though he was sure he could feel them to their tips, there was no movement against his hip, where they lay. Instead, something cold and hard twitched against his skin. He had heard about this from men who had lost limbs in battle. Ghost pain. His hand was gone—replaced by some clumsy tool of metal.

Brutus did not know why he was not dead. Perhaps Hugo and their sisters had saved him, but his one clear memory was of them lying in a bog grave, their bodies ravaged with wounds. Earth was being thrown upon their faces. Perhaps someone had kept him alive to prolong his torture. As his thoughts turned to his family, he was struck with the certainty that they were in mortal danger. He must act.

His memories were confused; he could not think clearly. Opening his eyes, he found his vision was blurred. The room around him looked large and bright, with tall rectangular windows that blinded him with their light. He was in a bed, and on his left side, on a small table, were what could have been small weapons or surgical tools. His hand clumsily grasped the largest, a saw of polished metal. As he sat up, his unfocused eyes picked out the shape of a man lying in a bed a few feet away to his right. Brutus could see no details, but the man was not moving.

That was when he looked down at his right arm and saw the claw attached to it. The claw opened as he lifted it, and clicked closed as he pushed it away. What sorcery was this? He gaped in horror, but stayed silent.

Then he noticed the man standing to his left. The man's left hand held a short white stick from which smoke was rising lazily. His right hand was in his hair and he was staring at Brutus in what looked like awe.

"My God," the man said in a low voice. "You're awake!"

He was dressed in strange, straight-edged clothes unlike any Brutus had seen before, and he knew now that he had fallen into foreign hands. He was among enemies. A violent rage came over him, old battle instincts coming to the fore. His powerful muscles bunched, the hand holding the saw swung back.

Gerald stumbled backwards an instant before the naked seven-foot-tall medieval ogre, with gold needles protruding from his skin, slashed at the young doctor's neck with the bone-saw. Brutus let out a cry of savage aggression as the saw embedded itself in the top of the table. He pulled it free, his newly awakened body moving with a raw but cumbersome power. Staggering forward, he made to attack again.

"Wait! Wait! I can take you to your family!" Gerald cried.

The giant hesitated, breathing heavily. The fist holding the saw was poised in midair.

"That's what you want, isn't it?" Gerald said softly. "To be with your brother, Hugo, and your two sisters, Elizabeth and Brunhilde?"

Brutus was still for a moment, but then he nodded.

"Yhheeess," he croaked with vocal chords that hadn't worked in centuries.

"Come with me then, and I'll take you to them."

Brutus stood unmoving for what seemed like an age . . . and then lowered the blade. Gerald could see just how weak the giant was; the initial effort of the attack had emptied him out and it was taking all his strength to stand upright. But maybe he had enough left in him to make it to the elevator. Once Gerald had walked him down to the cellars, he was sure the ogre would have no fight left in him and could be subdued with a minimum of effort.

"That's it," Gerald said in an encouraging voice. "That's a good fellow. You'll be safe with me."

Brutus rested his right arm on Gerald's shoulders, causing the younger man to stoop under the giant's enormous weight. The claw opened and clicked closed again, inches from Gerald's face. He patted the arm nervously and started to lead his research subject towards the door. Brutus's fingers loosened their grip on the saw and it clattered to the floor.

Clancy woke to see Gerald crumpling under the weight of the ogre, one giant arm wrapped around his neck. Slowly, to avoid attracting attention, the manservant swung his legs off the bed.

Brutus slipped and lost his footing, bringing his whole weight down on Gerald's shoulders. Gerald let out a loud grunt as he tried to remain standing. A moment later, Clancy piled into

Brutus, knocking Gerald aside. The young doctor watched in despair as Clancy charged the howling giant straight towards the window and, with a crash of glass, shoved him through. Clancy nearly followed him out, but Gerald darted forward, grabbed him and pulled him back. They both leaned out of the window to see the remains of the ogre splayed on the ground several stories below. There had been no conveniently placed gargoyle this time.

"Well . . ." Gerald gasped, straightening up unsteadily. "That's the end of that."

Gulping air, he nodded his thanks to Clancy. The pale-faced footman sank back onto the bed, clutching his bandaged chest. Gerald hurried out of the door and along to the elevator, eager to see if there was anything of Brutus's body to salvage.

"I suppose that was one way of getting him downstairs."

Francie had gone to great pains to assure his father that the Wildensterns would not be coming after him. Shay found it hard to believe: the Wildensterns were not known for their forgiveness. It was only after Francie had informed him that Master Nathaniel not only knew the full story of the botched robberies and had kept quiet about it, but had also promoted Francie to the position of groom in the engimals' stable, that Shay finally had to admit that it sounded like they were in the clear. Even so, he persisted, it was all a bit fishy if you asked him.

Francie still felt a wave of cold fear come over him when Patrick Slattery walked in as they were sitting over pints of stout in McAuley's. Shay went tense beside him, gripping the edge of the rough-hewn table. But the bailiff was a changed man. McAuley's was the local for many of the Wildenstern staff, and word had got round in the week since the catastrophic train wreck that Slattery had been fired by the family and that his name had been blackened by rumors of murder, so he could not find work anywhere else. Everyone knew that the disaster on the railway had been caused by Trom and everyone knew who drove the bull-razer. Slattery's expensive suit was dirty and disheveled and he wore bandages on his head and one hand. There was a sullen look in his eyes that dared anyone to give him grief. Despite his loss of status, he could still inspire fear. He stood by the bar and ordered a whisky, downed it in one and then demanded another.

Francie was struck by a sudden need to empty his bladder. He slid out from behind the table. He had to walk past Slattery, and the bailiff glanced down at him as he made his way out. He imagined the man's gaze drilling into his back as he unlatched the door and stepped outside. It was a damp night; a light drizzle was falling and Francie trudged through the mud round to the back of the pub. There was always a stench from the outhouse so he avoided it, choosing to relieve himself into the hedge behind it.

Someone came out after him: he heard footsteps in the mud and then the sound of two horses trotting towards the pub. There had been no sign of them on the road when Francie had come out; they must have been down under the trees at the bend. The outhouse door opened and there was an indrawn breath and a curse. Francie recognized Slattery's voice just a few feet away. He froze. He didn't want to go bumping into that fellow in the dark. Before the door could close again, the horses drew up.

"Patrick Slattery?" a man called out.

"Who's askin'?" Slattery snapped back.

"A friend of Eoin Duffy's," the man replied.

Francie flinched as a shot rang out and then another. Something heavy fell against the outhouse door and there were three more shots. The horses whinnied and their riders shouted and then they were gone, galloping away into the drizzling night.

Francie cautiously looked round the end of the wall. Slattery lay dead against the toilet, his body across the threshold, his chin pressed against his chest as if he were asleep. Men were coming out of the pub; there were excited shouts, questions and fearful warnings.

"Jaysus, it's Slattery," someone said. "Someone's done 'im in."

They formed a semicircle around the corpse, and for some time there wasn't a word. They took off their hats, shifting their feet and looking uncomfortably at one another. Then, at last, Shay said:

"Sure, it was the best cure for 'im, God rest 'is soul. Let's get 'im out of there now—it's no fit place for the deceased."

And so men who had despised the bailiff while he lived gathered to lift his body up and carry it inside, finally treating Patrick Slattery with all the consideration, respect and diffidence he could have wished for . . . had he not been dead.

SUFFER NO WEAKNESS

EPILOGUE

THE NEW PATRIARCH

DAISY WAS WAITING IN A CHAIR by Roberto's bedside when he finally regained his senses. He had been feverish for more than a week, racked by pain from his injuries. His sleep was troubled by nightmares, and when he woke, he would suffer delusions brought on by his agony or the laudanum given him to ease it.

Even as she nursed him, she wondered about their future. How could she forgive him for his infidelity? It was hugely humiliating for her and the greatest betrayal of her trust. If word got out about it—as it surely would—she would hear whispers and muffled laughs wherever she went. But worse was the knowledge that she was trapped in a marriage with a man who did not love her—who was in love with another man, one old enough to be his father. She had heard of this kind of thing before, of course; the upper classes had all sorts of strange habits, but Roberto was her *husband*. She'd be giving him a piece of her mind, he could count on that.

Then one day he opened his eyes and looked over from his bed at his wife and smiled weakly, and she knew that it was an argument that could wait until he was better prepared for it. As a friend, she owed him that much at least.

"How are you feeling?" she asked, smiling back at him.

"I'm starving . . . Thirsty too," he replied. "Other than that . . ."

His voice drifted off as he tried to move his legs. A look of sorrow came over him.

"Gerald says there might still be hope," Daisy told him, getting on her knees by his side and taking his hand. "You have your ancestors' blood in you. He said anything is possible."

"Having met my ancestors, I'm inclined to agree," Berto snorted. "That said, I'm not sure I'm happy having their blood crawling around in my veins. Heaven knows what it's getting up to in there. Is everyone else all right? Tatty? Nate? What about Clancy? Did he make it?"

"They're all fine," she reassured him. "Although Clancy refuses to stay in bed even though he still has a hole in his chest, and Tatty ordered a suit of *boy's clothes* to be made for her the other day. I'm not sure quite what to make of that. Nate and I have been busy putting the house in order for you."

"What do you mean?"

"Darling," she said, squeezing his hand. "You're the Patriarch now."

"Oh, bugger," he sighed.

The door opened and Nathaniel peeked in.

"Bloody hell! He's back from the dead!" he exclaimed, rushing across to his brother.

"God! Don't say that!" Berto protested, grinning as he clutched his brother's hand. "There's been quite enough of that, I think. What . . . what's happened to them, anyway?" His face went suddenly somber. "Are they . . . ?"

"It's over," Nate told him, his hand going self-consciously to the fast-healing wound in his side.

And it *was* over, for the most part. They saw no reason to trouble Berto yet with the news that Elizabeth had escaped somehow, despite her injuries, and that Gideon was trying to have Nate exiled for his very public duel with Hugo. A blatant breach of the Rules of Ascension, he argued, even if Hugo had instigated it—not that the family were in a mood to listen to him. They still weren't sure whether or not he had actually sent the telegram to the Viceroy. The British were outraged over the train crash and were demanding answers, and the entire family were at each other's throats over the whole affair.

Abraham and his two brothers were gone too. The last time Daisy had seen them was boarding a ship for Southampton, from where they hoped to find passage to Kenya. They had said something about wanting to kill a lion.

Daisy had been pressing Nate to help her persuade Berto to do away with the family's barbaric Rules once and for all. And he seemed inclined to agree with her, although they both doubted if it could be achieved so simply. It was more likely to take generations to filter all the conspirators, traitors and murderers out of the family. Gerald continued to insist that, as a woman, it was none of Daisy's business anyway.

Not that he was very interested himself. He had personally disposed of Brutus's body in the house's boilers and was now immersed in his studies to investigate the so-called "intelligent particles." Whatever Nate and Daisy decided to do about the family's traditions was apparently of no concern to him.

But it seemed that Berto, even in his fragile state, was one step ahead of them.

"If I'm going to be in charge, I want to change a few things around here," he said abruptly. "I'm tired of all this one-upmanship and back-stabbing. It's absurd, the way we live in fear of one another. There's no need for it and it . . . it just gets in the way of everything. I'm absolutely sick of it. It's time this family just got along with one another. I'm going to put a stop to this fighting once and for all."

"Absolutely!" Nate said, clenching his fists. "You're absolutely right, Berto! And if they don't want to stop, then by God, we'll *make* them."

And that, thought Daisy, is why some things will never change.

ACKNOWLEDGMENTS

I was never sure how this book was going to read, so I'd like to show my appreciation to all the people who helped me to see it from the outside. That goes particularly for my family: Mum, Kunak, Marek, Erika and Darius as well as Joe and Suzanne. I owe a special thanks to Maedhbh Rogan, for her sound advice, input and support throughout. I'm grateful to Conor Kostick, who checked over my peculiar portrayal of history—any mistakes or complete fabrications are entirely mine. Any really good ideas are mine also.

My agent, Sophie Hicks, continues to steer me through the world of international publishing with expert ease, ably assisted by Edina Imrik and the rest of the folks at Ed Victor Ltd. I'm indebted to all the book-loving people I've met on my travels, who've spoiled me rotten with their enthusiasm and educated me in so many different facets of this passionate industry.

And finally, a special thanks to Emma Pulitzer and Tim Travaglini at Open Road Media, for their work on the US edition of this book, and for their diligence in making sure I was involved in, and kept informed of, every stage of the process.

Thanks to all of you.

ABOUT THE AUTHOR

Oisín McGann was born and raised in Dublin and Drogheda, County Louth, in Ireland. He studied art at Senior College Ballyfermot and Dún Laoghaire School of Art, Design & Technology. Before becoming an author, he worked as a freelance illustrator, serving time along the way as a pizza chef, security guard, background artist for an animation company, and art director and copywriter in an advertising agency.

In 2003 McGann published his first two books in the Mad Grandad series for young readers, followed by his first young adult novel, *The Gods and Their Machines*. Since then, he has written several more novels for young adults, including the Wildenstern Saga, a steampunk series set in nineteenth-century Ireland, and the thrillers *Strangled Silence* and *Rat Runners*.

A full-time writer and illustrator, McGann is married, has three children, and lives somewhere in the Irish countryside.

THE WILDENSTERN SAGA

FROM OPEN ROAD MEDIA

Available wherever ebooks are sold

OPEN ROAD
INTEGRATED MEDIA

Open Road Integrated Media is a digital publisher and multimedia content company. Open Road creates connections between authors and their audiences by marketing its ebooks through a new proprietary online platform, which uses premium video content and social media.